To Brigid Coady and Deborah Harkness,
a blessing of writers

No man ever steps in the same river twice,
for it's not the same river and he's not the same man.
HERACLITUS

Praise

'The queen of the contemporary Cornish novel'
Guardian

'Vivid and beautifully written,
Liz Fenwick is a gifted storyteller'
Sarah Morgan, bestselling author of *One More for Christmas*

'Atmospheric, emotional and full of mystery –
an absolute pleasure from page one'
Veronica Henry, bestselling author of *The Beach Hut*

'Pure escapism at its best'
The Sun

'A wonderfully evocative story, packed with secrets and emotion'
Judy Finnigan, bestselling author of *Eloise*

'Engrossing and romantic – a perfect holiday read'
Rachel Hore, bestselling author of *Last Letter Home*

'With a gifted storyteller's talent for crafting compelling
characters and putting them in alluring locations,
Liz Fenwick's books invite readers to … explore a dramatic
terrain of love, family, and friendship. With wit and skill,
Fenwick illuminates the small, often overlooked moments
that shape and define a life. These are tales that draw you
in and keep you engaged until the last page is turned'
**Deborah Harkness, No. 1 bestselling
author of the All Souls Trilogy**

'Full of emotion and mystery'
HELLO!

'Ideal for fans of Kate Morton'

Liz Fenwick was born in Massachusetts and after ten international moves she's back in the United Kingdom with her husband and two mad cats. She made her first trip to Cornwall in 1989 and bought her home there seven years later. She's a bit of a global nomad but her heart forever remains in Cornwall. For more information visit lizfenwick.com. Or find her procrastinating on Twitter @liz_fenwick.

Also by Liz Fenwick

The Cornish House
A Cornish Affair
A Cornish Stranger
Under a Cornish Sky
A Cornish Christmas Carol
The Returning Tide
One Cornish Summer
The Path to the Sea

The River Between Us

Liz Fenwick

ONE PLACE. MANY STORIES

HQ
An imprint of HarperCollins*Publishers* Ltd
1 London Bridge Street
London SE1 9GF

www.harpercollins.co.uk

HarperCollins*Publishers*
1st Floor, Watermarque Building, Ringsend Road
Dublin 4, Ireland

This paperback edition 2021

1
First published in Great Britain by
HQ, an imprint of HarperCollins*Publishers* Ltd 2021

Copyright © Liz Fenwick 2021

Liz Fenwick asserts the moral right to be
identified as the author of this work.
A catalogue record for this book is
available from the British Library.

ISBN: 978-0-00-829057-3

MIX
Paper from
responsible sources
FSC™ C007454

This book is produced from independently certified FSC™ paper
to ensure responsible forest management.

For more information visit: www.harpercollins.co.uk/green

This book is set in 10.85/15.5 pt. Sabon by Type-it AS, Norway

Printed and bound in Great Britain by
CPI Group (UK) Ltd, Croydon, CR0 4YY

Abbotswood Cottage

Stables

Shell House

Tennis Court

Holy Well

Dairy Dell Cottage

Swimming Bath

River Tamar

Ferry

Ferry

Black Rock

Duke's Drive

Boatman's Cottage

PART ONE

Sometimes you find yourself in the middle of nowhere, and sometimes, in the middle of nowhere, you find yourself.

—UNKNOWN

Case 752

14 March 2019

Saint-Waast, France

- Madame Marie Auch, while installing drainage to a field, uncovered the remains of two bodies.
- Also recovered one signet ring and one Duke of Cornwall's Light Infantry badge.

According to the War Diary (WD) for the DCLI, four soldiers and one officer were reported missing presumed dead on 2 November 1918 in this area. Special mention is made of Captain St Loy.

- Captain Edmund St Loy, the Earl St Loy
- Sergeant William Bowman
- Private Zachariah Carne
- Private Samuel Lyons
- Private Benjamin Skewes

Action: Review records for enlistment details, begin relative search.

Chapter One

2019

At the start of her new life, Theo stood alone on a medieval bridge spanning the Tamar, shivering in the mist and murk, neither in Devon nor Cornwall. That was Theo, never taking a side – but she had to now. Epic adventures always ended or began with a river, she reminded herself, as she walked across the bridge towards the Cornish bank, whether it was the Styx, the Seine, the Thames or the Tamar.

According to the sign illuminated by her phone, Horsebridge had been built in 1437, and at this moment she felt older than it and certainly less solid as her finger traced the cold stones. It was midnight, the witching hour, and she stood, bone-tired, looking at her ancient Volvo estate with a flat tyre and a jack that was rusted to uselessness. A sensible person would have checked before setting off on a long journey and she hadn't. If her car wasn't blocking the bridge, she would have gone to sleep in it, praying that things would not only appear brighter in the morning with the dawn, but they actually would be... somehow. This flat tyre was only a small delay. It wasn't final or fatal. It was flat and fixable.

Fortunately, she had phone signal and had been able to

call for help. The irony hadn't escaped her that emergency assistance was on its way to a Mrs Piers Henshaw, who didn't exist anymore. Yesterday the decree absolute ending her marriage had come into effect.

Above an owl cried. No moon, no stars; just a soft mizzle. A few miles from here there was an old cottage. It was hers. She'd bought it, sight unseen. No doubt her mother, given the opportunity, would say that was typical. On the basis of nothing more than a few fuzzy pictures and the reasonable price tag, Theo had bought the cottage. It seemed to need her, and if her brother Martin was right, she needed the cottage too. Living there would be a fresh start. She pulled out her phone and looked at the details again while she waited.

Boatman's Cottage

First time to the market in seventy years. A delightful two-bedroom cottage with ten acres of woodland on the Cornish bank of the Tamar in an area of outstanding natural beauty. Built in 1819, the cottage requires modernisation.

Originally constructed as part of the Duke of Exeter's estate, Abbotswood, and designed in the picturesque style by Sir Jeffrey Wyattville, the cottage was used as staff accommodation until the 1950s. The dwelling consists of a large reception room, a kitchen, a pantry, a family bathroom and two double bedrooms. There are several small outbuildings in need of repair.

The ten acres of woodland rise from the banks of the Tamar and up the hill behind. The wood consists of native and several

large specimen trees planted following the plans of noted land-
scape designer Humphry Repton.

The cottage is reached by a permissive drive along the Cornish
bank of the Tamar, accessed after crossing Horsebridge when
approaching from the north.

The Royal Inn was closed, and the few houses about were in
darkness. The sound of an engine grumbled in the distance.
Theo saw a vehicle's headlights tracking across the wide
floodplain on the Cornish side, picking out two boxing hares.
Such a thrilling sight. She hoped that their courtship would
be successful.

The dual beams of light left the hares in peace, and she
watched as the vehicle came closer. Jumping in her car, she put
the lights on to signal the driver. It couldn't be her saviour in
the form of a rescue repair man because the thing approaching
looked more like a decrepit Land Rover. It would be her luck,
with her car and trailer obstructing the bridge, to encounter
an old farmer on his way back from a night on the town.
The oncoming vehicle pulled right up to the bonnet of her
car and a tall person climbed out of the driver's side. The
shape loomed in silhouette. She clutched the steering wheel
and took a deep breath.

'Can I help?' the man asked, bending down to the slightly
open window.

'Not sure.' She shrugged, pointing to the front passenger
tyre. 'I have a flat.'

'A spare?' He pulled a torch out from his pocket and
switched it on.

'Yes, but the jack is rusted shut.'

'Shall I have a look?' he asked.

She swallowed. He was being kind and his voice reminded her of her son's. 'That would be wonderful. Thank you.'

He stepped away, and in the dispersed light it was clear he was all of thirty with dark hair and a bright smile. She climbed out of the car to join him.

Turning the jack over in his hands, he said, 'That's beyond a bit of WD40 and I don't think the one for the Landie will be any good.'

'Agreed. I've already called for assistance.'

'Have they said when?' he asked, returning the jack to her badly packed car, which was stuffed with the remains of her old life.

'Within two hours.'

He laughed. 'Woman alone, after midnight, blocking the road. That's good.'

'Yes, isn't it.' She laughed along with him.

'Allow me to introduce myself, I'm Hugo Mounsey.'

'I'm Theo...' She hesitated. 'Pascoe.'

'What brings you to Horsebridge at midnight?' He glanced at the trailer. 'Holiday?'

'Not a holiday.' She laughed, remembering her last proper break in Cornwall years ago... just her and her son David. 'I'm moving here.'

'Welcome to the Tamar Valley,' he said.

'Thanks.' She leaned on the bridge, looking down at the water she couldn't see. Both of them were becoming damp in the mizzle that was fast turning into proper rain. She glanced at him. 'You don't need to stay.'

He chuckled. 'Well, I could go to Greystone Bridge, but

that would take some time and I don't like the idea of you waiting here on your own.'

'Predators in the area?' She glanced over her shoulder into the darkness.

He laughed. 'Definitely... wild animals galore. Shall we sit in the Landie and keep dry and warm?'

She followed him and climbed into the passenger side of the old vehicle; it smelled of earth, damp dog and comfort. Weary, she closed her eyes and allowed herself a moment to relax. It would all be fine when she reached her new home.

It was past three a.m. when Theo finally manoeuvred her car and trailer along the rutted mud-filled track that was her new drive. In spite of her exhaustion, she kept her eyes wide open, peering through the heavy rain, looking for Boatman's Cottage.

She parked beside Hugo, who, she had discovered during their wait, was the manager of Abbotswood Hotel across the Tamar in Devon. She had been there years ago with her paternal grandmother, Claire Pascoe. A sharp stab of grief ran through Theo with the memory. Grannie had died a few days ago. Right this moment she could use a large dose of her grandmother's optimism and outlook. Climbing out of the car and into the heavy rain, she wasn't so sure about her rash purchase.

In the Defender's big headlights, she saw the gutter hanging from the house like an arm open wide for a hug but with an artery cut and gushing. Water rushed down in torrents, not only from the gutter but also off the roof, drowning the sides of the cottage. It was her new home, her new start and it looked more worn and broken than she felt. What in the name of heaven or hell had she bought? The survey had said it was sound and she supposed the great stones that made up the walls were strong enough to last until the next coming. But the roof, the window frames – and the floorboards too, she imagined – were all in doubt.

Hugo walked towards her with a large golf umbrella and she was grateful for his presence. 'I always wondered what this place was like,' he said, turning to her.

She brushed the rain from her eyes. 'Do you know anything about it?'

'Not much.'

She squinted at her home. It was nearing four in the morning, and she'd been in her car for too many hours. As her torch picked out the looming shape that was her new home, she thought tears might be mixing with the rain. What on earth had made her think she could do this on her own? She was a fool, as her mother had always said. The cottage in front of her proved it.

He touched her arm. 'You've had a long day. I can offer you a bed at the hotel and hopefully this won't look as... challenging in the daylight.'

She laughed, not quite hysterical yet but she could feel it bubbling up. Tempting as the offer of the hospitality was from a complete stranger, although a nice one, she wasn't taking that route, no matter how tired she was.

'Thank you but this is my home.' Theo glanced at it. She would sleep in the car.

'If you're sure.' He touched her arm and she noted the concern in his expression.

'I am,' she said with more certainty than she felt.

He handed her a business card. 'My mobile is on there.' He smiled. 'Don't hesitate to ring.'

'Thanks.' She tucked the card into a pocket, safe from the pelting rain, and watched him head to his 4x4 before she turned back to Boatman's.

Buying a house sight unseen was the most reckless thing she had done in a long, long time. She promised herself it would be an adventure.

Chapter Two

The pain in Theo's hip broke through her dream of sitting at a café in Paris with the sun warming her face. She opened her eyes and groaned. The gear stick pressed into her left hip and her head rested on the steering wheel. But the morning sun shone, and the bonnet of her faded red car glowed in the light filtering through the branches of the trees. Soon leaves would begin appearing. The words the estate agent had used were 'a bijoux retreat from the world'. It looked nothing like that at the moment; more like the setting for a noir film with the woodland smothering the cottage one bramble at a time.

She sighed. There were many things she had to look forward to… like summer by the river and creating a garden.

Uncurling from behind the steering wheel and opening the car door, she stood and took a deep breath. The air was sweet with the scent of damp earth. Raindrops beaded on branches backlit from the rising sun like magical fairy lights. The bright-yellow petal of the *Ficaria verna*, lesser celandine or pilewort, covered swathes of ground under the trees. She hadn't loved the plant at her former home, Higston Manor, but had tolerated them because they were early flowers for the bees. However, she adored the name pilewort… so descriptive.

Right now, the happy flowers brought colour to the woodland floor.

Birdsong filled the air along with the rush of the fast-flowing Tamar. This soundtrack calmed her. Buying a remote cottage in need of work rather than a safe bungalow was impulsive but she relished the challenge. After all, Higston had been in a dire state when her ex-husband Piers had bought it for a song: his words not hers. With four years of careful planning, and living only in the three heated rooms, she had – with a team of skilled builders and Piers's money – transformed the house into the jewel it was today. She evaluated the cottage. This should be a lot easier, but she was fifty-four now, not twenty-five.

As if to remind her, her back ached from the ridiculous sleeping position. She stretched, longing to make a start on pulling the woodland away from the cottage. Brambles and bracken vied with overgrown trees. This didn't worry her. It was a task she was more than up to, but the house... that would be a different issue without local knowledge of tradesmen and the seemingly bottomless coffers that she'd had with the Higston renovation. At least the slate roof in the daylight appeared whole. That was a relief. And the gutter needed reattaching, nothing more. She could do that once she bought a ladder. In her hand she held the key. She hadn't been brave enough to venture inside in the dark. But now with a need for coffee and the loo she was ready.

The front door was ajar. She hadn't noticed this last night. Animals? Squatters? Taking a deep breath, she pushed it all the way open. The hinges complained. She added WD40 to the ever-growing shopping list in her head.

The large room was bare except for an old mirror. She ran her finger along the wood panelling that covered the walls. The grain was fine, but it was dry and in need of oil and elbow grease. She stepped back, seeing the room as a whole. The connection of the cottage to the Abbotswood estate across the river was obvious. Even years later, she could picture the beautiful wooden panels in the hotel's hall. But unlike the hotel's wide floorboards, beneath her feet the large thick slabs of slate reminded her of gravestones. Not a good thought. Turning around she studied the massive fireplace. The proportions were way off kilter. It would look more at home in a castle. Perhaps an exaggeration, but nonetheless she could stand in it.

Walking through the room, she opened a door that led to the kitchen. Here she was confronted with the 1800s. It belonged in a museum. No, it belonged to her, but maybe she too belonged in a museum. She laughed, adding a camper stove to her list when she spied the state of the rusting Cornish range that had featured on the estate agent's list of desirable fixtures. She snapped a picture with her phone and sent a WhatsApp message to Martin and David captioned:

Arrived in the early hours of the morning. Slept in the car. Looking at this cooking breakfast might be a challenge, but all is well. xx

She hoped it would send as the signal was sketchy.

A huge ceramic sink sat under one of the windows looking out to the west onto trees, which, even though still bare, let in little light. Her heart and her true skill lay with what was outside the cottage but the inside of it was the first priority. She pulled out her phone and began a proper list.

To Buy:
- **Ladder**
- **Woodworm treatment**
- **Linseed oil**
- **Wood soap**
- **Vinegar**

Her mind wandered and she started to write a list of all the plants she wanted for her future garden. With little effort she pictured hydrangeas with their delicate lace cap flowers scattered among the trees; and, for a soft scent and rich colour, *lonicera*. Honeysuckle – the way it wildly grew from the hedgerows – always reminded her of Cornwall. Would David see or feel the connection to the idyllic childhood holidays? He'd been a support through the divorce but distant. She longed for their earlier closeness, yet she understood that it was difficult for him. Even at thirty-two, divorcing parents and the arrival of your father's love child were awkward at minimum, and made more complicated because he worked with Piers at the long-established building firm Henshaw and Son. Hopefully this discomfort would ease with time.

With Piers's pride in the growing baby bump on his secretary, no one questioned who was at fault in the divorce. But even without her mother's bitter words she knew in her heart it was never only one sided. She had made it easy for him to stay and he had made it hard for her to leave. Through the lawyers he'd pleaded poverty because of the business and

16

its constant need for money, yet when pressed he wouldn't sell Higston. So, she let him have his grand manor and his dreams of being more important than he was. She laughed drily. David had mentioned recently that Piers had traced his lineage back to a baronet, and his mistress to a lord, and the couple had taken DNA tests to see if they could connect the missing dots. Piers had always longed to be more than he was.

She was under no such illusions as the middle-class daughter of a vicar and not the brightest spark in the box according to her mother who'd descended from a long line of academics. That was the one thing Theo had never been: academic. Unlike her mother who had a PhD in Classics, her brother who had a PhD in Astrophysics and their late father who had a PhD in Theology. Theo was a continual disappointment. Her Latin was restricted to plants and in the end she had never finished her degree from the agricultural college. She sighed, still regretting the last bit the most. What she was… was a loving mother, a gardener, a floral designer and she had tried to be a good wife. Could she have been more? Best not to think about it.

Her phone beeped. David had messaged her.

Oh, Mum. You OK?

She responded.

Yes all good. Xx

He replied.

Phew x

In the trailer she had her cuttings; later she would take them out. That last day at Higston, she'd walked through her garden stretching down to the upper reaches of the Thames for the final time, taking cuttings. Foolish really. She'd had no garden for them then or home for her for that matter, nor had she known what the divorce settlement would be. But it was clear the old manor and her garden would be hers no more no matter what. She had insufficient income to sustain the upkeep. The heating alone was the equivalent of someone's yearly wage. With the settlement, when it was finally all released, she would be able to live carefully.

But losing Higston still stung. It had been part of her life since David was three and the longest she had lived anywhere. The challenge of restoring the remains of its neglected garden had lifted her and used every skill she possessed. She had created something special. No doubt Piers's mistress would rip it all out.

Taking a deep breath, she left behind thoughts of her beloved garden and returned to the to-do list, then stopped. If she wrote it, it would be overwhelming and an obligation. Instead she would throw herself into the work, then she wouldn't be a success or a failure each day but take the days and the tasks as they came.

Her phone beeped with Martin's reply.

Good thing you like a challenge, sis. X

She laughed and quickly typed.

Hmmm. Time will tell but exciting nonetheless. xx

She went through the door off of the kitchen to the back of the cottage where she found the larder and the bathroom. The old bath in front of her still had its enamel and, to her relief, the high-rise loo worked. The pipes creaked and groaned ominously as the cistern refilled. A plumber was definitely required, and as she walked back towards the kitchen, she spied an ancient fuse box above the door. Dead flies fell on her when she peered inside. She hadn't seen one with wired fuses like these in decades. According to the estate agent's details it was supposed to be functional.

Back in the kitchen she climbed the stairs, praying woodworm hadn't made them unsound and she wasn't taking her life in her hands. On the small landing, she despaired of the peeling, yellowed, floral wallpaper. That would go and a soft white paint would brighten it no end. She flicked the light switch. A brief moment of illumination, a loud pop then darkness. So much for the electrics. So much for a coffee or a tea.

The left-hand door led into the larger of the two bedrooms situated above the sitting room. The floorboards were wide and dark. The room was dual aspect with a large window facing north towards the river. Once it might have had a view of the water but no longer. However she could hear it. Across the room from the south-facing window, the view consisted of trees and the rising hillside. Light was going to be an issue, but she could resolve it with lamps, fresh white paint and a tree surgeon.

The smaller bedroom was similar, but it wasn't entirely empty. It contained a simple wooden chair and a built-in cupboard on the left of the normal-sized fireplace on the end wall. She would set up her study here where it would have afternoon sun from the west-facing window. She could picture it all done up and not as it was at the moment with cobwebs, woodlice and droppings, which she hoped were mice and not anything more sinister.

Downstairs she tried the kitchen ceiling light and nothing happened. She reset the main switch and still no electrics. Pulling out her phone, she texted Hugo. He might be able to recommend an electrician and a plumber. She also wanted to thank him for his help in the early hours. A reply came almost immediately, and she called and left a message with both tradespeople.

That done she checked on her plants in the trailer, setting them out in the dappled sunlight for a few hours. She grabbed the cleaning equipment from the car, trying not to feel overwhelmed by the task in front of her. After all, she had taken on four acres of wilderness and a dilapidated house before and made them both shine. But then she'd had plenty of money: Piers's money from the business he'd grown developing new properties all over the country. That had paid for the skilled heritage workmen and the gardeners. Once, she and Piers had been full of promise and plans. Back when they'd met, she was in her final year at agricultural college and he was learning the business from his father. Oh, the ideas they'd had, with him building the new houses and her developing the gardens around the new estates.

That was history. Boatman's was all down to her. She rolled up her sleeves and began scrubbing down the kitchen and the bathroom. The work was hard, but it left her with little time to think other than planning her future garden. *Osmanthus delavayi* would add much-needed fragrance, with its white flowers in spring. Certainly better than the caustic scent of bleach currently assaulting her nose. And maybe adding a *Viburnum plicatum*, or the wedding cake tree, *Cornus controversa*, would add some elegance with its white flowers in May.

In a matter of hours both rooms gleamed as much as possible, given their age. For the next task she headed up to the spare room with her mind still on the garden. It was safe to think of the garden. If nothing else, reciting the Latin names of plants blocked all other thoughts, and plants carried no emotion for her other than joy. With plants she was safe. They could rip her skin, bring up a rash or even kill her, but she knew where she stood with them and what they needed.

She decided to clean the built-in cupboard first, as then she would be able to unload some of her things. With dustpan and brush she began at the top; years of accumulated dust and dead insects piled up in the rubbish bag. She scrubbed until her hands hurt. Her knees ached too as she scoured the bottom shelf. Martin would say her knees ached because she didn't kneel enough and pray. But a Jesuit would say that. She smiled thinking about him. Martin was the rebel of the family. Her devout Church of England father, the Rev Thomas Pascoe, had been initially horrified when Martin had announced his intention to become a Jesuit priest in the final year of his PhD. She chuckled.

Scrubbing with renewed vigour for laughing at her father's reaction, she acquired a splinter for her effort. After extracting the piece of wood, she took a closer look at the bottom shelf. There was a plank askew. She tried to fit it back, but it wouldn't go. Pulling it out, it was clear the nail had sheared.

Using her phone's torch, she shone the light in and saw not the rest of the nail but a metal box. A secret hiding place. She grinned. As a teen she had hidden her things from Martin under the loose floorboard in an old rectory where they had lived briefly.

Theo pulled the box out and sat back on her heels. Would she find treasure or simply a teenage diary? She put it down on the floor and the lid popped open like a toothless mouth.

And, of course, there were no gleaming gems. She found some letters tied together in faded blue silk ribbon. A quick look showed most were unopened. A few were a faded green. The one on top was addressed to a Des Jenkins, Gate Cottage, Abbotswood Estate. Probably love letters, given they were hidden. What would they tell her about the previous occupants of her cottage? She looked about the simple room, half expecting to see people waiting in the corner.

It was almost six p.m. and her joints complained as she stood, taking the box downstairs with her. She propped it on a pile of her belongings in the sitting room and she heard her phone beep. It was another message from David checking on her. She smiled and replied almost truthfully that all was well. She might not have heat or electricity but the weather was mild. Her son was thinking of her and the cottage was hers entirely; that was all that mattered.

Theo's wandering thoughts were interrupted by the electrician returning her call. He would try and come tomorrow morning. She set out candles for the evening. She wasn't sure living in the 1800s was her thing, but candlelight could be flattering, and she needed that if the mottled mirror was reliable at all. Earlier she had put up the camp bed in the living room, along with a folding chair. Several boxes acted as tables, and, as she lit the candles, the wooden panels seemed to glow in the gentle light. It would be beautiful when she had restored them.

Her stomach growled. She picked up her pasty, taking it outside, and followed the path down to the river's edge. The setting sun reflected off the windows of the hotel opposite. It sat proud on the rise of the hill. Abbotswood's sturdy stone was all cast in a golden light, softening it and highlighting its charming irregular shape. From this distance it looked like a fairy-tale cottage, but it was far larger than most cottages.

Leaning against a tree trunk, she ate the pasty and crumbs covered her top. The peppery taste instantly transported her to a wide stretch of beach with Grannie. Pasties, ice creams and sunburn. She'd been six and her mother was about to have Martin so Grannie had taken her to Cornwall. It had been the first of many magic holidays wandering beaches, visiting old houses and gardens. Claire Pascoe, school matron extraordinaire, had been a wonderful grandmother and was always on hand with a willing ear and sensible advice. They had shared a love of Cornwall and visiting gardens. Grannie had been so vital it had seemed she would go on forever.

Theo missed her so much. Buck up, Grannie would say. You can do this. Her funeral was next week. Theo, Martin, and their mother Virginia would meet with Grannie's solicitor and pack up her apartment in Saltash. All this brought back the loss of her father ten years ago. Theo was grateful her father hadn't been around to witness the fallout with Piers.

Grannie, unlike Theo's mother, had been understanding about the collapse of Theo's life. Her mother's words still stung: 'The failure of the marriage was your fault. You weren't good enough.' Theo flinched hearing the next bit as clearly as if Virginia were standing here and delivering it. 'He never would have knocked up his mistress if you had given him another child or had taken sufficient care of his needs.' The sad thing was that Theo had wanted another child but it had never happened, despite her 'seeing to his needs' as her mother had put it.

The sky was darkening when she walked back to the cottage. Despite time out for a two-hour shopping expedition during the day, she had achieved a great deal. Standing outside the cottage, the air was cool and scented with the pine. All around the wilderness had encroached, obliterating what once would have been a cultivated landscape according to Humphry Repton's plan.

Now, two hundred years on, it had a certain stateliness about it. Squinting into the twilight, she longed to begin work on making a woodland garden, but it would have to wait. She went to the car and put her tender young plants back into the shelter of her trailer. April could be cold. It was too soon for them and for the garden. Their time would come.

Inside she wound up the radio that Martin had given her as a housewarming present in case of power cuts, or, as in now, no power. Theo opened the bottle of aged whisky, which was a treat to herself. Raising the glass, she toasted her new beginning. Despite the fact that the cottage needed several coats of paint, furniture and God knows what else that she hadn't considered, in the candlelight it looked welcoming.

Radio 3 provided a soundtrack of Puccini as she sank into the camping chair then pulled a candle and the metal box she had discovered earlier closer. She grabbed her reading glasses and took a sip of the whisky wondering what she would discover.

Opening the first envelope, she found no note or letter, but a green envelope enclosed. As she pulled the page out of that, her hand shook a bit when she saw the date and the location.

France
30 September 1915

My Lady,

We arrived in France months ago and went straight into battle. It should have been beautiful. Summer should have been everywhere, but nature only gives me glimpses that it hasn't abandoned us. Swallows gather above on their journey south and are beautiful like at home. A reminder that somewhere life continues. It is hard here with the sound of the heavy artillery to think of normal everyday things. I can't even call to mind the quiet of the riverbank.

The lieutenant tells me news of Penhale. He is well and has grown into his role for one who had never planned to fight. But you know this. Most of the officers including the NCOs are a good lot, which is lucky as being here is not. Yesterday I lost two men I'd signed on with. Do you remember Timo Tonks who worked in the kitchen garden? He died yesterday as did a fine young farmer from Bodmin.

Like the news above I have attempted to write letters to you. I have written many and not sent them. I have been trying to understand but I do not. It only makes sense if we were a lie as you said we were. But my heart won't accept that. I do not have your learning, but I thought I knew people. I could tell whether they had the right temperament for fishing. You had the right way about you. You caught the fish and you caught me, heart, body and soul.

I go through the motions of being alive, but I am not. I may breathe, I may eat, I may sleep but I only exist. Your betrayal has taken the future from me. Despite the late summer days and blue skies, all I can see is bleakest winter. Trees barren, fields unproductive, where before the sky above was an endless wonder. Now it is neither blue nor grey, nor dark nor bright. It is simply there, and I am in a limbo that is more like hell because I can never be with you. You have married. I am alone. I had given you my heart, my promise, and you had given me yours.

I still remember your words when I last saw you, which were so different from the words you had spoken in passion – how could those words of love have been lies? That's what torments me when darkness falls, and the guns go quiet. My sleep-starved distorted mind plagues me and I remember your hands on me. I remember you calling out my name. Not his name but mine. And yet your words can never be unheard.

I am still full of anger so I don't know why I am writing other than I must. I talk to you in my head all the *time. I hear your laughter and mostly I ache. I ache from my innards to the last hair on my body. I tell myself to let go but I can't so I hate myself. The sooner this war kills me the better. It will be the only way to be free.*

Z

Theo dropped the letter onto her lap and picked up her whisky glass. Taking a glug, she let it burn in her mouth before swallowing. *It will be the only way to be free.* Had the lady in question seen the letter? Had they lived here in the cottage? Who were they? Was Z the boatman of the cottage's name? She took a last glance at the remaining letters while she stifled a yawn. As intriguing as they were, she knew she needed to sleep and reading in candlelight wasn't all that easy.

But the emotion in it lingered as if physically touching her. She blew out the candles, trying not to imagine this Z and his lady here, but when she crawled into bed, zipping up the sleeping bag, she felt them all around her. She shivered and the healthy slug of whisky in her didn't dull her thoughts or warm her cockles. A fire would warm up the room, but she didn't dare light one until the chimney was swept. She had to be patient. In time the cottage would feel like home and not like she was on a camping trip. She snuggled into the sleeping bag that was supposed to keep one warm on Arctic expeditions.

There was an upside to everything: she just needed to find it.

Chapter Three

Theo's eyes opened wide. Her body tensed. There was something or someone walking upstairs, making a lot of noise. It sounded like it was moaning as it moved. Did she lie still and pray that if she didn't budge it would leave? But she was so hot she was going to self-combust and burst into an explosion of heat that would do a nuclear power station justice. Who needs another renewable energy source when all you needed was menopausal women with night sweats and daytime flushes?

With some wriggling, she freed one arm and undid the zip on the sleeping bag. The noises upstairs became louder. Right about now it would be good to have someone with her so she didn't have to face whatever was upstairs alone. Hell, even Piers had been useful at this sort of thing. But her ex-husband wasn't here. She was and she was alone.

This had been a lovely thing hours before, listening to the music she wanted to and not having to talk or watch television. But now, as she flung a leg out of the sleeping bag and onto the cold slate, she would rather have someone here. She shivered as she sat up. Even her heat had deserted her at this crucial moment. Standing, she pulled on her coat, grabbed the torch, and found her shoes. Whatever was moving and moaning upstairs was not disturbed by her presence.

The worst she could face was a rat. That was all. It wouldn't be a ghost despite the moaning that sounded like old Marley. She didn't believe in ghosts, but she did believe in rats. She had seen them often enough. Normally darting around the compost pile. She walked carefully into the kitchen, shining the torch around into all the dark corners just in case. In case of what she didn't know. She could shout the house down and no one would hear her. And why would anyone be lurking in a freezing kitchen in a cottage in a wood in the middle of nowhere. Come to that why was she? Because she was a fool.

'You love Cornwall,' she replied aloud to the voice in her head that sounded like her mother. 'It's perfect… just across the border, not too far.'

On each step upwards, she paused, listening, praying, and not really breathing. She could picture what she must look like… a mad fifty-something woman with bedhead hair damp from night sweats, wielding a torch like it was a sword. She started to laugh – not the mad hysterical sort but the punch-drunk kind. One night in her own home and she was fit to be committed to the nearest asylum.

The door to what would be her bedroom was shut. It had been open earlier. No doubt the noisy wind had closed it. Maybe that was the sound that had woken her. She turned the handle and, stealing herself, she pushed the door inch by inch. The beam of light from her torch wobbled. Good God she was a mess. It would be a rat if anything at all. She was far bigger than a rat.

With the door fully opened, two yellow eyes stared back.

Theo screamed. The thing jumped up onto the window bar. It was nearly eyeball to eyeball with her. When her heart relodged itself in its normal spot, she realised she was looking at a large cat. Not as big as the beast of Bodmin but big, furry, and clearly unafraid of her. The animal gave her one last look then jumped onto the floor and sauntered out of the door.

Theo collapsed against the wall. A bloody cat had been trapped and had been pacing. A moan exploded into the room. She jumped again. 'Get a grip, Theo,' she said aloud. She walked to the north-facing window and pulled it firmly closed but a cool draught wound around her fingers. The putty holding the thin glass was missing. Here was the cause of the noises. She had nothing with her that could fix it now. Another trip to the hardware shop was on the cards, the first of many, she suspected.

Closing the door firmly behind her, she went to the kitchen, longing to make tea. Instead she took a sip of water and prepared to crawl back into her sleeping bag only to find the very large cat sound asleep on top. She hoped it didn't have fleas. When she prodded it, the cat opened an eye and glared.

'Look, mate, this is my bed.' Theo lifted the sleeping bag and the cat adjusted accordingly.

'Well, I did want company,' she said to no one in particular. She shimmied into the sleeping bag. The cat curled into the bend in her legs when she rolled on to her side into the foetal position, hoping for some sleep before the sun rose.

Dawn arrived with the cat kneading her stomach and the birds not quite in tune. Coffee was the one thing on her mind and the one thing she didn't have. Hopefully the electrician that Hugo had recommended would turn up first thing.

The cat settled just as Theo wanted to move. Theo shifted and he, or was it a she, opened an eye and glared. Judging by its size and the length of its fur, this creature wasn't a stray cat. It had the look of breeding about it with its big tufted ears. Maybe a Maine Coon or a Norwegian Forest cat. Either way it would have a home somewhere and her little cottage wasn't it. She put a tentative hand out and stroked its head. The purr began low and soft but soon reached the point that she was surprised the camp bed wasn't shaking.

'OK, cat, I need the loo. You can have the bed.' She slid out. The cold of the floor travelled up her legs so swiftly she was afraid her heart would stop. She quickly found her shoes. However, if she'd thought the floor had been cold in the sitting room it was nothing on the bathroom. Yesterday she'd scrubbed the bath and looked forward to the moment when anything but ice water would flow through the taps.

Back in the sitting room, she dressed in haste, stealing a quick glance in the old mirror. She ran her finger on the edge of the bevel connecting herself to something that had lived here longer than she had. Turning, she watched the cat curl into the sleeping bag. It opened one eye but didn't move until they both heard the sound of a vehicle. Theo glanced at her watch: 8.30 a.m. If this was the electrician, she was impressed, but looking at the ancient Defender she didn't think that was the case.

The vehicle parked behind hers and a young woman climbed out. Her blonde hair was tied back but a piece had come loose and rested on the side of her tanned face. Even if Theo hadn't spotted the serious boots, she would have known this woman worked outside and relished it. There was a glow of confidence that covered happy outdoor people.

'Morning,' she called, pulling out a large thermos and a bag. She strode towards Theo and the house.

'Hello,' Theo said, hiding her surprise as she walked towards her.

The woman studied the house. 'I'm Gayle, the head gardener over at Abbotswood.'

Theo smiled.

'When Hugo told me that Theo Pascoe had bought the boatman's cottage, I had to come and say hello and find out if you were *the* Theodora Pascoe.'

Theo laughed. 'I'm not sure about the *THE*, but, yes, I was a garden designer of sorts.'

'Of sorts!' Gayle was beside her now. 'You've exhibited your designs at Chelsea and won a gold medal.' She drew a breath and continued, 'Your garden at Higston Manor, perfection.'

Theo held her smile in place. Even her gold medal winning design hadn't been seen as an achievement by her mother or by Piers. 'That was years ago; fifteen to be precise.' Making her use her maiden name for her flower dabbling, as Piers had put it, had backfired on him. The Chelsea gold and then the book on the flower arranger's garden were in her maiden name. His face had gone puce when he had been addressed as Mr Pascoe at one function.

'And now you create flower designs,' Gayle said.

Theo sighed, leading the way into the cottage. 'No, now I do derelict house repair.'

Gayle chuckled and handed her the thermos. 'Hugo thought you might need coffee as you don't have electrics.'

Theo raised an eyebrow.

Gayle laughed. 'Small world around here and he also sent some fresh croissants from the kitchen.'

'My God, he's a saint.' Theo sniffed the air, savouring the buttery aroma.

'Hmm, he's not bad.'

Theo was about to disagree but decided against it. She twisted the top of the thermos asking, 'Will you join me?'

Gayle glanced at her phone. 'Love to.'

In the kitchen Theo grabbed two mugs off the nearly bare shelves. Two plates, two glasses, two forks and so on. Everything she had collected over the years that she thought she had needed for a happy life was no more. Now she was the owner of charity shop finds and it was better than before. Freedom.

Back in the sitting room she spied Gayle stroking the cat. 'Do you know him or her?' Theo asked.

'No, but what a beautiful animal.'

'Yes.' Handing her a mug, Theo said, 'Sorry, I don't have any milk.'

'I think there's some in the bag with the croissant,' she said.

Theo dug in and next to the still warm croissants was a small glass milk bottle, two pots of jam, a tiny jar with brown sugar and a container of butter plus napkins and a bamboo knife and spoon. Attention to detail.

'Croissant?' Theo asked. The aroma was divine.

'No thanks, had bacon and eggs earlier.' She looked around the room. 'I remember coming over to take a look at this when I first started working at Abbotswood.'

'And?'

'It was shut up so I couldn't see much.' She took a sip. 'People said it was haunted.'

Theo laughed.

'Is it?' Gayle asked.

'Well, if you'd asked me in the early hours, I might have said yes, but that was when I discovered the ghost cat—' she paused to stoke its head before she continued '—locked in the bedroom and the wind moaning through a gap in the window.'

Gayle laughed. 'A good night's sleep then?'

'Absolutely.' Theo rolled her eyes then asked, 'Do you know any of the history of the cottage?'

Gayle shook her head. 'Not much. It hasn't been used in years and I wondered who would buy it when we heard it was for sale.' She took a sip of the coffee. 'Hugo may know something or be able to at least put you in touch with the archivist for the Duke of Exeter.'

Theo tilted her head. 'That would be good.'

'I know he'd spoken to her regarding the history of Abbotswood when he was putting the potted history of the house together for guests.'

'That makes sense,' Theo said, cradling the mug in her hands and looking out at the towering trees. She turned back to Gayle and asked, 'Do you have the name of a good tree surgeon?'

'Yes.' Gayle smiled.

'I knew you would.' Theo inhaled the coffee again before asking, 'How is it to work on a Repton garden?' Abbotswood had been Theo's first Repton garden and, though only ten years old, Theo had fallen in love with it, and she remembered Grannie telling her what was special about it. The setting of the house in the landscape so that it had presence yet felt entirely natural to its environment. It elicited the emotion that Repton wanted from a landscape. What made the biggest impression on her then had been the dingle, a sound garden created by controlling the flow of water down through the valley and finally into the Tamar. She had raced over the bridges and through the tunnels all made to look natural and enhance the landscape.

'Now fine, but when I started, I was afraid to dead head.' She laughed. 'But it's kind of magic to keep the design alive, still creating the impact he sought.'

'Have you seen the red book for Abbotswood?' Theo asked, recalling her studies and poring over a few of them. Repton had made a red book for the landscapes he had designed.

Gayle nodded. 'There's a copy in the hotel. You should come over and have a look.' She tucked a strand of hair behind her ear. 'You might even find out what the plans were for the space around the cottage.'

'What a brilliant idea.' Theo grinned. 'How long have you been there?'

'I began as a junior gardener straight out of college.'

In the distance Theo heard the rumble of another vehicle making its way to the cottage. 'That will hopefully be the electrician.'

'Yes, my uncle.'

Theo's eyes opened wide. 'Very small world.'

'Small community.' Gayle grinned.

Theo placed her mug on a box and walked out to greet the man who could be her saviour.

Gayle followed her. 'I'll send Jim over later to have a look at your trees.' She gave her uncle a kiss on the cheek before she disappeared into the old Defender.

'Mr Thompson,' Theo said.

'Rich, please,' he said holding out a hand.

She took it. 'Theo Pascoe.'

'Pleased to meet you and I'm glad someone's going to live in this old place. Been needing it for a long time.'

'Do you know any of its history?' she asked.

He shook his head. 'Two sisters owned it most recently. My mother may know more. She used to work at Abbotswood. I'll ask her if you'd like.'

'Yes, please.' Theo smiled and then continued, 'I looked at the fuse box and it appears like it was done pre-war... First World War, that is.'

He laughed. 'Let's have a look then.'

She stopped as they passed the fireplace. 'Before we do, you don't know a chimney sweep by any chance?'

'Happens my nephew is one.'

'Gayle's brother?' she asked.

'No, my sister's son. Here's his number.' He reached into his pocket for his phone. After a few taps he handed it to Theo who quickly snapped a picture of the contact details. Her phone had become her brain. It kept not only the contacts and lists but visual aids and reminders of inspiration or necessities. She wasn't sure what she had done before she'd had it.

'Thanks.' Theo handed his phone back and led him to the old fuse box before she dialled his nephew. If she was lucky, she may have light and warmth before long. But then she heard Rich's low long whistle as he opened the fuse box. Maybe she wouldn't.

*

Well, things were only half bad or half good depending on how Theo looked at it. She had electric power to the kitchen. The whole cottage needed rewiring, but she had expected that. She hadn't anticipated the cost, nor had she thought she would now be restricted to light and power in one room only. However, she had that, and she could charge her phone and boil a kettle. She could cook using the two-burner hob she had bought. Washing herself would be a brisk experience. Laundry would be trickier but the nearby town had a laundrette.

In the late afternoon, Rich's nephew, the chimney sweep, had arrived and from the main chimney he dislodged years of debris including old birds' nests and several small skeletons of the animal variety. Thankfully no human ones. It was now clean but in need of repointing and preferably lining. He'd said under pressure that it was mostly safe to have a fire as long as it was not left unattended and that she needed smoke and carbon monoxide alarms. She had laughed rather too heartily when he mentioned she didn't need to worry too much about ventilation at the moment. If she replaced the windows with double glazing, then it would become an issue.

Right now, as she looked at the fading light through the old glass, she didn't think she'd be rushing to replace it. In the top right pane, she made out two letters intertwined: A Z... the beginning and the end. She went to it and used her hankie to wipe the grime from the pane. Was this done by the Z of the letters? Resting her head against the window, she connected herself to those that had lived here before her. A and Z had, and no doubt others too, including the cat who laced its way through her legs, leaving a trail of long grey hair on her black leggings.

Her phone pinged with a text from Gayle.

Fancy a drink at the pub tonight and the chance to meet a few locals?

Theo was tempted but a yawn arrived to call her to her senses.

Can I take a rain check? Am absolutely shattered and wouldn't be much company.

Theo's phone vibrated with Gayle's response.

Of course. I asked Hugo about the archivist. He'll send the details. Keep in touch!

A swell of excitement rose in her. With a bit of luck and some digging, she might discover Boatman's history. Another message arrived. Hugo sent her the details of the archivist for the Duke of Exeter. After a quick reply thanking him, Theo glanced at the box containing the letters. There was no time like the present. She began an email.

Dear Ms Jones,

Hugo Mounsey of Abbotswood Hotel has given me your contact details. I have recently purchased Boatman's Cottage on the Cornish Bank of the Tamar, which was once a part of the Abbotswood estate. While I was cleaning, I discovered a stash of letters hidden in the bottom of a cupboard. I have not yet read them all, but they were written during WW1 by a man signing the letters Z to someone he refers to as his lady.

I would love to discover who they are if possible and if they lived here at the cottage. I would also be grateful of any other information you have regarding the cottage.

Yours sincerely,
Theo Pascoe

She added her phone number before she pressed send then dropped the phone onto the wooden table. She had found it in the lean-to shed along with two chairs. While the electrician had worked his magic, she'd cleaned and polished them. Now the sitting room contained her camp bed along with the table and chairs. Her maternal grandmother's silver candlesticks looked perfect on the old oak table. As would have the beautiful blue and white old willow plates she had collected over the years to fill Higston Manor. She had furnished the house with care and love so that it matched the garden she had created. Theo stood and shook off the 'might have beens'. Higston and its garden were gone.

With the fire going all afternoon the room had some warmth now, but she suspected that most of the heat was heading up the chimney. However, the room had come alive with a fire, as if the soul of the place had returned. The cat was already curled up on the camp bed. It had eaten its dried food in one go and seemed to have settled in for the night. Theo had buried the present of the dead mouse she'd found earlier, in the far reaches of what would become her garden. For the first time in ages she felt the urge to design, to create, to make her mark. She had been treading water and living on past laurels for a while. The messy divorce had sucked her dry.

Restless, she opened a box of her things she'd brought in from the trailer. On the top was the old, battered, red Edwardian Baedeker's guide to Paris. It acted like a portal to a different time. She stroked the cover while she sat down by the fire with a glass of whisky. She had treasured this old book for so long, yet it had no value despite its age. The cover was faded and the spine ripped. Some pages were dog eared and the map nearly falling out. Yet her hand held it as if it was as precious and fragile as a new-born. It represented the old her, the more adventurous her. The one she had lost all those years ago.

Theo shivered, remembering, but she was not in the warmth of the sun on a June day in Paris in 1986. She was sitting alone, alone with a cat, in a not quite derelict house in Cornwall. She stood, throwing another log on the fire. She had wasted so much time marking it. The changing seasons in the garden and the doorframe in the utility room that recorded David's growth from toddler to man were her key markers. But, rather than continue to simply mark time, she would now use it. She could be like Grannie who lived until a hundred and hadn't wasted a moment.

Chapter Four

Theo leaned against the door jamb, watching the plumber, and praying that the ancient contraption wasn't as bad as it looked. The plumber laughed as soon as he spotted it. She paled. Laughter meant one thing... unsalvageable.

'Well, in my time I've seen old and vintage, but this boiler classifies as truly antique.' He shook his head. 'It's so old it should be listed.' He chuckled to himself. 'Coal-fired and hasn't been used in my lifetime, at a guess.'

'So, it can't be fixed, or it's not worth it?'

'I wouldn't want to try, and coal isn't clean...' He trailed off and Theo pictured pound signs going up the flue.

'Then what are my options?'

'Well,' he said, pulling the pencil from behind his ear, 'you'll need a boiler that could be either gas- or oil-run as you've got enough room for a tank but whether they would come down the track to fill it is another problem.' He glanced at her. 'So, I think liquified gas in canisters would be the answer.'

'When the new boiler is in, can heating be installed?' she asked.

'Radiators?' He looked about the room.

She glanced down, before saying, 'I was thinking more underfloor heating.'

He looked at the large slabs of slate under his feet. 'Doubt if there's anything but earth under these. Mighty expensive to lift the floor and lay concrete and insulation. Then are you going to use electric to do it or put in pipes?'

She sighed. 'Well, then radiators, the old iron type.'

He scratched his ear. 'Hmm, that would be doable.'

'Cost?' she asked, afraid of the answer. It would be easier not to know, but those days of ignorance and someone else paying the bill were behind her.

'I'll have to get back to you on that.' He adjusted the pencil behind his ear.

'OK, and how long would it take?' she asked, wincing in anticipation of the answer.

He looked up at the ceiling. 'About a week, once I'd started.'

'And when could that be?' She smiled at him, praying he'd say in a few days or in two weeks at the latest.

'July,' he said.

Theo cleared her throat. It was April. 'Not any sooner? I have no heat and no hot water.'

'I see your point, but I've jobs lined up.' He packed up his bag. 'Do you want me to put the figures together?'

Theo suppressed a sigh and said, 'Yes, please.' She put her best smile on and continued, 'If you have a cancellation please let me know.'

He looked at her as if she was insane and perhaps she was. In the short time living in the cottage, she was talking to herself and to the cat with no name. Theo was living the high life with nothing but fresh air coming in through every possible crevice. Why had she thought living in a cottage in the middle of the woods would be a good idea?

She watched with anguish as her one hope for hot water, let alone heat, disappeared down the track. She would soon have to take up wild swimming to become properly clean. With great care this morning she had washed her hair in the sink and fluff dried it because she was afraid her hairdryer would blow what electrics she had. Dry shampoo would become her best friend. She added it to her shopping list.

Standing by the kitchen sink, Theo tried not to despair about the boiler while the cat rubbed her calf. She had captured her, for it turned out Cat was a female, and taken her to the local vet, who had gone to where no person other than a vet should go. Cat was spayed thankfully but not microchipped. The vet had no record of this feline, who she thought was a Norwegian Forest cat. 'Well, Cat, it's just you and me again.' The animal looked at her and blinked then sauntered off to the warmth of the fire in the sitting room.

Theo stood hands on hips. No hot water, no heating. People had survived without and so could she. She would soldier on and the next thing to do was to move the camp bed up to the main bedroom along with the last of the boxes in the sitting room. A few days ago she had treated the floorboards for woodworm as a precaution and had painted the walls in a soft yellow distemper. The hint of colour warmed the room as did the heat from the chimney below.

After that job was done, she changed into a smart shift dress and flat court shoes before returning to the sitting room. It appeared empty despite the table and chairs and the boxes of her things. Tomorrow was Grannie's funeral and this afternoon Theo, Martin and their mother would meet with Grannie's solicitor. Martin had already said he had no need of any of Grannie's furniture, therefore Theo thought she might make use of some of it. It would be good to have reminders of her grandmother here at Boatman's.

Theo took a last glance in the mirror. It wasn't nearly as kind in daylight as it was in candlelight. In fact, it was downright frightening. These past months, the wrinkles had deepened with the stress of the divorce and she looked all of her fifty-four years. Martin was six years younger and didn't look his age at all. She laughed at her own thoughts then said farewell to Cat, promising to be back in time to feed her as she climbed in her car and set off to Plymouth and her grandmother's solicitor.

Martin was sitting next to their mother in the office when Theo arrived five minutes late, having been caught in traffic queuing into the car park.

'Sorry.' Theo took the chair beside Martin, nodding a greeting to her mother who did not return the gesture.

'Mrs Henshaw, would you like a coffee or a tea?' the solicitor asked.

Theo took a deep breath. 'I'm fine, thank you, and I'm Theo Pascoe now.' She raised her bare left hand and Martin sent her an encouraging smile.

'Sorry, I was unaware.' The solicitor folded his hands on the desk. 'Thank you for coming. We could have done this over the phone but, as you are all here for her funeral, it made sense to go through this in person.'

'Yes,' Martin said, looking every inch the priest in a dog

collar and black attire, but his biker leathers hanging on the back of the chair revealed a different side.

'Claire Pascoe updated her will after the death of her son over ten years ago.' He paused and looked solemnly at them.

Theo glanced in her mother's direction. Virginia Pascoe's mouth was set in a straight line.

'There is a bequest of a small oil painting for your son David, Mrs... sorry Ms Pascoe.' He opened a file. 'Her estate consists of two savings accounts and her flat plus its contents.'

Theo looked out the window as if she could see the flat from here, which was foolish. The two-bedroom flat was across the bridge in Saltash and her grandmother had bought it twenty years ago because it was on the ground floor and had a lovely view of the Tamar and the bridges crossing it. Theo had helped her to plant a garden that Grannie could maintain herself and could survive the strong winds that buffeted it. Up until her last day she had been tending it.

The solicitor took a breath. 'In view of your vow of poverty, Father Martin, she left the flat and the savings accounts to Mrs... Ms Pascoe.' He coughed.

'Please call me Theo or otherwise you'll end up calling me Mrs Pascoe like my grandmother.' Theo smiled at him.

He cleared his throat. 'Your grandmother wasn't Mrs Pascoe but Miss.'

Theo looked at Martin and he shook his head.

'Surely this is wrong.' Virginia put down her teacup.

'No, Claire Pascoe was clear: she was born Claire Pascoe and died Claire Pascoe.'

'I was not referring to that.' Virginia cleared her throat.

'That is nothing but history, and I am uninterested. I don't care if my mother-in-law had been… indiscreet. My concern is that the will is wrong.'

'No, Mrs Pascoe, I assure you it's not.' The solicitor placed his hands on the desk, giving her his full attention.

'She left everything to my husband.'

'That had been the case when he was alive, but on his death she altered the will.'

Virginia turned to Theo. 'Did you know this?'

Theo shook her head. There had been no love lost between Grannie and Virginia so this didn't surprise her.

'I don't believe you.' She rose and said, 'Martin, we will fight this.'

He laughed. 'No, Mother, we will not. I was aware of the will and, because I have taken a vow of poverty, I suggested she leave everything to Theo.'

Virginia sucked in air, picked up her handbag and said, 'Then I shall not waste my money on a hotel room this evening just to see her put into the ground. I'm heading back to Oxford now.'

Theo flinched with the force of her mother's look.

Virginia shoved her hand into her handbag. 'The undertaker had sent her tatty gold watch and garish paste ring to me. You might as well them.' She thrust a small padded envelope at Theo and left.

Martin laughed. 'Well, Mr Simmons, do you have any other revelations?'

He smiled. 'Not for this family.' He pushed an envelope across the table. 'Here are the documents that we stored for your grandmother. I understand from our earlier discussion you plan to sell the flat. Please keep me informed.'

'I'm not so sure about Martin not receiving anything.' Theo looked at Mr Simmons. 'It doesn't seem fair.'

Martin stood and said, 'Life never is, but I don't need anything, and you, dear sister, do.' He grabbed his leathers and led her out of the office.

The kettle on, Theo watched a sea fret moving in from Plymouth sound. Both the river and the bridges were being erased. The flat felt empty without Grannie's calming presence. Theo glanced over her shoulder longing to see her in the chair by the window but it was empty. Theo walked to it and ran her hand along the back feeling the indent of her grandmother's head from years of use. God, Theo missed her. Nothing would fill the void. Picking up a photo frame she studied her grandmother holding a five-year-old David's hand. She ran her finger over the image, trying to feel her again.

Grannie had kept her secrets close. They had never doubted her story. It was simply there. Her husband, John, a fighter pilot in WW2, had never made it back. Had Theo's father questioned it? She shook her head. Judging by her mother's reaction, no. She pulled down the teapot and two cups and saucers. There was only one mug in the flat and that was one David had made for Grannie. Tea tasted better in fine china, according to Claire Pascoe. Theo couldn't argue but mugs were far more practical.

She looked out the window and she could no longer see the bridges or the river. As she scalded the teapot with the boiling water, she couldn't help wondering had there actually been a fighter pilot called John? Obviously not John Pascoe. Or had Grannie simply had one night of passion that had led to the birth of Thomas Pascoe nine months later? Theo closed her eyes. These things happened. She brought her grandmother's image into her mind. A tall and elegant woman who was always neat with her hair in a twist at the back of her head. Her smile lit up her features, especially her bright-blue eyes. The few times Theo had asked about her grandfather, Claire had smiled wistfully. John existed even if only in Grannie's memories.

She put in two heaped spoons of loose tea – gunpowder to be precise – into the teapot. Grannie had loved the rolled pellets of this Chinese tea for her afternoon cup. She would take it with one lump of sugar. Theo picked up the silver tongs and wondered what on earth she would do with them. Surely only cafés and hotels served lump sugar these days, but not the neat squares of her grandmother's kitchen. Theo looked about the tidy space. The counters were clear and the only thing on display was an empty rose bowl. What did this tell her about Claire Pascoe of floral china, gunpowder tea, silver tongs and white sugar cubes for her tea?

While the tea was brewing, Theo walked again into the sitting room and sought out the painting David loved of an old bridge crossing a river. Dappled sunshine covered the ground and the water sparkled. It reminded Theo of Horsebridge. She stepped closer studying the small oil painting, but it only showed the bridge and the river, thus keeping its location a mystery. She lifted it off the wall to see if there was any information on the back. There was a label listing the gallery and the cost. Forty years ago, Grannie had paid £100 for it.

She must have loved it, for Grannie had always been careful with her money, never stingy but selective.

Using her phone, Theo took a picture and sent it with a text to David. He would be down for the funeral tomorrow even if Virginia would not. There was a huge sense of relief in this fact, if Theo were honest. Every meeting with her mother these days became a battle of some sort. Theo wasn't clear what they were fighting about any more.

Martin entered the sitting room and handed her a cup and saucer, saying, 'Imagine keeping that information a secret all of this time.'

Theo shrugged. She understood that sometimes things were best kept secret. 'The shame would have been a big motivator,' she said.

'Thank God some things have changed.' He opened the front of the desk, revealing all the cubby holes and little drawers that they had both loved as children. 'Will this work in your cottage?'

She nodded. 'Are you sure you don't want it?'

'I have Dad's.'

'True.' She smiled, thinking of their father.

He threw an arm over her shoulder. 'Do you want to keep it?'

'The flat?' Her glance narrowed. It had roughly the same square footage as the cottage. It was all on one level and it was near the main line to London. 'Are you saying I'm getting old?' She stepped back and hit him lightly on his arm.

'Well, if the shoe fits.'

'Beast.' She laughed. 'No, I don't want it. I love Boatman's.'

'No heat, no hot water and not much electricity.' He raised

an eyebrow then turned to the view. 'They're both by the Tamar.'

'Indeed, but I love my little place, even without all the mod cons, and they will arrive eventually.'

He turned to her. 'You could live here while you renovate.'

She looked at the beautifully maintained but dated decor, and longed for her wood panels and the sound of the river. 'No, thanks. You could use it as a bolthole.'

He shook his head. 'Not needed when you have a spare room.'

Together they walked into Grannie's bedroom. She opened the jewellery box on the top as she had done so many times as a child fascinated by its contents. 'Do you think she has a photo of our grandfather?'

'Great minds.' He grinned. 'You check in here and I'll go through the desk.'

The box yielded a lovely string of pearls, three unmatching rhinestone earrings, a bracelet Theo had made for her out of seashells and an odd collection of hair pins plus one beautiful tortoiseshell hair comb. Each of them told a story of a woman Theo loved but what was the truth.

At the bottom was the thin gold wedding band Grannie had worn for years. Theo picked it up and turned it in her fingers. She had helped Grannie ease the ring over her swollen knuckles fifteen years ago. What had she said at the time when Theo had said she could have it altered? 'No need for that. I know who I am.' Theo looked in the mirror above the dressing table and said aloud, 'You may have known who you were but you haven't been honest with us.' Theo sighed and put the ring back in the box. This was all harder than she had expected. Claire Pascoe had lived a long and full life. Theo wished it could have been longer but that was a selfish thought. Grannie had been ready and hopefully she was now reunited with her John whoever he was.

Next to the jewellery box was a picture of Theo's parents on their wedding day and one of Martin at his ordination. Opening the backs of each frame, she looked for others. Rather than clutter the surfaces with too many frames, Grannie had simply put one picture on top of another as new photos had arrived. Each frame revealed earlier images. She left them out for Martin to see.

Turning she scanned the simply furnished room. It contained a double bed, a nightstand, a dressing table and a chest of drawers. Theo ran through her mind what she knew of WW2. Almost everything had been rationed including paper. If there was a photo it would be small.

With little hope she went through the drawers, trying not to cry as her grandmother's scent of lavender and rose filled the air. Not today nor tomorrow but she would sort these things out. Picking up a heavy gauge silk scarf, she ran it through her fingers. The colours were a bit faded. Grannie wore it often, lifting whatever cardigan she had on from comfort to elegant fashion. Theo draped it on her shoulders and looked in the mirror. She saw both herself and her grandmother. A lump formed in her throat. Time was fleeting. She turned away and went to the nightstand. In the drawer was a bible and a prayer book. Flipping through the pages she found nothing. She put them back then plumped the pillows and smoothed her hand over the bed cover.

Martin stood in the doorway, watching her. She had

helped Grannie buy a new mattress only last year, but the wooden frame was far older. Running her hand over the headboard, she thought it might look good at Boatman's. She needed a bed; the camp bed was only a temporary solution. Straightening, she asked, 'Find anything?'

He shook his head and crossed his arms. 'There are old letters from us, pictures galore but all beginning from Dad's early years.'

She tilted her head to the side. 'None of her as a child?'

'No, not a one.'

'Disowned?' she asked, at the same time praying that this wasn't the case.

'That's one answer, but most unmarried women gave their children up for adoption at that time,' he said.

'And Grannie didn't.'

He leaned against the door frame and said, 'I looked through the documents that she had stored with the solicitor.'

'And?' she asked.

'Her old passports, her birth certificate and Dad's. Those were the key things.'

'What did they say?' Theo slipped past him into the sitting room and to the desk.

'Look for yourself,' he said, following her.

Pulling her reading glasses off the top of her head, Theo's glance went to her father's registration of birth and the place where his father's name should have been – it stated 'unknown'. Surely Grannie had known who the father was but then she stopped her train of thought.

'I did a quick google search. You couldn't put the father's name on the registration of birth without his signature.'

'Really?'

He nodded. 'They changed the law in 1953.'

'Even though she knew the father she couldn't record it.' Theo touched the word 'unknown' on the form.

Martin shrugged. 'We assume she did.'

Theo frowned.

'It was during the war. Things happened and not all of them good.'

Theo shook her head. 'Grannie loved Dad's father. She told me she had.'

'And you believe her with what we now know?' he asked.

'Yes, and you do too,' she said.

'Can't lie to you.' He laughed. 'Never have been able to, though God knows I tried.' He tapped his finger on Grannie's birth certificate. 'She was born in Truro and both her parents are listed there.'

She studied the documents, trying to put it all together.

He refreshed her tea and glanced over his shoulder. 'Looking at the weather, are you heading home or are you going to stay here tonight?'

She peered out the big picture window at the white wall of fog. 'I'm heading to Boatman's. Cat will never forgive me if I don't provide the required offering of fish-scented biscuits.'

'Then drink up and head off while there is some daylight left.'

'Will do.' She obediently drained her cup and placed it in the kitchen sink.

'Tonight, there is a takeaway fish and chips in my future and some time spent on Ancestry.com to see if I can shed any light on Claire Pascoe, woman of mystery, before I eulogise her tomorrow.'

She smiled. 'I think you may need her whisky supply, which is under the kitchen sink.'

'Under the sink? Who was she hiding it from?' he asked.

'Good question.' She stood on tiptoes and kissed his cheek. 'See you in the morning.'

'By the way, I forgot to say I thought you were gracious to let them do the flowers for tomorrow.'

She rolled her eyes. She hadn't had a choice. It was their church and Grannie had been one of the flower ladies; they wanted to honour her and Theo wouldn't interfere. Although tomorrow when she saw the results, she may not feel so gracious.

Chapter Five

Thus far today had not gone as expected. First there was a dead rat, a present from Cat who obviously thought Theo was struggling for food with the late delivery of dry biscuits last night. Then there was the email from the archivist of the Duke of Exeter. That had distracted her from the rat. The archivist said she would love to see the letters and could confirm that a Zachariah Carne had lived in Boatman's Cottage in 1913 and 1914. He had been a river keeper, the junior gillie on the estate, and he had not returned to the estate after the Great War.

This piece of history had led to her late arrival at Grannie's flat and no quiet time with either Martin or David who, between them, had completed all the set-up for the small reception after the burial without her help. On her arrival they had headed almost immediately to the service in the local church, St Stevens. But Theo had wanted so much from today, especially time with David. Funerals had a way of putting things into perspective. Hopefully his unease about the divorce had lessened since the arrival of Piers's new daughter six months ago.

She turned to watch David as he ushered the last old dear

out the door. He had been wonderful with them all, listening attentively to whatever they had to say. She, on the other hand, had been distracted. Her thoughts raced between Grannie's secret, wondering if Martin had unearthed anything on Ancestry last night and David's slightly hands-off behaviour with her.

Theo still clutched the newspaper that had been thrust into her hands. It contained the obituary of Claire Pascoe, she had been informed. She put it down and picked up the last of the cups and brought them to the kitchen. Martin had already begun the washing up. Picking up a tea towel, she began drying.

'That went well,' Martin said, casting her a glance.

She nodded. 'Bit quiet.'

'If you live to the ripe old age of a hundred there won't be many dancing a jig at your funeral.' He handed her the teapot.

She laughed. 'True but...'

'This is interesting.' David walked into the kitchen, holding open the paper she had put down.

Theo squinted at the paper. 'Grannie's obit?'

He shook his head and said, 'No, the article about the unidentified remains of two WW1 soldiers they've found in France.'

'Another mystery to be solved,' Martin said, letting the water out of the sink and reaching for the bottle of whisky below it.

David pointed to the page. 'Three soldiers and an officer from the Duke of Cornwall's Light Infantry had been reported dead in the area but never found.'

'Intriguing,' Martin said as he took out three tumblers.

Theo smiled. Grannie did enjoy a good single malt whisky. It was where Theo had acquired her taste for it.

'Yes, they are looking for relatives, specifically direct male descendants, for a DNA search,' David said. 'It would be great if they could find them and bury the men with their names.'

Theo peered over his shoulder, scanning the article. Her heart leapt. Zachariah Carne. She pointed to the name. 'This one, Zachariah Carne, could have been the gillie who lived in my cottage.'

Martin handed her a glass. 'Now that is interesting.'

'And this—' she tapped the article '—could explain why he never returned after the Great War.'

David looked between them both. 'How do you know all this?'

'I found a stash of hidden letters when cleaning,' she paused, thinking of the emotion in the one she had read. 'And the manager of Abbotswood Hotel directed me to the archivist for the Duke of Exeter whose ancestors built the estate back in the early 1800s.'

Martin walked to the door to the garden. 'It's a lovely evening – shall we sit outside?'

Theo and David followed. David handed the article to Martin who said, 'Hmmm, St Loy. Isn't that the family that owned Penhale?'

'Penhale?' Theo asked.

'I recall reading an article about it after a visit with Grannie. It was one of the first properties given to the National Trust after WW2.' Martin swirled the liquid in his glass. 'Grannie visited the property frequently.'

'Did she?' Theo remembered going once years ago with her. 'I don't recall her mentioning it.'

Martin nodded. 'She particularly liked the chapel there.' He raised his glass. 'To Grannie, an enigma.'

Theo lifted her glass. 'True.'

'What do you guys mean?' David took a sip of the whisky.

Martin looked to Theo. 'Shall I tell him he is from illegitimate stock or shall you?'

Theo turned from Martin's searching glance. 'You,' she said, while walking away to look at the view.

'It appears that Grannie never married her fly boy. She was born Claire Pascoe and remained Claire Pascoe.'

David smiled. 'Imagine keeping that a secret all these years.'

'Hmmm. Secrets are not all they're cracked up to be.' Martin raised an eyebrow.

'Come on, secrets are kept that way for good reason.' David stood.

'Normally people think so, but all it means is that you're avoiding the truth.'

'Is that bad?' Theo asked.

'In my experience, yes. Things fester and grow far worse hidden.'

'This experience comes from the confessional, no doubt.' David laughed. 'I bet you've heard everything.'

'Almost.' Martin tilted his head to the side and looked at Theo. 'Shining light on things may at first make them appear worse, but once the shock is over it can be resolved. None of us would have cared a bit if Grannie announced she never married her fly boy.'

'True,' Theo said, looking back to the flat and thinking of

all the questions she had for Grannie that would now never be answered.

'We still would have loved her and would have known more about him and therefore us.' Martin took a sip from his glass.

'Well, she loved him,' David said.

Theo turned around. 'How do you know that?'

'When I used to stay with her, she would talk to me about her life.' David grinned. 'And I listened too.'

Martin raised his eyebrows. 'Maybe we never asked... don't talk about the war and all that.'

'She was an only child and her father was a solicitor.' David swirled the whisky in the glass. 'Mind you, she never mentioned that she hadn't married her fly boy, as you called him. His name was John and he was Cornish too. That's how they met, she said.'

Theo sat back down. 'Where?'

David laughed. 'Gosh, you didn't know her at all.' He stood and went to the kitchen to top up his drink. 'Oxford.'

'Grannie was at Oxford.'

David nodded. 'She did two years then the war arrived. John was there too but they were only acquaintances at the time.'

'How did they meet again then?' Martin asked.

'A London nightclub.' He sat down. 'Can't remember the name but she recalled every single detail. By then she was working for the war office and he was in bomber command.'

'Well, that all fits with what she told us in brief,' Theo said.

'What else did she say?' Martin asked.

'Not too much but she had a great picture of them when they became engaged.'

'Where is it?' Theo asked, scanning the room.

David stood. 'Where's her handbag?'

'I put it beside the bed, but I went through it yesterday and there wasn't a picture in there.' She'd found an embroidered hankie, her bus pass, the battered brown leather coin purse and half a roll of extra-strong peppermints. It was the extra-strong mints that broke Theo yesterday. They were Grannie's weakness. She loved them and Theo knew she never allowed herself more than one a day. No doubt a legacy from the years of rationing.

David returned with the handbag and Theo watched him go straight to the side pocket. From there he pulled out Grannie's bus pass. She kept it in a beautiful, old, tooled, leather folding case. He opened it and Theo saw the bus pass as she had yesterday, but David pulled that out. 'Here. Isn't it a gorgeous photo?' He held the picture up and there she saw her grandmother as a young woman with a huge smile. Her hand was held aloft by the handsome airman by her side. The black and white image had faded and the features weren't sharp but there was no denying that this man was her grandfather. Martin looked like him. The other thing that was unmistakable was the engagement ring. It was huge on her grandmother's slender fingers.

David handed her the picture and Theo put on her reading glasses to take a closer look. Grannie's dark hair was down but rolled off her face in the style of the day. She wore a skirt and a jacket that nipped in at the waist, showing off her slim figure. John, clearly her fiancé, was in uniform. Behind them was the Thames. Looking at the faces, their happiness was obvious. She handed the photo to Martin saying, 'It's clear where your cheekbones come from.'

He smiled then studied the photo carefully. 'I remember that ring.' He looked up. 'She wore it around her neck.'

'Yes.' Theo grabbed her handbag where the padded envelope from yesterday was tucked. She opened it and scanned the letter from the undertaker. The heavy gold chain slid out first followed by the watch and the ring comprised of a large emerald flanked by two big diamonds. 'Here.' She passed it to David.

He turned it in his fingers. 'This must be worth a lot.'

She shook her head. 'Paste.'

'Why do you say that, Mum?' David asked.

'A ring of the size would be worth a small fortune.' She glanced at the photo again. 'He was a pilot and not some duke so a real ring of this size wouldn't have been in his reach.'

'Maybe it was his gran's,' he said.

Theo laughed. 'As my mother said yesterday, it's paste.' She slipped the chain with the ring around her neck where it settled by her heart.

'Do you think Grandpa knew?' David asked.

Theo and Martin looked at each other and said in unison, 'No.'

The carriage clock on the mantle chimed the hour and David glanced at his watch. 'Sorry I can't stay and help with the flat.'

'It's OK. The estate agent will be here tomorrow morning early and then Martin and I will know what we need to do.' Theo smiled at him.

'Thanks for understanding; it's just that Dad is on paternity leave.' He looked down at his feet.

Theo walked up to him and took his hand in hers. 'It's OK. I understand.'

He glanced at her briefly. 'Thanks, Mum, must go and catch my train.' He downed the last of his whisky and dashed out the door before Theo could say another thing.

She turned to Martin after David was no longer in view and asked, 'Is he OK?'

Martin cocked his head to the side and said, 'Give him time.'

She pressed her lips together.

'You can do it. He loves you and you love him but he's in an awkward place.'

She nodded. She must be patient.

Case 752
Status: Open
6 May 2019

Further examination of the remains indicate that it is of two men both approximately 23–25 years of age and approximately six foot to six foot one in height. This eliminates Benjamin Skewes as he was aged 35 when he enlisted.

DNA has been obtained from the remains.

Contact has been made with the family of Samuel Lyons and a DNA collection kit has been sent.

No family located for William Bowman yet.

Captain Edmund St Loy, the Earl St Loy, had one son who died in WW2 and without issue. We are contacting the relations of St Loy.

Chapter Six

As Theo reheated wild garlic soup she'd made yesterday, she looked around. Not long ago this place seemed alien and now, even in the light of one low-wattage bulb, it felt like home with red campion and cow parsley in a jug on the windowsill, Grannie's old kitchen table, and two Windsor chairs with their seats worn and shiny from years of use. They filled the kitchen along with the bright floral china on the open shelves. David's final painting for his A levels adorned the big wall dividing the kitchen and the sitting room, bringing much-needed colour and joy.

Grannie's flat had sold without even going on the market and now many of her things filled Boatman's and looked as if they had been designed for the cottage, whereas they had always looked out of place in the 1970s built flat. Theo felt alive here but she couldn't explain why. Somehow, she had sleepwalked her way through over half her life until she was pushed, kicking and screaming, into the cold bath of reality like the one she'd had this morning. A new boiler couldn't come soon enough. The joy of not having to use Gayle's washing machine would be a gift too.

She poured her soup into a large mug and went out the

back door of the cottage to check the bonfire. A small trickle of smoke rose from it and the ground around the cottage was in the full flush of spring. It was late May and the ramsons vied with the bluebells. The pungent garlic aroma battled it out with the sweet bluebell scent but she loved them both. The wood violets and primroses were almost finished along the pathways. And this morning she had discovered a cluster of white wood anemones. Her heart had soared. Now that the tree surgeon had begun to work wonders, lopping off branches and clearing a few of the weedier trees, she could see where the garden had been. Sunlight bathed the cottage at midday and picked out the small rowboat she had discovered when clearing brambles. Testing its water worthiness was on her list of things to do.

With Gayle's help she had put together a cold house shelter on the west side of Boatman's for her cuttings then together they had raided a local garden centre for all the slightly damaged discounted pots. This year she needed to observe the garden and discover what was there before she made any big changes; she must confine herself to potted plants for this summer.

Back in the kitchen she put the kettle on and glanced at the box with the letters. Now that most things had been resolved with Grannie's estate, she could return to finding out more about Boatman's. The electrician was due in this week to rewire and would be bringing his mother. Theo was looking forward to quizzing her about the cottage's history. But this afternoon was for painting the second bedroom.

Her phone rang.

'Theo, I'm glad I caught you,' Hugo said. 'Are you at home?'

She squinted out of the window. 'I am.'

'I'm in a bit of a jam. The floral designer has gone down with stomach flu.'

'Oh.' Theo put her mug on the counter.

'Gayle mentioned you did this.' He cleared his throat.

'I… I'm very rusty.' It had been two years since she last worked properly. She glanced at the wildflowers on the windowsill.

'I'm in a bind. Tonight we have a fiftieth wedding celebration.'

She took a deep breath. 'I might not have the skill you need?'

'I'm sure you do and I wouldn't ask if the assistant hadn't lost his nerve,' he said.

She closed her eyes for a moment. 'OK. But you said the event is tonight?'

'Yes, the flowers are here as are the plans.'

She looked out the window and said, 'I'll come.'

'By boat?' he asked.

She laughed. 'Don't think so. Not sure the one I found will even float.'

'I'll send the gillie with one of ours to meet you.'

'OK.' Theo looked down at her bleach-marked tracksuit bottoms. She needed to change, and the painting would wait until tomorrow. 'I'll be on the quay in ten minutes.'

Beads of water pooled on the glossy leaves of the climbing jasmine. The scent reminded her of Paris in June. Theo stepped back, releasing the memory. Although it tingled across her skin, she needed to focus on the here and now. The effect of the jasmine in full bloom over the arch was stunning. It would fragrance the entrance to the tent for the anniversary party. Fifty years together was an accomplishment.

'Hello dear,' a proper yet husky voice said.

Theo turned around to see an older woman in a crisp white blouse with a chunky silver necklace about her neck. Her hair was close-cropped in a timeless style; pure effortless elegance.

'Are you the florist?' she asked.

Theo smiled. 'No, just the hired hand.'

'I've been watching you, and you're no hired hand.' She paused as she breathed in the scent of the plant. 'In fact, you look familiar.'

Theo tilted her head to the side. 'Really?'

'Yes—' the woman paused, studying her '—but it won't come to me right now.'

Theo smiled. 'That happens to me too. I'm Theo.'

The woman held out her hand. 'Jeanette.'

Theo took her hand, noting the bright eyes and the beautiful bone structure of Jeanette's face. 'Is this your celebration?'

'Heavens, no, my twin sister, Sophie's. I could never have tolerated one man for that long.' She chuckled.

'Fifty years is impressive.' Theo smiled.

'They met in Paris. I was there as a model and she had come to visit, or, truthfully, to spy on me for my mother.'

'To see if you were behaving?' Theo raised an eyebrow.

'I wasn't, not at all.' Her laughter began from deep within as a rumble and emerged glorious and gritty.

'Oh dear,' Theo said.

'Well, on the first night I took her to meet an English reporter I knew and the rest, as they say, is history.'

'And you?' Theo asked, securing the main stem with one more tie.

'Well, I stayed in Paris then went to New York and Rome.' Jeanette lifted a blue violet to her nose.

'Love?' Theo asked.

'Plenty of it but never the type that was meant to survive all the boredom of the domestic.' Jeanette's face had her life well lived etched across it. The laughter lines were the most pronounced.

'Ah, I see.' And she did. There was a caged energy about her and a mischief dancing in her eyes.

Jeanette returned Theo's scrutiny. 'Yes, I think you do.' She glanced at Theo's left hand with the indentation still very noticeable on her ring finger.

'You will be fine; in fact, I predict better than fine.' She placed a hand on Theo's arm.

'Thank you,' Theo said.

From the hotel a young woman waved a hand at them. 'I think that means I have a dirty martini waiting.'

'Enjoy.' Theo smiled.

'Oh, I intend to... and remember it's all in the intention.'

Theo turned back to the tent and the task at hand. With luck she would finish soon and might be able to squeeze in some decorating after all.

As Theo was walking back down to the river, she saw Jeanette coming towards her and asked, 'Was the martini dirty enough?'

'Indeed, it was.' The crow's feet around Jeanette's eyes deepened and the light in them danced.

'I can't remember the last time I had a martini.' Theo sighed.

'Now, that is a sin of the highest order.'

Theo laughed. 'I can think of others and may have committed a few more.'

Jeanette slipped her arm through hers in a conspiratorial way. 'Now that sounds like an interesting opening.'

'Opening?' Theo raised an eyebrow.

'Of our acquaintance.' She smiled. 'We are at the beginning of a brilliant friendship.' She raised her shoulders and shivered a bit. 'I can feel it in my very bones.' Jeanette stopped and turned to the river. 'You were about to set off in that little boat, weren't you?'

'Yes.' Theo had told the gillie that she would use it to make her own way back, if that was fine with him. He'd looked her up and down, assessing her rowing skills, and said she could give it a try.

'See, your life is intriguing already,' she said, waving a graceful, almost dancer-like hand towards the river.

'How?' Theo wrinkled her nose. Mundane, yes. Intriguing, not so much, unless having no hot water counted.

'You cross a magical river and you think nothing of it.'

The Tamar glistened in the afternoon light, reflecting the pale-blue sky above and fresh green leaves adorning the trees along the Cornish bank.

'Magical?' Theo asked.

'Don't you know the legend of Tamara from which the river takes its name?'

Theo shook her head, looking not for magic but at the force of the current. She would need to put her back into it to row upriver to the small quay. She untied the boat and held onto the painter. The boat tugged as if sensing the potential freedom.

'There once was a nymph who loved being in the sunshine.' Jeanette waved her hand. 'She was of such beauty that two giants, whom her parents feared, fell in love with her. They were called Tawridge and Tavy. She would frolic with them and wouldn't do as her parents wished and return to the dark cavern. They feared she would marry one of them.'

Theo pulled the boat back to the bank, envisioning the enchanted world that Jeanette's words were conjuring.

'One day, tired from play, they sat with Tamara between them and they all fell asleep. And this is where her parents found them.'

'Parental intervention?' Theo asked.

She nodded. 'Rather than have their beloved daughter marry one of their enemies, the giants, they turned her into a river. Her tears flowed as she became water that would always flow to the sea.' Jeanette bent to the Tamar and ran her hand through it. 'A river of tears.'

'What happened to the giants?' Theo asked, wrapping the rope tighter around her hand.

'Tavy woke first and, devastated, he went to his father who understood his despair, and he turned him into a river that always runs alongside his love but never touches her.'

'And the other?' Theo asked.

'Tawridge woke later and ran to an enchanter who turned him into a stream. In his rush he took the wrong direction, which led him away from his love.'

Theo squinted as a cloud pulled away from the sun. 'Poor bloke.'

'Do you see how magical it is?' She smiled.

Across on the Cornish bank the late afternoon sunlight picked out patches of deep-violet bluebells, bursting open from the day's light. 'Yes, it is a special place.'

'Fairies could live there,' Jeanette said.

Theo laughed, thinking of her little place with no hot water unless it came out of a kettle. 'It's not very glamorous.'

Jeanette shrugged. 'Who needs glamour? What you need is excitement and contentment.'

'Well, there has been excitement and I'm working on the contentment.'

'Excellent to hear,' she said.

'I live in Boatman's across the river. It's there out of sight as the hillside climbs.' Theo thought for a second. 'Would you like to see it?'

'Thought you'd never ask.' Jeanette smiled.

Theo helped her into the boat and released it. They floated away from the bank and Theo felt the force of the current, but, thankfully, as she pulled the oars back, the boat began to move, and before long she was securing the boat to the quay.

Theo turned to her guest and said, 'Follow me and mind your step.'

They walked the narrow path through the bluebells to the cottage in silence. The scent on the warm breeze was heavenly and Theo felt light like the white feather she saw floating down from the treetops. Jeanette picked it up then bent low to breathe in the bluebells. When she stood, she handed Theo the feather. 'You've been visited.'

Theo raised an eyebrow.

'An angel walked this way and—' Jeanette looked around before she continued '—love has walked this way too.'

Theo stopped and looked up to the cottage. Her glance sought out the window by the door. A and Z. The letters linked beautifully and below them on the window ledge Cat sat waiting. Since she had recently been bringing Theo decapitated animals, Theo chose not to leave a window open for Cat to wander through at leisure. Everything Cat did was at leisure, even hunting. She would lie in the bluebells, waiting until some unsuspecting creature passed by her.

Opening the door, Theo said, 'Welcome to my little home.'

'I've wondered about it.' Jeanette stroked the door frame. 'You know it?' she asked.

'Oh, yes, I spent many summers here with my family.'

Theo blinked. Jeanette could have said almost anything, and she wouldn't have been surprised, but this did.

Cat now wove through Jeanette's legs. Theo took a deep breath, trying to envision the cottage through Jeanette's eyes. She wouldn't find much changed. Grannie's two armchairs sat by the fire currently draped in white throws. There was also the large ottoman covered in a Turkish carpet that Cat had claimed as her own.

'I'd wondered who had bought it.' Jeanette scooped up Cat and moved toward the fireplace where she stroked the lintel as if it were her lover.

She turned to the window and said, 'Aardvark and Zebra.'

'Who?' Theo asked.

Jeanette chuckled in a deep throaty way that spoke of years of two packs a day. 'My sister and I created a story about a love affair between an aardvark and a zebra.' Her finger traced the letters. 'But the truth is always more haunting.'

'I'm confused.' Theo shook her head.

'I'm sorry.' She smiled. 'I don't suppose you could offer me a drink and I'll tell you a story.'

'But of course.' Theo looked around. 'Tea?'

'Something stronger perhaps.' Jeanette slipped into the armchair while Theo went in search of her good whisky, intrigued beyond words. She returned to Jeanette, carrying two glasses. Cat was curled up on Jeanette's lap, purring, and a letter from the metal box was in Jeanette's hand.

She looked up. 'You found these?'

Theo nodded.

'I thought they might have dissolved into the building once we had put them back.' She lifted the thin sheet of paper. 'We were never allowed to open the unopened ones. My mother said not to. But reading it now, my God what heartache.' Jeanette cleared her throat and read it aloud.

30 July 1916

My dark lady,

The birds may be singing but I don't hear them. I have shut out all beauty and let the sound of guns and men's dying screams fill my thoughts. They match how I feel. How could I have walked into this? I knew from the beginning that we were not meant to be together. There was no possibility it could have worked. That we could have escaped. That was only ever a dream.

Just like the dreams I had as a boy when I led your horse and fantasised that you were my friend, and not his. I should have known. But the heart never listens to the head. Love does not conquer all.

I try not to think of you but even if I work until my body will move no further, once it stops my mind is filled with you. Sleep does not bring relief nor does boredom during the endless hours when we can do nothing but watch the beetles shuttle across the bottom of the trench. I relish hard physical labour when it comes. I want my back to strain as I dig and my hands to blister from the repeated movement of the handle.

Anything at all that will prevent me from thinking of the feel of your skin, the taste of your lips and the sound of your pleasure. In the whisper of the breeze I hear your laughter. In the flight of a falcon I see your grace. Nature gives me no reprieve. I found you in the woods, walking among the fading bluebells and emerging foxgloves. How angry you were then at your unjust banishment to paradise. Yes, it is paradise, not the hell you thought. Here is hell. My grandmother always said hell was being kept from her loved ones. Here in this trench I am with my brother but away from you.

Now the mud is deep and the boredom relentless and I am kept from you. No matter what I do I can never be with you. You made certain of it. You married him. He walks past me and I see his pity. So yes, I am in hell in every form except for the flames. The flames come at night as I dream. Our passion consumes me.

I've licked the pencil and the lead tastes bitter. Therefore the words I am writing are bitter too. I am a fool, and I live to do the bidding of my lover's husband. Why him? I do not understand.

Z

Jeanette's hand shook as she put the letter down. Theo remained standing, holding the glasses. Eventually she found movement and gave Jeanette her large measure of whisky.

'I need this.' Jeanette raised the glass to the light.

'Agreed. Do you know who it is?' Theo asked.

Jeanette shook her head. 'My mother did.' She looked at the window with the letters entwined and took a long sip. 'Which is why she scolded us and told us to put everything back.'

'How did you come to holiday here?' Theo sat opposite her.

Jeanette smiled. 'Oh, my mother was the youngest daughter of the 10th Duke of Exeter and when the estate needed money, they sold bits off, and she bought Boatman's.'

'Did I buy the cottage from you?' Theo asked.

Jeanette smiled. 'In a way. The cottage and a few other bits and pieces were tied up in a complicated trust that only resolved recently, hence the sale.'

'I see.'

Jeanette laughed, saying, 'There's no way you could. It took me years to unravel things. Her estate proved to be complex like her life.'

'How so?' Theo studied Jeanette.

Jeanette snorted. 'Well, as a start she lived until the ripe old age of a hundred and four.'

'Wow.'

'She was completely with it until the end.' Jeanette smiled. 'Now, what have you done to the place?'

Theo stood. 'Not a lot is the simple answer but let me give you a tour.'

'Wonderful.' Jeanette hopped up, disturbing Cat, who did not appreciate the movement. 'Do you have plans for in here?'

'Other than to eventually find a small sofa, sort some heating, no.'

'Agree with you on that completely.' They walked through to the kitchen and Theo turned on the light. Jeanette looked up and down. 'You'll need to update this.'

'Agree.' Theo took a deep breath, thinking of the work and the disruption.

Jeanette laughed and studied Theo more closely. 'You have the look of someone I knew, however it escapes me now.' She laughed. 'Unlike my mother, my memory is failing. Although my mother's life was unusual, very unusual, especially for her time. I lived life a bit harder, shall we say, and that, I think, has taken a few of my brain cells.' She turned to Theo, smiling wickedly, before saying, 'I think it was a good trade.'

'I bet it was.' Theo grinned.

'I hope you have lived and lived fully.' She stepped closer to Theo and Theo fought the urge to turn away. 'Hmm, well, there is still time.'

Jeanette chuckled and studied David's painting. 'That is beautiful and very, very good.'

Theo nodded, thinking of all that talent unused now. Who knew when David had last picked up a brush? No time she guessed if he was running the business while Piers was away being a new father. Grannie's carriage clock chimed from the sitting room.

'Good lord is that the time?' Jeanette held her wrist.

'Afraid so.'

'I don't suppose you could drop me on the other side?' Jeanette asked.

Theo nodded and they walked out in the beautiful evening together. As Theo made yet another trip across the Tamar she suspected her muscles would remind her all about it tomorrow.

Chapter Seven

Theo replied to David's text checking on her then looked at the metal box as she tidied everything away for the electrician's visit. Jeanette hadn't told her what she knew, but they had arranged to meet this afternoon and Theo couldn't wait for the electrician's or for Jeanette's visit.

In the kitchen she boiled the kettle and made a thermos of coffee and one of tea that would hopefully provide for her and her guests while the electrics were down. She had picked up some homemade cake at a local farm. Placing everything on the sitting room table, she adjusted the irises in the mason jar she had placed there earlier. They too had come from the local farm. Theo discovered that they grew flowers commercially, carrying on as many farms had in the past in the Tamar Valley with market produce, be it apples, cherries, pears, and, of course, early daffodils.

Maybe after the cottage and garden were restored, she could work with the farm and their flowers. Possibly running courses. She wasn't sure she wanted to provide arrangements for weddings and other events again. She had loved doing that for years, but she was rusty and would she be good enough now, having had nearly two years out? Doubt always crept in.

Her phone rang. 'Hello Martin.'

'Just checking on you in the wild west.' He laughed.

'Still alive and best of all the whole cottage should have electrics from today or possibly tomorrow at the latest.' She glanced about the sitting room. Candlelight was lovely but for reading in the evening impractical. She had found two wonderful lamps made from old candelabra. The bases were creatures – sort of firedrake meets dragon meets lion – with the tails rising to support three candles or now two candles and a light bulb. She had polished the brass and she couldn't wait to see them glowing with electric light.

'Great. So I can come and visit?'

'Do you need electrics to do that?' Theo walked through to the kitchen.

'Yes, and hot water and Wi-Fi.'

She laughed. 'Dream on.'

'I need a tent then?' he asked.

'Not that bad. It's one step at a time. Electrics first then the heating engineer.' She paused. 'What have you been up to?'

'Finished teaching for the summer and now becoming an amateur genealogist.'

'Really?' she asked.

'Yes. I've found out about Grannie and her parents and their long Cornish heritage.'

'Brilliant.' She walked out the back door to check the plants.

'And I've taken a DNA test.'

She stopped. 'Good God, whatever for?'

'A colleague managed to track down his birth mother and father this way.'

'You're searching for John?' She watered the plants and deadheaded the parsley that had already run to flower. 'Tricky without a last name.'

'Doing my best.'

'Can you find out that much?' she asked.

'Yes and no. Can I come tomorrow?'

'Of course.' She laughed. 'I haven't painted the room yet.'

'Camping it is then.'

'Not quite. You have a bed and a roof.'

'See you tomorrow afternoon.' She heard the phone click and noticed her battery was low. She plugged it in and hoped the electrician wouldn't arrive until she had some charge. She should have thought of that last night.

The sun had come out and Theo sat outside with Mrs Thompson, Gayle's grandmother, who was a delight. What was not a delight was the sounds of Mrs Thompson's son and his apprentice coming from the house. Repeatedly she was drawn away from this charming woman to consult on whether they could cut through the wood panelling to bring the cables through, this being the easiest and cheapest option, but there was no way she would have those panels cut.

This led to a long discussion on how to achieve electrics into the room. One answer was to go through the bedroom and then down to the sitting room and the other was to lift the floors. She asked for estimated costs and the expected results. While they worked that out, she suggested they tackled the utility room, bathroom, bedrooms and outdoor sockets to cater for the existing shed first and the planned greenhouse.

With a notebook open and tea poured, she asked Mrs Thompson what she remembered about the cottage and working at the big house.

The woman smiled. 'The cottage didn't belong to the house by the time I was there. It belonged to Lady Constance.' She raised an eyebrow in a meaningful way that Theo assumed she was supposed to understand.

'Was this a problem?'

'Oh no, but Lady Constance was a bit of a black sheep.' A smile hovered on Mrs Thompson's mouth.

Theo thought of Jeanette and thinking possibly the acorn doesn't fall far from the tree. 'Do tell.'

'Well, she never married.' Mrs Thompson put her cup down.

'I see.' Theo wasn't sure that she did.

'I don't suppose you do because she lived with another woman.'

'Oh.' For the time this must have been most unusual. Who was Jeanette's father?

'There was always talk about Lady Constance that the family thought the staff didn't hear, but of course we did. Her brother, the 11th Duke, Francis Neville, was a delight and adored her, but his wife didn't approve. Lady Constance went to Oxford in the mid 1920s and her companion went with her. Lady Constance became something of an expert on butterflies.'

'Impressive.' Theo was trying to fit this all into the little Jeanette had revealed. She had implied her mother had led a quiet life, but Theo could imagine compared to Jeanette's it might have been. 'Her daughters?'

'We never heard who the father was. He never appeared when Lady Constance and family would stay here in the summer.'

She would need to ask Jeanette about her father. She looked at the cottage then asked, 'Anything else about the cottage?' Theo pointed to the windowpane with the letters etched into it.

'No.' She smiled. 'The Nevilles were good people to work for. I was sad when they sold the estate off and the fishing syndicate took it on for a bit.'

'Did you continue to work there?' Theo asked.

'No, soon after I was married and had my hands full.' She smiled. 'You married?'

'Was.' Theo put her pen down.

'Widow?' Mrs Thompson asked.

Theo shook her head.

'Got a bad one, did you?' Mrs Thompson asked.

Theo laughed. 'I think he might look at it the other way around.'

'They always do dear, they always do. Women are always blamed but it takes two, it does.' She rose to her feet as her son came out, swiftly followed by the apprentice.

'Nothing more we can do today. Need some parts and I need to put together the costs for you.'

Theo asked, 'Do I have any electrics at the moment?'

Rich nodded. 'As you were before.'

Mrs Thompson placed a hand on Theo's arm. 'My mother was a lady's maid here during the First World War.'

Theo's head shot up.

'She didn't say much about it because she'd been accused of stealing.'

85

'Stealing?' Theo asked.

'Yes. But she hadn't and thankfully Lady Alice found out she'd been accused and brought her to Penhale and made sure that she was OK.'

'Lady Alice? Lady Constance's sister?'

Mrs Thompson shook her head. 'I don't think so. My mother thought the world of her, but there had been something scandalous that she would never speak of.' She smiled and climbed into the van with the help of her son.

'Thank you.' She waved them off and went to investigate the electrics feeling more confused than ever. Who was Lady Alice?

Theo was sweeping the dust up when Jeanette appeared. 'Well, hello.'

Theo smiled at Jeanette, who was carrying a bottle of wine and a basket.

'I was correct in guessing that things hadn't gone to plan today.' Jeanette put everything on the kitchen table.

Theo nodded as she straightened then emptied the dustpan.

'Well, it's a glorious evening and I brought dinner and wine as I'm later than expected.'

Theo smiled. 'Thank you.' She bent over, putting the dustpan away and Grannie's ring swung out from her shirt.

'That's quite the rock!' Jeanette said. 'Did the ex give you that? Not surprised you kept it.'

Theo laughed, lifting it up so that Jeanette could see it. 'Not from the ex but my grandmother's paste ring.'

Jeanette's nose wrinkled and she held the ring to examine it. 'I may not know many things but—' she paused to slide her glasses on '—I know the real thing when I see it.' She let it drop back onto Theo's chest.

Theo lifted the chain over her head, saying, 'Take a closer look. There is no way my grandmother could have had an engagement ring of that size and quality.'

Jeanette lifted the ring towards the ceiling light and said, 'Do you have a magnifying glass? I can't make out the maker's mark.'

Theo dug into her grandmother's sewing basket. The small circular glass was encased in decorative silver and caught the light casting a prism on the wall.

Jeanette took it and, after examining the ring, said, 'As I thought. Not paste. It's a Garrard's piece and it's familiar.'

'Oh God, are you about to tell me my grandmother was a thief?' Theo took a deep breath. 'Mind you, we just discovered that she never married.'

'I think there is a story emerging here and she sounds like a wonderful woman.'

Theo nodded and opened the wine.

'Tell me about her,' Jeanette said, taking the glass from Theo.

'First, if this isn't paste, what would an emerald of this size and clarity be worth?'

Jeanette shrugged. 'I'm no expert but at least fifty thousand pounds, maybe more.'

Theo gulped.

'But let's not talk about that. I have an idea.'

Theo frowned, not wanting to stop talking about the ring.

'Are you free tomorrow afternoon?' Jeanette asked. 'It's too late today sadly.'

Theo shook her head. 'My brother Martin will be here.'

'Excellent, he can come too.'

'I'm confused. To where?' Theo unpacked the basket, spying a quiche and salad.

'To Penhale, which I think may answer your questions about the ring and explain why you look more familiar to me by the day.' Jeanette took a sip of her wine.

'I'm confused.'

'I do do this to people.' She grinned. 'I rather enjoy it.' Her deep throaty laugh emerged and Theo decided she would follow along with her. She didn't think she had much choice about it either.

Chapter Eight

Martin had rung from a service station to say he was running late. Jeanette was talking to Cat in the sitting room while Theo was making coffee. She wasn't sure how this trip to Penhale would go. Martin was intrigued, but then he always was. Unlike her, he looked at everything as something to discover. She should try and be more like him but she didn't have his mind, as her mother made sure Theo knew.

She carried the tray into the sitting room.

Jeanette was looking at the old Baedeker's. 'What a beautiful guide.' She looked up and smiled.

'Yes, it was given to me a long time ago.' Theo took a deep breath, feeling the sun on her back and fizzy excitement in her stomach thinking about it.

'Looking at you in this moment you've changed. There is a spark in your eyes that I haven't seen before. Tell me the story please.'

Theo cleared her throat. 'It's nothing.'

'It's not nothing. Your hands are shaky and you have flushed. I sense something momentous, like a forbidden love affair.'

Theo sat in the chair opposite Jeanette. 'A painter bought

me the book from one of the bookstalls on the banks of the Seine in June 1986, two weeks before I married.'

Jeanette picked up the pot and poured them both a cup. 'More please?'

Theo shook her head.

'I know there's more. It's written on your face. You had an affair with this dashing French painter; he painted you in the nude and seduced you.'

Theo closed her eyes.

'I'm right, aren't I?' Jeanette grinned.

Theo shook her head no.

'I am. Don't forget I know the lure of Paris, the lure of painters, photographers and, well, let's be honest, men in general.'

'He wasn't French.'

'Oh, how intriguing. Did you know his name?' she asked.

Theo's eyes opened wide, affronted, but then smiled. 'Only his first, Patrick.'

'Delicious.' Jeanette laughed. 'I am pleased for you.'

'He did paint me, nude and…'

'I can imagine, having been in the same position myself… many times. First it's the exposure, then it's someone looking at you that closely.' She sipped her coffee. 'Then it's how do they see you and then each brush stroke on the canvas is… a caress.'

'Umm, well,' Theo said, picking up her cup. She hadn't allowed her mind to travel this route in a long time. She had blocked it. It was the past. It was wrong. She'd been foolish. She winced, hearing her mother's voice especially in the final word.

Theo had been engaged to be married and she'd slept with another man. On her return to the UK, she had planned to call the wedding off, but Piers had beaten her to a confession. At their favourite pub on the banks of the Thames, he confessed that while she'd been away finishing her dissertation on the Trocadero Gardens in Paris, he'd been sleeping with his father's secretary. He'd said it hadn't meant anything, it was just sex. Could she forgive him? She'd sat dumbstruck and looked into his eyes. This was the man she'd thought she loved and had agreed to marry. Could she forgive him knowing she was guilty too? She had cheated too, although she couldn't say it had just been sex; it had been passion and freedom.

She'd turned the engagement ring on her finger and had forgiven Piers and had put Paris and Patrick behind her. Marrying Piers was the right thing to do. If she didn't, he would think she hadn't forgiven him, and she had. He would have declared that she was unkind and cruel and she wasn't. He deserved a second chance. She did too but she didn't ask for it. Marrying him and promising to make everything perfect going forward was her way to atone. Paris and Patrick were moments to remember, nothing more.

Of course, marrying Piers had meant proving her mother right. Because of Theo's pregnancy she had never finished her dissertation, never received her degree and had been crowned a throwback woman, becoming a housewife and mother for years. Her education, what little she had in her mother's eyes, had been wasted. Even when she had begun designing it was viewed as a hobby, and the worst thing about it was that she had gone along with it. More fool her.

'Oh, you have gone far back.' Jeanette chuckled. 'Did you meet him at the bookstall?'

'No, he had been painting in the Trocadero gardens all week while I'd been working there.' Theo smiled. It was safe to think of it now. It couldn't hurt Piers or... David. 'He followed me my last day and he bought *Gaudy Night* for himself and the guide for me, haggling with the stall holder over the best price.'

'I'm loving this. And then did he sweep you away to his garret, quoting Donne and other such things that Wimsey did?'

'No.' Theo laughed. 'I wanted to pay him for the book, and he said to buy him a drink.'

'And you did.'

Theo nodded. On the longest day of that year, Paris had been breathless and so had she, for she had lived as she had never before or since. She lived fully, forgetting that she wasn't enough. In Patrick's eyes she had been everything. It was the scent of jasmine that always brought the night back to her. It grew around his balcony window.

She focused on Jeanette and the here and now, stepping away from the rabbit hole of her Paris past. Jeanette was turning the old guide over and opening the map. 'You know you could have the book repaired a bit. It's all coming apart.' She ran her finger down the back cover where the paper had become detached. Theo hadn't opened the book in years. She had simply kept it to remind her of the brief moment in time.

In Patrick's studio she had found hundreds of sketches of her. All that week as they had smiled and nodded to each other from a distance he had not been painting the garden as she had thought but her.

'Hello, what's this?' Jeanette slid a photograph out. She turned the picture over then showed it to Theo. Two men stood side by side facing the view not the photographer. Shoulder to shoulder, back of hand to back of hand.

'Lovers,' said Jeanette.

Theo nodded, recognising exactly where they stood in the gardens.

'Had you seen this before?' Jeanette asked, taking the photograph back from Theo.

'No.'

'How wonderful. I love it when old books reveal a bit of their past. Do you think these two lovers were using the guide as they cavorted about Paris in love?'

'Could they do that then?'

'Oh my, yes. The French were much more sensible about love and sex and all the variations it takes. Homosexuality wasn't illegal there. I think it was decriminalised back in the late 1700s.' Jeanette looked at the picture again, running fingers along the almost non-existent space between them. 'It's such a shame the UK took so long. So much heartache, and all so unnecessary.'

Theo nodded, wondering about the two men just as Martin arrived. She jumped up to greet him and a huge smile covered Jeanette's face. Jeanette, like most women, was instantly in love with her celibate brother. She could also see his enchantment with Jeanette.

'Sorry I'm late. I was held up leaving London.' He unzipped his leather jacket and Jeanette was transfixed. 'Is there any coffee left? I could use a cup before we set off.' He grinned and walked up to Jeanette. 'Hello, Theo has told me all about you.'

Jeanette gave him her hand. 'I doubt that and I'm deeply saddened that you are a priest. It is such a God-awful waste of such beauty.'

Martin laughed. 'So I've been told, but rest assured I sowed my wild oats before I found my vocation.'

'Thank God for that.'

'Indeed,' he said, sitting in the chair that Theo had occupied. He looked at home. She might be lucky to move the two of them on to the planned visit to Penhale.

Chapter Nine

Theo, Martin and Jeanette stood in the hall courtyard, behind them a medieval gate and in front of them the great hall. Déjà vu. Theo had stood in this spot with Grannie when Theo was around fifteen. Theo shivered and Martin sent her a look. Was he feeling the same? The history of the house was fascinating with its medieval origins but there was something else about it.

'I love this place and it shows how two world wars had changed much about the past way of life.' Jeanette marched through into the hall. 'It's such a lovely mix of medieval, Tudor and the garden is all about the 1800s.' She kept walking and both Martin and Theo travelled behind.

Theo swivelled her head, taking in the coats of arms on the walls and vaulted ceilings of the great hall. She wanted to stop and absorb the atmosphere but Jeanette strode on through it and said, 'Everyone thinks my mother was the rebel of the family and in some ways she was but her cousin Alice... she was the true rebel. As the only child of the 9th Duke of Exeter, she confronted the king and queen about women's rights and she fought on until women were given full suffrage.'

Jeanette paused as they entered the old dining room. The

wall in front of them was covered in tapestries and Theo was drawn to the beautiful garden scene portrayed. She stepped closer to study it, listening to Jeanette with half her attention.

'But that wasn't the end for her radical ways. She used her station to bring publicity to causes from women's rights, to gay rights, to the fight for racial equality. She was tireless.' Jeanette paused. 'Now do you see why you reminded me of someone, Theo?'

Martin let out a low whistle. 'Bloody hell, Theo, when did you pose for this?'

The blood left Theo's face. She turned, expecting to see a portrait of her starkers on a big red armchair, but what she saw was herself in a golden gown that clung to her body, accentuating her curves and showing off her porcelain skin. A blue silk wrap looped over her arms, setting off her blue eyes, and on her left hand was Grannie's ring. The portrait was exquisite. It radiated beauty and grace. Very different from Patrick's painting of her, not that she had seen the finished piece. Somehow, she imagined that the experience hadn't been the same for Lady Alice. 'That looks like me as a young woman,' she said, stepping closer to check if she was hallucinating. But even up close it could be her with slightly lighter hair. The plaque read:

LADY ALICE, COUNTESS ST LOY,
PAINTED BY PHILIP DE LASZALO 1918

The note under the painting said that the portrait was on loan from the Carew Family.

Jeanette slipped her hand through Theo's and said, 'Uncanny, isn't it, and have you seen her left hand?'

Theo nodded, unable to speak.

'Now do you think it's paste?' Jeanette asked.

Theo placed her hand to her chest where the ring sat. 'I guess not but how would my grandmother have it?'

Martin stepped closer. 'It looks similar.'

'I've done a bit of research.' Jeanette led them through to a flight of stairs to the red room. 'And I believe that you are wearing the St Loy Emerald.' She stopped in front of another portrait. It was as arresting. The plaque read:

LORD EDMUND, EARL ST LOY,
PAINTED BY PHILIP DE LASZALO 1917

The portrait managed to be sensitive yet haughty but somehow still approachable. It was the sadness, or was it the acceptance in the slightly hooded eyes that created the feeling the painting aroused? They had a story to tell and part of it, she suspected, might be quite wicked. His mouth was full and expressive.

'Such a sad fate,' said Jeanette.

'What happened?' Theo asked.

'Well, he died days before the end of the Great War.' Jeanette rubbed her bare arms. 'Such a tragedy. Whole estates and villages signing up together and dying together.' She left them and went to speak to the volunteer.

Martin turned to Theo. 'Do you remember that article in the local paper about the soldiers' remains?'

'Yes,' Theo said.

'It could be him.' He stepped closer to the painting.

'It could be the gillie who lived in Boatman's too.'

'True.' He waited for Jeanette to re-join them. 'Can we go to the chapel?'

Jeanette nodded. 'Sudden urge to pray?'

He laughed. 'Always.' Looking at him now, he was anything but a priest in his Nirvana T-shirt and leather jacket and jeans.

'In view of all this—' Jeanette waved her hand then took his arm as they walked to the chapel '—I'm dying to know how you are connected to the family.'

'Me too,' he said, stepping aside as a couple exited the chapel then they all entered the holy space.

There was a certain sound of silence in empty places of worship. Theo knew it well. The hushed whispers and chanted prayers of the past paused, giving the lack of sound a weighted feel. Afternoon light fell in through the west window by the altar. Martin dropped to his knees and the look on Jeanette's face was priceless.

Theo began to search the small chapel. If Grannie had come here frequently, there had to be a reason. On the wall she found a list of all those from the estate lost in WW1 and a separate memorial for Captain Edmund St Loy, the Earl St Loy. She moved slowly to the next memorial.

Martin was now at her side. 'Are you thinking what I'm thinking?' he asked her.

She nodded.

SECOND FLIGHT LIEUTENANT
JOHN ST LOY,
THE EARL ST LOY

LOST OVER FRANCE ON 23 MAY 1940

'Jeanette, are there any photos of John?' Martin asked.

'Of course. His half-brother Toby will have them and then there is a portrait of him, which is in the National Portrait Gallery. You do look like him, you know.' She tilted her head. 'It's in the cheekbones.'

'Any other St Loys?' Theo asked.

'He was the end of the line. As Lord Edmund's father had been an only child as had his father before him.' Jeanette smiled. 'But I think I'm looking at the Earl St Loy.'

'That would be entirely wasted on me, and what we do know is that our grandmother never married John.'

'Such a shame but clearly the intention was there if he had given her the St Loy Emerald. That was a form of contract although not as binding as it once had been.'

Theo touched the plaque, tracing John's name, wondering if this could be the case. David hadn't been far off when he'd said what if the ring was his gran's. But what did it all mean? Did it matter? Then she thought of Piers being so proud of his lineage and she smothered a laugh. An earl tops a baronet and a lord, and Lady Alice had been a duke's daughter. Piers may never know this information but she did.

'I don't know about you two, but I'm parched and tea will have to do. Let's away to the café and I'll call Toby but I will have to warn him that you, Theo, look so much like his mother it's uncanny.'

*

Theo yawned. 'I don't know about you, but I'm shattered. And I'm beginning to feel this family history lark is a bit like Pandora's Box.'

She turned to Martin, who was sitting on the front step of Boatman's and scrolling on his phone. On this June evening it was still light at nine. Jeanette, with her glass in hand, joined Martin on the step. Theo needed to find some garden furniture other than the one folding chair she had. The summer was promising to be lovely and something more comfortable would be a welcome addition to the cottage.

'Thank you for today,' Jeanette said.

'I think it should be the other way around.' Theo took a sip of wine. 'Of course, we don't know for certain, but you may have answered the question regarding the identity of our grandfather.'

'It's definite,' Jeanette said, peering at Martin's phone. 'Yes, that's John's portrait. Clever you.'

Martin said, 'Genes will out, I suppose.'

'According to one of my sister's children, they are everything. They gave me a DNA testing kit for my seventieth birthday.'

Martin turned to her. 'And have you done it?' He handed the phone to Theo. The portrait of John was certainly the same man that was in Grannie's photo.

Jeanette grinned. 'Of course. Had the results months ago.'

'Have you had your results back yet, Martin?' Theo asked, handing his phone back.

'Two days ago.' He rose. 'Let me grab my laptop.'

'Have you done yours?' Jeanette asked Theo.

Theo shook her head. 'No point really.'

'It's fascinating. It appears many a lineage is not as direct as it should be.' Her dirty laugh filled the air then she took a sip of her wine. 'Speaking of which, do you have those letters still or did you send them to the archivist?'

'I posted them yesterday. She'll send them back once they have been photographed.'

'Well, when they are back we can have a good read, for I do think Z's lady is Alice.'

Theo looked at her. 'Why do you say that?'

'The timing.' Jeanette twisted the wine glass in her fingers.

Theo nodded.

'And my mother hadn't been surprised by what we found and—'

Martin came back outside, holding his laptop and his phone. 'When are you going to get the internet here?'

Theo laughed. 'When the electrics are sorted.'

'Well, by connecting to my phone I'm on my results. Do you know which company you used?

'Twenty-three something.'

'Good, those are the results I've had in.'

'You did more than one test?'

He nodded. 'Did you make your profile public or use a pseudonym?'

'My name.' She studied the screen. 'This, of course, assumes that my mother was actually her father's daughter.'

'Or that Alice was her father's, and so on,' Martin said.

Jeanette pointed. 'There I am.'

Theo squinted at the screen. 'Wait. Am I understanding

this correctly? You believe that your grandfather wasn't the father of his children.'

'Not an uncommon occurrence. Marriage then was more a business arrangement. Love rarely entered into the equation. Once the male heir appeared, and possibly the spare, the pressure on both sides was off. All the children would bear the father's name but not, as we now know thanks to DNA, the genes.'

'Oh,' Theo said.

'It was a working arrangement and sometimes proved useful for the wives to stray if they hadn't had success on the conception front.' Jeanette sipped her wine. 'Especially if it wasn't a love match as it frequently wasn't.'

Theo shook her head, trying to take it all in.

'In law any child born in a marriage belongs to that father,' Martin said. 'And being Jeanette's genetic third cousin roughly—' he pointed to the screen '—doesn't prove that John was our grandfather.'

'No, but maybe we could ask Toby.' Jeanette topped up her glass.

'That could connect to Alice but he's not a St Loy.'

'True.' Theo peered at the screen not understanding what she was looking at, but she was certain Martin did.

'But of course,' Martin said, opening a new window on his laptop, 'there may be one St Loy we can test.'

'Who?' Theo asked.

'The MOD possibly has the remains of one and I think we have a reasonable argument to approach them.'

'Good thing this DNA wasn't around in the past. Many a great family wouldn't still be going.' Jeanette laughed.

'At least I knew from the start that I was illegitimate and have no idea who my father was, and, of course, I've never done anything of value.' Jeanette waved her hand.

'I think you are being hard on yourself.' Theo gave her a searching look.

Jeanette snorted. 'Not at all; well, maybe I added a bit of beauty and a bit of fun and possibly, on occasion, kindness.'

'Then you have added more than most,' Theo said.

Jeanette turned to her. 'Well, you have too.'

Theo shook her head and turned from Martin, who was watching her closely.

'You have a gift.' Jeanette placed a hand on her arm then raised her glass. 'You create magic, beauty with flowers.'

Theo shook her head. 'My mother and my ex-husband considered it a hobby.'

'For God's sake, forget Piers, and forget Mum too.' Martin closed his laptop.

'I wish I could,' she said.

'I saw you alter the flowers on the table in front of my sister's place setting. You added tulips to it… enduring love.'

The corners of Theo's mouth turned up. She had done that. Fifty years of marriage represented stamina at the very least, but those whom she had met who had celebrated that milestone had expressed enduring love.

Jeanette glanced at her phone. 'Damn. Toby's away in the States on an epic road trip with his daughter and her family. He'll be in touch when he returns.' She pursed her lips. 'Well, we know who you are; we just need to connect the dots, as they say.'

Theo laughed and the windowpane caught her eye. A and Z. Alice and Zach or Aardvark and Zebra?

'Now, Martin, would you be so kind as to row me across the river. I have one more night of pampering then back to my abode. It's now filled with all my mother's papers, which I think I mentioned. I'm the only one who can read her writing.' She sighed, kissed Theo on both cheeks, and took Martin's arm down to the river.

Theo followed behind and stared across at Abbotswood, wondering about Lady Alice and her own possible connection to her. It didn't matter in the overall scheme of things but something inside fell into place.

She was meant to buy Boatman's — that much she knew.

PART TWO

'How do you know I'm mad?' said Alice.
'You must be,' said the Cat, 'or you wouldn't have come here.'

—ALICE'S ADVENTURES IN WONDERLAND,

LEWIS CARROLL

Case 752
Status: Open
10 June 2019

Still searching for the family of William Bowman. Another media request for help planned.

The DNA from Samuel Lyons's great-nephew did not match.

We have made contact with the family of Zachariah Carne's brother's family after a newspaper appeal. DNA test sent.

Chapter Ten

1914

'I think you should be considering the Marquess of Ware,' Lady Alice's aunt, the Duchess of Exeter, said, putting down the delicate silver cake fork in her hand.

Alice watched her mother, the Dowager Duchess of Exeter, digest this suggestion. Alice could think of nothing worse. The marquess in question was vile.

'Possibly, but Ware is…' Her mother's mouth flattened with the word and Alice focused on controlling her breathing. Old was what she should be saying. He was forty if he was a day.

'Of course, there is always Lord Edmund, if he could be persuaded.' Her aunt's mouth twitched.

Her mother sighed and Alice knew that even though Edmund would become the Earl St Loy on his father's death, that wasn't good enough to reset the balance of power between her mother and her aunt. Nor was Ware. The competition between these two women was fierce since the reduction in her mother's status in society following Alice's father's death four years ago. The whole thing was wrong, all of it. There was little she could do about anything, but she had a plan.

The cherubs frolicking on the tapestry on the morning

room wall behind her aunt reminded Alice of the painting in the classroom where Miss Parkes had first spoken to her about Votes for Women. Life as she knew it had changed in that moment. Her time at school had no longer been an exile from Nanny Roberts, but a call to arms. It had become the chance to study, to change the world and the course of her own life. From then on, Alice had been biding her time and for the past few months she had done all that was expected of her exactly as she should. Her presentation at court was soon and she must be patient, which was not a virtue she possessed. The divine dresses she had been acquiring for the season and beyond were compensation for all the waiting.

Her mother, Olivia, when she was not pursuing her latest lover, was plotting Alice's marriage this season to no less than a duke or even better the Prince of Wales. Therefore, she had not stinted on Alice's wardrobe. Her mother wanted the best possible match. That didn't mean the best possible husband for her daughter. These things weren't necessarily compatible, or even desirable, from what Alice had seen.

Her aunt was waving her hand up and down. 'Dear heavens, Constance, can't you be more like your cousin, Alice,' her aunt said, picking up her cup. Her voice was so sharp it cut into Alice's thoughts.

Constance's face was the colour of beetroot, and it didn't suit her. Poor Constance. Crumbs were scattered down the front of her cousin's bodice and covered the book in her lap. Alice's glance narrowed. If only her aunt would be quiet and leave the poor child alone.

'We'll have no trouble in finding the right husband for Alice, but you, Constance, will be a problem if you don't improve. It's not as though you are blessed with beauty.' The duchess eyed her daughter, who twisted her fingers together in her lap until they went white.

Alice caught her cousin's eye. The tick in Constance's cheek worked hard as she sought control of her emotions. If Alice didn't leave the room at this moment, she might declare her devotion to the suffrage and tell her aunt to be kinder to her youngest daughter. If she did, it would certainly change the conversation and Constance wouldn't be the problem any-more. But Alice wanted a larger audience so she took a deep breath, stood and extended a hand to her cousin, saying, 'Constance, take a walk in the garden with me.'

'That's good. Listen and learn from your cousin.' Her aunt smiled. Turning to Alice's mother she said, 'You know Henry was correct. Sending her to school has done her no end of good.'

Her aunt would not say that if she knew Alice's thoughts. Of course, Alice wasn't supposed to think, but school had taught her how to do that. She supressed a smile, took her younger cousin's hand, and led her through the French window and down the steps to the garden of Exeter House, one of the largest in London.

It was still damp with rain that had just stopped. Looking down with dismay at her shoes, Alice stuck to the path rather than go across the lawn, hating that everything about her life limited her, including her shoes, although pretty.

The air smelt of cut grass and the cool air dulled the blazing colour on Constance's cheeks. Her eyes were still downcast. Once they had reached the far end of the garden, Constance looked up and said, 'Thank you.'

Alice smiled. Her cousin had given her a reason to leave the over-warm room and the wretched discussion about marrying Alice off to whoever had the best title, the most land, or the most money. She had no intention of marrying. She shouldn't have to. She had money, or, more correctly, she would have money once she was twenty-five or married. But if she married the money would be in her husband's control and not hers. She exhaled loudly and Constance gave her an inquiring look, but Alice couldn't speak directly about this.

Alice would be eighteen in a little over a month. Old enough to marry. Old enough to bear children. But not old enough to think, according to her mother, her aunt, her uncle, and society. If her father were still alive things would be different. She would be free. She knew it. He had indulged her, according to her mother, and possibly ruined her, according to dear Nanny. But at least Nanny had said those words with love. Alice could not say the same of her mother's words... ever.

Miss Parkes said all women should be in control of their own destinies and that should begin with the right to vote. Women were not chattels to be listed among the items that men owned. And yet, listening to her mother and her aunt, it sounded as if it was something she should be aspiring to. She huffed as she sat down on the bench under the cover of a barren rose arch.

Constance watched her. The poor girl was thirteen and a bit lumpy at the moment. It would hopefully pass. Constance was good-natured and Alice enjoyed her company. If her cousin would smile, it would go a long way to reaching her aunt's goal of marrying her off. But didn't Constance and all women deserve more?

'You have only recently returned from Paris,' Constance said, sitting down beside her.

'Yes.' Alice pulled a camellia bloom towards her and sniffed. No scent. This always felt a disappointment. How could a bloom be so visually perfect and sensually so flat? She released it and the branch swung back. Once still, the whole bloom dropped onto the grass. Nearby the lilacs were coming into full flower and making up for the camellia's lack of perfume.

'Was it wonderful?' Constance linked her fingers together on her lap.

Paris. She smiled. 'Yes.' She liked the way men looked at her there. They were more direct. Her mother was flirtatious with the men but forbade Alice from even looking. But how could she not? Flashing eyes, beaming smiles and an obvious sense of wanting to know more about her, not only because she was Lady Alice Neville, daughter of the 9th Duke of Exeter. No, they were interested in her because she was a woman and that was exciting.

'Did you truly convince your mother to let Paul Poiret design your presentation gown?'

Alice allowed herself a small smile of triumph. 'Yes, but I had to have the rest designed by Worth.'

Constance nodded. 'I wonder who will design mine.'

Alice peered at her. 'In five years styles may have changed?'

'Do you think so?' Constance worried the fabric of her skirt. She still had her hair down. It wouldn't be that way for long. This would be her last summer of freedom. Alice missed that childhood liberty.

'The styles have changed since Beatrice came out last year.'

Alice considered her bossy cousin. Beatrice, Constance's elder sister, was abominable and continually looking down on Alice now that her father was the Duke of Exeter. Alice had never been hateful to her when she could have been. She wrinkled her nose. That wasn't true. She and Edmund St Loy, her childhood friend of so long, had once put a large house spider down Beatrice's back. But it was only a house spider and Beatrice had overreacted. Nanny had sent both Alice and Edmund to bed without supper. She smiled remembering both her and Edmund's stomachs protesting loudly at their emptiness. He was such an ally.

Last year Beatrice had married Viscount Fancot, who was twenty years her senior. Alice could only imagine how horrid it all was. But her aunt had been delighted. It wouldn't happen to her. Alice would make certain of that. She thought of all the eligible men she had met thus far, and they were dire, but she played along as best as she could. It was all about power. Both her aunt and her mother wielded what little they had over her and tried to do the same over each other.

In the corner of a far flowerbed, late Pheasant's Eye daffodils bent in the breeze. Their scent drifted towards them, reminding her of Edmund's family home in Penhale. She had spent a great deal of time there as a child, carefree days running riot with Edmund while their mothers gossiped and their fathers hunted. She particularly remembered sitting on a beautiful grey pony. She had been so jealous that Edmund hadn't been required to have anyone lead his pony, but she had. Even then she had been made to feel less... less able.

This whole thing was ridiculous. She stood and smoothed her skirt. She didn't want to be married and didn't want to play this charade of the season, despite the dresses, but she must for the time being. It served no purpose being impatient, but she was. She could learn something from Constance: resilience. Her aunt was always beastly about Constance yet the child never acted out. Alice would never have managed it.

'When will you be heading to the country?' Constance said, standing as well.

'After Henley, I imagine,' Alice lied. Everything would change after her presentation and then she would be free.

'Scotland?' she asked.

'Most likely.'

'Not Devon?'

Alice shook her head. She would have preferred to go to Abbotswood and enjoy the countryside, but that was painful. That was where her father had died in a riding accident. That was where she thought of as home and it wasn't hers anymore.

Constance frowned. 'You don't sound excited.'

'It's all nonsense.' They walked forward towards the gardeners, who were trying not to be seen and yet still do their work.

'How is it nonsense?' Constance followed her a step behind.

'I don't want a husband.' Alice pursed her mouth. She could say this to Constance. Even if her cousin repeated it no one would listen to a thirteen-year-old girl. This Alice knew from experience. Girls don't matter, her mother had said.

Constance grabbed her arm. 'But you need one.'

'No,' she said and stopped walking. 'No, I don't.'

'But don't you want love?' Constance asked, eyes wide.

Alice sucked in air; her cousin had been reading too many novels. 'Don't be foolish. Marriage isn't about love,' she said and looked at Constance. 'It's about power and property.' Constance's pupils narrowed as she took in the information.

'I don't want love, I want freedom.' There, she had said it aloud.

'But love is important.' Constance tilted her head and Alice felt like a bug being inspected because it hadn't acted as it should.

'Love isn't important. It may be nice but freedom is everything,' Alice said, hearing Miss Parkes's words in her head. Her mother appeared on the steps scanning the garden. She was still a beautiful woman and she used it to her advantage. Alice wanted more than that, so much more. Her mother's glance fell on them both as Nanny Roberts appeared at the dowager's side. She hadn't seen Nanny in two years and Alice had missed her. Alice and Constance without a word, quickened their pace back to the house.

Dearest Sylvia,

I hope this letter finds you in better health. A constant cough is most worrisome. Have you seen the doctor? Has he said what it is? Do make sure you are keeping warm and away from all draughts.

I have arrived at Exeter House and it is bursting as the London season is in full swing. I have this moment seen Lady Alice. How she has changed in this time away from me. Gone is the slightly wicked child and now she stands a confident young woman. But there is something troubling me that I can't explain. Behind the sophisticated veneer something is going on. I have seen this before. She was one to always have her way and I can be certain that her time at the school has not removed this trait from her. Her dear late father indulged her, and I too may have as well. She, of all the children I have raised, has been allowed to have her own way more than she should have.

Of course, I pray I am wrong and the child will find the right match this season and her uncle will release me from his service to look after Alice's children when they arrive. For I promised her father that I would look after her and that duty will never finish until I draw my final breath.

In other news, young Lady Constance is growing at a great rate. She is mature physically for a child of thirteen and I'm not sure her mother has noticed, even though I have been at pains to point this out to her. The duchess is far too taken up with the current gossip and her jealousy that Alice has been hailed the debutante of the season whereas poor Lady Beatrice limped behind last year, and is now struggling to produce an heir for the viscount. Lady Beatrice is a fine woman but has none of the vivacity or intelligence of Lady Alice. Of course, this will be Lady Alice's downfall if she is not careful. I hope there is a good match out there for her. I know the family is discounting Lord Edmund because of his tendencies but I feel he would be the perfect husband for Lady Alice.

I can hear you asking how I am? Well, I have been better, my dear sister, but I am here and I am being allowed

to witness the triumph of my dear girl's season. This brings
me great joy and energy that I had forgotten I had.

With all my love,
Eve

Up on the fourth floor in the nursery, Alice found Nanny. She was at the desk, writing. Alice tiptoed across the bare floorboards, ducked around the eaves and past the rocking horse that her father had given to her. Many things on the shelves had been hers or her father's but they were no longer. Everything without question became her uncle's four years ago including her future until he handed her to another man. Her chest tightened.

Bold building blocks sat neatly on the shelf beside Humbert Bear. She picked him up. He smelled of dust and honey. Her nose wrinkled. Who had last loved him? Constance? Francis, the youngest of her cousins? No one? She held him tight then she walked up to Nanny, who had turned from the desk and was studying her. A smile spread across Nanny's face.

'Had you forgotten him?' she asked.

Alice nodded and sat in the rocking chair next to the desk. Once, Nanny would have held her as she rocked, to soothe her after a skinned knee or banged elbow. Alice had always been rushing at things. Impatient to move on and up and out. But, like the corset that bound her breasts and restricted her movements at fourteen, they now wanted to place a ring on her finger and tie her further. Downstairs she had overheard her uncle and her mother again discussing the potential candidates. Every day it was the same, week in and week out. Who would offer? Who would they entertain?

'What's wrong, Lady Alice?' Nanny asked.

Alice pulled the bear closer, feeling the prickly stubble of the plush fur against her chin as she hid from Nanny's scrutiny. 'That obvious?'

'To me.' She leaned forward and placed a finger under Alice's chin. 'What have they said?'

'Marriage.' Alice stroked the bear's head.

Nanny dropped her hand. 'Of course.'

How could she make Nanny understand? She hugged Hubert tighter.

'You don't like the offer.' Nanny put her pen down.

Alice looked through the worn ears of the bear. 'No one has offered… yet.'

Nanny's gaze narrowed. 'Is this the problem?'

Alice shook her head. 'I don't intend to marry.'

Nanny chuckled. 'Dearest child, we both know that your intentions do not matter.' She picked up one of Alice's hands from the bear. 'The best you can hope for is to be married to a man who is tolerable.'

Alice pulled her hand away. How could she have thought that Nanny would understand. Nanny was part of the problem.

'Now, I agree from all I hear that the Duke of Cleveland is objectionable, but he is more than solvent and has vast estates. Things could be worse.'

Alice rose to her feet still clutching the bear.

'Child, you have to marry. That is your duty… and your

right.' Nanny looked down at her left hand, moving the bare ring finger.

'It is the one right I don't want.' Alice turned and left the nursery with Humbert. Nanny of all people should understand, but she was as bad as her mother and the rest of them. Only Miss Parkes understood her. Alice knew what she had to do at her presentation in a few days' time. It was clearer now than ever before. While she had a voice, she must use it.

Dearest Sylvia,

I am pleased to hear you are feeling better and that you have followed all my advice. I can picture you in the garden surrounded by the roses.

Here in London the garden is advancing by great leaps and bounds. The wisteria is finishing. It always reminds me of a dress you once had, the pale shade of blue with a frill at the neck. These are such happy thoughts.

Lady Alice has just visited me here in the nursery. She clung to her father's old bear as if her life depended on it. I thought for a moment she was the child I had known but no, someone has replaced her. The fire remains in her eyes and in her heart. I haven't figured out what is going on in her clever brain but she has taken against marriage.

This is new. No child I have ever raised has rebelled against their duty. But something tells me that trouble is brewing. If something does indeed take place, it is on her mother's watch. That, in truth, says it all. The dowager duchess has never cared for her daughter nor had she for her husband. I still remember the eight-year-old Lady Alice's sobs as she kept repeating, 'I'm not good enough. I'm not enough. I'm a girl. Daughters don't matter. I'm not enough. I'll never be enough.' When I finally calmed her down it turned out she'd heard one of the frequent arguments between her parents. Bitter. There was little love between them at the time. He'd turned to drink because of his wife. Poor mite knew then what her mother thought of her and the dowager's views haven't changed. But enough said about that.

Young Lady Constance continues to delight and the duke's youngest, Lord Francis, is a kind and gentle soul. There is talk that he isn't the duke's child but with the two elder sons His Grace had no worries. I have spoken with his tutor, who is pleased with his progress. The boy heads to Eton this year.

I am awaiting a role. I doubt I will be sent to Lady Beatrice as her mother-in-law wishes to have her woman on hand. I believe there is little love lost between the two women.

I am grateful to be here in London to watch my charge fly and she will, for her beauty is assured as is her poise. If she can hold her rebellious nature in check, she will make it through the season with the husband of her choice and not her mother's. Somehow I must feed this thought into her head. She mustn't think that she needn't marry, for she must. If she is clever then she will learn if she acts appropriately then she has the right to choose. She simply needs to look at the possibilities. The Duke of Cleveland is keen. He is extremely wealthy, and cares for hunting more than anything else. She could do worse but there are better choices. I will do what I can from the distance of the nursery.

If you have time, make me a sketch of the blooms in the garden at the moment and I will write with details of the presentation as I have them.

Yours always,
Eve

Chapter Eleven

There were twenty motorcars ahead of them on The Mall and God knows how many behind. Not a cloud appeared in the evening sky and normally this would lift Alice's spirits, but all it was doing was cooking her despite the open windows. Beneath her gloves her fingers swam in sweat. Her mother's fan moved languidly, not doing anything other than pushing the hot air in Alice's direction.

In the distance the gates to Buckingham Palace were closed. Soon they would open, and all the debutantes and their chaperones would rush inside as best they could, like it was handicap day at the races. In a way it was. Who would be the winner? Not Alice. In less than an hour the course of her life would change. No longer would she be competing in this insane quest for a husband and the best part was that she would have done something for others. Each act, however small, in the fight for equality was important. Doing this would make her existence worth something. It wouldn't be decorative, it wouldn't be to bear children, it would be to help herself and all other women. That was what she needed to focus on. Not the heat, not the beauty of her gown or the feathers in her hair.

She will speak for the cause and will go from voiceless, useless, and decorative to powerful. This coming change was exciting and terrifying in equal measure if her stomach was anything to go by. But strangely it wasn't excitement or fear that she felt. It was power. It shimmered in her.

The only thing she could compare the feeling to was the hope she had had before her first kiss. She and Edmund had tried it after seeing her cousin kiss his fiancée. The anticipation had been far better than the reality. They had both stood still, lips touching, waiting for something, but nothing had happened. Edmund had stepped away and declared he might have to marry her if anyone had seen them. As if on cue, bushes beside them had rustled. Edmund had said it was only the gillie's son and he wouldn't tell. She wasn't so certain, but the boy had disappeared, leaving her wondering if he'd truly been there. The thought of being watched had been more exciting than the kiss. It had been entirely unsatisfactory.

'Alice!' Her mother pulled her arm. 'It's time.' With a straight back and a firm step her mother led her down The Mall, through the gate and into the palace. The sound of footsteps filled the air and her mother looked neither left nor right but focused on her goal. The neutral mask on her mother's face did not encourage Alice to ask her thoughts.

Each step brought her closer to her future. She slowed her breathing so she would be calm and graceful but most importantly nothing must give away her intentions. She wanted to remember every detail from the flowers to her fellow debutantes.

Footmen opened the doors to a salon next to the throne room. After the great rush of movement, they all stood still.

Silent except for hushed whispers, suppressed coughs, and the rustle of silk. It was enough noise so that Alice couldn't hear her own heart thumping nor the band playing next door. The smell of nearby gardenias was both intoxicating and repugnant. Unlike the other chaperones about, her mother was motionless and watchful. Did she know? She couldn't.

For a moment Alice struggled for breath in the heavy air. Sweat trickled between her breasts. What were they waiting for now? A day of endless pauses. She wanted it done. The longer they stood there, the more her throat closed. She was fifth in the line, waiting. Her dress glimmered in the low light and her pearls lent their radiance to her skin. Even her uncle had seen fit to comment on how well she looked.

The door opened when the first debutante entered. They all shifted forward and Alice caught sight of herself with the feathers on her head. She resembled a bird ready to be hunted. Her mother straightened the pearls at Alice's neck while Alice listened to quiet words of encouragement uttered to others behind her. She looked over her shoulder to see the line of her peers snaking behind. She would do this for them as much as for herself. Things moved again as another debutante was announced. Not too much longer to wait. She risked a glance at her mother who was fully focused on the open door.

Finally it was only Lady Blomfield and her daughter Mary in front of them. George V and Queen Mary sat under an ornate canopy with a circle of duchesses to one side. Alice was related to many of them and they would witness her actions. She would be respectful, but she would be heard. It was almost her moment.

Mary Blomfield dropped her train and the footman spread

it out with a stick. He reminded Alice of an old-fashioned shepherd sorting sheep. What had the American ambassador called the presentation? 'The best-managed, best-mannered show in the world.' The international press would be here. Alice's actions would echo across the globe.

Through the gap in the door, Alice watched Lady Blomfield curtsey in front of the king and move towards the queen. Mary reached the point where she should go into a deep curtsey. She stood and Alice feared that an attack of nerves had overcome her but suddenly Mary fell to her knees saying, 'Your majesty, for God's sake do not use force…' Before Mary could finish she was swiftly removed by two gentlemen at arms.

Alice swayed. The dowager duchess grabbed Alice's hand tightly and the music rose in volume so that neither Alice nor anyone else could hear a thing. Her stomach flipped over and the footman beckoned them forward. Alice didn't move. Mary had done it. She had spoken to Their Majesties. Everyone was trying to proceed, ignoring what had happened. How could they? What should she do? This was her moment.

With her mother's sharp elbow, instinct kicked in. Alice dropped her train and the footman prodded it into place. All blood had left her face. They expected her to go through with this. Alice shuddered. Her mother sent her a look. It said don't be ridiculous. And she was right. Alice could do this in her sleep. She wasn't concerned about tripping or walking backwards.

'Her Grace, Olivia, the Dowager Duchess of Exeter, and the Lady Alice Neville.' Her mother glanced at her then entered the room with head held high. Her mother curtsied first then Alice hesitated before she did the same. As she rose to standing, she looked the king directly in the eye while her mother was curtsying before the queen. His face was blank. She moved on and bowed before the queen who did not even glance at her. Queen Mary's views on the 'furies', as she called the suffragettes, were well known.

'Thank God that is over with.' Her mother fanned her face. 'Can you believe what that Blomfield girl did? Really, of all times.' She tutted and Alice wished it had been her. It should have been. She should have done it as well and then they wouldn't have been able to continue. Now she would have to rethink, re-plan, and all the while continue with this terrible farce.

Her feet hurt and she was tipsy, in fact she was more than tipsy. Debutantes weren't supposed to drink alcohol, but someone had spiked the fruit punch they were allowed and suddenly the dull ball had become much more fun. Alice stood on the balcony, breathing in the scent of jasmine on the night air; no – it was nearly two o'clock – morning air. What was she going to do? Mary had taken Alice's moment. She must make a plan, but her head wasn't as clear as she would like.

'Escaping?' a deep voice asked as its owner stepped further onto the balcony and she saw the familiar face of Arthur Carew.

'Definitely.' She slipped her shoes back on as elegantly as she could. The sensation of feeling undressed covered her skin.

He lit a cigarette. 'I can't blame you.'

She laughed then hiccupped.

'The punch was that good?' In the light spilling out of the ballroom she could see his raised eyebrow.

'That obvious?' she asked.

He chuckled. 'Not until that moment.'

'That's good to know,' she said then smiled.

'Have you enjoyed this evening?' he asked, before drawing deeply on his cigarette. When he exhaled the smoke caught the light and created a halo around his fair hair. She tilted her head and looked at him, looked at him properly. He was tall and handsome and was said to be exceptionally clever and one of the best MPs in the country.

'The punch helped,' she said.

He laughed. 'That bad.'

'It feels like the county show and the other debs and I have all had our hair brushed and ribbons attached, trying to win a prize.'

'And have you?' he asked, leaning on the balustrade.

Lifting her chin, she said, 'I don't want to win.'

'How interesting.' His keen glance studied her face. 'What do you want, Lady Alice?'

'Votes for women.' She didn't have to think at all. It was so important. Men had to be made to see it was important.

'You agree with Mary Blomfield?'

'Yes, the force-feeding of the suffragettes in prison must stop and women must be given the vote.'

'I see.' He tapped the ash off his cigarette over the balcony onto the deserted path below.

'Do you, do you really?' she asked, studying his intelligent face.

'I have supported the cause,' he said.

She leaned back. This was true, he had.

'Women aren't less.' She pulled her shoulders back.

'You are right.'

She peered at him. He was listening and he agreed with her. 'Thank you.'

'I will continue to support votes for women and for all men too.' His glance met hers.

'Will we have to wait long?' she asked, liking the way his blue eyes looked at her mouth.

'That I can't say. Some things take time; worthwhile ones definitely do.'

'Thing, there you are,' Edmund said, popping his head out the door as the band began again. She smiled at his use of his pet name for her. 'Come on, I know I'm not the duke you're after, but you owe me a dance.' He looked at Arthur. 'You don't mind, do you, Carew?'

'Not at all.' Arthur bowed and she took Edmund's hand back into the cattle market with one last look at Arthur Carew, who smiled as he watched them leave.

Chapter Twelve

It was ten past ten and the sky was still bright. The air was warm when Alice alighted from the motorcar at the Royal Albert Hall. Tonight's Anglo-American Peace Centenary Ball marked the treaty of 1814. Everyone who was anyone from both sides of the Atlantic was here, including six members of the royal family, and, most importantly for Alice, the king and queen.

Pilgrims entered the building ahead of her and Alice tried to see who was under the neat bonnets. Every costume had to relate to themes of the Empire or the New World. Alice and her mother climbed the stairs and in the distance Alice caught sight of Lady Astor as Columbia while Lady Maud Warrender as Britannia looked fierce with her metal breast plate. As one of Britannia's warriors, Alice was relieved she didn't have to manage that along with the helmet, which, on this warm evening, was a bit unpleasant.

Alice stumbled and her mother sent her a look. Managing her St George's shield, her large plume and holding her skirt was causing a balance issue for her, even though she regained her footing. Her mother was decked out as Kentucky for the presentation of the States. She too had a shield and wore a helmet circled in stars.

Inside the main hall she scanned the crowd, looking for Edmund. He shouldn't be hard to find if he was truly wearing a full feather headdress. She was riveted instead by the sight of Christopher Columbus or, more correctly, Roland Hill. There was even a tableau of the Santa Maria. Her glance quickly fell on Sir Walter Raleigh and his Virginia settlers. The Royal Albert Hall had never held such a multi-coloured array of costumes.

Alice spotted Arthur Carew dressed as an American frontier trapper with a racoon hat adorning his head. He nodded to her and she smiled. She spied several other of Britannia's attendants and breathed with relief. For the moment it was best to be part of the crowd. Today Alice felt no fear, no nerves, only impatience.

'Thing!' A reddish-brown Edmund in glorious headdress loped in her direction. He might be two years her senior but dressed as an Apache warrior he looked like the child she had known.

'You look extraordinary.' She held back a giggle. He somehow looked taller than he was. It must be the headdress.

He bowed, holding his tomahawk to his naked but painted chest. 'Why thank you.'

'Do you intend to skin anyone tonight?' she asked.

He scanned the crowd and his glance fell on someone across the hall. A smile spread across his handsome face. 'Only if I'm lucky.' She couldn't see who it was because the press of people was too great.

'Now, Thing, you will save a dance for me.'

'Always,' she said, turning to look at the band. They were already well into the first set of music and a few dancers were moving in the centre of the room. The parade was at midnight. It must be about eleven now. Her goal was to avoid the Duke of Cleveland and to establish a direct route to the royal box where she could speak to the king and queen directly. This was Alice's chance. They could do something about this awful state of affairs. Force-feeding these women in prison was intolerable. The American papers said the government shouldn't do it, but the response was the suffragettes shouldn't be allowed to starve to death. The correct answer was that women should be given the vote.

A tap on her shoulder brought her out of her thoughts. Her cousin Beatrice stood beside her, dressed in an Indian sari in glorious shades of green. It suited her. 'Cleveland is looking for you,' she said.

Alice wrinkled her nose.

Beatrice pursed her lips then said, 'You might as well accept your fate.'

Alice shuddered.

'Do you think that you can marry for love?' Beatrice raised one eyebrow.

'No.' Not marry at all was the plan Alice continued silently.

A corner of Beatrice's mouth lifted. 'Good, marrying for love is so middle class.'

'So, you have no love with Fancot?' Alice studied her cousin, seeing the rise in colour in her cheeks.

'Oh, there is plenty of that until the heir appears.' She glanced down at her flat stomach. Beatrice's childless state had occupied much of the conversation between their mothers. Constance was stuck listening to many inappropriate conversations because people forgot she was there. She had collected almost as many secrets as the servants.

'Lady Alice.' The feel of the Duke of Cleveland brushing up against her hardened her resolve. After tonight he wouldn't have anything to do with her and for that she was already grateful.

'A dance?' His whisky-tinged breath poured over her. She turned around taking in his costume: a Puritan, a drunk Puritan. Alice had not had any wine with dinner nor at the soiree her aunt had held at Exeter House before the ball. She didn't need her wits to be addled, but right now being a little bit drunk might make everything easier, especially dancing with Cleveland, as his hand slid down her bare arm. She didn't even have the defence of gloves as he forced his fingers between hers.

He towered over her with his wide-brimmed hat and his white collar was covered with stains of red wine. Her stomach turned as she let him lead her to the dance floor. Fortunately, the music was upbeat, a foxtrot, and he couldn't hold her too close. She discovered her shield could work in her favour as she slipped it between them frequently. As he flung her around, she caught sight of her aunt and her mother smiling at her.

A quick glance confirmed the king and queen were in the royal box. Their Majesties had not opted for costume as such, but looked the part anyway, presiding over the celebrations of peace between the two countries. It was a show of strength. The empire was still spread far and wide.

'Lady Alice,' the duke said, leaning down towards her ear as the music slowed.

'Your Grace.' She pushed back from him adjusting her shield between them.

He belched then said, 'You appear very fierce this evening.'

She needed to be.

'Such fire.' His glance narrowed as he tried to hold her hand.

She turned away, spotting Edmund in conversation with a fellow Apache warrior. Was that who he had been eyeing with such hunger earlier? Cleveland grabbed her hand. She didn't pull it away and played the role. At least if he was holding her hand then he wouldn't be groping her bottom.

'I intend—'

She interrupted him. 'Sorry, Your Grace.' She stepped back. She didn't want him declaring himself here or anywhere.

'Please call me Cleveland.' He stepped closer.

Her eyes opened wide. Somehow, she had to stop him. Not here. Not now, not ever.

'Sorry, Your Grace.' He grimaced and she continued, 'I mean Cleveland; I have promised Lord Edmund this next dance.' She pushed through the crowd until she reached Edmund.

'Dear God, Thing, you look like you've been hunted rather than the other way around.'

'Dance, now,' she whispered.

He dipped his head to the gentleman with whom he was speaking and led her onto the dance floor. 'Right, what happened?'

She glanced about, making sure Cleveland wasn't near, before she said, 'Oh lord, he was about to propose.'

'Ham fists himself?' he asked.

She nodded. The music pushed them around the room and her shield rested on Edmund's bare back as did her bare hand. It should feel uncomfortable touching him this way, but it didn't at all. She had known him far too long for any awkwardness to come between them. He was as close to having a brother as she would ever have. Their mothers were the best of friends and had gone through this terrible ritual of the season together. They had both done their duty when it came to marriage and bearing children, but the countess had provided an heir and her mother had only provided a daughter, a girl. Alice closed her eyes for a moment. Was that all she was?

'Thing, don't go silent on me. Did he propose?' he asked, guiding her across the floor.

'No, thank goodness. I ran away.' She laughed.

He pulled back and studied her face. 'Not like you to run away.'

'True.' She nodded.

'Much the better way to handle things though. So, how are you going to turn Cleveland down?'

She pressed her lips together.

'You're not going to say yes.' He pulled back to look at her face more closely. 'Please tell me you aren't going to marry him.'

'I don't intend to marry anyone,' she whispered.

He blinked. 'Ah, yes, so you have said.'

Out of the corner of her eye she saw Cleveland moving towards her uncle. She could only hope that her uncle would be too busy to listen to him tonight or at least for a while. As much as she disliked Cleveland, she did not want to mortify him.

The music stopped and they were called into position for

the parade. Everyone in the royal box moved forward to watch the proceedings. Alice found Lady Maud and her fellow warriors, all fifty of them, then proceeded across the floor.

Once they were done with the procession, the photographer assembled them for a photo. As soon as that was taken, Alice slipped through the crowds and climbed the stairs, passing several attendants who didn't even look at her.

She was about to do something so outrageous, so absolutely right, that surely someone must see it in her face or feel the energy coming from her. Fear tingled along her exposed skin, but it was the strange elation that shocked her. Power ran through her. She almost flew down the wide empty corridor as everyone's attention was still focused on the end of the parade.

Her gown flapped behind her and the shield slipped loosely against her sweaty palm. She was dressed as a warrior and she would be one. Votes for Women. End the injustice of force-feeding. That was all she needed to say. She mouthed the words, practising as she approached the box. The door was open and, from below, the previously muffled sound blasted through, pushing her back. Raising the shield slightly, she pressed against the volume of the band playing Pomp and Circumstance. She would have to shout to be heard.

As Alice entered the box, the queen turned from the crowd and stilled. Her eyes narrowed then she spoke to the king who put a hand on the queen's arm. The king turned and stared at Alice. She froze. The music below rose. Alice wouldn't be heard but she had to act now while she was alone with them. This was her chance. The queen glared at her and looked as if she was about to speak but the music reached a crescendo.

Everything inside Alice tensed while she waited for the

final drum beat then she shouted, 'Your Majesties.' She gulped before she continued in a more moderate voice, 'Please end the force feeding. Votes for women.'

The queen paled. The hall went silent.

Alice saw the crowd below staring at the royal box. A hand from behind grabbed her and she lost her balance, falling to her knees before she was lifted out of the box and down the back stairs.

She had done it.

Chapter Thirteen

Alice hadn't spoken more than a yes or a no since they had departed London hours ago. Poor Constance had been roped into accompanying her, along with Nanny Roberts. Alice felt bad for Constance being rushed out of town, but her cousin didn't appear troubled by it. They were clearly under the impression that Constance would be a good influence on her. How swiftly things had reversed.

Her family's parting words circled in her head. They had spoken as if she hadn't been standing right there.

'She is a disgrace,' her uncle had said.

'She will never find a husband now.' Her aunt had sounded almost gleeful.

'What a hare-brained thing to do.' Her mother's voice was still so clear she could be sitting beside her, but, no, her mother wasn't with her as Alice was sent into exile.

Alice bristled. She was not stupid or ill informed, but she might be impassioned or impetuous.

The coach that had picked them up from the railway station turned sharply and Alice slid into Nanny who was snoring. Poor Nanny had been chosen to guard her during her banishment to Abbotswood. God forbid that her mother inconvenience herself and leave the delights of the season.

'Devon is the place for Alice. There's no one there at this time of year and soon this debacle will be forgotten,' her uncle had said.

There had been more muffled words as she left the house, but she picked out beautiful, headstrong, and foolish. Even now that last word in particular stung the most and she set her mouth into a straight line. Foolish. Foolish because she wanted suffrage for women. That wasn't foolish. And she'd been right to speak to the king. Force-feeding was wrong. So much was wrong, including the order to hide her in deepest Devon.

The sun broke through the low cloud as they turned onto Duke's Drive. Once she had been excited to come to Abbotswood. When she was small, roaming the woods and swimming had made her happy. Nothing had confined her. She'd ridden, hunted and yelled to her heart's content.

Now, as she looked out the window, the Tamar was there. It reminded her of all she had lost. At fourteen her father had died, and her hair was tied up and her movements restricted. A year later she had been taken from Nanny's charge and sent away.

Everything had altered on her father's death. Abbotswood had become her uncle's home, where his rules applied – and they still did. Back in the summer after her father's death, when she had come to Abbotswood with Nanny the last time, she'd fought all the constraints placed upon her. She'd hidden in the woods as often as she could. She'd listened to her cousins, William and Charles, frolicking but hadn't been allowed to join in, even when Edmund had been visiting. She had become an alien being.

Light refracted on the surface of the river. At least here in the lands lost between Cornwall and Devon she wasn't on view. With a bit of luck, she would be forgotten; that could work in her favour.

They passed the first ferry crossing. In moments Abbotswood came into view. It sat high on the crest of the hill across the river. The lawn tumbled down in front until it reached the water. Her memories raced and rolled down to the riverbank then breathless dashed back up to a tea table groaning with cakes. Now, in the afternoon light, the stone glowed golden. For a moment Alice let more memories fill her. It would be easy to picture her father standing by the long border watching her running through the course he'd set up for her made from garden stakes.

They passed the boatman's cottage and came to the ford. Despite having been advised they were arriving, there was barely a soul about. But everything had happened with undue haste, which was no doubt why they were met by the carriage and not the motorcar. She leaned out of the window and hailed the coachman. 'I wish to alight.' A shadow crossed his face, but he stopped, opened the door and helped her down.

'Do you want company?' Constance looked up from her book.

'No, thank you.' She stood on the bank looking into the clear water and breathing in the cool air. The river hadn't changed but of course that wasn't true. It was never the same from moment to moment. Behind her, woodsmoke rose from the boatman's cottage, and it scented the air. When she was small, she would visit the cottage with Edmund. The old woodsman who lived there was a fine storyteller. She and Edmund used to argue over which of their fathers owned more of the river. Now she knew that the Duke of Exeter's estate was far bigger than that of the Earl St Loy's at Penhale but the St Loys were an older family.

Unlike the seclusion of Abbotswood, boats could make their way up to Penhale's quay and carry away the rich minerals and the produce of the market farms. But here at Abbotswood there was no industry. There were tin and copper mines nearby in both Devon and Cornwall yet none of this was visible from Abbotswood... except a small glimpse from the Swiss Cottage. That sat high up on the ridge above the river and from its heights the tors of Bodmin were visible. The nearest mining was down past Horsebridge where arsenic was drawn from the earth.

The Tamar divided the two counties but not the Abbotswood estate. As a child she used to pretend that once she had crossed the Tamar, she had entered a sacred magical world where fairies lived and dreams came true. It would be good to still believe in such things.

Yet her heart lifted. The bright new leaves cast a green light on the ferns covering the ground. The rain of yesterday had made much of the path muddy and she picked her way to the cottage. As she reached the door it swung open. A man, tall and haughty, looked down on her. Dark-brown hair curled behind his ears. He was not the prince she once sought in these woods but someone not much older than herself. When he reached the path, he spoke. 'How can I help, my lady?' He looked down at her feet.

'You live here?' she asked.

'I do, my lady,' he said, bowing his head.

'Are you the new woodsman?' she asked.

'The gillie,' he said.

'Tucker?' she asked, thinking of the man who, along with her father, had taught her to fish.

'He is slowing down due to gout and I am working with him.' He looked at her directly. 'I'm Zach Carne.'

'I see.' She studied him. He saw through her, she was sure of it. He saw not Lady Alice Neville but something wild. Something that belonged in these woods and nowhere else. She had forgotten that creature that had run free.

She took a last look at the gillie and the cottage then turned. Her shoe caught and she stumbled. A ready hand caught her.

'Thank you,' she said.

Carne bowed his head in acknowledgment. He was close. He smelled of woodsmoke and rosemary. His hand still steadied her. She straightened then his hands fell away and she forced herself to step away down the path back to the river.

'Alice!' Constance's voice travelled across the Tamar where the carriage had stopped after crossing at the ford.

'May I assist you to the quay?' he asked.

'No, I shall be fine.' She met Carne's look for a moment. There was no deference there.

He bowed his head. 'As you wish.' His eyes met hers again and she shivered. She put one foot in front of the other until she reached the quay, not looking back for she knew the new gillie was watching her. Her skin tingled where his glance lingered on her neck.

The boatman stood ten feet from her with hat in hand. 'Excuse me, m'lady. The carriage is waiting for you on the other side.'

She sighed and nodded. She would have to leave the magic of this wood, leave Cornwall and head across the Tamar. Taking the boatman's hand, she stepped on board the small rowing boat with care then perched on the stern bench seat. The river was in a lazy mood, gently making its way out to sea. Midges and dragon flies moved above the surface as if there were no fish lying in wait below. But she knew there were. And as if one heard her thoughts, a salmon rose and stole a dragonfly. Further downriver she spied the gillie as he walked along.

In the woods behind her, she made out the outline of the cottage. Years ago special trees had been planted here, but right now the beauty came from the last of the bluebells. It would have been a carpet of purple-blue a month ago. The perfume was gone now but they would bloom again next year. It was one thing she could look forward to, the fragrance of bluebells. She stared across the river to the house. No, that wasn't true. Abbotswood had a library. Bluebells and books. It would have to do.

Alighting on the Devon bank she took a deep breath and began to walk towards the house when Nanny leaned out of the carriage window and said, 'There you are.'

Alice stopped. She would have preferred to walk up to the house, but she climbed into the carriage and it made its way up to the house that had been her four times great-grandparents' hunting lodge. Out of the window the sky darkened behind the house, but to the front the sun broke through. It blinded her as it shone off the windowpanes, not allowing her to see inside. Was someone there looking out as she looked in? No, that was foolish; of course she was being watched. It was a Thursday in June and instead of being the toast of the season she was here at Abbotswood in disgrace.

The carriage reached the courtyard and stuttered to a halt. Unlike the great Palladian house upcountry that was the seat of the Dukes of Exeter, Abbotswood was crafted in the picturesque style so beloved of the time almost a hundred years before. It was meant to blend into the landscape and to look more like traditional buildings with different roof lines and to be subordinate to the landscape. She looked over her shoulder down to the river and across to the Cornish bank. Smoke rose through the trees from the old cottage and the hillside appeared more like Scotland as it had been planned.

The house always reminded Alice of her childhood drawings with everything a different size including the windows. None of the pleasing symmetry of so many houses existed here. This was a fairy-tale cottage on a grand scale surrounded by an enchanted wood as if it had walked straight out of a story book. She stepped out of the carriage, onto the cobbles. A cough echoed against the stones beneath her feet and the walls of the house and stables. 'Lady Alice.'

She turned, forcing a smile as she said, 'Burton.'

The butler stood tall. He looked much as he always had but a few grey hairs had appeared. She shouldn't be surprised. It had been three years since she had seen him, and he served someone very different now.

She strode through the door into the hall. Despite being June, the fire blazed and its light danced off the wood-panelled walls. As her eyes adjusted to the low light, she picked out the familiar details as she moved towards the flames. The circular table sat in the centre as it always had. The vase was filled with roses, and their sweet scent vied with the woodsmoke.

'We have put out refreshments in the library, unless you would like to go to your room?'

Alice froze for a second. Had he been instructed that she should be sent to her room? No, she was overreacting. She turned and stepped towards the long corridor that led to the children's wing.

'No, my lady. Her Grace instructed that you should be in the main house.'

Alice paused. Somehow that sounded like a death sentence. All fun was henceforth banished from her life. She took a deep breath. He was only following orders. 'I'll have tea before I go up.'

'Very well.' He bowed and she fled to the library, with Nanny and Constance trailing in her wake. A quick glance confirmed that this haven hadn't changed. Despite being called a cottage, Abbotswood's ceilings on the ground floor were high and the windows large to provide sweeping views of the countryside and the river.

She removed her gloves, picked a delicate cake off a plate and flopped into a large armchair, her uncle's favourite. It guarded the three windows that bowed, providing a spectacular view. For the time being it was going to be hers. With just Nanny, Constance and the servants, Alice had the house and the gardens almost to herself.

Staring down to the river to the bend, she watched the gillie she had met earlier walk the bank. No doubt it would be salmon for dinner tonight. She released a long slow breath. Over the past hours she and Nanny had exhausted every possible safe topic of conversation. Dinner would be challenging along with every other meal. Thankfully she didn't have to be so careful with Constance.

Alice hopped up and grabbed a book off the shelf. Books might be her salvation, but not this one. Turning it over she slipped the *Lives of the Saints* back onto the shelf and searched for something more entertaining. The spine of *Pride and Prejudice* slid under her fingers. No, she would not read that. It would only point out how precarious her situation was. She was not in search of a husband. Her finger paused.

A match might still be made without her input.

With that thought, her hands fell to her side.

Chapter Fourteen

Burton showed Alice to a room she didn't know. It was not one that her parents had used nor her grandmother. The walls were covered with wallpaper painted with swallows and pheasants and so many butterflies. It was as if nature had flown inside. The fire was blazing to counter the cool air of the early evening. Above the fireplace was a large looking glass and she peered at the tired woman reflected there. Her lack of sleep showed in her paleness and the purple shadows under her eyes.

She turned away, drawn to the large south-east-facing window, which opened onto a small balcony. The room sat above the dining room which gave her a commanding view of the long border currently filled with summer perennials and colourful annuals with the rose walk above it and the river below. But her eyes were not drawn to the view but the curl of smoke coming from the woodland across the river. Who was this new gillie?

'Alice,' Constance said, walking into the room and stopping by the bed.

Alice turned and smiled at her cousin.

'Nanny is going to take her dinner in the children's wing as she is feeling unwell.'

'Shall I go to her?' Alice asked.

'It's her chest. She coughs a lot and has trouble finding her breath sometimes.' Constance paused. 'She is resting now. We'll have dinner at eight in the dining room.' She grinned.

Alice knew why. This was not normal for her cousin. At thirteen this was unheard of but with only the two of them it made some sense and of course Constance was senior to Alice. She would preside, despite her age, if she was allowed to the table. Alice smiled as she said, 'I'll see you at eight.'

Constance nodded and almost skipped out of the room. Alice turned back to the window. It was now six thirty. She had time for a walk. Without another thought, she slipped downstairs and outdoors without encountering Burton or anyone else to impede her freedom.

She sped past the orchid house and the brewery, which was long out of use. Water tripped down the hillside, enticing the visitor through the different areas of the garden, but she wanted none of the created landscape with its streams and waterfalls. She longed for the wild wood and the possibility of being alone and unwatched, which was hard with fifty gardeners about.

Foxgloves. She stopped to admire them. They acted as spears of colour while the wild honeysuckle scented the air, sweet and reminiscent of her childhood. This was where Alice's father had been happiest. He had relished his time here… mostly fishing.

With slow steps she wandered the main garden landscape from the top waterfall so noisy she couldn't hear her own thoughts, to where water diverted and rushed down rockeries and under bridges more quietly. She stood and stared up at the giant sequoia and a towering Douglas fir, feeling like a small child. Her hand clenched longing for her father's. Tears fell and she stumbled on, not wanting to feel, but not able to avoid it. She paused to peer through the bamboo grove, remembering laughter and her father's love.

The clock on the coach house chimed the hour. She hid under the weeping beech, drying her face and composing herself to go and check on Nanny. The evening breeze scented with roses dried the last of her tears and she headed to the children's sitting room.

She stopped before the opened French windows. Nanny was sound asleep in a chair. Her book lay open on her lap. Alice carefully backed away, not wanting to wake her. She ran her fingers in the water channel that bordered the parterre which filled the children's garden. The water reflected white cumulous clouds filling the blue sky. The sun was still high. It would make more sense to eat a light meal in her room rather than dress for dinner. She didn't have the energy for the unnecessary effort to be formal.

Continuing around the house, looking down to the river, she entered through the hallway between the sitting room and the morning room. The sounds of the dinner preparations drifted to her from the kitchen. With heavy feet she went upstairs, longing for sleep. The maid was waiting for her when she reached her room. Through force of habit she let herself be dressed. Constance was excited, therefore Alice would make an effort. The maid fixed the clasp on her pearls and Alice viewed herself in the glass. A bored woman looked back at her. She hadn't looked further than doing the deed and freeing herself from marriage. Now she was trapped and there were seven years ahead of her before she would receive her inheritance.

Walking down the main staircase, she considered what she might do to fill her time? Thankfully it would not involve the Duke of Cleveland, but given time her mother might find another candidate. The scandal would only remain vivid for so long. She could strive to become a blue stocking. Although she was in possession of some intelligence she was not a scholar.

Constance stood at the bottom of the stairs, her eyes shining. 'Ready?'

Alice nodded and followed her cousin into the dining room, her least favourite room in the house with all the crests of all the families that the Nevilles were connected to by marriage prominently displayed around the room crowning the tops of the wooden panels.

Constance looked up from her plate. 'I love this room.'

Alice opened her eyes wide. 'Why? I have always found it a bit dreary.'

'Because I love to sit here and dream about who I will marry and seeing their coat of arms on the wall.' She grinned. 'He will be handsome and kind.' She sat straighter. 'And he will adore me and I will love him forever.'

Alice looked from Constance's beaming face to the arms on the wall. She doubted any of these plaques represented love. There wasn't a great family in the kingdom that the Nevilles weren't connected to. Each coat of arms silently shouted 'do your duty'. Constance clearly saw them differently.

'I imagine yours when you marry will be right there.' Constance pointed to a space near the door.

'I shan't marry and you will have that place next to your sister's.'

Constance smiled then pulled a bone from her fish. Alice wasn't sure how Constance held this fantasy of love. Surely she'd heard the reality from Beatrice.

'If you don't marry,' Constance said, as their plates were cleared, 'will you study?'

Alice raised an eyebrow.

'You've been to a girls' school and I'm sure you have learned much.'

Alice took a sip of her water. 'I have.'

'I intend to study insects and go to Oxford.'

Alice put her glass down. 'Duke's daughters do not go to Oxford.'

Constance pouted. 'Whyever not. The book on butterflies I'm reading was written by Lady Arabella Carvon.'

'And did she go to Oxford?'

Constance's eyes narrowed as if she was trying to read the page in her mind.

'Possibly she had and then she married a baronet who was also interested in bugs.' Alice took a sip of water.

'Lepidopterology is Lady Arabella's speciality.'

Alice nodded. She wouldn't disabuse Constance of her dreams of marrying for love and going to Oxford. Everyone needed dreams. After all, Alice had dreamt of being a fairy princess once.

'Today I spotted a comma and a Camberwell beauty.' Her face flushed. 'I need a net though.' She paused to look at Alice. 'Do you think the gillie might have a spare net that I could use and adapt?'

'The gillie?' Alice tilted her head and studied her cousin.
'Yes.'

Alice pictured the young man she had met earlier. 'Shall I ask him about the net for you?'

'Yes, please.' Constance grinned.

Dinner finally finished Alice rose and wandered outside. She breathed deeply. The air was freshly touched with rain. Strolling the lawn covered terrace, she admired the long border in the fading light. Above, the rose-covered trellis covered the walkway, and the perfume floated on the gentle breeze. The sound of the stream pelting down the hill through the gullies and waterfalls filled the air. It was only as she approached the small hexagonal building containing the riches of geological specimens and shells that she could hear the Tamar.

Climbing roses and honeysuckle covered the outer walls and ran riot over the roof. The fragrance was sweet. Standing beside the entrance to the shell house, as the grotto was referred to, she looked down and watched the river water bend and seem to break as it reached Black Rock. Although the surface looked still, it moved with some force on its way out to the sea. She envied the water's freedom.

She took a few steps on the pebbled path to the door of the house and turned the handle, but it was locked. This had never been the case before. All her old excitement about this little building and her times in it with her father – talking about the shells and minerals – evaporated. She tried the handle one last time before she turned back to the house.

The lamps had now been lit in the library and in her bedroom. She couldn't see the children's wing from here, but she was certain Nanny was sound asleep even though it was only ten. The poor woman wasn't feeling at all well. Alice had never recalled Nanny having a moment's illness in her childhood. Surely looking after Constance and Francis couldn't have been that arduous. By now Constance would be curled up in her own bed with a book. Alice would have to do the same, even though the sky was still bright. It was mid-summer's eve in a few days, and in the normal course of things she would have been dancing at the Midnight Ball. She paused and looked at the pale sky. Both the feeling of missing out and relief battled inside her.

Chapter Fifteen

The mist hung in the air as Alice walked across the tennis court. The sun had just risen and if she were still in London, she would only be getting home. Instead she was in Devon and had gone to bed at ten and had woken with the dawn chorus. No one had expected her up. The maid hadn't even been in to light the fire. Poking about in the bedroom, Alice had found her cousin William's pyjamas in the bottom drawer and had pulled on those and his dressing gown. Her feet were bare. She hadn't been barefoot outside in years. The damp grass between her toes tickled and she rolled the bottom of the pyjama legs up to the middle of her calf. If anyone saw her, they would be shocked. But it was four in the morning and no one was about as she headed down towards the river.

She came to the old swimming pond where the mist hovered inches above its surface. Loose blades of grass that had collected on her feet floated on the surface when she tested the water. She had learned to swim here and the cold water called to her. Alice glanced around. No one was about. She shed the dressing gown and the pyjamas, leaving them hanging from the metal handles of the ladder. Standing for a moment on the edge of the pond, she imagined she must look like a marble statue in the mist. Goosebumps covered her skin.

Alice took a shallow dive into the pond and gasped as she surfaced. It was far colder than she had expected. Every bit of her was tight and complaining. She swam from one side of the pond to the other, ignoring the tangled weeds wrapping about her limbs and caressing her stomach. As she reached the metal ladder ready to climb out, she heard a footstep. She froze.

Alice was swimming naked. If she were discovered, she would be sent further away than Devon. Eyes squinting, she scanned the giant gunnera that protected the privacy of the pond. Aside from the pounding of her own heart, she heard another footstep and saw a boot. It wasn't moving nor was she. Who was there? If it was anyone from the house they would turn away and protect her modesty, but this boot faced her. What was she going to do?

Alice began to shake with the coldness of the water. She had to climb out or she would freeze. Taking a deep breath, she held the handle on the old ladder and climbed out. She didn't look ahead. It would be best not to know who had witnessed her swim. Quickly she pulled on the pyjamas. The fabric stuck to her damp cold flesh. Finally she thrust her arms through the sleeves of the dressing down. Only then did she look up and see the top of the fishing rod move away.

Wrapping the dressing gown tighter about her body, she walked up to the house, careful not to acquire too much grass or dirt on her feet. She must slip into the house without being noticed. She had only arrived yesterday and it was as if prison bars had been placed around Abbotswood. This was a far finer prison than Holloway, but it was a prison nonetheless.

She shouldn't feel this way; after all, it was she who had acted. It had been her decision alone. Not even Miss Parkes had had a part in it, although she had planted the seed; Alice had chosen to act and when to do so.

Yet she felt forsaken, which was an odd word and an odd feeling. As she neared the house, in all its grand cottage orné glory, she had never been more alone. Here in deepest Devon there were no near neighbours, and Tavistock was miles away. Her mother had washed her hands of her, not that she had ever had much to do with her before. Thankfully Nanny was still with her.

A shutter moved in the children's wing. It was Nanny, perhaps, or maybe Constance or simply a servant. No matter who it was, Alice had been seen. She raced the last stretch to the house and found Burton by the door. Alice took a deep breath. She would not be cowed. Head high she walked through the door held open by the butler.

'Good morning, Burton. Has tea been brought up?'

'Yes, m'lady.'

She sailed past him, leaving damp footprints on the floor like an energetic puppy. She didn't wait for him to say any more but fled up the stairs and into her room, where she startled the maid who was poking the fire.

'Good morning.'

The maid stood and bowed. 'Would m'lady like a bath?' she asked, keeping her eyes looking down as the water pooled about Alice's feet.

'Yes.' Alice picked up the teapot and poured. She drank it

without milk or sugar in a large gulp. Heaven knows what the maid had thought when she had found the bed empty. There was no place for her to go and swimming wouldn't even have been considered. Alice hadn't considered it either and now she was cold through. The maid went into the bathroom and Alice stood by the window, looking out towards the sunrise. She shivered, not because of the cold, but because by the riverbank she spied the gillie walking.

'M'lady, your bath.' The maid held open the bathroom door.

Alice put the cup down as the gillie looked up. He stopped walking and stood staring at the house. She was certain he couldn't see her now, but he might have seen more than enough of her already.

Herring, kippers, kidneys. Her stomach rolled. Despite the early morning exercise, she didn't need or want all this food. After much indecision Alice filled a bowl with porridge and sat at the far end of the long table. From there she could look out onto the garden. It was a riot of colour and the roses were at their peak.

Constance burst into the room and Burton followed with the papers. On the top was the *Bystander*. It was now Friday and too soon for them to report on the ball. When they did her name would not appear, but she knew as well as anyone that her name would be on everyone's lips, including the monarch's.

'You went for a morning swim.' Constance looked over her shoulder as she piled her plate high with eggs.

'Yes, very refreshing,' Alice said, smiling at her cousin.

'Wasn't the swimming pond a bit...' Constance waved a piece of bread in the air.

'It was cold and refreshing. I highly recommend it.'

Constance sat opposite her with a thump. 'You certainly have a great deal more colour in your face.' She squinted at her. 'Yes, this morning you look more yourself. Nanny thinks you were affected by a fever of some sort.'

Alice looked up from the porridge. 'Does she?'

'Yes, she does, I heard her telling your mother on the telephone last night.'

Alice put her spoon down. Her distant gaolers were receiving a full report. She stood, saying, 'I'm going for a walk.' She glanced at Constance's open mouth and resisted the urge to close it for her. 'Would you like to join me?'

'No, thank you.' She looked at her breakfast plate. 'Nanny might. She's in the small room overlooking the garden, writing to her sister.'

'I'll stop by and ask.' Alice went down the long corridor, bracing herself to hear a lecture from Nanny before she would be allowed out.

Nanny sat at the small table by the window. Sunlight reflected off the fountain, in which two woodpigeons happily bathed. Bright cosmos were coming into flower in the fan-shaped parterre that made up the children's garden. Pinks and whites danced on the morning breeze. Alice, listening to Nanny cough and wheeze, paused to admire them.

Nanny scribbled with great speed and without looking up, she said, 'I hope you enjoyed your swim this morning; and, if you choose to do so again, find appropriate attire. Either myself or Constance will go with you.'

Alice stilled. 'I prefer to go alone.'

'If you decide to swim naked every morning, I assure you, you will not be alone.' Nanny continued to write.

How did Nanny know she swam naked? Of course, she knew because her clothes would have been sodden and instead they were simply damp.

'I...' Alice's voice trailed away as she didn't know what to say.

'Yes, you may go for a walk on your own for the present time, but this may have to be reviewed,' Nanny said, as a cough rattled her birdlike frame.

Despite her concern for Nanny's health, Alice bristled. What was she being punished for, the swim or for offending the king and queen? She stared hard at Nanny, trying to see what she was thinking, but Nanny continued on with her letter.

Walking out of the room and into the large vestibule at the base of the main staircase, she stopped to compose herself and she heard Nanny cough again. She looked better this morning but the cough was persistent and worrying.

'I expect you back in an hour,' called Nanny.

'Yes, Nanny.' The pleasure in the bright morning dimmed as Alice strolled towards the dairy dell where the 5th Duchess of Exeter had played at being a milkmaid, as had every daughter of the house since. She was no exception but right now that didn't appeal because she didn't want to play at life; she wanted to live it and not just live it on the surface.

Alice stopped at the bridge which crossed the stream running through the garden and fed the dell pond. The morning mist had disappeared and the water glistened in the sunlight. Her heart lifted.

She turned and sought out the holy well tucked on the side of the lower pond. The structure was covered in foliage and green moss as if it was becoming part of nature. Yet as she pushed back the ivy, the carved stones showed their beauty. Once she imagined they would have been in a church and not over a water source.

Aside from the statue of the Abbot presiding high on the west-facing wall of the house, these stones housing the holy well were the remaining thing at Abbotswood that hinted at its distant past, aside from its name. The land had been owned by the Abbot of Tavistock until Henry VIII had dissolved the monasteries to the benefit of families like the Nevilles. Once the well had been renowned and pilgrims on their way to Rome and the Holy Land would stop here en route to Plymouth and the next part of their journey.

As a child Alice made wishes here. Then, she wanted to be a fairy princess. Now she wasn't sure what she wanted. All that had moored her had disappeared. A few days ago, everything had been clear.

She bent down and dipped her hand in the water, pulling it up quickly when she heard footsteps behind her.

'Can't keep you away from the water, m'lady,' the gillie said, looking at her like the men in Paris had.

She flushed. If she had thought he hadn't seen her she was wrong. She wobbled on the slippery stones. His hand shot out to steady her, but she drew back. Her breath stilled as she looked up into his dark eyes. But the hunger there disappeared, and he helped her over the water running from the well into the pond.

'Have you worked here long?' she asked, smoothing her

hands over her skirt, trying not to think about what he had seen this morning.

'No, only since December.' He looked directly at her. He knew her. This morning's swim but more than that. Her face flushed at the thought of what he might have seen. 'Do you need any more assistance?' he asked.

'No.' She pursed her mouth. He bowed and turned from her. She watched him walk away with a swagger in his gait. He was far too confident to be an under gillie for Tucker and his accent was softer. Who was this river keeper?

'There you are.' Constance stood with hands on hips. 'Nanny said she'd seen you walk this way.'

'Did she?' Alice's eyes narrowed as the gillie climbed into the boat and crossed the Tamar. She didn't move from the spot until she couldn't see him, but she knew he had gone to Boatman's Cottage. The ever-present smoke rose above the trees on the other side. It was probably alight when she had made her way down here hours before, but the smoke had been disguised in the morning mists.

'Yes, she thought you might be bored and in need of company.' Constance smiled and adjusted the book under her arms.

Alice continued to look across the river. 'Yes, I think she is right,' she said, turning away from the river and looking first at her cousin and then at the house. 'I think it's time to take up fishing again.'

Constance took a step back. 'Fishing?'

'Yes, I used to fish all the time with my father when we were here.' Alice set off towards the house. 'The fish are rising.'

'Oh,' Constance said, racing to catch her.

Yes, fishing would be the answer to the boredom.

Dear Sylvia,

How wonderful to hear all your news and that you are now well enough to walk to the village. Keep resting and do not stress yourself too much. Has the doctor diagnosed the problem and has he prescribed anything?

We are now ensconced at Abbotswood and I cannot begin to tell you how wonderful it is to be here again. The air is fresh, and I can see the colour return to Lady Alice's cheeks. Her mother and her uncle had wanted to send her to the Highlands, but I suggested this, and they eventually agreed, taking it on as their own idea.

Away from her mother and the influence of others, Lady Alice will remember her duty and who she is. I know I only gave you a little information as to what caused her fall from the debutante of the moment. At the ball where her uncle expected the Duke of Cleveland to offer, the foolish girl chose to admonish the king and queen regarding women's votes.

Now, if I am honest, I understand what she has done and why, but what she doesn't see is how precarious her situation now is. Her actions suggest there are mental issues to her uncle and these same actions make her mother desperate. Indeed the dowager duchess is so desperate that she might arrange an even more unfortunate marriage. If the child thought the duke repulsive, she didn't look at the others who were vying for her hand.

I have already seen her regression into her childhood ways. This morning she was swimming naked in the pond as if she were a young girl and not a marriageable woman. This is not in fact bad but good. Being here is removing the veneer put on her by that wretched school. They filled her head with unnecessary nonsense. My role now is to bring the child back to her senses so that next season, although not the shining star she was this year, she will have some say in choosing the man to be her husband.

And yes, my cough has returned. The hasty journey wore me out, but I hope with the good weather we are now having it should lessen. I will write more once we have truly settled into life here in Abbotswood.

Your loving sister,
Eve

Chapter Sixteen

Alice and Constance entered the house together. Alice's mind was on fishing and she was about to ask Burton about it but he said, 'Lady Alice, your mother is on the telephone.'

She went to the handset in the closet off the hall. 'Hello, Mother.'

'Alice, how is Nanny?'

Alice forced as much brightness as she could in one word. 'Improving.'

'Good, I don't want you unsupervised.'

She glanced around. 'Mother, there is no one here, nor is there anyone for miles.'

'People are still talking,' her mother said, taking in a deep breath. 'Your picture was the frontispiece in *Country Life* this week and the *Bystander*, *Tatler* and the *Spectator* have reported what you have done. Thank God your uncle has managed to keep your name out of print, but everyone knows and talks of nothing else.'

'I see.' Alice pressed her lips together.

'The pitying looks I have been subject to.'

There was nothing Alice could say to this so she asked what she had been longing to know. 'When can I come to

London?' Although she loved Abbotswood, she missed the entertainments of London, especially the museums, theatres but most especially the libraries and the newspapers. She had no access to *The Suffragette* or the *International Woman Suffrage News*. But it wasn't only that: how could she effect any change from here in the middle of nowhere? After the ball she had thought she would be content to have done her part, but she wasn't and longed to do more.

'You will stay at Abbotswood for the foreseeable future,' her mother said with force.

'But...' She looked down the hall where Burton was standing, listening to the conversation. Unsupervised. She would be lucky to find a moment alone.

'No arguments. Your uncle and I are in agreement. It is the only way to quash the scandal.' Her mother's voice trailed away.

'Yes, Mother.' Alice was about to say goodbye but her mother hung up and Alice placed the handset down, frustrated. She walked through to the morning room, trying to make a plan. The one thing, along with fresh air, that Alice had plenty of was time. How could she fill it? She couldn't write letters supporting the cause because everything she did at the moment was scrutinised. But if she was going to be here for months, she must do something. Just then she saw the young gillie carrying a large salmon towards the kitchen.

Alice rang the bell and looked out the window while she waited. When she was younger, the appeal in the sport lay in pretending to be a fish rather than in the catching of it. She hadn't liked to eat fish much at the time, but her tastes had changed.

A discreet cough announced Burton's arrival. She turned

and smiled. 'Burton, I'd like to go fishing. Would you tell the gillie, please?'

He paused before he spoke. 'I'm afraid Tucker is down with gout.'

She looked him directly in the eyes and said, 'Well, there must be someone who can assist me.'

'I'll speak with Johns and see if young Zachariah Carne is up to the job.'

Alice drew her brows together. This didn't make sense. 'Why wouldn't he be?'

'He's not long come to us from Penhale where he was working with his father and brother.' He shifted.

'Then he should be well trained, as the earl wouldn't have employed him otherwise.'

'Very well. When?' he asked.

'In an hour,' she said.

He bowed and left. Alice knew that she had made him do something he didn't want to do, and she wasn't sure why. He surely didn't think she couldn't be trusted with the gillie. Heavens, what did people think of her. She was for women's suffrage not indiscreet liaisons with the gillie. Free love may well be favoured by a part of the movement but surely there needed to be love?

Burton had arranged for her to meet the gillie down by the river. The morning was warm, and her heavy clothes were more attuned to Scottish summers than Devon ones. She stopped halfway to the river to adjust the waist of the skirt, which had slipped despite the maid's best efforts to tighten it sufficiently. To her left, the branch of a birch tree moved. The leaves wobbled but the air was still. She turned fully when it wavered again. Stepping closer, a young jackdaw peered at her, its eyes black and soulful. Above a kestrel circled and she turned to the jackdaw again to warn him, but he was gone.

It was now the first of July and her days went slowly as the nature around her moved swiftly. Her mother was wrong; people would have moved onto other news now, despite the recent coverage of the ball. London was full of events to discuss and then there was all the talk of what was happening in Ulster and the actions of her fellow suffragettes in their battle for women's votes. She didn't pine for London but missed being a part of something.

In Abbotswood she was woken to bird song and a small blue tit tapping on the window. She liked the little bird, but it would have been better that she had slept until noon and the day would have been half over. But no, she woke to the dawn chorus and when her blue tit arrived, she headed to the window slowly so as not to startle him. He would stop and stare at her much like the young jackdaw of moments before. But the tit's eyes weren't soulful. They were mischievous. Each morning he would cock his head as if to say, 'Still a bed, are ya? What a waste of a day.' Then he would fly away before she could agree with him. It was a waste of a day, a week, a summer, a life.

This morning she would catch fish or at least she hoped she would. She hadn't done this since she was still wearing her hair down. Life was simpler then. She had roamed freely without adults watching her every step. Now she knew that, even though Nanny wasn't well enough, she would be at the window watching for her return, as would Burton.

Once she reached the river she stopped and waited. Her life was spent waiting for something. Seven years until she came into her money. Seven years waiting. Yet standing here – with the sun breaking through some light clouds and in the woods across the Tamar the dappled light gave the woodland floor the appearance of a Turkish carpet with greens and deep browns – she didn't want to lose a moment of it. Out of the corner of her eyes she saw the gillie approaching. She turned to him and she asked, 'Which beat?'

'Which one do you wish, my lady?' He bowed slightly.

'Where do you suggest?' She drew a deep breath.

'I would suggest that Black Rock might be the spot this morning.' He held his hand out, indicating the direction as if she didn't know it.

'Thank you.' She set off, not sure why his attitude was irritating her but it was. For no reason she could pinpoint she felt peevish as she studied the water as it swirled and eddied past the outcrop of stone. Alice stopped, frustrated, wanting to scramble down onto the rocks as she had in the past. But then she hadn't been encumbered with long heavy skirts or corseting that resisted her movements.

The gillie jumped down the incline then turned and held out his hand. She had no choice. She needed assistance and took his hand as he led her sidestepping out onto the rock. He released it. Her hand fell to her side, but she could still feel the strength of his fingers on hers. She looked down into the water, hoping that her colour hadn't risen too much. It was nothing for a gentleman to take her hand, but here she was, flushed… because of the gillie holding hers.

'Burton informs me that you have done this before,' he said.

'Fishing?' Her glance flew up to him then away as she said, 'Yes, I have.'

He handed her the rod. She felt it flex. The intricate fly on the end danced, the pheasant feather catching the light. But this was all different from the last time. Then the rod had been shorter. Now she was holding something altogether different.

'Would my lady like some assistance?' he asked.

Alice held her breath. She didn't like the way he said my lady and she didn't want help, but it would be wise to take it. Those easy days of fishing here with her father and the old gillie seemed distant. Standing here with the new one, everything was confused.

'Shall I show you?' He held his hand out for the rod he'd given her. Her hand tightened on it. She wanted to be capable, but she wasn't. She gave it to him with more force than she intended, and he leant back nearly falling but he didn't say a word.

'Hello,' Constance called out from the bank and Alice swung around, nearly unbalancing herself and the gillie. They swayed as if they were dancing and she laid a hand on his forearm to steady herself while her cousin scrambled out onto the rock without any problem. But Constance's skirts weren't as long or as full.

'Caught anything?' Constance looked from the gillie and back to Alice.

'Haven't begun.' Alice withdrew her hand from the gillie's arm.

'Nanny thought I might enjoy this.' Constance wrinkled her nose as she studied the fly on the end of the line.

'Did she?' Alice didn't believe that Constance would enjoy it at all.

'Yes, she did, and Burton suggested that I join you.' Constance pushed her hair from her shoulder and onto her back.

Alice pressed her lips together, keeping in the things she longed to say. A red admiral butterfly flew past her cousin's face and she chased it back onto the riverbank where it landed on a daisy.

Alice turned to the gillie. 'You were about to demonstrate...'

He bowed his head and she stepped back. Lazy bugs skimmed the surface in the morning sun. With ease he cast the line and she watched not the progress of the fly but the movement of his arms and shoulders. Her glance travelled up the back of his sun browned neck to the curl of his dark hair.

He turned and his gaze met hers. The silence grew between them. His eyes were not entirely brown but had flecks of green, the green of the summer's long grass and the gold of a hay field. His mouth was full and the corners were turning up as if he found something amusing.

The rod bent sharply, and the line pulled. 'Would you like to bring in the fish?'

Alice glanced at the rod and the pull on the line. 'Yes, I'd like to try.'

She took three steps to stand beside him.

'Place your left hand above mine,' he whispered.

She tried to avoid touching him, but it was impossible. Her arm pressed against his.

'Now bring your right hand.' His voice was low, meant only for her.

Alice did and found herself pressed against his side. Despite the fabric of their clothing, she was conscious of every move of his muscles as he released his right hand. The pull on the line distracted her but not enough. A keen awareness of his every movement filled her senses as he held the rod with his left and had moved himself behind her. Only their left arms and fingers touched but she was aware of the line of his body so close.

With all her concentration, Alice focused on the fish that was on the end of the line. She would not think how close the gillie was or how he still smelled of woodsmoke and rosemary and... soap. The rod bent further and she leaned back, coming into contact with the solid strength of the gillie.

'You have him, my lady,' he whispered. His breath was so close to her ear it touched a nerve and her body tensed.

'I've got him!' Constance ran as fast as she could along the bank while keeping her clasped hands together, holding the butterfly between them.

Alice pulled sharply and the fish found its freedom. She fell back against the gillie and his free hand swung out until they were both balanced and not touching. She released the fishing rod and went as best she could to her cousin, hoping in her excitement that Constance wouldn't notice how high the colour was in Alice's face.

It flamed, as did her thoughts.

Chapter Seventeen

'Hello.' Nanny smiled as Alice entered the children's sitting room. She detected a hint of colour on Nanny's cheeks that hadn't been there this morning.

'You look better,' Alice said, as she bent down to kiss her. Nanny's continued ill health did worry her. Nanny coughed into her handkerchief but it was gentle.

'I sat in the garden for a bit.' Nanny pulled the shawl closer and picked up her needlework.

'Well, it's done you good.' Alice sat opposite her.

'As has the fishing for you.' She stared at Alice and Alice prayed she didn't look flushed.

'I'd forgotten much.'

'Not surprising. It's been years and you were young then.' Nanny's glance hadn't left Alice's face as if trying to read her thoughts. Alice stopped herself from thinking about the gillie.

'What is the gillie like?' Nanny asked.

Alice looked out the window. 'Silent mostly.'

'Is he no help?' Nanny asked.

'He says the minimum required to achieve his purpose.'

Nanny laughed. 'That sounds like a virtue in a gillie.'

Alice smiled. 'I supposed it is.'

'You were so long, Burton was concerned about you,' she said, laying her needlework aside.

Alice straightened her shoulders. 'I may want votes for women but that doesn't mean I can't be trusted with a gillie.'

'That's what I said to him.' She peered over her spectacles and smiled.

Alice's heart filled. Nanny knew her so well.

'Did Constance enjoy it?' Nanny asked.

Alice laughed. 'No. She chased butterflies.' Alice sat on the nearby chair. 'I don't think she can be still for long enough.'

'You were the same.' Nanny's eyes crinkled with another smile.

'True.' Alice picked up Nanny's hand, reassured by its warmth.

'We had a call from Lord Edmund at Penhale. He heard that you were in residence.'

Alice stood. 'Is he not in London?'

'He said he needed a break from all the parties and the heat.'

'Will he be visiting?' Alice walked to the centre of the room.

'I believe he will.' Nanny rested her left hand on the base of her throat before she coughed.

Alice clapped. 'Now, that is something to look forward to.'

'I thought you'd be pleased.' Nanny clasped her hands together.

'I am indeed. Now rest so that you can enjoy Lord Edmund's company as well.' Alice kissed Nanny's cheek.

'I will.' Nanny closed her eyes and Alice slipped away, stopping briefly by her bedroom to retrieve her book, a collection of P G Wodehouse's short stories. Burton hovered in the hall and Alice wanted to scream 'go away' but said nothing. He was doing his job. Before he could enquire about her intentions, she grabbed her hat and gloves and fled. It was all unbearable, but, unlike London, she could escape outside and a photographer wouldn't be waiting.

In the courtyard she turned left and headed up the steps into the woods. Before long she was out of breath and needed to stop. It was hot and her clothing itched. She longed to shed the layers and take a swim. She turned down through the garden towards the dairy dell, listening to the sound of water cascading. Crossing one of the ornamental bridges, she looked down through the tree ferns to where she could see a gardener bent low over one of the beds. God, she was never alone.

It wasn't his fault so she smiled as she went past and came to the pond by the dairy, thinking about what Arthur Carew had said about wanting all men and women to have the vote. She paused for a moment. None of the many people who worked here at Abbotswood had the vote any more than she did. Arthur was right. It should be universal suffrage. All these people working for her uncle were no different to her.

She ventured across the bridge and up the steps to the small thatched dairy. Unlike the shell house, this domain of her childhood was open. Once inside, the silence was astounding. The door swung closed behind her and the coldness of the place covered her skin. She shivered as if she could see ghosts moving through the pristine interior. Rubbing her arms, she left the inside to walk along the balcony.

'Lady Alice.'

She started and the gillie's hand touched her arm.

'Burton sent me looking for you,' he said.

Alice's pleasure at seeing the gillie evaporated with the butler's name. 'You've found me.'

His glance met hers and her chest tightened. It was such a direct look. It was a man looking at her as a woman. Not even her suitors in London had dared to stare so boldly at her. She should reprimand him, but the words wouldn't come. She looked away, up towards the house. Burton was standing with binoculars in his hand.

'Did Burton have a message?' she asked.

'Yes, Lord Edmund will be arriving this evening,' he said, stepping away from her.

Alice smiled. 'Thank you.' She paused, needing escape. 'Is the fishing good now?'

He glanced past the pond cottage to the Tamar. 'It might be upriver. When you were taking luncheon, I walked a mile and the conditions looked good.' He studied her.

A mile away from Burton. The gillie already carried a pack and her rod. 'Fine, take me there.' And then, thinking of the gardener, said, 'Please.'

He looked up from under his long lashes and the sunlight caught the gold in his eyes. He held out his arm and she took it and they walked along the bank in silence. She left her hand resting on his forearm. Below the thick fabric of his jacket she felt his strength. There was something wild about him. She couldn't say why she sensed that, but she did feel his pent-up energy. He limited his stride so that she could keep up with him. Her boots were pretty and the most practical thing she had with her, but they were not made for trekking through the countryside.

'Tell me,' she said, casting a sideways glance at him, 'does your disenfranchisement bother you?'

He stopped and turned to her, frowning.

'Sorry, lack of a vote.'

'I knew well what disenfranchisement meant but I was considering my answer.'

'Oh, I'm sorry.' She withdrew her hand from his arm. 'I meant no offence. I wanted to know… was curious.'

'To know how the servants feel?' He opened his eyes wide and took a step back, studying her.

'Hadn't thought of it quite that way but yes, I guess I do.' She paused. 'You see, I am still filled with anger at the injustice of it all.'

'You have no need to waste your anger for me. I am happy with my lot.'

Alice blinked. This was not what she had expected. 'How can you be? Just because you have no land, you have no power.'

He turned to the riverbank. 'I have the river to work on and His Grace is fair.'

Alice opened her mouth to say more but stopped. He pointed to the old stone steps leading down to the water. Here the Tamar flowed slower, the Cornish bank was further, and the water was clearer. She scanned the surface, looking for the sunlight to bounce off her elusive prey.

'My lady.' He handed her the rod. He stood on the step behind her. She loosened her shoulders and cast the line, but it caught on the bank behind.

The gillie freed it and said quietly, 'If I may, my lady.' He placed his arms around her and his hands over hers. He drew the rod back and then, with a flick, released it. The fly landed downriver by the bank, where the water slowed even further.

They stood together and she barely dared to take a breath and yet she felt the rise and fall of his chest. After some time, her own breathing began to match his. She didn't know how long they stood like that but a tug on the line set them both moving. He began to reel it in with his arms still about her. Her lungs were filled with the scent of woodsmoke and... him.

She closed her eyes as he leaned into her as the rod bent further. The fish was resisting. His hand gripped hers as the battle went on. Her fingers hurt but it was the sensations of him pressed up against her that concerned her. This was wrong. She should step away, make a fuss, but the salmon on the line appeared out of the water.

'Well done,' he said, as he stepped back from her and let her bring the fish in the rest of the way while he readied the net. He took the rod from her. 'A respectable size too.'

'It's your fish,' she said.

'No, it's not.' He put the fish into the basket.

She huffed, not wanting to argue but not sure what else to do with the feelings inside. 'It's my uncle's fish.'

'This is true. Would you like to continue?' he asked.

Her mouth was dry. Would he stand so close to her again? It was best if she went back because she did want him to be that close to her again. 'No, that is enough for today.' She looked him in the eyes. 'Thank you.'

He half bowed and then gathered the equipment before leading the way along the bank back to the house. The clouds that had lingered from the morning had cleared and the sun beat down on her heavy clothes. She stopped when they reached the bathing pond. If she were alone, she would strip off and swim. She looked at the gillie's back and wondered what he would look like unclothed. He turned as if he had read her thoughts. She tried but she couldn't lose the images in her head of him undressing her and himself.

'Go on without me,' she said, waving her hand to fan her face. 'I'm going to stand here in the shade for a bit.' Her voice sounded unnaturally high-pitched.

His glance narrowed. 'Are you feeling well? Shall I fetch one of the maids?'

'That won't be necessary.' She turned from him and looked fixedly at the gunnera. Once she was sure he had gone, she took off her boots and stockings. The feel of the cool grass on her feet was exquisite. In moments she had reached the water's edge and there she placed one foot at a time in until her body temperature began to drop to a more normal level. He had seen her here. Then she thought of his breath on her neck minutes before and her temperature climbed as a flush covered her. She must not think of it. It was nothing. He was doing his job. That was all.

Chapter Eighteen

The maid did the clasp on the pearls and Alice looked over her shoulder to thank her. She must be about the same age and Alice was overcome with remorse that the maid had been looking after Alice since she'd arrived and Alice knew nothing about her, not even her name.

'Thank you for your help.' Alice smiled. 'What's your name?'

'Susan, my lady.'

'Thank for your assistance this evening, Susan.'

Susan bowed and when she looked at Alice again Alice made sure that their glances met. She wanted to ask Susan so many questions. She couldn't rush in but she longed to know how Susan felt about women's votes.

Now was not the time to ask. Edmund was waiting downstairs. She didn't need to adorn herself for Edmund but somehow it was the correct thing. This dress was one of her favourites designed by Lady Duff Gordon, otherwise known as Lucille. The way the white fabric draped in the skirt, revealing a hint of her right leg, was divine. It appeared as if her bodice had been wrapped in deep black. Where the satin met it folded richly, rising to her right shoulder and trailing down her side in two different lengths in striking contrast to the glimmering skirt.

She opened the box containing her paternal grandmother's tiara. It was part of her legacy to Alice. She would never be able to wear the intricate laurel diadem fully assembled on her head unless she married. Thankfully it came apart and it could be worn as a necklace or as a brooch.

As she handed the brooch to the maid, to Susan she corrected herself, to pin into place, she recalled the story behind the tiara. Her grandfather had the tiara made for his bride, Daphne. Among the laurel leaves design were small diamond flowers. Her grandmother had said that, as he'd presented her with the piece, he'd told her how she had won his heart and he'd hoped that she would wear it on their wedding day to show the world she had been victorious. Her grandmother had. She had also told Alice the story of Daphne who was turned into a tree to escape the lustful advances of Apollo. Alice scowled. Cleveland. How could they have even thought of marrying her to him? Her own father would have done what Daphne's had and protected her from such a fate; she was certain.

But she would not think on her fate for the moment. She would enjoy Edmund's delicious company. And tonight there would be wine. Burton never offered her any if she was alone with Constance and Nanny. Despite her eighteen years, he treated her as if she was still in the nursery.

'You look beautiful, my lady.' Susan smiled.

'Thank you.' Alice took one last look in the glass before she went downstairs to the drawing room where a fire was blazing.

Nanny was tucked up in a chair with Edmund leaning low beside her in conversation.

On seeing her he stood. 'Well, Thing, how are you?'

'I'm here.' She sent him a look.

'I can see that and looking more beautiful than ever. The country suits you.' He took her hand and bent low over it, but his lips did not touch. Always so proper when others were around them. So unlike the Edmund behind the polished veneer. Her Edmund was fun, free and fabulous.

'It's wonderful to see you.' She grinned.

'Desperate for company is what I heard.' He winked at Nanny.

Nanny smiled. 'I thought this would cheer you up, Alice.'

'It has no end.' Alice tucked her arm in Edmund's and led him to the sofa opposite Nanny where they sat. 'Tell me all the news from London. Is everyone still talking about me?'

'Yes, but they are also chatting about Maud Dalrymple who has accepted the proposal of a man three times her age.'

'No.' Alice made a face. 'Is he well connected or simply rolling in money?'

'The money won this one, I'm afraid,' he said, pulling a silver cigarette case from his pocket.

'Has anyone caught your eye yet, Lord Edmund?' Nanny asked before taking a sip of her sherry.

'I'm saving myself.' He placed a hand on his heart and Alice laughed.

'For our lovely Lady Alice.' Nanny smiled.

Edmund raised his glass. 'Of course.'

'Well, it will have to be next season now,' Nanny said.

Alice took a deep breath and turned to Edmund. He had it

easy. His father's estate would come to him and his only duty was to produce an heir. Something her own father had failed to do. Begetting a daughter wasn't good enough although her father had never made her feel that way.

Burton came into the room. 'Dinner.'

Edmund stood and walked over to Nanny. He helped her to her feet as Constance entered the room looking peaky. 'Edmund, how lovely to see you but...' She paled and placed a hand over her mouth and dashed out of the room.

Nanny glanced at them and said, 'I won't be joining you after all but attending to this one.' She disappeared.

'Hope it's nothing serious,' Alice said. 'Something she ate, perhaps.' Constance hadn't eaten luncheon. She drew her brows together trying to remember breakfast.

Edmund held out his arm for Alice to take it. 'Left on our own, Thing. What mischief shall we get up to?'

'Mischief is in short supply around here.' She sent him a sideways glance.

In the dining room, Burton was rapidly removing Constance's and Nanny's place settings and was about to transfer Alice's to the far end of the table. 'That won't be necessary, Burton. You may leave that where it is,' Alice said.

'But Lady Alice.' He hovered.

'Have no worries, Burton, I shall look after Lady Alice very well.' Edmund put his most serious expression on. Alice held her laughter as a footman pulled out her chair. It would have been dire to have been seated on her own down the far end. At least this way they could have decent conversation without speaking so loudly the whole host of servants would hear. Edmund always had the best gossip.

Burton poured the wine, giving her no more than a mouthful in her glass while filling Edmund's fully.

He leaned and whispered, 'Being kept on rations, I see.'

'Afraid so.' She raised her eyes to find Burton watching her closely. She put on her sweetest smile.

The first course of watercress soup arrived and Edmund said, 'You have missed such exploits, Thing.'

She put her spoon down and her heart sank a bit. 'Do tell.'

'Well, Lady Diana Manners and her corrupt coterie are causing the normal stir, but everyone has been talking about Iris Tree and Nancy Cunard who were arrested for swimming in the Serpentine after a ball two nights ago.'

Alice opened her eyes wide. 'And?'

'Oh, all back to the usual. I saw them last night at the Devonshires' before the theatre.'

Alice pushed her soup away. They were arrested and they were still in London. They had been harmlessly foolish and she had spoken for others. She sighed and, not wanting to know anymore of London, asked, 'How is Penhale? Next to Abbotswood, it is my favourite house.' They had spent many happy days there together as children. Although much smaller than the house up country that she had once called home, Penhale was beautiful and intimate by comparison. Edmund was lucky it was his.

'It is well. The magnolias put on quite a show this year.'

'Your mother must have been pleased.' Alice smiled. The countess was a sweet woman. Alice had never understood the friendship between their mothers as her own mother was far from sweet.

The second course was served, and Burton added a taste

of red wine to her glass. The corners of Edmund's full mouth turned up as Burton poured him a full glass. Edmund was by far one of the most handsome men she had ever seen with his black hair and grey eyes. Her mother had called him pretty as a boy and that prettiness had developed into the most striking of looks. He turned to her once Burton had moved from the table and smiled as he swapped his glass with hers.

She put her hand over her mouth to stop the laugh from emerging. It was like their childhood when they ate in the nursery and he was always being fed more so he would fill out. He would pass the cakes to her. What was it about her that made people want to give her less? Did she appear greedy?

She took a sip of the wine. It was delicious. Edmund leaned forward and whispered, 'Tell me what exactly came over you to speak to the king about such a thing.'

Her chest rose and fell as she lived it all again not sure where to start.

'Not that you weren't correct, but it was a splendid ball and went on until the sun rose. You missed all the fun.' He looked at her over his wine glass.

The breath she had been holding in slipped out and she sank back against her chair. 'I was filled with the need to help my fellow women.'

'Indeed.' He raised an eyebrow. 'All you did was set yourself back. Do you think the king doesn't read the papers or talk to the prime minister?'

She twisted the wine glass in her fingers before taking another sip. 'If I could live the night over again, I would say the same thing.'

'Now then, that is truly reckless, but I am glad you followed your heart and spoke up for what you believe in.'

She looked for signs of irony on his face, but it was open. He was being honest and she wouldn't expect anything less from him. They had always told each other their secrets. She wondered if his were still the same as those he'd confided in her years ago. People change. She had. She had gone off to school seeing her future one way; then, with the help of Miss Parkes, she had seen that there could be other possibilities. Especially one not bound up on marriage where she would have no autonomy and no control over her own body. But who had she been fooling? She was the daughter of a duke even if he was no longer around. She had no other possibilities than to marry and to marry well. And she couldn't think of anything duller.

'I hear you have been fishing,' he said.

Her cheeks warmed and she took a quick sip of her wine.

'And I can see you enjoyed it.' He laughed. 'May I join you tomorrow?'

'Of course,' she said, taking another sip of wine

The footman left the room for a moment.

'Alone at last?' He grinned.

'It won't be for long. I have never been so watched as I have this visit.'

'Well, Thing, you chose to make a name for yourself, to have a reputation.' He raised his glass.

'That doesn't mean I will go off with the gardener,' she said.

'It's been known to happen.' He laughed.

'Don't be ridiculous.' She pursed her mouth.

'You are quite right. Only a European-crowned prince would turn your head.'

She laughed. 'More likely to turn yours.'

'Naughty one, Thing.' He grinned.

She leaned back. 'Not from where I'm sitting.'

'No, I can see that.' He stood and went to the decanter, returning to fill both their glasses before the footman came back. 'I do think dear Nanny feels I would make you a good husband,' he said, sitting down.

'Ah, you've come to offer for my hand, have you?' She smiled.

His glance met hers and his face became serious. 'If I were to marry it would be to you.'

She reached out and gave his hand a squeeze. That was a high compliment. He did not care for women in that way. 'You have the freedom not to marry and no one will think anything of it.' She twisted her napkin.

'Oh, they will, and sadly I must marry at some point.' He paused and looked into his wine. 'But I shall put the objectional task off for as long as possible.' He raised his glass to her. 'Here's to you finding the right match. You have certainly done an admirable job of putting off many of the suitors who were attracted to your rank alone.'

She considered Edmund over the rim of her glass. He too had to marry at some point and do his duty; he needed an heir or the earldom would end.

Burton noisily came back into the room and ended any further interesting conversation. They finished the meal, discussing tomorrow's weather and if the fish would be obliging or not. Edmund excused himself to have a cigar in the garden and Alice went to her room.

As she was undressed, she watched the burning end of Edmund's cigar as he walked down the long border.

'Did you have a lovely evening?' the maid asked as she undid Alice's shoe.

'Yes, Susan, and Lord Edmund is on good form.'

Susan looked up as she slipped the other shoe off Alice's foot. 'He's so handsome.'

Alice nodded while Susan removed Alice's stockings.

'Will you marry him?' Susan put her hand across her mouth. 'I shouldn't have asked that, my lady.'

Alice looked up and laughed. 'I don't intend to marry.'

'You are like me, my lady, if I may say so.'

'You may, and why won't you marry?' Alice asked, standing.

'I would lose my position.'

Alice turned to her. 'Yes, this is true. But if you married you could be a housekeeper.'

'Not as glamorous,' she said, putting the shoes in the wardrobe and bringing Alice her nightdress.

'But more powerful.' Alice held her hands up. Susan slid it over her head then Alice sat again.

'I hadn't thought of that.' Susan pulled the clips out of Alice's hair.

Studying Susan from her reflection in the mirror, Alice noted what a pretty woman she was, with her sprinkling of freckles across her nose and her soft brown hair. 'Are you interested in someone?'

Susan looked down at her hands holding Alice's gown, her face flushed.

'You don't have to say.'

'Thank you, my lady.' She bobbed and disappeared with the gown. Alice stood and went to the window. Another figure joined Edmund. She squinted into the dim light. It was the gillie. Why was he there? But then she remembered that they would be known to each other from Penhale. The sound of their laughter was carried on the breeze and a thread of something like jealousy arrived with it. Edmund was her friend and Carne was her gillie and she didn't wish to share either one of them.

She half expected someone to tell her to come away from the window, but she remained watching them, trying not to feel the emotions running through her that she couldn't explain.

Chapter Nineteen

Ignoring the tea on the table, Alice dashed to the window and pulled the curtains back to see the low rays of the rising sun piercing the mist filling the river valley. Timeless or without time, a subtle difference. Abbotswood was unaffected by the passage of years. Only the height of the trees marked time here. She was looking forward to today more than she had anything in ages. Taking a deep breath of the cool morning air, the joy in her drained away as she breathed out. Constance. Was she improved or further sickened?

Alice grabbed the teacup. She didn't want to miss a minute of this day; even if it didn't include fishing with Edmund because she would have no chaperone, it would still include time with him.

She stood before the glass and washed the essential bits. Tonight she would have a bath but right now she wanted to be outside. However, dressing took ages. Layer after layer she was wrapped up tighter than a package at Christmas. After the maid put the skirt over her head and secured it, Alice spied her old creel that had been found in a toy box. The willow basket had been made especially for her and in truth was more ornamental than useful. But mixed with dust engrained in the willow it held memories of her youth, her father and her old expectations. He had called her his princess and she had glowed. But now she knew that princesses and consorts had no real power.

'Susan, do you know how Lady Constance spent the night?'

'The doctor has been called as a precaution, my lady.' As soon as the last button was done, Alice raced down the stairs, hoping to find Nanny, and that last night nursing Constance hadn't sent her into a relapse and that her cousin was on the mend. There was no sign of Nanny or Edmund in the dining room. Alice walked to the children's wing where she met the doctor.

'Morning, Lady Alice.' He paused in the doorway.

'Lady Constance?'

'Stomach flu. She is simply tired out but is on the mend.'

'Nanny?' she asked.

'Ah, yes, I believe she has asthma. I have spoken with her before about this, but she insists it is nothing.'

'What can we do?' Alice asked.

'There are cigarettes I have left with her, made with a form of belladonna, which should soothe the air passageway, but above all avoid extreme emotion.'

Alice nodded.

'Both of them need to rest for the next few days.'

'Thank you,' Alice said then she watched the doctor depart.

She returned to the main building where she found Edmund chatting to Burton. She debated the best course of action for the day. There was nothing she could do for either Constance or Nanny at the moment.

Edmund gave her an encouraging smile as she strolled into

the dining room. This morning there was porridge, kippers and bacon. She didn't feel like any of it. Her excitement for the day ahead had evaporated with her concern for Nanny. Asthma, the doctor had said. That explained the cough and the wheezing.

Edmund walked up to her and placed a hand on her shoulder. 'Cheer up, Thing, and eat something. Zach says the fishing will be good today. I've asked Burton to have our luncheon brought out to us.'

'I'm not sure I should?' She looked up from the bowl she was putting porridge into.

'I assured Burton that Zach Carne was chaperone enough and that if I had any intentions at all they were honourable.'

Alice laughed.

'That's much better and both Nanny and Constance need rest.' He placed a kipper on his plate. 'Today will be wonderful and you have the best gillie around here.'

'You know him well?' The memory of the two of them laughing last night ran through her thoughts.

'Grew up with him and he shared my school room until I went to Eton.' Edmund laughed. 'He was the brighter of the two of us. Loved Shakespeare.' He rolled his eyes. 'Truthfully he should have gone to Eton, not me.' Edmund filled his plate with kippers. 'His father is a gem and his brother will be taking over from him in due course. Abbotswood was lucky to acquire Zach, for I think he's better than his brother, Brindley.' He looked around as the footman entered with the coffee. 'Don't you remember him?'

She ran through memories of Penhale and said, 'No.'

'He was always with me and therefore us when you visited.' Edmund filled his plate from the sideboard.

Alice thought back to her many visits to Penhale. She tried to picture the gillie from then, but she couldn't picture him younger and less virile than he was now. Her thoughts were interrupted as Burton entered with the papers.

'I'm not sure I want to read them,' Edmund said, putting sugar into his coffee. 'It's all becoming a bit tense in Europe.'

'Do you think it will come to war?' she asked.

'I hope not.' He stood and picked up some toast. 'The day is beautiful. Let's enjoy it and let's not think about the bad things. They will find us whether we enjoy today or not.'

Alice looked at her bowl, not feeling hungry but knowing she needed to make an effort. She had lost weight in the time she'd been here. All the walking and not enjoying the meals in this room. The maid had commented on it. Maybe being out all day today she would work up an appetite but somehow she didn't think so.

'Don't look so glum. You'll be set free soon and be the belle of the ball again.' He sat then placed a finger beneath her chin.

Alice shook her head and his hand fell away. 'I don't want that.'

'Hmmm, we have truly changed.' He picked up the newspaper. 'A few years ago that was all you wanted.'

'I know.' She shook her head. 'But I want much more than that now.'

'Votes for women.' He looked over the top of the newspaper studying her. 'It will happen.'

'Do you think so?' she asked.

'I do.' He put the paper down.

She smiled and forced some more porridge down her throat, eager to spend the day enjoying Edmund's company.

The morning's fishing had been unsuccessful, but Edmund and the gillie had had a marvellous time. The laughter Alice had witnessed of last night was replicated today. They worked together without words, each anticipating the other's movements. Edmund engaged as much with the gillie, Zach, as he called him, as he did with her. In fact, she would say he treated him as an equal and there was an intimacy to their constant banter. Continuous snippets from *Romeo and Juliet*, with the gillie taking the part of Romeo and Edmund, Mercutio.

Despite her amusement, she couldn't explain the unease she felt. No, not unease but the realisation that she was an intrusion to their enjoyment. She didn't have Edmund to herself nor did she have the gillie's attention either.

The gillie placed the luncheon basket down and looked to Edmund. 'I dream'd a dream to-night.' He cast a glance at her.

Edmund sat next to her and said, 'And so did I.' He opened the wine.

'Well, what was yours?' the gillie asked.

Edmund beckoned him to sit with them, saying, 'Dreams often lie.'

'Did your tutor teach you nothing but Shakespeare?' Alice asked.

Edmund laughed. 'He was overly fond of it and would set us tasks of performing most days. I preferred it to the Latin. Zach excelled at all.'

The gillie looked down.

'Come now, Zach, you were a far better student than I ever was.' Edmund handed Alice some wine.

Zach glanced up, his eyes dancing, 'Stop there, stop there.'

'Thou desirest me to stop in my tale against the hair.' Edmund raised a strawberry dramatically.

'Enough.' Alice held up her hand, smiling.

The gillie glanced at her and then dropped his eyes.

She ate her lunch listening to the chatter about Penhale and reminiscing about some of the things they had done as children, including setting a trap designed to send a bucket of apples down on the gillie's elder brother's head. Their laughter was contagious and the wine mellowed her mood, taking away the slightly irritable feeling that had plagued her thoughts. She shouldn't be jealous of Edmund's friendship. It was clear they respected each other and she shouldn't be surprised by this. He didn't treat her less because she was a woman, therefore his not doing that with his servant made sense. Perhaps that was why he gave the greater part of Romeo to the gillie, or maybe it was because Mercutio had the better lines.

Alice wandered into the garden after Edmund's departure. She couldn't believe how hot it was. Here, in the upper reaches by the dammed stream, she had found a bench to sit on and read. It was a book of Shakespeare's sonnets. All the banter between Edmund and the gillie had given her a taste for the Bard's work. She let the book fall open. This was a trick she had discovered when she was at school. It would always open to the most read pages. Sonnet 30. She hadn't expected that. She turned to the front of the book to see if there was an inscription. It had been her father's.

She ran her fingers over the writing then turned back to the poem. She read aloud:

> *When to the sessions of sweet silent thought*
> *I summon up remembrance of things past,*

And then another voice said the next two lines:

> *I sigh the lack of many a thing I sought,*
> *And with old woes new wail my dear time's*
> *waste:*

Alice's mouth fell open. The gillie stood before her. Despite all the earlier Shakespeare it was different hearing him recite the lines of the sonnet. It unnerved her.

'Sorry to disturb you, my lady, but Nanny Roberts is looking for you,' he said.

'Thank you.' She closed the book as she stood. He didn't move away. Did her expression show her surprise?

'It's not my favourite sonnet.' He pointed to the book.

She held it out to him.

He flipped the pages and then looked at her. 'I much prefer this one.'

Zach pointed to Sonnet 130 and handed the book back to her. She quickly scanned:

> *My mistress's eyes are nothing like the sun*

'I see,' she said, not seeing at all but feeling. She closed the book with her finger marking the page to read later, to search for meaning, because right now she didn't understand anything, most especially herself. She took one last glance at him before she set off down to the house. Despite longing to, she didn't look back and she didn't stop until she reached the house. Inside the door she paused and opened the book and read the sonnet in full, mouthing each word. The last two lines:

> *And yet, by heaven, I think my love as rare*
> *As any she belied with false compare.*

Alice closed the book and turned into the children's wing, hearing the gillie's voice say the words of the sonnet in her head. She stopped when she saw Nanny sitting by the window reading. Beside her were the cigarettes that the doctor had suggested.

Nanny looked up from her book. 'Where have you been?'

'I was reading in the garden.' Alice smiled, coming closer to check on Nanny's condition.

Nanny tilted her head and glanced out the window.

'Not there; it was far too warm. I walked up to where the Douglas fir grows and sat on the bench under it.'

'Cooler?' Nanny asked.

Alice nodded.

'The gillie found you?' Nanny raised an eyebrow.

'Yes, he did,' Alice said.

'Good.' Nanny looked at the book in Alice's hand. 'I thought he might.'

Alice frowned. That was an odd comment.

'Did you see your photograph in *Tatler*?' Constance asked,

as she walked into the room appearing much rested and recovered.

Alice had been afraid to look. 'No.'

'It was of you walking in the park with my father.'

'Not the one with you and Beatrice?' Alice asked.

Constance glanced down. 'No.'

Disappointment was written all over her face and Alice reached out to her. 'It will happen in time.'

'Indeed it will.' Nanny took Constance's hand. 'I'd like to take a walk.'

Outside in the children's garden the early evening sun was still hot, and its rays reflected off the water channel encircling the flower parterre. During Alice's childhood, small boats filled the water channel.

'The boats are still in the cupboard,' Nanny said, reading her mind.

'That could be fun.' Constance grinned.

Alice laughed.

'Sorry, Alice,' she said. 'I know you wouldn't want to do that.'

'I could be tempted,' she said, giving her cousin a smile as her glance followed the gillie down on the riverbank.

'I imagine you could be, Alice,' Nanny said.

Alice turned her attention back to the children's garden. She must remember that Nanny could read her thoughts easily.

Chapter Twenty

The first week of July had disappeared much as today was moving towards evening. In the distance, the tors of Cornwall loomed. Alice sat on the veranda of the Swiss Cottage. Tea had long been cleared and she should head back to the house and dress for dinner. She despaired, thinking of the conversation to be had with Nanny and Constance. Over breakfast it had been about butterflies. As lovely as they were, she would rather talk of poetry than of insects.

Rising, she picked up her diary, which these days consisted of walks, more walks, and the odd fishing trip, rather than who she had met and what she had worn. It was better; she was marginally more in control here. The abundance of nature around granted her some freedom. She debated what route she would take back to the house... the high path and then along the drive, or she could descend to the river and follow its progress until she reached the house. That would take some time. She couldn't escape the feeling that she was only filling the hours. What was she waiting for? Her mother had been right all those years ago when she had told her father that Alice wasn't good enough and it was his fault he had only produced a girl. That's all she was and, even though Miss Parkes had told her more was possible, Alice was left in limbo.

Grabbing the book of Shakespeare's sonnets, she walked down the outside steps to the lawn. She noted a maid was still in the kitchen. How did she feel? She had a job, a role unlike Alice. Alice existed, nothing more.

Scrambling over a boulder in a most unladylike fashion, she made her way down the steep hillside, thankful no one had witnessed her skirt about her waist when it had caught on a bramble. Order restored, she stopped and sat on a stone by the river. She rolled her neck back and looked up at the pale sky above. It was the time of evening when the swallows emerged to feed on the plentiful insects. Above them she could pick out Venus appearing.

A cough sounded and she shot up to her feet.

'Sorry, m'lady,' Zach said.

Since Edmund's visit she had stopped thinking of him by his role alone. He had become Zach in her thoughts. He moved so silently that she never heard him arrive, but she always watched him depart. He glanced at the book of sonnets in her hands.

'Would you like to borrow it?' She held it out to him, remembering what Edmund had said.

He took the book from her hands and ran his fingers across the marbled end pages. 'Thank you, but it is too fine a book.'

'But you like Shakespeare.'

He looked up from the book. A slow smile spread across his face as he ran his fingers down a page. 'I do.'

She shivered.

'It is getting late and you are becoming cold,' he said.

'I'm fine,' she said.

He held the book between them.

Her hands remained at her sides. 'Please borrow it.'

'I have memorised them all or almost all of them,' he said, still holding the book out between them.

'Have you?' She could only recall one or two fully.

'It was a means to have them with me at all times,' he said.

She opened her eyes wide, taking in his features more closely. 'You loved them that much?'

'No, not love.' He returned her scrutiny, his glance resting on her slightly parted mouth. 'They expressed things I didn't know how to put into words or even that they could be.'

She tilted her head to the side. 'I don't understand.'

'Words give meaning to things but sometimes naming something or speaking of it takes away from it too.'

'Oh.' She looked at the book between them.

'Your book,' he said.

Footsteps in the distance disturbed her thoughts. No, that wasn't true; he did. She took the book from him and their fingers touched. She inhaled and he stared. He too felt it. She had been stung yet there was no nettle. But, like the nettle sting, the feel of his fingers remained long after the brief contact.

She sensed his regard as she walked towards the house. Zachariah Carne was an enigma. He recited Shakespeare easily, knew this stretch of the river as if he had always walked its length and was so at ease with Edmund that it had shocked her. They joked, laughed and spoke without words at times. She'd been taught not to notice the servants but that was wrong. It was so obvious, but she had been blind.

Now Zach filled her vision. Every touch of his hand set her skin tingling; even after the briefest of contact, the feeling remained.

Alice had caught nothing until this moment and the fish on the end of the line was too young. With deft fingers Zach had freed it from the hook. He looked at her and without words she knew what his question was.

'Set it free,' she said.

'Thank you, my lady.' He bent to the water and held the fish in his hands. It stilled. She held her breath. He had been quick in untangling it; it couldn't be dead. She bent low and put her fingers into the water and stroked the fish. It moved and Zach opened his hands. The fish wriggled again and set off down the river. He looked at her. Their heads were so close. His breath caressed her cheek. She glanced down at his lips, for the intensity in his glance was too much. And yet looking at his mouth was no better. She couldn't move. She was caught.

His head came towards hers and she leaned in, slipping. One foot twisted and caught in the rocks below the water's surface.

'I'm sorry,' he said.

She winded as she shook her boot. He helped her up the bank and it was clear that the boot was going to be a problem. It chafed. She limped. He took her arm and they went on a short distance. 'This isn't going to work.'

'May I help?' he asked.

She shook her head. 'You will not carry me back to the house.'

'I could,' he said.

Looking at his broad shoulders and strong arms, he spoke the truth. Being that close to him wouldn't be good at all. She stopped that line of thought. 'That may be true, but I will simply remove my boot.' She sat on a fallen tree and began unlacing.

He moved her hands aside and pulled the swollen laces loose then slipped off the boot. The stocking was sodden, red, and stuck to her foot. His hand pulled the wet fabric from her calf.

'Thank you,' she managed to say.

He looked up. 'There is blood on your stocking.'

'Yes.' It throbbed but other feelings were overtaking the pain. He pressed his fingers against the spot and she squealed.

'Perhaps we should look at what's causing it.'

Alice nodded and all thoughts left her as his fingers loosened the ribbon holding her stocking. His fingertips touched the bare skin as he rolled the stocking down with care. With the white fabric bunched between his tanned fingers he carefully pulled it away from her foot. A gash of angry red sliced across her lower calf. Whatever had cut her leg had not torn the stocking. He rolled the stocking the rest of the way down, and let it fall to the ground while he held her foot. A bruise was already forming across the top of her instep. He turned her foot with care to look for further injury, checking each toe. Her heart hammered and she took in a sharp breath.

He looked up. 'Pain? You must have twisted it when you slipped.'

She shook her head. Words were not possible. His touch

had taken them from her. It wasn't pain she was feeling but something entirely different. It travelled up her leg to where moments before his fingers had touched and went higher still.

'I'll get some water to wash the blood away.' He placed her foot down on the grass with great care. It tickled and itched but it didn't remove the lingering feeling of his fingers. That was like good wine. Once on her tongue she longed for more.

She examined her stocking and her leg. The feelings in her weren't caused by the injury. It was him. He walked towards her with his gaze intent on only her. He watched her like he did the river, looking for each nuance and ripple across the surface. Every breath she took he noted, each movement he saw and every word she spoke he listened. She felt it all.

He fell to his knees and lifted her foot again. That tingling began again and she gulped. Did he feel it too? His glance met hers and held. His eyes seemed black as the iris had become large. Endless pools of darkness beckoned. The song of a lark broke the spell. He opened his flask and poured cool clear water over her calf.

With the blood cleared, it was obvious that something had ripped her skin. It was not deep but sore. With a clean cloth he patted the wound dry.

'I am sorry.' He picked up the ruined stocking.

'Why are you sorry?' she managed to mumble, when she wanted to say, please, put your hand back on my leg.

'You fell and I should have caught you.' He looked down. 'Your stocking is ruined.'

She swallowed. 'Had you not been there it would have been worse.'

He looked at her for a moment then down at his hands holding the flimsy fabric spotted with red.

Constance came running down the hill. 'Oh no, what's happened?' Her glance travelled from Alice's bare foot and leg to the gillie's hands holding the bloody stocking. She dropped her net, freeing a butterfly.

'I slipped and cut my leg.' Alice took a breath. 'Nothing dire.'

'How are we going to get you back?' her cousin asked.

'I'll walk,' she said.

'With one boot on and the other off?' Constance tilted her head to the side. 'No, that will not work.' She turned towards Zach. 'Can you carry her?'

He nodded, bent down and scooped Alice up into his arms. The breath left her body and it wasn't from the impact against his chest, but his proximity. This close he smelled of lavender as well as woodsmoke.

Each step he took brought her against him. The muscles in his shoulders hardened under her hands as he climbed the hill. Constance raced ahead, Nanny stood in the French windows watching while Burton viewed them from the lawn. She closed her eyes and breathed in his scent, wanting him to walk right past the house.

'You will need to be more careful.' Nanny looked at Alice's bandaged leg.

'Yes, it was a moment of lost concentration as... I released a young fish.' She thought not of that moment but what had followed afterwards.

Nanny's gaze narrowed. 'Maybe you shouldn't be fishing.'

She took a deep breath. 'I'm here. The fish are in the river. I've read most of the worthwhile books in the library. I paint appallingly and my needlework is dire, your words not mine.'

Nanny leaned on the back of a chair; she still was not in full health. 'I take your point, but we can't have you injured.'

Alice waved her hand. 'I twisted my ankle and cut my leg; that is all.'

'You were carried to the house.'

'At Constance's insistence.' She looked away, remembering the feel of his arms about her. It would have been simpler to remove the other boot and walk back to the house. Although being barefoot would have raised eyebrows, it wouldn't have caused the furore that being carried into the house had. Burton's face had been thunderous and Nanny's disapproval forceful. Nothing she had said had made the situation any better. Constance was in a state of heightened alarm.

The previous week's *Tatler* lay on the table. Was this why Nanny was agitated? Alice sat down and picked up the magazine. Swiftly flipping through the pages until she reached *In Town and Out*. There were photos with the caption 'The "Perfect Peace" Ball At The Albert Hall'. The first photos were of Lady Lowther, Lady Churchill, Miss Peterson and Lady Newborough. Alice's heart didn't know whether to stop or speed up. It did a strange combination of both that caused her to feel peculiar as she stared at a portrait of the Viscountess Curzon.

It was on page twelve that coverage of the ball began in earnest. Under the headline 'Some of the Gay Throng who Celebrated the Hundred Years' Peace with Dance and Song and Supper', there was a picture of Edmund in his Apache headdress with his friends as part of the photo entitled 'Five o'clock the next morning – still Merry and Bright!'.

Her stomach fell unpleasantly. Normally she would have been in that photograph. Under that was a portrait of Lady Warrender as Britannia and on the opposite page there was a picture of Alice standing behind Lady Warrender entitled 'Waves for Women – Long May Britannia Rule Them.' Alice's blood rose. Reading the small print, her ingress into the royal box was altered to invading Britannia's throne and providing comic relief.

She looked up from the paper to find Nanny studying her. Her uncle must have paid handsomely in some way to keep her name out of it.

'I hope it was worth it.' Her gaze didn't budge but Alice matched it. Despite being ridiculed in *Tatler*, it had been worth it; she had played her part.

'Your mother and uncle are still scrambling to save your reputation.'

Alice pressed her lips together. She might want to say it was their own reputations they were concerned about and not hers, but it was best left unspoken. Nanny knew her thoughts.

'Do you want me to marry the appalling Cleveland like Mother does?' she asked.

'No, I didn't say that, and this action you took wasn't about that, was it?' Nanny arched an eyebrow.

She crossed her arms. 'No, it wasn't.'

'Then don't say it was.' Nanny walked around the chair and sat.

Alice pushed herself to a more upright position. 'Nanny, women should have the right to vote.'

With a slow shake of her head, Nanny said, 'I agree with that but not with what you've done.'

'What else could I have done?' she asked.

'Use your position to influence.' Nanny fixed her with a look.

'Who could I influence? No one listens to me.' As she said the words she thought of Zach. He listened to her. And Edmund did as well. She ran through all the other people of her acquaintance and eventually fell upon Arthur Carew. He too had listened, and he was a member of parliament.

Nanny smiled that smile Alice had seen so many times when Alice had given her thoughts away on her face. 'See, you could still make a difference without affronting the king.'

Alice huffed. The whole thing was being pushed under the carpet. She had done something. Yet *Tatler* had called it a comic incident. Suffragettes weren't comic.

'My child, you have done your part; now step back and think about your future.'

She looked to the older woman. 'What future?'

'You have everything you need to make yourself a happy future.'

Alice squinted but saw nothing but clouds rolling in from Cornwall.

'You have beauty, breeding and money.' Nanny held up three fingers.

'What good are any of those if I'm not allowed to do as I want? I'm not trusted to choose for myself,' she said.

'You can choose, but you have to do so cleverly.' Nanny clasped her hands together like she used to when Alice had been very stubborn and wouldn't understand something as a child.

Alice lowered her bandaged leg to the ground. 'I don't want to marry Cleveland.'

'That I understand, and I doubt if he would have you now.' Nanny sent her a sideways look. 'But you never know with his type.'

'Thanks.' Alice crossed her arms in front of her chest.

'You do have some say in who you marry.'

'I don't want to marry.' Alice rose to her feet, feeling her cut's newly forming scab pull.

Nanny pursed her mouth. 'Why ever not?'

'Because I would be simply changing the person who has control over my life.'

Nanny pressed her lips together.

'See, even you can't argue that fact. If I want to be in charge of myself then I simply must not marry.' Alice hobbled to the window, trying not to wince as she put weight on her ankle.

Nanny shook her head and said, 'But what sort of life will you have?'

'A free one.' Alice pushed the window open in order to see further to the right as she heard Burton talking.

Nanny laughed bitterly.

'You don't agree.' She turned back to Nanny.

'Freedom is an interesting thing.' Nanny studied her.

Alice moved to the chair opposite Nanny. 'You are free.'

'Am I?' she asked.

'Yes.' Alice stood up again. 'You are free to go where you wish, dress as you choose, seek out those who interest you.'

'That is what you see, but in reality I am tied to this family for my living.' She waved both hands out to the side as if she were about to dance.

Alice studied her. 'What do you mean?'

'I'd have no home without the Nevilles.' Nanny brought her hands back down on the arms of the chair.

'But I thought the cottage was yours.'

'No, it is through the favour of your uncle that I have it.' She wheezed and Alice recalled that the doctor had mentioned that she should have no emotional upset.

Alice picked up a china dog from the mantlepiece. 'Have you no money of your own?'

'I have saved but not enough to have a home and put food on the table.'

'I see.' Alice turned the porcelain creature in her fingers, noting the collar about its neck. 'Money provides freedom.'

'This is true,' Nanny said.

Alice placed the dog down. 'It provides power too.'

'Yes, but there are other ways to have power.' She tapped her fingers together. 'Youth and beauty provide some, as does intellect.'

Alice snorted. 'All passing but money remains.'

Nanny nodded.

'I simply need to bide my time until I gain control of my own.'

Nanny rose to her feet. 'You are eighteen.' She walked to Alice. 'Headstrong, intelligent and beautiful.' She placed her hand on Alice's arm. 'Seven years is a long time to behave.' Nanny walked out of the room, leaving Alice staring into the mirror above the mantle.

Seven years to wait for her own freedom. Behave. Avoid marriage. She could do it. She could trick them all.

Chapter Twenty-One

This field was covered in long grass and filled with wild-flowers. The yellow vetch and the wild carrot glowed in the fading light but always Alice was drawn to the blue of the cornflowers. She bent and picked one before walking further upriver and away from the watching eyes of the house. Constance hadn't wanted to walk and Nanny was too weary. The cigarettes that the doctor had given her had seemed to ease Nanny's breathing but she was still not on full form. Alice had spent the past week as the perfect model of a lady. She, of course, had hated it. But it had meant that tonight when she had said she needed to take a walk, she had been allowed to go on her own. After all what trouble could befall her on her uncle's land? Everyone within miles and miles worked for her uncle in some way.

A fish jumped and Alice walked closer to the water's edge, remembering her last fishing excursion and how it had ended. Even now she could still feel Zach's fingers on her legs. She shivered and looked across the river. Light glowed from the cottage window and the tell-tale trail of smoke rose above the trees. Was he there, reading by the fire? Reciting more poetry? He puzzled her. He wasn't like old Tucker who was calm and soothing. Everything about Zach was exciting despite his quietness. She had noticed that he could be still anywhere, but she could only achieve it here by the river. The water calmed her mind.

The cry of an owl as it swooped down the valley toward the river interrupted her thoughts. She looked up doubting she would spot the bird, for the sound carried here. Someone could be speaking on the opposite bank and it could sound as if they were right beside you. It had always fascinated her as a child when she'd listened into what people were saying. Now she wished it wasn't true. She wanted people to keep their secrets and for her own to stay safe. Not that she had any.

She walked on, picking up a pheasant feather. She ran it through her fingers. Silky and smooth. It was from the male, beautiful and showy.

'My lady.' The gillie stood in front of her. She looked over her shoulder. With the lights on in the cottage, she had expected him there.

'I heard something and came to investigate,' he said.

'Poachers?' she asked.

'Possibly.' He looked to the sky. It was now the colour of brushed blue velvet growing darker by the moment. Stars were beginning to appear.

'You're about late,' he said.

'Yes, fresh air after dinner.' She looked at the space between them. One step closer and she would be able to see the full colour of his eyes.

'Lady Constance?' he asked.

'Tired.'

'You are well?' He looked at her.

'Yes, though Nanny has been concerned for my ankle.' She pushed her foot out and rotated it. 'But it's fine.'

He looked down and Alice flushed, twisting the feather in her hand.

'Shall I escort you back to the house?' he asked.

'That won't be necessary.' She looked over her shoulder. Light gleamed warm and yellow from the windows.

'As you wish.' He went to the rowing boat and before long he had crossed the river and was out of sight.

The house was in silence when she returned. Only Burton was lurking and once he was certain she was on her way to her room he disappeared. She then crept to the children's wing, hoping Nanny and Constance were asleep.

In the sitting room, she dug to the back of the cupboard and, as she had hoped, her fly-making equipment was still in a basket. Taking it, she went back to her room. It had been years since she had done this, but her fingers remembered their task. She waxed the thread and created the dubbing before she took the marabou. This she had made from the silk threads from a frayed edge of a scarf. She split the thread and wedged the marabou in it, before wrapping it around the shank as her father had taught her.

Next came the feather. She selected a few colourful pieces and secured them to the shank before trimming them. She completed the tying off and viewed her fly. Despite the time elapsed she still remembered. Part of her wanted to run down the hall to her father's room and show him what she had done but those days were no more.

She turned the fly, watching the colour in the feather catch the candlelight. Tomorrow she would fish again. Standing by

217

the river provided great solace and peace. How could anyone disapprove of that? She could say that most of the possible marriage candidates would approve of her love of the sport.

She placed the fly on her bedside table and blew the candle out. Her curtains remained opened and she stared at the sliver of a moon while the cry of an owl carried on the breeze along with the scent of woodsmoke.

Nanny scowled. 'I thought you had abandoned this foolishness after last week.'

'The weather is fine and last night I rediscovered my love of making flies.'

The creases beside Nanny's eye deepened as she looked on the intricate lure. 'I'd forgotten you did this.'

'My father...'

'Yes, you can't sew in a straight line, but you can make these delicate things.' She examined it, turning it so that the feather caught the light. 'Mind what you catch,' she said as she walked to the window. 'I'll send Constance down to you shortly.'

The weather was a perfect July day. Alice didn't wait in the courtyard for Zach. Her new fly resting in her creel along with Shakespeare's sonnets. Not that the two went together, but the small book fit beautifully into the creel and the red leather binding caught the red in the feather.

She cantered down the hill with her skirts flying behind her until she reached the water. Her cheeks were pink from exertion. Zach was walking along the bank, watching the water.

'Morning,' she said, breathless.

He turned to her.

'Which beat today?' she asked.

'The river is slow and lazy on this summer's morning. I think down by the bend where it narrows.'

He set off downriver and she followed, hoping that the conditions would be right for dry casting. Excitement she hadn't felt in years bubbled through her. She wanted to run to the beat, not take this gentle pace. Everything in her urged her forward faster. She swished past him and picked up her speed.

'My lady,' he called out.

She glanced over her shoulder, seeing not him but Burton on the lawn with glasses watching them. She pressed on faster. Was there nowhere where eyes didn't watch her? She scanned the opposite shore where dense trees hid the hillside. There she could be unwatched, unseen, almost invisible.

'We have passed the beat,' he said softly. He was not far from her. She stopped and he bumped into her.

'Can we not try one further on?' she asked, searching his face for what he was thinking.

'We could but you may not find the fishing as successful,' he said.

Her mouth twitched. Of course, that was what this was about for him. 'True.' She looked back. They were finally out of sight of the house. She pointed and he nodded. The river widened after the bend and its pace slowed slightly. He took her hand in his to assist her down the bank, only releasing it as he scanned the surface of the water. She opened her creel and with care she picked up the fly and placed it on her palm, holding it out to him. He looked from it to her and back again.

'Beautiful,' he said.

'Thank you.' She smiled.

'May I?'

'Yes.'

His fingertips brushed her palm as he picked up the fly. Her breath caught. He raised it to the light and moved it between his fingers. The pheasant feathers gleamed.

'Where did you find this?' he asked, turning back to her.

'I made it last night.' She pulled her shoulders back.

Again, he looked at the fly then to her. 'It's wonderful.'

'Thank you.' She tilted her head to the side. He didn't appear surprised that she had made it. 'Are the conditions right?'

He studied the river again while she held her breath, trying to see it through his eyes. Her father and Tucker had taught her much about it, but she had never seen them look at the river in such a way. His glance caressed the surface of the water as he tried to peer into its depths.

'Yes,' he said, taking the rod and removing the old fly. His fingers moved deftly, undoing and tying the knots with ease. Once he had finished, he glanced at her and then the river again.

'It would be best if we went further down and crossed to the other side.'

She took a deep breath, looking at the edges of the wild wood. She nodded.

'Wait here while I get the boat.' He placed his creel down and he was gone before she could reply. Before long he was back and helping her into the boat. The journey to the other side was swift. He made light work of the crossing. His arm muscles tensed with each stroke and she forced herself to look at the water and not him. Yet, out of the corner of her eye, she saw the fluid movements propelling them along.

He secured the boat and helped her ashore. His hand held hers for a moment longer than was necessary and she missed it when he moved away to ready everything.

The stones they stood on appeared as if tumbled into the river but she knew better. Their flat tops had been organised for those who didn't wish to become wet. When young she had stood with her father waist deep in the river, waiting. But now this would be unseemly. But she remembered the chill and the press of the current against her legs.

He jumped onto the first stone, holding out his hand. She clasped his and they made their way to the furthest rock. He broke the contact as he checked the river. His stillness while he watched was mesmerising.

Zach turned back and their faces were inches from each other. Flecks of amber highlighted the deep, dark brown in his eyes.

'My lady,' he whispered.

'Yes.'

He handed her the rod and stepped away. She exhaled, thinking of the rod and the line and the fly. She cast. The fly rested on the surface and they waited. Neither moving. The air too was still and hot. A fish came to the surface near the rock, but her fly was further away. She reeled it in and cast again this time, landing it closer. Again, they stood so close to each other that she could see the rise and fall of his chest.

The fly went down and they both tensed as the rod bent with the pull. Slowly she began to bring the line in. She lost her footing in the fight with the fish. He caught her and wrapped his arms about her and together they brought the trout closer, his body against hers. She should be focused on the fish but the feel of him took over her thoughts. They moved in unison, leaning into the tug and drawing back, the fish joining in their movements.

'Slowly,' he said.

'Yes.'

The fish was now below the stones; the colours of the trout reflected in the sunlight.

'I'll get the net.' His words tickled her ear and when his body left hers, her legs trembled.

He crouched low and scooped the fish, bringing it out of the water. Drops sprayed as the trout writhed. He dispatched it swiftly and removed the hook. Weakness ran through Alice as her adrenalin dropped. He looked up then took her hand, leading her into the shade of the bank. She rested against a tree. Although the fish was large and had fought, she shouldn't feel this way.

'My lady.' He laid the rod and fish down and came to her side, handing her a flask. The smell of strong spirits rose from it as he released the top.

'Take a sip,' he said as he stepped closer. His eyes were darker now; all the amber was lost in the cool shade of the trees. 'It will help.' He smiled. 'I've not seen a trout that size here at Abbotswood and only once at Penhale.'

She lifted the flask to her mouth, not taking her eyes off of him. The liquid burned yet there was a sweetness to it. She handed it back to him, licking the tingling liquid from her lips. He was focused on her mouth. Her lips filled as if pressure had been applied to them.

He closed the flask and slipped it into his jacket pocket. 'If you are ready perhaps we should head back to the house.'

She nodded. Words were not possible. He helped her into the boat then rowed them upriver to the house. In the small confines of the boat her ankle rested against his. She glanced down but then caught sight of the movement of his thigh muscle as he worked against the current. As he watched over his shoulder, she took the chance to study him. Strong thighs, lean torso, broad shoulders. She swallowed.

He turned, catching her glance. He didn't look away. Her mouth opened to speak, to say something, but she couldn't. Blood pounded through her and she didn't understand.

He broke the contact between them and tied the boat up. Climbing out, he first took the fish and the equipment. Then, leaning in, he held her outstretched hand. Threatening storm clouds were moving swiftly from the south towards them. A big fat drop of rain hit their clasped hands. Thunder rumbled then lightning forked over the hillside behind her. He pulled her swiftly from the boat. Their bodies crashed together, winding her.

'My lady.'

'Yes,' she said as the heavens opened, and together they raced towards the house.

Chapter Twenty-Two

Alice rose and paced the length of the room. The restlessness within her would make her insane. Burton walked into the room. She stopped halfway across the floor.

'Do you still wish to fish this afternoon?' he asked.

She stared at him. In this weather? 'No.' She looked out the window. The rain was heavy, and the visibility was reduced to ten feet.

'Very well. I will send the gillie away,' he said.

'No, send him to me, please.'

He bowed his head and left the room. She resumed pacing until she heard a cough. She took a step towards Zach then stopped. He was soaked.

'Why don't you stand by the fire.' She held out her hand towards it.

'You wished to see me,' he said.

She nodded then looked up. His glance held hers. 'I wish to fish,' she said.

He made to move, but she stopped him by saying, 'Not now but when the rain ceases.'

'Very well.' He stepped away from the fire.

'Do you think the rain will stop?' she asked, not wanting him to go.

He paused and looked out the window. 'Unlikely.'

'Lighten up?' She moved towards him as she spoke.

He stepped back. 'Possibly.'

'Good.' She glanced out the window to the lashing rain and made out the shell house. 'I may while away the time in the grotto,' she whispered.

He bowed his head and left the room before she could say another word. She moved to the door, but she couldn't follow him. That would be foolish and she mustn't be. Anything but that... wilful, stubborn, reckless, arrogant even, but never foolish. But she wanted to be foolish.

Burton stood by the door and Alice waited for him to say something. But he remained silent.

'Yes, Burton?'

'Lady Alice.' He bowed his head but said no more.

'Burton, I can tell you have something to say.' She stood still and tall.

'His grace would prefer that...'

She lifted her chin. 'My uncle would prefer what?'

'He would prefer it if you refrained from fishing.' He did not look directly at her but rather over her shoulder.

She held her hands tightly together. Her uncle liked fishing. This made no sense. 'He has always encouraged me in the past.'

Burton coloured. 'Yes, Lady Alice.' He looked past her out the window.

'The weather isn't good today but tomorrow I will fish.'

She expected him to leave but he remained standing there. 'What is it, Burton?'

'It would be best not to fish,' he said.

'Why ever not?' She walked closer to him. 'The river is there, the fish are there and the gillie unoccupied.'

'But it's not Tucker.'

'No, it is his junior.' She watched him closely. 'Ah, that is the problem. He is young.'

Burton cleared his throat. 'He is Cornish.'

She did not like the connotation. 'I will confer with Nanny to see if she feels it appropriate.' Burton hadn't moved. 'That is all, Burton.' She turned her back on him and picked up the book she had been reading earlier in the day. Part of her seethed and part of her was sorry for him. But at the moment the angry part was winning.

The wind had dropped as she walked down the long border. The clouds about were no longer solid but broken up, and the heavy rain had become light. The drops pooled on her cloak. Her stomach tightened as she approached the grotto. Had she actually suggested that he meet her here?

In front of the door, she saw a beautiful magpie feather. After she had picked it up, she said, 'One for sorrow, two for joy, three for a girl, four for a boy.' She ran her fingers down the feather, pushing off the rain drops. 'Five for silver, six for gold, seven for a secret never to be told.' A twig snapped and she looked around. No one. She walked to the grotto door. It was ajar. 'Eight for a... wish.' She pictured Zachariah Carne with his deep, dark eyes. 'Nine for a...'

'Kiss.'

She jumped. The voice came from inside the shell house. Alice pushed the door open and asked, 'Do you remember what ten was for?'

'I have heard many things?' He looked at the feather in her hand. 'Ah, that explains it.' She held it out to him.

He took it and ran his fingers over it, causing the colours to change from blue to green to black.

'The gamekeeper had been shooting them this morning,' he said, handing it back to her. 'They have been eating the pheasant eggs.'

She nodded. 'I thought I'd make another fly.'

'I've brought some things for you.' He turned and picked up a basket from the bench. Alice spied a large array of threads and hooks.

'Yours?' She looked at him.

He nodded.

She sat on the bench and examined the items. She looked up and said, 'This is wonderful.' She held a peacock feather in her hand.

'Yes.' He smiled and her breath hitched. She lifted the basket onto her lap.

'Please sit.' She tapped the space beside her on the cool stone bench niched into one of the six sides of the grotto. She didn't look up but felt the warmth of him as he settled beside her, hip to hip and thigh to thigh. All around them on the walls were glistening crystals and great seashells but she couldn't take her eyes from him. He reached into the basket and pulled out some blue thread and a needle. She took out the wrench and handed it to him. She found the wax; positioning the hook in the wrench he held, she began waxing and spinning the thread. Once she had covered the shank, she stopped and met his glance.

'We have done this before,' she said.

'Yes.' His glance didn't leave hers.

It all came rushing back to her. Every time she visited Penhale as a child he'd been there. She had thought of him then as Edmund's shadow. But seeing him now he was far from shadow. He'd led her pony. He'd been beside her as now, holding the hook as she'd made her first files under the gillie's instruction. He'd stood on the side watching when she and Edmund had swum together in the river. He'd always been there, and she'd never really seen him until now.

Her fingertip snagged on the hook. She gasped. He dropped the wrench and took her hand in his. He lifted it to his mouth and kissed it, keeping pressure on the wound. She should take her hand away, but she couldn't move. She didn't want to.

He lowered her hand. The blood had stopped. She looked from her finger to his mouth. There was a bit of blood on his lip. She brushed it off. Their glances met. He leaned in as she did. Their mouths touched. She tasted blood and him as the kiss deepened. The basket rocked on her lap as she tried to move closer.

He cupped her face in his hands and kissed her again and again. The hinge on the door creaked. They pulled apart. Her hands fumbled, picking up the thread. He grabbed the wrench.

'There you are.' Constance stood in the doorway, rain falling off her and pooling around her feet. 'Nanny wondered what on earth you could be doing alone in the shell house for so long.' She studied them sitting side by side. Alice dropped her shaky hand into her lap.

'But you are not alone,' she said, looking at Zach.

'No,' Alice said, straightening the basket on her lap. 'We are making flies.'

Her cousin walked up to them, peering into the basket at the feather and threads. 'Oh.' She picked up the magpie feather, running her fingers down its length. 'This is beautiful, but doesn't it mean bad luck?'

'No, only seeing one bird alone means bad luck or—'

'Sorrow,' Constance said, interrupting him. She pointed to the top of the feather. 'There's blood on here.' Her brows knitted together as she brought the feather closer to her face. 'Fresh blood.'

'Yes, I pricked my finger on the hook.'

'Tisk, you should be more careful, Alice.' Constance stood in front of them and Alice sensed confusion coming off of her in waves.

'Would you like to watch and then try making one of your own?' Zach asked.

She shook her head. 'No, I think it's a beastly thing trying to trick the fish into thinking that it's a real fly.'

He laughed. 'How else do you catch fish?'

'I don't like them.' Constance shivered. 'I eat them because I have no choice.'

Alice rose to her feet. She glanced at him for a moment then walked to her cousin. 'Are you cold? Do you need to head back to the house? You are soaked through.'

'Have you found me another net?' Constance watched Zach.

'I have, Lady Constance. Shall I bring it tomorrow?'

She nodded then turned to Alice. 'Nanny wanted to see you.'

Alice studied her cousin's face for a clue about what she was thinking. 'You hadn't said.'

Constance tugged at the tie at her neck holding her cape. 'Your mother telephoned.'

Alice's hands clenched. This was never a good thing. She peered out the open door at the rain then turned to Zach and said, 'Thank you for the help.' His glance met hers. She didn't want to leave but she must. 'If the weather is fine tomorrow shall I meet you by Black Rock at ten?'

He bowed his head.

Alice took Constance's arm and they dashed back to the house.

From the dining room window, Alice could see Burton watching their progress and a chill ran up her spine while raindrops rolled down her face.

Chapter Twenty-Three

Alice eyed *The Suffragette* dated 17 July 1914 with elation while Susan helped her change out of her wet clothing.

'Thank you. How did you acquire this?' Alice asked, touching the paper.

'A friend of a friend, my lady.' Susan looked down.

'Well, it doesn't matter. Thank you, however you did it.'

Susan smiled and Alice scanned the headlines. Mrs Pankhurst was released from prison, The Great Meeting was to be held, and more on the forced feeding. Nothing had changed. She sighed then spied Arthur Carew's name where he was commended. He was true to his word.

'Please hide this away and I'll read it later.'

'Of course.' Susan bowed and Alice went to see Nanny in the small room overlooking the children's garden.

She detoured through the library and pulled out the book of Shakespeare's sonnets again. If she was going to have to sit with Nanny then she needed something to occupy herself so she wouldn't think of Zach's kisses. She didn't want to hear what her mother had said. It wouldn't be good.

In the small drawing room, she stopped to admire the wallpaper. Large birds filled the room and as a child she would pretend that she was in an exotic garden or remote jungle, and not in a drawing room with wallpaper older than the house. Touching the tail of one of the birds she thought about her four times great-grandmother. She too had been a duke's daughter with a mother who'd wanted more from her. She too had been trapped in a cage but she had flown free here at Abbotswood.

'There you are.' Nanny looked up from her needlework.

Alice forced a smile. She would not think about the shell house and the kiss. She lowered her eyes.

'Constance tells me you have been tying flies,' she said.

'Yes.' Alice's voice croaked.

She touched Alice's hand. 'You were quite good.'

Alice nodded, still looking down. Nanny read her too well. She would know and Alice wanted and needed to keep this to herself.

'I'm pleased you've found something you enjoy here aside from fishing.'

Alice looked up at the tone in Nanny's voice. Was it a hint of mirth?

'Your mother has confirmed again you will remain here for the foreseeable future. They will hope for the best for the next season.' Nanny's tone dropped to disapproval. 'You know how risky that is, despite your beauty.'

Alice took a deep breath. 'Yes.' She had heard the stories of women who didn't find a husband in their first season. A fate worse than death was a possibility… spinsterhood. The spare woman who no one knew what to do with. She opened her mouth to say this was what she wanted but then closed it when she saw Nanny's face.

'It is not the fate for you.' Nanny picked up her sewing and cast her a glance. 'You are too full of life and... love, to be self-contained.' The last words came out in a low tone laden with meaning. Alice tried to decipher what it was. Self-contained. Too full of life and love.

'Nanny... you know—'

She interrupted. 'I know you well.' She paused, peering at Alice. 'I know what you would say you want. But you don't know what freedom is. I don't think you know what being alone is either.' She held up a hand before Alice could say anything. 'There is no such thing as freedom in this world.' She placed her hands on her lap and looked directly at Alice. 'There are levels of freedom that come from money, sex, status, but no one is free, not even the hermit in the desert. Remember that, Alice, and think on what level of freedom you can attain, for you will never be free.'

Alice sucked in air then rose to her feet. She didn't need to listen to Nanny; she was wrong. Alice could be free. She left the room and walked down into the main hall. The rain had stopped, and she marched straight out the door and past the stables up into the garden.

Thoughts raced around in her head. With each step, her foot hit the ground harder until her teeth jarred and she was lost in the tall trees and far from anyone. She stopped and filled her lungs with pine and eucalyptus-scented air. Behind her lay the house and Cornwall and in front of her trees and ferns and damp wet earth. Was this the only way to be free?

A twig broke and she turned. Zach stood a few feet away. Had he followed her? She lifted her hand to acknowledge him. The red book of sonnets in her hand flashed. He looked directly at her. She didn't turn away as he came closer.

'I saw you leave the house,' he said as he stopped beside her.

'You followed me.' She held the book in front of her chest.

'Yes, I was concerned.' His voice trailed away.

'Why?' she asked; her glance kept straying to his mouth.

'Because you looked angry and troubled and...' he stopped.

'And what?' She was breathless as if the climb she had made had caught up with her.

'You were in trouble because of me,' he said.

She smiled slowly. 'No, making flies is acceptable.'

'Is it?' He moved closer.

'Apparently,' she said.

'Shall we try some more?' His fingers traced hers on the book.

'We shouldn't,' she whispered.

'I know,' he said.

She stepped closer to him. 'You could lose much more than me.'

He swallowed and she watched the movement of his Adam's apple. This – them – was forbidden on many counts.

She shivered. His hand moved to her arm. It was wrong but she wanted to kiss him again. She rose to tiptoes, bringing her face closer to his. High above, the chatter of rooks filled the air. They were being watched. She stepped back. 'I don't think we are alone.'

He took a step away and bowed slightly. 'You may be right.' He didn't turn, but continued to look at her openly. She saw something in his eyes and she wanted the same thing. She shouldn't. She mustn't. But she did. As the sound of the footsteps came closer, she held the book out between them and thrust it in his hands and said, 'Thank you for returning my book.' She cleared her throat. 'I was distressed when I realised I'd dropped it.'

He bowed again but kept eye contact. The gamekeeper appeared at their side.

'Everything 'right, m'lady?' he asked.

'Yes, Evans.' She began walking back down the hill, listening.

Evans said, 'Bit far from the river for you up 'ere.'

'I was seeking out new feathers,' Zach said.

'Ah, that makes sense.' Evans's voice trailed away.

The sound of running water coursing down to the small waterfall drowned out any further conversation. A dragonfly whizzed past and she pushed a loose strand of hair from her face. He still had her book. She smiled and wandered alone to the dairy dell.

After dinner Alice found the book of sonnets sitting on the round table in the hallway. She was about to pick it up when Burton appeared.

'The gillie left this for you.' He stepped closer, towering over her. 'He said you had dropped it in the wood.'

'I had. He was returning it to me when Evans met us.' She picked it up and turned her back on Burton. Everyone in this house was a spy of some form or other. She would have to be very careful.

In the library she sat by the window, looking down on the river and across to the woods. The smoke spiralled above the trees. She longed to be with him. Opening the book, she flipped through the pages until she found a swallow feather tucked into Sonnet 29. She read the opening lines.

> *When, in disgrace with fortune and men's eyes,*
> *I all alone beweep my outcast state.*

She smiled and ran her fingers down the silky feathers as she read aloud the last lines.

> *'For thy sweet love remembered such wealth brings*
> *That then I scorn to change my state with kings.'*

Looking across at the woodsmoke, she knew what she would do.

All household noises had stopped. It was midnight. She had done this many times as a child when it was nothing more than an adventure, but this time she would be more than reprimanded if discovered. Her bare feet were silent on the stairs as she skipped the fourth one down that creaked. She continued down the corridor and slipped out of the servant's door to the courtyard. The nearly full moon was hidden behind cloud, but she knew the way. The hat on her head disguised her fair hair and dressed in her cousin's breeches and coat, she hoped she would not be recognised if seen.

Once out of sight behind the tree, she put on her shoes. The path was slippery as she made her way to the small boat on the bank. It was much easier clambering into the boat in trousers and the cut of the jacket and shirt made for easy rowing across the river. She climbed onto the quay and secured the boat. Above her an owl cried and Alice stilled. She was risking everything but knowing that didn't stop her as she took the path to the cottage. She stubbed her toe then stopped. What was she doing? He hadn't invited her.

A swallow feather tucked into a sonnet wasn't an instruction or an invitation. She took a deep breath and walked forward. A yellow glow came from the cottage. Someone was still awake. Taking small steps to avoid making any noise, she approached the window. Multiple feelings raced through her vying for top position. Fear, exhilaration and something she couldn't acknowledge to herself yet it ran through her. She saw him on his own by the fire, reading. Desire, need, want. Motionless, she stood contemplating his beauty. If she could paint, she would paint him with the shadows on his cheeks and under his eyes. He looked up. Their glances met and both of them remained still until she pulled off the hat and he came to the door.

He took her hand, leading her into the cottage. With his other he traced her face and neck. He closed the door and pulled her into his arms. 'Hello,' he said before he kissed her, lacing his fingers through her hair.

When he lifted his head, she pulled it back and kissed him, pressing her body closer to his. He pushed the coat from her shoulders and the shirt she wore opened up, revealing her breasts.

He inhaled and lifted her into his arms and carried her through the kitchen and up the stairs. He turned right into a small room and laid her on the bed. 'You are so beautiful,' he said, his breathing ragged. She took his hand and placed it on her bare waist.

'Are you sure?' he asked.

'Yes.' She looked in his eyes. She was as certain as she had been of anything else in her life. She kissed him and pulled him to her.

'A swallow feather, Sonnet 29,' she said and rolled on her side.

'You came to me.' He traced the line of her neck.

'Yes.' She took his fingers and kissed each one. 'Did you know I would?'

'I'd hoped.' He pressed his lips to her collarbone.

'We must be careful.' She sat up, pulling the sheet with her. Why she was worried about her modesty when he had kissed every part of her, she wasn't sure, but now the need to hide filled her.

He rose and the candlelight illuminated his beautiful naked form. His face, neck and arms were brown from the sun while the rest of his skin was almost glowing white. A hunger she couldn't explain filled her. She was entirely different from the person who had walked through the door. An old-looking glass hung on the wall. It appeared as though it had once been in the main house but a knock or two on the frame had relegated it here. She stood, bringing the sheet with her and peered in it. He stood beside her, woman and man. Despite the ache of longing in her, she was strangely complete.

He laughed. 'Are you a ghost or simply a vision?' He pulled her into her arms. The sheet she held did nothing to disguise his desire.

'I'm neither.' She drew a deep breath, pressing her hips into his. 'I'm a woman.'

'Yes, m'lady,' he whispered before nibbling her earlobe.

'You can't call me that, not... not after...' His mouth trailed down her neck and thinking of anything but him was difficult.

'What should I call you but my lady?' he asked, as he slipped the sheet from her hands.

She closed her eyes as his hand touched her breast, his thumb teasing her nipple. 'No, that puts a divide between us,' she managed to say.

'You are the lady of my heart, and now—' he paused and placed his hand on her heart '—my soul.'

'Then call me by my name,' she whispered.

He shook his head.

'Please. I can't be with you if you put the title between us.' She placed her hands on his waist.

His hand cupped her face. 'As you wish, Ali you shall be.'

She smiled. That was what her father had called her. She hadn't heard it in years.

'And what will you call me?' he asked.

'My lover.' She took his hand and led him towards the bed.

'I am that.' A slow smiled spread across his mouth.

'My heart.' She pulled him on top of her.

He brushed her hair from her face. 'I hope.'

'My everything.' She couldn't say more for his mouth was on hers and when he stopped, she said, 'Zach, how will...'

'I don't know but somehow we will.' He stroked her collarbone. 'But now we need to get you safely back into the house before they notice that you've gone.'

She sighed. He was right but she wanted nothing more than to spend the night and the rest of her life in his arms. There had to be a way. He took her hand, leading her from the bed. Handing her the britches, he helped her to secure them, put one of her arms through the shirt, followed by the other. He buttoned the shirt across her breast. She couldn't breathe with the desire filling her as he tucked the shirt into the waist. His fingers caressing her skin with each move until he took her hand and led her down the stairs. The kitchen was in darkness, but the oil lamp still burned by the chair he had been sitting in a few hours before. He picked up the jacket and assisted her into that. Finally, he lifted her hair and twisted it before fitting the hat on her head. Her disguise was in place.

'You make a rather beautiful boy,' he whispered into her ear, which he then kissed. 'But I know better.' His hand slipped between the coat and the shirt and touched her breast.

She gulped. 'That's not going to help me to leave.'

'No?' A smile played across his mouth as he took her hand and led her out into the darkness. The air was cooler and the scent of the trees sharper after the smell of woodsmoke in the cottage.

'Tomorrow by Black Rock,' she said, watching him as best she could in the darkness. He stopped when they reached the riverbank where he looked at the clear sky. It was deep and dark. The moon had slid across the sky and was no longer visible. Stars flashed in a great swathe above. A night had never been this perfect.

'Yes, I'll be there at ten.' He kissed her slowly then helped her into the boat. He untied it and tossed the line to her. She set off, filled with a strange sadness. Because she knew he was there, she could pick him out of the shadows on the far bank as she rowed to the northern one. Tying the boat up, she knew he stood there still watching. The distance between Devon and Cornwall had never been so great.

She waved then fled towards the house, hugging the tree line in order not to be spotted. There was a lightening on the horizon. It was later than she thought.

PART THREE

'I could tell you my adventure – beginning from this morning,' said Alice a little timidly: 'but it's no use going back to yesterday, because I was a different person then.'

—ALICE'S ADVENTURES IN WONDERLAND,
LEWIS CARROLL

Case 752
Status: Open
1 July 2019

William Bowman's family has been located and DNA has been requested. Further investigation has revealed that Sgt Bowman had been sent to search for Captain St Loy and he never returned.

The DNA did not match from the nephew of Zachariah Carne.

Chapter Twenty-Four

2019

The windows were wide open, and the air was still heavy with the day's heat. Theo finished arranging the hydrangeas, white Japanese anemones and the orange crocosmia for the table. In half an hour, Jeanette, Hugo and Gayle would be coming to dinner. Her first proper entertaining at Boatman's. And this, of course, was possible due to the rewiring and the boiler being installed, including underfloor heating, thanks to Grannie. Basically, her life had been transformed and both she and the cottage looked far better for it.

Everything was ready, including a large trout caught this morning on the Tamar. Sadly not by her hands but by one of the guests who hadn't managed to return it to the water in time. The guest hadn't wanted to eat it, therefore Theo had become the lucky beneficiary when she met the gillie by the river.

This afternoon she had made a green bean salad with chillies and garlic then poached the trout in white wine and prepared local strawberries to be adorned with clotted cream; Cornish clotted cream as they were in Cornwall. She had been lectured on the differences between Devon clotted cream and

Cornish today. Although she could see the colour difference, they both tasted divine. Also divine were the cheeses. There had been so much choice, but she had settled on Helford Blue, Yarg and Vulscombe goat's cheese.

Cat jumped on the counter. She was still adjusting to the collar and bell that Theo had insisted on for the sake of the local shrew and bird population. As compensation, she treated Cat to stupidly expensive gourmet cat food three times a week. But Cat thought the trout looked good too. Twice Theo had nearly lost it to the beast. Currently it was hidden under tin foil and two tea towels.

With the flowers on the table laid for four, Theo sat and took a deep breath. The word hovering around in her mind was 'home'. She turned her head and noted the letters back from the archivist on the side table. She had been reluctant to delve into them again. Maybe because her gut told her the lady in question was her possible great-grandmother and it felt like prying rather than simply discovering something about the people who had lived in Boatman's. But she knew Jeanette was fearless about everything and would dive straight into the letters once she saw they were back. Jeanette had built Lady Alice up into something of a hero and a quick Google search hadn't lessened that impression.

She took the top letter off the pile, noting the rusted brown spots on it. She fervently hoped it wasn't blood but in her heart she knew it must be. Those poor boys and men lived through hell, and Zach sounded as if he was in another type of hell on top of it all. She put it down and went to the kitchen to check on the new potatoes.

'Hello.' Hugo's voice arrived before he did in the kitchen.

'Wow, you have made progress.' He noted the fridge in the corner and the old Cornish Range had been refurbished but Theo had also acquired a second-hand cooker that was easier to use. She stopped and looked at the cottage through his eyes. That first sighting in the early hours of the morning it had looked derelict and to some extent it had been, but although not yet finished it was her home.

Hugo handed her a bottle of champagne and Gayle came in with a potted plant.

'A daphne?' Theo asked.

'Yes, from a cutting I was allowed to take from Penhale two years ago. I thought that, with all the tree clearing you've done, you will have about the perfect amount of light for this beauty. And the scent, oh the scent...' She grinned and Theo watched the expression on Hugo's face. Something had happened between them, she was certain. They had taken their time about it from what she could tell. In many ways the polished, almost urbane Hugo seemed a mismatch for the outdoor practicality of Gayle but they sparked, and a small part of Theo was jealous; no, not jealous but wistful. She thought of Patrick and Paris. It never would have worked as a long-term thing, but the possibility lingered in her mind.

'This is perfect,' Theo said, and walked through to find Jeanette in an armchair, reading.

Jeanette turned the letter over in her hands. 'May I read another?' Jeanette asked.

'Of course, if you can bear it.' Theo placed a hand on her shoulder.

'It's a glorious evening. Why don't we sit outside?' Hugo asked.

Theo nodded and said, 'And if Jeanette would oblige, she can read you a piece of history from a hundred years ago.'

'I'll grab the champagne.' Gayle dashed into the kitchen and Hugo followed. Theo noted his hand taking Gayle's for a moment before he collected the glasses. As they went outside Jeanette leaned in and whispered, 'Think we need to find a new hat.'

'That serious?' Theo turned to watch them come out of the house.

'I've seen the signs before.' She winked.

In the newly cleared space in front of the cottage facing the river, they all sat down to the long refectory-style table and two benches. Theo was immensely proud of them because they were made from the wood of her trees by the hand of another cousin of Gayle's. And, best of all, Theo had been able to assist in the design and the making.

As Hugo opened and poured the fizz, Jeanette slipped out the single sheet of paper and read aloud.

10 September 1917

My lady of the depths,

This morning as the sun rose the blue sky was reflected in the water. I turned to tell Fred, but the words died in my mouth. For it was not Fred I wanted to share the beauty with but you. How had I dared to dream? I knew from the start that you could never be mine and yet... and yet I'd dreamed. When you looked at me, I didn't see artifice, I didn't see lies; I saw a woman I loved. I, a simple man, loved you, a simple woman. You were not a lady; you were my wild river nymph filled with laughter and love and passion. I don't know what haunts me more. Is it the loss of your touch, your voice, your glance, your presence in my life, or your words? Your words that encouraged me to feel I was more. That I could be more.

Can I continue to pretend that if it weren't for this wretched war that we would have fled together to build a new life for you and me. Would that your dancing eyes could be looking down on me now. But you would be horrified by the filth of the trenches that will no longer wash off. It has gone beneath the skin and stained my very being indelibly as you have. I try and wash you out of my mind, out of my heart, out of my soul, but you remain steadfast even if in person you are not.

Your betrayal cuts so deep I care not for my own life. The thought of him holding you in his arms goes through me like the bullets I have seen pierce my comrades' bodies. And in the distance, I see him, our smart officer, laughing with one of the men. I want to hate him, but he is a good officer and asks nothing of us that he doesn't give of himself. But he is not giving me the one thing I want, I need… you. God, how I delude myself thinking you could still be mine. That once the war is over you somehow will be again. But you are married and that I must always remember.

Z

'Gosh.' Gayle picked up the envelope and turned it in her hands. 'It's not addressed.'

'I'm beginning to think he never intended to send them,' Jeanette said, before taking a sip of her wine. 'He was clearly a deep-thinking and feeling young man.' She paused. 'And his use of language is poetic even.'

'I thought the same, listening to it.' Hugo took the envelope in his hand and turned it over. 'These green envelopes were used when you didn't want your immediate officer to censor the letter.'

'Really?' Gayle stared at him.

'Well, remember, many of the men came from the same place. He might want to say things to his loved one, to be passionate without his boss back home knowing that he wanted to make love to his daughter.' His voice broke a bit and Jeanette caught Theo's eye and smiled knowingly.

'Z'. Hugo touched the letter at the bottom. 'You found the letters here?'

'Yes,' Theo said, topping up everyone's glasses. 'I believe he was Zachariah Carne who was the under gillie at Abbotswood in 1914.'

'It was definitely Alice,' Jeanette said.

Theo nodded.

Gayle leaned in. 'Don't be a tease.'

'Well, Lady Alice – my cousin, it seems – almost definitely is Theo's great-grandmother. She was sent here to Abbotswood after she confronted the king and queen about the right for women to vote.'

'How utterly brilliant that Abbotswood has radical links.' Gayle grinned. 'And how wonderful that you bought Boatman's, Theo, and found these letters.' Gayle raised her glass. 'Here's to new friends, an old cottage and a forbidden love.'

'I'll drink to that, especially the friends and forbidden love,' Jeanette said, gently touching her glass against the others.

Hugo's phone pinged. 'Sorry, I have to take this.' He wandered off and Theo noted Gayle's glance followed him.

'I'm going through my mother's papers, endless quantities of them, to try and find some more information for Theo and her brother Martin.' Jeanette's eyes twinkled. 'Have you met him yet, Gayle?'

Gayle shook her head.

'He's a priest but think of *The Thorn Birds*, if you know that story.'

'Oh, like *Fleabag*.'

Theo snorted her champagne. 'My Martin is a scholarly Jesuit.'

'Oh, to be a bit younger and seduce him from his devout ways.' Jeanette cradled her glass and Theo looked into her own and away from Jeanette's enthusiasm.

Hugo returned. 'Sorry, I've got to go. Crisis re: tomorrow's wedding.' He took a sip of his champagne and continued, 'I have a huge favour to ask, Theo.'

She nodded, waiting.

'Karen is the emergency room. She's broken her foot.'

'Oh no.' Theo took a deep breath, knowing what was coming.

'They are operating tomorrow.'

Theo put on a smile. 'Of course I'll take over. I'm sure it will be a matter of following her plan.'

'I need to head back now because the bride is in a fit over something.' He shook his head. 'And she doesn't yet know about the flowers.'

'Don't tell her.' Jeanette stood up. 'It will make things worse and a little white lie has saved many an event.'

'True.' He laughed. 'I'm sorry.' He looked at Theo. 'You've gone to all this trouble.'

'No problem and I'll need an early night if I'm to sort tomorrow for the bride.'

'Oh, Karen said that her assistant will be in the courtyard at seven with the flowers and the plan. She also says thank you… as best she could as the pain relief drugs were kicking in.'

'No worries.' Theo stood. 'Off you go, Hugo, and ladies if you follow me, we will gallop through the meal as I want to be tucked in bed with the dishes done by nine thirty.'

'Yes, ma'am.' Jeanette dashed into the cottage and Gayle followed with a last lingering look at Hugo.

'I'll send Wilf back with the boat.' He called over his shoulder. 'And are you up to rowing tomorrow or should I send him in the morning?'

Theo paused. She glanced through the trees. It was time to test it out. She could do this, all of it, row her own boat and do the flowers.

'It should be fine. Have the coffee waiting, please,' she said, waving him off. Her phone vibrated in her back pocket. She pulled it out, about to answer, and saw that it was her mother. Theo didn't answer it but let it ring out. She wasn't going to let her mother ruin her first night entertaining in Boatman's.

Chapter Twenty-Five

1914

Alice stood by the window. The fire was low. The sun would rise soon. It was time for her to head back across the river. With her whole heart she wanted to stay here always. At the sound of Zach's quiet footsteps, Alice's body tensed in anticipation of his touch. He stood behind her, not quite touching her. Without turning she leaned against his bare chest. The linen of the shirt she wore offered a new texture to the feel of his skin. Her breath quickened. The glass pane in front of her fogged.

'I want to stay,' she said.

'That is my wish too.' He lifted her hair and kissed her neck. She pressed her hands against the window. His kisses trailed from her neck to her shoulder. The linen fell away and his hand slipped round her ribs and found her breast.

'Zach,' she managed to say, her fingers leaving a mark on the condensation.

'Hmmm.' He pulled the shirt free from the britches, sliding his hand across her bottom.

'This is not helping me think.'

'I wasn't trying to help you think but to feel.' He laughed. 'Sometimes you think too much.'

'I do, and...' She couldn't think or speak when his hand had made its way between her legs. Her fingers splayed to support herself and she pressed her hips back. He dropped to his knees, pulling the trousers down and brought his mouth to where his fingers had been.

She bit her lip in order not to cry out before she fell onto him, bringing him to the joy he had just given her. They lay entwined on the floor, not saying a word as their heartbeats returned to a more normal pace. Outside, the birds began to stir, and Alice rose. Zach collected her clothing from the floor and helped her to dress.

'I hate leaving you.' She kissed his shoulder then looked out the window. It was still dark. In the fogged windowpane she wrote A and Z. She turned to Zach. 'I can be here always this way.'

He frowned.

'Do you have a sharp knife?' she asked.

'Why?'

'We are going to carve our initials into the glass.'

He smiled. 'You're crazy.'

'Quite possibly but this way we will always be here together.'

He left her for a moment and returned with a fishing knife. She took it from him and tested it on the bottom pane to discover how much force she needed. Zach stood close as she drew her A. He took the knife and interwove his Z.

'A and Z, the beginning and the end.'

'I don't want it to end,' he said, kissing her, 'but you do need to go now.'

In haste she pulled on the jacket and thrust the hat on her

head. They raced to the river's edge and she rowed across in the growing dawn light.

The day's fishing had gone well; the lovemaking even better. Alice was halfway up the hill to the house when she spotted Edmund on the lawn. Her smile disappeared. She cast a quick glance at Zach. His full mouth pressed into a flat line. Moments before he had been kissing her. Once they had secured the first catch of the day, and Constance was off with her new net, they walked far downriver to be sure they were alone. Here they'd kissed and laughed in the cover of the woods. With fern fronds as her pillow, he'd made love to her again, and afterwards they had eaten cheese on thick slices of bread while he'd read from the book of sonnets.

'Thing, you return at last?' He walked down to meet them. 'Hello Zach. A good day?' He smiled and the sun came out. He linked his arm through both hers and Zach's while they made their way the short distance to the house. 'My two favourite people together.' He glanced at them both and said, 'I hope you haven't caught something other than sunshine.' He touched Alice's cheek. 'You are a bit pink.'

She felt her face and it was flushed. Was it that or was it from the contact with Zach's stubble last night? She hadn't dared to peer into the looking glass this morning for fear of what she might see. She should have. No wonder Burton had given her an odd look this morning. Once she had hidden the clothing and climbed into bed, Susan was soon about the room. Alice had slept until almost ten and rushed off to the river without breakfast, which had been greeted with much silent disapproval.

Edmund dropped Zach's arm. 'Off to Penhale soon. Is there anything you'd like me to bring?'

Zach shook his head and made his way around the house. Edmund led her into the drawing room where tea was waiting, as were Nanny and Constance.

'Isn't this a wonderful surprise?' Nanny smiled at the two of them.

'It is.' Alice forced a smile. Constance glanced up from her sketch book and sent Alice an inquisitive look, but didn't speak when Alice sat down across from Nanny. If her skin was red, she didn't need it closely inspected. She took the proffered teacup and drank swiftly. Her thoughts raced around while she studied Nanny, Edmund and Constance. Once she would have said they were all on her side, but now no one but Zach was. A plan was in place to meet again this evening as they had done most nights. She smiled remembering carving their initials. Reckless but seeing it there made it feel more real – more permanent.

'What is the news, Edmund? *Tatler* and the *Sphere* only provide so much information.' Nanny coughed as soon as she finished speaking. Alice's glance narrowed.

'Have you heard from Isabelle, your cousin?' Edmund asked Alice.

She shook her head.

'She is to marry Viscount Barnes.'

Alice beamed. 'I'm pleased for her.'

'And I believe you will be relieved to hear Cleveland is to marry Martha Mayhew, the American heiress.'

'Now that is a pity,' Nanny said.

'I wouldn't have married him.' Alice put her cup and saucer down.

Nanny sent her a look. 'You don't have a choice in such matters. Your mother and your uncle were working hard to have him offer for your hand again.'

Alice sat back in her chair.

'You look quite pale,' Edmund said.

'Yes, I feel a bit faint by the thought I was almost sold off to that buffoon.'

'Alice!' Nanny put her cup down with more force that was necessary, and the china rattled.

Alice clenched her hands together on her lap. 'I am not a piece of property to be bought and sold.' She stood, casting a furious look at Nanny and left the room, heading straight out of the house. She couldn't bear to be in it for one moment longer. It represented everything she didn't want. Power, position and submission: hers.

Her need to get away was overwhelming. How? She saw Zach heading towards the fishery. The one thing she was certain of was Zach and he was the one thing they wouldn't ever allow her to have. She would find a way.

Dressed for dinner, she stood at the library door, listening. Edmund was chatting with Nanny.

'Yes, I can stay a few days, there's no rush,' he said.

'Good, you have always been able to talk to her when no one else could,' Nanny said.

'She is a wonder, a joy and wilful... which is part of her charm.' Edmund chuckled.

'It may well be, but she must see that she has to do her duty.' Nanny's voice rose.

Alice didn't want to hear any more. She walked into the room with a smile on her face. She had taken care with her appearance, which would please Nanny. Pearls with a large diamond clasp glistened at her neck and diamond clips adorned her hair. The gown was in a dusty blue, which set off her eyes. She was the vision of what a woman of her class should look like, not a woman dressed as boy as she would be later. Later meant Zach and freedom in the cottage.

'Beautiful as always, Thing.' Edmund bowed. It was years ago that he began to call her Thing. She had asked him why and he said it was because she wasn't an ordinary girl for she could shoot, fish, climb, ride and run like a boy. None of that was true anymore. Her ability had diminished when her access to all of those things had been limited by the need to be a lady. It had been restricted further when her father had died; her Thing self had died too. But Edmund always reminded her of those times.

'Handsome as always,' she replied, noting the cut of his jacket and white waistcoat. Edmund was slim and elegant, oozing poise with every movement. He would be on her side if she spoke to him. He would understand. He always had in the past. But she must not tell him. 'Is Constance joining us?' she asked.

Nanny nodded. 'She had her nose in a book on butterflies and has lost track of the time, I imagine.'

Alice took the glass of sherry from Burton.

'I was saying to Nanny the weather looks set to be fine and I fancy some fishing. I'll be staying a few days.'

Alice took a deep breath. 'How lovely. Is the fishing not acceptable at Penhale this time of year?'

Edmund sent her a surprised look. 'The water is more affected by tidal influences.'

She raised her eyebrows, hoping Nanny hadn't seen it. But thankfully Constance came dashing in, skidding to a halt in front of the fireplace, followed by Burton.

'Dinner,' Burton said. Edmund helped Nanny to her feet. She coughed quietly. Alice was relieved the medication was continuing to work.

Once seated at the table, Alice indicated that she didn't want any of the wine that Burton was suddenly pouring liberally. She needed her wits and her senses clear for later.

'Constance says you caught a fish right before lunch.' Nanny looked up from her soup.

'Yes, a good size trout.'

'But you continued fishing.' Her gaze never left Alice.

'I'm afraid other than hooking a few I was unable to land any of them.' Alice clasped her hands together tightly on her lap.

'Is the gillie not up to his job?' Nanny put her spoon down. 'I know he came here with your recommendation, Lord Edmund.'

Alice curled her toes. Nanny was the one fishing. 'Nothing to do with the skill of the gillie, but down to my skill and the fact that the fish are particularly wily at this point in July.'

'Yes, definitely more challenging at this time of year.' Edmund raised his wine glass, pausing to say, 'Really only another week of decent trout.'

'I expect you are heading to Scotland shortly.' Nanny

took a spoonful of her tomato soup, dislodging the watercress on the top.

Alice was positive the soup was delicious. She had seen the tomatoes collected this evening on her way back from her walk. The weather had been fine and the fruit warm and fragrant when she had stopped to watch. But although she had consumed half the bowl, she couldn't remember the taste.

'Yes, soon,' he said.

Alice listened with half her attention to the conversation between Edmund and Nanny. He had always been a favourite of hers.

'Alice?' Nanny was staring at her.

'Sorry.' Alice bowed her head.

'I asked you a question.' Nanny's voice was stern.

'I'm afraid I had wandered off in my thoughts.' Alice smiled as today's catch, the trout, was cleared. 'All the fresh air has made me a bit tired.' She faked a small yawn, placing a hand over her mouth. 'I'm sorry.'

'Well, you'll sleep well tonight.' Nanny's glance narrowed.

'I'm looking forward to tomorrow's fishing, Thing.' He smiled at her. 'I should think that you are something of an expert now.'

Alice cleared her throat. 'Well, there isn't much else to do.'

'You've been making flies,' Constance said and all eyes turned to her 'Yes, Alice and the gillie were making them.'

Edmund raised an eyebrow. 'I forgot your skill. There is no end to your talents.' His mouth twitched. 'Just the thing to catch a husband.'

'What I was thinking.' Nanny's eyes narrowed as she looked across the table. 'Isn't Lord Buchan looking for a new wife?'

Alice sputtered. Lord Buchan owned a vast chunk of the Highlands, but he was fifty and whiskery. 'No, thank you.' She wiped her hands on her napkin before standing. 'If you will excuse me. I'm feeling a bit unwell.' She once had understood this whole protecting and growing the family focus, but now she saw no sense in it. It had made her property, and – if she didn't marry and marry well – worthless property. But it was in her power to change this. 'A bit too much sun, I think.'

Nanny paused. 'I thought you looked a bit burnt.' She shook her head. 'Not good for your complexion.'

Edmund stood. 'I shall miss your company, Thing, but see you at breakfast.'

Alice nodded and forced herself to walk at a sedate pace from the dining room. Now all she could do was wait.

Susan stood quietly with her hands clasped. 'My lady, you will—' she paused and stepped closer '—be careful?'

Alice sent her a sideways glance. Susan was very well aware that Alice wasn't spending her nights in her own bed and Susan had made sure William's clothes were cleaned and kept hidden. This was the first time she had spoken about it.

'I will be, Susan.'

'It's just that things can happen and people might find out.' Her fingers twisted tight.

'Thank you. I will be careful.'

Susan bowed and left, and Alice sat in the dark, making plans.

It wasn't until one o'clock that the house had gone dark. Edmund was something of a night owl, but Zach would know this and would understand her tardiness. The waning moon was bright tonight as she rowed swiftly across the river. She didn't want to be seen. Her biggest fear was the gamekeeper, especially tonight as she had a bag with her, but thankfully there had been no talk of poachers. If she was lucky, he was tucked in his bed and not on patrol. Besides, poachers would be foolish to be active around the house with family in residence.

Zach stood waiting by the door. Before she could speak, he kissed her. Several minutes later he pulled away and closed the door behind them. Only the light of the fire lit the room. On the table two glasses were filled with an amber liquid. Beside them were bread and meat. She walked to the table with a lump in her throat. It was so real, so homely. It was everything she wanted. If only they could live together here. It would be perfect.

'I loved our lunch today.' He followed her. 'I wanted to enjoy another meal with you.' His thoughts echoed her own. She stroked his face as he held out a chair for her. He had moved the table away from the window. No one could see them without entering the cottage.

She lifted the glass to her nose and sniffed. It was strong and smelled of fresh apple.

'Cider brandy.' He shrugged. 'It's all I have. I would love to give you wine.' He looked down. Almost without thought her hand raced to his and she threaded her fingers through his before she lifted the glass to her lips, not looking away from him, and tasted the sweet fiery liquid.

'It's perfect.' She licked her bottom lip to catch the last drop. 'It's like you.'

He frowned.

'Refined yet untamed, fresh and sweet and delicious.' She laughed.

'That's quite poetic,' he said.

'It's the way you make me feel.' She took another sip. 'With you I am free, I am me.'

'Who are you, Ali?' he asked.

'I'm… I don't know.' She stood.

'You are my lady.' He smiled.

'No, please don't say that.' She shook her head. 'I've heard enough of that today and I have a plan.'

'A plan?' He leaned back in his chair.

'Yes, but I need to know if you love me.' She reached across the table for his hand.

He took her hand. 'Yes, with everything in me.'

'Good, for I can't do this without you.' She took another sip of the brandy.

'Do what?' he asked, rising to his feet.

'I'm leaving.'

His face fell. 'You're leaving Abbotswood?'

'Not just Abbotswood but England.' Her fingers tightened their grip on his. 'I want to leave England and go somewhere where I'm not Lady Alice Neville and you're not my gillie but my equal partner in life.'

'You want to marry me?' He stepped closer.

'You haven't asked me?' She held her breath, suddenly afraid.

He stared for a long moment before he said, 'I… I never dared to hope.'

'Hope, hope please.' She placed a hand on his heart.

He went onto one knee before her. 'I have loved you for so long.' He took a breath. 'I have dreamt of you every night. In those dreams I have loved you.'

She leaned down and kissed him. How had she not seen him all these years? She had been blind to so much.

'When you kissed me, I thought I could not want for anything else. I could have died then and there and been happy.' He took her hands in his. 'Then you came to me, gave yourself to me freely.' He shook his head, his eyes filling with unshed tears. 'And yet now here you are offering me everything.'

'Yes.'

'Ali, my heart, my dream, my everything. Will you do me the greatest honour and become my wife?' he asked.

'Yes, I will.' She pulled him to his feet and kissed him with all her love and hunger for him. They fell to the floor and their legs entwined. She wanted all of him now, but he stopped, pushing her hair from her face. 'Not here on the floor.'

'Why not?' Cool air filled the space between them.

'I want the first time I make love to you as my fiancée to be perfect.' He took her hand and pulled her to her feet. Silently they walked to his bedroom and he pulled the door closed behind them. He led her to the looking glass and they stood side by side.

'We are the only ones who can witness our vows to each other at the moment.'

She studied him.

'Will you be my wife?'

'I will. Will you be my husband?' she asked.

'I will.' He turned from the looking glass and took her face in his hands. 'Thank you for loving me.'

She laughed, feeling freer than she had ever done. He slipped the shirt from her shoulders and led her to the bed.

Downstairs she heard the first birds stirring, though it was still dark; she grabbed a piece of bread, suddenly famished.

'How will we do this?' He ran his fingers through his hair.

She reached for her bag on the back of the chair and pulled a blue box from it. He looked from her to the box.

'It is one of the few things that is fully mine.' She smiled.

'I am,' he said.

'I am grateful.' She kissed him then opened the box. The diamonds reflected the low firelight and cast rainbows on the walls. He gasped. His fingers touched the tiara.

'This will provide our passage and the funds we need to escape.'

'It's yours?' He ran his fingers along the leaves. 'Laurel?'

'Yes. My grandfather had it made for my grandmother when she won his heart.'

He nodded.

'We need to find a way to sell it.' She closed the box. 'I know there are such places in London but there must be ones closer.'

'Exeter,' he said.

'Yes.' She smiled. 'I'm sure I can find a way to convince Nanny we should go to Exeter.'

'Papers?' he asked.

'More difficult but there has to be a way.'

'Maybe…' His voice trailed away.

'Yes?'

'I may know someone but…' He stopped speaking.

'I have more jewellery that we can sell later, when we arrive wherever we are going.' She met his glance.

'America,' he said.

'Yes, America.'

'Yes, please, the west.' He smiled.

'Far from here and all who know us.' She paused, her mind racing through what facts she knew about the United States. 'West it is and a state where both men and women have the right to vote. Maybe California.'

'My rebel.'

'Is it wrong to want equality?' she asked.

'No,' he said.

She picked up their plates.

'Leave them.'

She shook her head. She was about to embark on a new life incredibly different from the one she lived now. It was time to begin to learn. 'No, let me.'

He dropped her hand and went ahead of her into the kitchen. An oil lamp sat on the windowsill and cast enough light for her to look at the room clearly. It contained nothing more than a sink, a stove of sorts and a counter with a shelf below it. It was clean. The cooking pan was already washed and drying on the side. She went to the sink and turned on the tap. Cold water filled it and she began to rinse the plates. 'Small steps,' she said.

'You have never washed a thing in your life, including yourself.' He kissed her neck to take away the sting of his words. She had never dressed herself except for these midnight journeys.

'Will you teach me?' She turned in his arms.

'With pleasure but only...' His voice trailed away.

'Only what?' She pulled back, trying to read his expression.

'If you let me bathe you first.'

Desire ran through her. The thought of water and him mixed. She kissed him hard, pressing her body against his. 'Yes.'

Outside the growing sound of birds pulled them apart. She had stayed too long. Together they raced through the cottage grabbing her coat and not stopping until she was in the boat and he was pushing her out into the current.

Chapter Twenty-Six

Yawning on her way down to the river with Edmund at her side, Alice tried her best to be alert. Constance was bringing up the rear.

'Troubled sleep?' he asked.

'It would be if she had read the papers,' Constance said, jogging to come abreast with them.

'How so?' Alice stifled another yawn as she asked.

'Don't you pay attention to anything but yourself or your angling?' Constance placed her hands on her hips.

'War is in the air.' Edmund took a deep drag on his cigarette.

'Surely it won't come to that.' Alice had glanced through the papers most days; since the grand duke and his wife had been assassinated, things had become perilous, but she had faith that they would sort this out. No one needed war.

'I wish I had your confidence, but I am sure it will be short and sharp,' he said, dropping his cigarette onto the path and crushing it with his boot.

'I hope so, Lord Edmund.' Constance moved in front of them, walking backwards. 'But are wars ever what people say they are?'

'You have an old head on the body of a young person.' He smiled at her. 'Nothing escapes you, not even the obscurities of foreign politics, clearly.'

Zach stood by the riverbank, waiting. Alice looked quickly away. Every part of her called out to him but she must not betray him, them, their plan.

'Morning, Zachariah.' He slapped Zach on the back in a jovial manner. 'How does the river look on this fine morning?' Edmund glanced up at the blisteringly blue sky.

'The water is getting a bit low, but I have seen trout rising up by the pool.'

'Excellent, lead the way.'

Sweat trickled down Alice's back as they moved through the heat of the late morning. Edmund had asked for permission to remove his tie and told Zach to do the same. The clear running water beside them looked inviting, but they all walked on in confining clothes in the sweltering heat. The pool gleamed with the blue of the sky above and green from the towering trees. Not a cloud was seen to provide relief.

'I'm going to sit there.' Constance pointed to an old oak, and Alice, for a brief moment, was jealous. If she and Zach were alone they could escape to the far side of the river and rest in the shade of the trees. But instead she was studying the river while Zach readied their rods. On hers she noticed he'd finished the fly they had begun together. He saw her looking and smiled briefly. It was important. Nothing should appear out of the ordinary to anyone.

'There we are,' Edmund whispered and pointed. Trout were about. Zach moved between them distributing the gear, his glance trained to the water. It was so clear by the bank Alice could count the stones. But it was towards the middle of the pool off the Cornish side that Alice cast her line. Her fly sat poised above a rising trout, but it took the midge nearby. So the morning went. The fish were wary and she was about to give up when one took the fly and then she began the merry dance to land the fish.

Zach was close beside her and his breath mingled with hers as they worked to catch the trout. The closer it came the more it fought. She needed all the skill that Zach and her father had taught her. Finally, it was in reach. Zach grinned as he netted the fish. Their glances locked for a moment before Edmund's voice broke through. 'Well done, Thing. You haven't been idling by the river at all.' He looked at the two of them and then turned to Constance in the shade of the tree, her head down, intent on whatever she was reading. 'First catch goes to Alice. Are you sure you won't join in, Lady Constance?'

She shook her head without looking up from her book.

Zach pointed to the far side and Edmund nodded, casting his line. Zach stood a foot away, watching the fly on the surface of the water. A trout surfaced and took a real one. Edmund reeled the line in then cast again.

Alice's fingers played with the feather on the fly. It had taken a beating and she should use a different one. This one would require freshening if it was to catch another trout.

From her creel she pulled out a fly. Turning it over in her fingers, she recognised it. It was one her father had made. It must be eight years old. She couldn't use it. It was one of the few things of his she had. The red spine of the book of sonnets caught the sun. She would keep this too and not return it to the library here. Touching the book, she remembered her tiara. She'd left it at the cottage last night. He would have hidden it she was sure. He would be arrested if he was found with it. That had been careless of her. She must speak with him about it.

She selected a different fly and removed the damaged one before replacing it. She turned back to the men. Silently they worked, with Zach anticipating Edmund's moves. His family had been working for Edmund's family for decades. There was a bond that came from that. Soon another trout was in the bag.

'Well done,' she said, grinning. This would be easier from the other side. Just as she was about to suggest it sunlight picked out a rising trout. Without thought and in a fluid movement, she cast to land the fly directly above it. It took the fly and in moments she was dancing with the fish again. It was winning. She struggled to achieve the right balance of bringing it in without letting it wriggle free. This trout was older and tougher than the previous causing her to slip. It was proving stronger than she was. Zach was beside her in an instant, his arms about her, steadying her and the line. Together they moved to bring the fish towards the bank. Edmund appeared with the net. Zach stepped away from Alice and took the net. He bent low and Edmund held Alice by the waist, keeping her safe but letting her pull it in alone.

Edmund dropped his arm and whispered in Alice's ear. 'Well done, Thing. But be careful not to slip up.'

Alice shivered as he stepped away from her.

'I'm in need of luncheon,' Constance said, peering in the basket now holding three trout. 'But not fish.'

'I think that would be a good plan.' Edmund looked to the

sky. 'It would give me a chance to cool off. For us all to.' He looked at Zach then Alice.

Alice wasn't hungry although she was hot. The last thing she wanted to do was sit down in the dining room. No, she wanted cheese and bread and love.

'The trout are still rising and I will stay… if you won't miss me.' She gave Edmund her most charming smile.

'I understand the thrill of the hunt,' he said, taking Constance's arm. 'Just remember it is just a chase.' Alice narrowed her glance as she watched them walk away. Constance was chatting and Edmund nodding. He was no doubt learning the intricacies of butterfly mating.

Once they were out of sight she turned to Zach. 'Shall we cross to the other side?'

He smiled, gathering the equipment. They walked further upriver until they came to a boat. Leaving the fishing gear against a tree on the Devon bank, Zach rowed across to the woodland and the cool shade. Once they were alone, Alice pulled him to her. It had been torture to have him close all morning but not to touch him, to kiss him, to make love to him.

His passion met hers. Before long her skirts were up and he was in her, holding her against a tree. She climaxed and he followed. They collapsed onto the woodland floor, lying together among the ferns. Her ears were filled with the sound of her heart, the river and the birds above. His fingers laced with hers as they lay shoulder to shoulder, returning to normal with all the pent emotion spent.

'Zach?'

'Hmmm.' He rolled onto his side. His fingers circled her ear then trailed down her neck resting on her still heaving breast.

'I didn't dream last night?' she asked.

'No more than I did,' he said.

She closed her eyes for a moment. 'I love you.'

'I love you, my lady.'

She pursed her mouth but turned it into a smile. 'Oh, the tiara, I forgot it last night.'

'I know.' He shuddered. 'I buried it outside the cottage.'

'Is it safe?'

'Yes. I wouldn't jeopardise our freedom.'

She smiled and pulled his head to hers and kissed him. 'I want to be your wife so much it hurts, and I count the days until we can be in America.'

He sat up, pulling one knee towards his chest and wrapping an arm around it. 'It may take some time to put everything in place.'

'I mentioned a trip to Exeter to Nanny in passing this morning. She seemed receptive.' Alice placed a hand on his leg.

'Good.' He grabbed the basket and took out a piece of bread, handing it to her, then some cheese. From his flask he poured a bit of the cider brandy.

'When I come tonight, I'll collect the tiara. I don't know when Nanny will give the go-ahead but I must be ready.'

He nodded and she watched him rip a small piece of bread and then match it with the cheese. Everything he did was considered. Even his loving her was that way.

He looked up and stared at her. 'Ali, I loved you so long and I still cannot believe my dreams are real and won't disappear with the morning light.'

Alice took his hand in hers. 'It is well past midday. The sun is high, and you have just made love to me.'

In the distance they heard a dog bark. Quickly they gathered their things and moved closer to the shade by the bank. If they were seen together it must appear perfectly correct. Simply a gillie and his angler taking refreshment in the shade. They didn't say a word as they worked in unison until they sat ten feet apart as the gamekeeper came upon them.

'M'lady.' He bowed his head. 'Carne.'

'Evans,' Zach said. 'The temperature is much cooler this side.'

The gamekeeper looked about. 'Aye, it is, but I think the fishing is better from the other where you left the rods.'

'It's been a good morning.' Alice rose to her feet and the gamekeeper's stance changed.

'Pleased to hear that, m'lady.' He bowed more formally and walked away. She watched his back. He turned once to find her still observing him. He took their boat and crossed the river. Alice crossed her arms against her chest, saying, 'He's an awkward soul.'

'Indeed.' Zach came closer to her but was still too far for her liking. However, she knew they couldn't risk anything now. Together they gathered the small picnic.

She was no longer hungry but filled with anger instead. Her resentment grew as they walked along the bank shaded by the trees to reach the other boat. His hand would brush past hers but they didn't touch. Everything was appropriate for a lady and her gillie and she didn't like it one bit.

Case 752
Status: Open
16 July 2019

Sgt William Bowman's remains have been identified and the family have been notified.

DNA test dispatched to Fr Martin Pascoe SJC PhD.

Chapter Twenty-Seven

2019

The alarm sounded. Theo thrashed about until she'd found her phone. It was five thirty. Cat wasn't even pawing her face. But Theo was taking over for poor Karen today and she wanted to be on the ball.

Cat beat her down the stairs and sat on the countertop, waiting.

'Cheeky,' she said, filling the food bowl.

Cat scoffed down the fish-scented pellets. Why Theo had bought the fish ones she didn't know. It gave Cat the worst morning breath; well, anytime-of-day breath. But her coat looked better for it, as it had after she'd eaten the skin from her mackerel the other night.

Her phone rang. It wasn't even six. It must be an emergency. She answered without looking at the name. 'Hello?'

'Are you deliberately ignoring me?' her mother asked.

Theo pressed her lips together before answering. 'No.'

'I rang last night,' she said.

Theo put the kettle on. 'I had friends over.'

'What, entertaining already in your little cottage?'

'Yes, I was.' Theo pressed her mouth into a flat line.

'It's all sunshine and flowers now that summer is here but come winter your little folly will be dark, dank and dire.'

Theo looked at her slate floor and considered her under-floor heating, which would ensure that Theo would be snug and warm all winter.

'Surely this isn't the reason for your call?'

'No.' Her mother took a deep breath. 'I'm selling the house and I need you to get rid of your things.'

Theo rubbed her eyes. She had left home at twenty-two; she couldn't imagine that her mother had anything of hers.

'Well, what do you want me to do with them? I can no longer afford to keep this house on since your grandmother snubbed me.'

Theo took a deep breath. 'Is it much? Could you send it?'

'There are two boxes of books and bits.'

Theo still couldn't imagine what was in them.

'Fine, I'll transfer the money for the cost of sending them.'

'What about my time?' she asked.

Theo began to speak then stopped and asked, 'What is your hourly rate?' She couldn't believe things had come to this.

'Well, including going through the stuff already... oh, and I can't believe you slept with a man before marrying Piers, but that only confirmed to me that you take after your father's mother and not my side of the family—'

Theo interrupted her saying, 'You read my journals?'

'Of course.'

She released all the air in her lungs and counted before saying, 'Fine, please send me the boxes and I'll transfer the money including your hourly rate.' Theo would not engage further and was grateful she was more like Grannie than her own mother.

'Make the amount five hundred.'

'Fine.' If that's what it took to be done with her mother she would pay the price.

'Why your father kept them in the first place I don't understand but then he was always soft on you.'

Theo bit back the words she wanted to say and instead said, 'I have to cut you short but I have to be at work in an hour. Goodbye.' She shut the phone off and looked around her home. Her mother was wrong on many counts, but she still managed to take the legs out from under her every single interaction. She was fifty-four; it shouldn't happen but it did. Today would require all her focus and that required strong coffee and a good breakfast after she transferred the money to her mother and sent her the address. Hopefully Theo would not have to suffer another call.

The sky was washed grey and the ground damp. The wind tickled the leaves of the bamboo. Sometimes she had to pinch herself, living this close to Abbotswood and this garden. She had gone through Repton's red book for Abbotswood with Gayle but there hadn't been much about Boatman's sadly. But looking across the Tamar the specimen trees showed his mark clearly. And now the wind lifted the leaves of the trees and the hair on the back of her neck. A warning or a promise.

She walked down the hill clutching the necessary greenery to finish the tables for the wedding party. It was a day of promise for the couple. Her own had been lovely but in view of both their infidelities before the wedding they never should have gone ahead. Breathing deeply now, the scent of the pine needles filled her lungs. She was alive and must live here in this moment.

She turned left and walked into the courtyard. The clock rang the hour and the sound of wheels crunching over the drive greeted her. She froze then pulled back in the cover of a shrub when she saw the licence plate. She hadn't met the bride or seen the guest list, but she knew that Range Rover and registration number. Piers was here and that would mean his mistress and possibly child would be too.

Theo dashed through the house to the long border where the tent was set up. She worked quickly so she could check the bride's bouquet and make adjustments to the flower crowns for the little girls. But she must flee before she could be seen. It's not that she couldn't face Piers; it was more that she didn't want to. He did not belong in her life now.

She stood back. The setting was perfect, and the flowers only enhanced it. The brief had been simple: white and green. Elegant and understated, and possibly a little too virginal for Theo's taste. She would have liked to have seen some passion somewhere. However, she was pleased with the result and she hadn't broken the brief from Karen.

'Mum.'

Theo swung around. David stood in morning coat clutching a top hat. He shuffled from one foot to the other. Theo ran through a list of possible people who would invite both David and Piers but she came up with no one.

'What on earth are you doing here?' he asked, looking around.

'The flowers,' she said.

He waved at his girlfriend, Natasha, in the distance. 'God, this isn't going to help anything.' He ran his fingers through his hair. 'I haven't got time to explain right now.' He glanced at his watch. 'Look, I've got to go but I'll call you tomorrow, OK?'

'Sure.' She smiled at him and watched until he had joined up with Natasha. It must be awkward for him to even be in the same place as both her and Piers. She didn't mind but she had no desire to see her ex. She picked up the last few branches, wondering if he were staying here tonight and if he would visit tomorrow. She longed to show him the cottage. It was hard to believe it was now the end of July and David hadn't yet seen it but with him covering everything during Piers's extended paternity leave she understood.

Back inside in the corridor to the kitchens, she checked her phone. It was dead. She stopped by reception and asked them to give it a bit of charge for her. Piers's voice reached her and she flinched. The sooner she could cross the Tamar and be back to the safety of her own cottage the better. She was due to attend to the bride and her flower girls at one and it was now 12.45 p.m. It was unnerving to be presented with the possibility of seeing Piers but once back in Boatman's she could forget again. It was her place and not tarnished by her past life.

Tucking her hair behind her ear, Theo tapped on the bedroom door to the suite. She could hear laughter and the popping of a champagne cork. All was as it should be. She smiled as the door opened wide then she tilted sideways, held up by the door jamb.

The bride stood in a pristine white satin gown that clung to her beautiful figure. Her nails and her lips were fire engine red, but she paled beneath her tan as she stood open-mouthed.

She looked more shocked than Theo. Theo nearly dropped the flower trug with spare blooms, flower crowns and the bouquet.

'You,' the bride said. Theo could have echoed the same word if she had a voice, but she was struck dumb. She had spent today arranging the wedding flowers for her ex-husband and his mistress. No wonder David had looked uncomfortable. No expense had been spared on this wedding. She had seen the details this morning and this was all paid for, no doubt with money that should have been Theo's final payment months ago. It was all clear.

'Get out!' The bride marched up to Theo and pulled the bouquet out of her hands, smashing the delicate white roses on the doorframe. Soft petals fell to the floor. 'See what you've done!' She waved the bouquet in the air and more petals fell to the ground like confetti.

'Tina, chill. What's the problem?' A woman covered in too much fake tan took the bouquet away and handed Tina a glass of champagne.

'This.' She pointed at Theo. 'This… this… is Piers's ex.'

'And you hired her to do your flowers?' The woman whistled.

A wild laugh threatened to explode out of Theo. She pressed her lips together.

'No, I hired the best, Karen Smith.'

The woman looked closely at Theo. Theo stood tall and looked her directly in the eye.

'So, where is this Karen?' she asked.

'Yesterday while loading the flowers into the van she fell and broke several bones in her foot.' Theo paused and looked at Tina, daring her to say something ridiculous. 'As we speak, she is in surgery.'

'Oh.' The woman looked at her more closely. 'And you are qualified?'

'Yes—' Theo paused, pushing aside her mother's voice saying she wasn't '—more than qualified, and Karen asked me to step in so that the bride wouldn't be let down.'

'I don't want her near me.' Tina knocked back her champagne.

'That's fine by me. I'll leave these here.' Theo lifted out the flower crowns and the spare blooms and placed them just inside the room.

'You're here to wreck my day.' Tina spun around and her eyes narrowed.

Theo laughed drily. 'Funnily enough today has been all about making the bride's day beautiful. The irony is I had no idea who the bride was.' She took a step backward and once in the hall she moved at a brisk pace away from the room, stifling her inappropriate laughter. It really couldn't be better. Tina's day was ruined because everywhere she turned were flowers that Theo had put together. If she had planned it, it couldn't have been better. She almost wished she had.

In the long hallway back to the main house, she bumped into Hugo.

'You, as my grandmother would say, look like the cat that had the cream.'

'Oh, I have and let me tell you it was good.' She smiled, but then put a hand on his arm. 'I'd better warn you. Today's wedding...'

He tilted his head. 'Yes.'

'It's my ex's wedding.' She shook her head, trying to erase the whole thing from her mind, but it wouldn't go. Not long ago she was still married and thought she had some form of happiness. But her eyes were open now and she wasn't going to miss the rest of her life. She would face life head-on and live it.

He coughed. 'No.'

Theo nodded, still smiling. 'I think the bride might be upset that I have done her flowers.'

He laughed. 'Oh God, no.'

'Indeed.' She glanced at the empty trug in her hands. 'I was going to stick around in case anything needed a quick fix, but maybe Gayle could stand in and prevent another outburst from the bride.'

He winced. 'Was it bad?'

'So bad it was beautiful.' Theo couldn't supress her grin.

'You owe me a drink,' he said as he dashed to the front desk to send someone in search of Gayle.

Theo walked the remainder of the long corridor away from the former children's wing. There was something peaceful about all the wellington boots and waterproofs lined up. She slipped out the door to the courtyard as a big fat drop of rain hit her on her nose. Those boots and coats might come in handy if the rain picked up. She looked heavenward and let the rain hit her face. She felt damn good and she knew she shouldn't, but she did. She almost skipped as she set off down to the river and to her boat.

Chapter Twenty-Eight

By the time she reached the river the rain had picked up. What had been a grey summer's day for a white wedding was morphing into a washout and Theo didn't feel a bit bad. She should; she knew she should. With that acknowledgement she stuck her hand in her pocket and cursed. She'd left her phone charging at the reception desk. Looking up to Abbotswood she debated whether she would risk being seen, but she had no choice. In her bag of things tucked in the boat, she pulled out her wide-brimmed waxed hat and lightweight cagoule. With those in place she strolled back up the hill, hoping it would disguise her appearance should the bride glance out the window.

The rain stepped up a gear and the sky showed no lightening, only solid grey cloud heavy with rain, and not the soft gentle rain of summer but full on angry rain. She laughed. They said that rain on your wedding day was a good sign, but she doubted the bride felt that way.

Finally in the courtyard, she entered through the door into the kitchens, trying to be as invisible as possible. She bumped into Gayle.

Gayle jumped. 'What the hell!'

'Sorry.' Theo gave her a rueful smile.

'I know it's not your fault but that woman.' She shuddered.

Theo chuckled. 'Yes, and thanks for stepping in.'

'No problem. Your son is a bit of all right,' she said.

Theo smiled. 'Yes, he is.'

'He reminds me of someone, but I can't place it.' Gayle collected her raincoat and headed out to the tent, no doubt to secure things from the wind that had suddenly arrived and hit the kitchen windows with a bang.

Hopefully once this wedding was over David would feel more at ease about the divorce. With that thought, she dashed to reception to collect her phone.

At the desk Piers stood huffing, puffing and giving the receptionist hell about something… possibly Theo. Theo remained out of sight and tried to see him with anything but dismay. It was hard but she needed to try. There had been good times and laughter. The saddest thing of all is she would have stayed even though she had known about his affair with his soon-to-be-wife and the others before. He provided security. He had bought Higson Manor, which had been the muse that had opened her up and brought part of her to life. It had given her a purpose aside from David. For that alone she'd tolerated the infidelities. What a desperate state of affairs. She held her head high. She could and would be gracious.

'Congratulations on your wedding, Piers, and your new daughter.'

He spun around. She watched him try and control his emotions as there was a witness who looked like she'd been pulled through the hedge backwards. His face was puce, and he was far from the handsome man she'd married over thirty years ago. He had succumbed to the middle-age spread far worse than she had, and he couldn't blame menopause.

'Theodora, you are here,' he managed to say.

'Indeed.' She smiled politely.

'Just to ruin things,' he said in a low tone.

She laughed with no humour or lightness. 'Fine words from a man who couldn't run his own life.' She had made sure everything had gone smoothly from the perfect meals to the correctly starched shirts. She had been his housekeeper and occasional bed partner. Why hadn't she seen it? Because she had believed she wasn't good enough. That she was lucky to have him. She had been afraid of life without everything he offered. 'No, I live less than a mile away. You have ventured into my world not the other way around.'

'This explains the text from Tina.' He waved his phone about.

Theo smiled. 'Yes, I've done the flowers for your wedding. May they bring you every happiness, all the happiness you deserve.' She paused, watching him figure out what he could say in front of others. 'I'll grab my phone, Jane, and I'll be on my way.' She gave the receptionist an encouraging smile. The poor woman had watched the farce while trying to hide her dismay. She held out the phone.

'Thanks for charging it for me,' Theo said, before turning to Piers and stepping closer to say, 'Best wishes on your second wedding day.' She turned and strolled towards the kitchen. Her hand shook but he wouldn't be able to see that. Switching the phone on, it pinged what seemed like hundreds of times. They were all messages from Martin. Most consisted of 'Don't visit Abbotswood today'.

Your ex is remarrying. Don't let the buggers get you down. Love you. M.

Theo clutched the phone to her heart. At least she hadn't lost her self-respect or, more correctly, she had finally found it.

Outside in the squall she walked head down against the wind and the rain. The river might be too rough to cross and that was saying something. What could she do?

Someone tapped on her shoulder and she nearly screamed. Hugo stood in a poncho, holding out a key. 'Go and stay at mine. Terry will give you a lift. This weather is set to get worse.' He smiled. 'And there's a tree down blocking the road.'

'Thanks. You're a star.'

'No, simply a friend.' He dashed away. Theo didn't envy the rest of his day managing a wedding in a marquee on the lawn with a pissed-off bride and groom in the middle of a fierce storm.

In this howling gale, Hugo's home, the Swiss Cottage, looked like a welcoming hobbit house. From the short walk down to the cottage, she was soaked through. Inside the kitchen, Theo shook like a dog.

Peeling off her outerwear, she hung it to dry. But she was still too wet. Leaving the kitchen, she opened the door to her right at the bottom of the stairs. This led into a room with bunk beds. Across the hall she found the utility room, but it was immaculate without even a folded towel to be found. She stripped off down to her knickers and bra and placed her clothes in the tumble dryer. Goosebumps covered her skin. She needed to find something to put on while her clothes dried. Knowing he wouldn't mind, she ventured up to find his room. There must be a dressing gown or something.

On the first floor she found a small dining and sitting room. She didn't linger but went up another flight. The first door revealed a bathroom and the next was a long room with sloped ceilings on both sides. She struggled to stand straight and she wasn't sure how Hugo could except in the centre of the room.

Despite the rain outside and her damp state she went straight to the mullioned window to look down. The weather had closed in entirely. No river, no Cornwall, no Boatman's. The heavy rain had erased the world. The wind battered the window and Theo shivered. She turned, hoping he had a dressing gown or something else visible. She didn't want to look in the cupboards or drawers. That would be a step too far.

On the back of the door she spied a dressing gown, but that was not what had her rooted to the spot. On the wall by the door was a large oil painting. A naked woman sat in a red armchair. Moonlight fell over her shoulder. Theo couldn't breathe. Couldn't move. It wasn't a sketch. It was a large oil painting and even from this distance she felt its power. Its promise. Sexual tension crackled off of it. She had seen the sketch, which had been beautiful, but in the years that had followed she had forgotten the photographs he'd taken. He must have painted this from them or maybe, just maybe, the memory of that night had made as much of an impression on him as it had on her.

Finally, her feet moved. She reached out and touched the thick oil paint. It was less emotive this close when she could see each brush stroke but then she knew with each one he had touched her again. Her mouth dried. In the far righthand corner of the painting she saw his signature. Patrick Mounsey.

Her legs wobbled and she backed up to the bed and sat staring at it. Patrick Mounsey. He must be related to Hugo. The room swayed and she leaned back on the bed, waiting for everything to settle.

He'd promised he'd never sell the picture. She laughed. Of course that hadn't meant he couldn't give it to someone. She was grateful that Hugo hadn't made the connection. She blushed like she hadn't in years. This young man had a painting of her starkers in his bedroom, but then it was not the type of painting you hung in your sitting room. Maybe she should be offended that he hadn't recognised her. She laughed. What a contrary creature she was.

Taking a deep breath, she grabbed the dressing gown and straightened the bed out of habit. She felt exposed in a way she never had, not even when Patrick had been taking the photographs. She took a last look. It wasn't that the picture was sexual. In fact, her pose, although inviting, was shy. Maybe that was why it felt the way it did to see it and to see it here hanging in the bedroom of a young man she knew.

Dashing downstairs, she added her bra and knickers to the tumble dryer then ventured into the kitchen and turned on the kettle. She was chilled through and longed for a hot toddy. What a day it had been.

A quick check through the cupboards showed no whisky, but she was sure he must have some. She padded upstairs and into the small panelled dining room and not seeing anything there she opened the door into the sitting room. There under the bookcases on the far side of the fireplace she found his whisky, wine, and about any other tipple she could put a name to. Taking the bottle of blended whisky, for she wouldn't put a single malt into a toddy, she stood and looked at the painting above the fireplace. She managed to catch the bottle before it hit the grate. Placing it carefully on the floor, she studied Patrick's self-portrait. And when Theo could look from him to the rest of the paintings, she saw the painting of her leaning against the studio wall.

The expression on his face showed loss. But also something more. Those eyes were familiar. She had seen them uncomfortable and awkward a few hours ago... David's eyes. Theo bent to pick up the whisky and went downstairs. She poured a healthy glug into the mug. She needed it... first Piers then the paintings. Before pouring the hot water in she took a big sip. Her past in Paris was not a dream. But it was real, and seeing Patrick's self-portrait she had seen David. All these years she had dismissed any thought that David could be Patrick's. Hell, she hadn't even known his full name. Patrick Mounsey.

Adding the hot water to the mug, she wondered if she had enough signal to do an internet search. She wasn't sure what it would tell her. Did she want to know? Wasn't it better not to know? But it might reveal who Hugo was to Patrick.

With her hot toddy in hand, she went back to the sitting room and looked for clues. There was a picture of Hugo and his mother, but no photographs of a father anywhere, not even a formal graduation shot. That was enough for her to dash up to the top floor and try to get enough signal. Back in Hugo's bedroom by the window she had four bars of 4G, and she typed in his name. Patrick Mounsey.

He had a Wiki entry and that was a good starting point, but part of her didn't want to know. It had been thirty-three years. He remained a mystery but because of David she needed to know. Maybe he hadn't been in Hugo's photos because he was an uncle or his parents had divorced. She looked at the screen. The top line listed year of birth 1962 and year of death 1990. She released a long slow breath. Four years after they had met. So young. She scanned the details without taking them in until she reached family. He never married but he had one brother. Hugo must be his nephew.

She closed the browser and walked slowly through the room. Stopping at the painting of her, she saw the woman she had been through his eyes. It was all promise and possibility. A week later the woman had been lost forever. She ran her finger over his signature. She had never told him how she felt, how he had made her feel. She could have written. She could have explained she was engaged. Instead she stole away as he slept, taking the guide to Paris. No note, just a kiss and she had gone. No wonder there had been sadness on his face. He had felt the love as much as she had. Love at first sight. Her heart had known it, but she hadn't listened.

In the sitting room clutching her toddy, the earlier joy of having scuppered Piers's wedding without any ill intent had disappeared. The weight of loss settled on her and pinned her to the sofa. Tears came but she brushed them away. She had grieved for the loss of Patrick years ago and put it away the day she married. But somewhere in the back of her mind Patrick had lived and there was always the possibility that somehow she would meet him again. Now she knew he wasn't there, and that small flame of hope was extinguished.

Chapter Twenty-Nine

1914

It was half past midnight when Alice stole from the house taking a different route to the river and across it. Although she knew differently, she felt the house had eyes, but it was in darkness and only the scent of extinguished candles and oil lamps filled the air. Here on the Cornish bank the air was brisk. Rain was coming. She hoped that it would hold off until she was back in the house.

She crept to the cottage, wishing Zach was outside waiting for her; instead she heard voices. Edmund. What on earth was he doing there?

'For Christ's sake, Zach, this isn't a game,' Edmund said.

'I know that.' Zach's voice was measured.

'What do you think you are playing at? If I can see it don't you think others can?' Edmund asked.

'No one sees us together,' Zach's voice dropped away.

'That's not true. You walked her back to the house today and there were ten of us viewing the spectacle. God, you both were bloody glowing in the afternoon light.' Alice watched Edmund move to the fireplace.

'Do you know what will happen to her?' Zach asked.

'Nothing.' Edmund swung around and Alice caught sight of his face in the light from the fire. She had never seen it this solemn. 'No, that's not true; there is already talk that she is unstable and that if they don't find her a husband fast they may send her away.'

'No.' Zach's voice rose.

Alice's hand went to her throat. She sank to the ground, her ears pounding.

'And then there's you. What they will do to you doesn't bear thinking about and I won't be able to save you.'

Silence. Alice crawled to a nearby bush, trying hard to think clearly. Edmund mustn't see her here. The door swung wide and Edmund stormed out. He turned. 'Zach, I'd do anything for you but for God's sake don't be a bloody fool. Don't ruin both your lives.' He marched off down to the river.

Alice shook as she watched the silhouetted Zach run his fingers through his hair. She needed to run to him, but she must be certain that Edmund had gone. She could only hope that he wouldn't come and seek her out back at the house. As Zach was about to close the door, she sprang to her feet. He stopped.

'Zach,' she whispered, running to him. He didn't pull her into his arms but stood back and let her into the cottage, closing the door behind him. Edmund's words were there in Zach's tense stance. She felt them too, but she wouldn't let them win. She loved him.

'I heard.' She held her hands close to her sides and took a seat at the table.

His eyes opened wide.

'Yes, possibly not all, but enough to know why you are there and I am here.'

He sat down beside the food on the table. Again he had prepared a midnight feast for them. This time there was a bowl of raspberries with the ham and bread. She fought the urge to cry. They must keep their heads.

'All is not lost,' she said.

He ran his fingers through his hair again. 'How can you say that?'

'Because Edmund knows both of us; he sees more.'

He sat opposite her. 'Nanny?'

Alice took a deep breath. 'She has not been out with us.'

'But you heard what Edmund said and I can't… can't let that happen to you.'

'I did too but there is no evidence. We must go forth carefully.' She stood.

'How?' His chin dropped down.

She flexed her neck, clearing her thoughts, pushing the fear aside. 'No more fishing for a start.'

He nodded. 'How will we communicate?'

She rubbed her hand across her mouth as she looked about. 'With feathers and flies and books if necessary.'

He rose to pace around the room. 'It could work.'

'We need time to sell the tiara, find papers, book our passage.' She took a deep breath. 'There is no plan to move me from here. I will be perfect.' She laughed. 'I will sit inside and sew and read and make flies. I will accompany Nanny on short strolls around the gardens, leaving the book of sonnets behind.'

'We need a code.' He rubbed his neck. 'I had one with Edmund as a child.'

She shook her head. 'He would know it.'

'But he won't be staying.' He paused by the fire.

She prevented herself from walking into his arms. They needed to think, to plan. 'True.'

He looked at her with eyes full of emotion. She couldn't hold back. She went to him, but stopped, keeping a distance as they could be seen in the window. 'I am still your fiancée. I will marry you and we will leave here and go to America.'

'I want that with all my heart,' he said.

'I do as well.' She turned and walked to the stairs. 'We may not have another chance. Please come and love me.'

'Yes,' he said, following her up the stairs.

The rain was heavy as she crossed the river, but the sky was brightening already. It had taken longer than they had anticipated to adapt his childhood code, but they had done it and he made a map showing where they could leave their messages. Once the boat was secured, Alice slipped along by the swimming pool. She had done this once and it would be the only way to cover her actions. Even now smoke rose from the chimneys of the house. Everything rested on her playing the role of the perfect lady. But before that, one last hurrah to cover her wet tracks.

She stripped off and dove into the lake. Her skin contracted with the cold, but she swam in big messy strokes across the water. Weed tickled her legs, reminding her of Zach's hands on her skin. She dove under and swam lower to let the plants caress her breasts. She surfaced at the steps and grabbed hold of the ladder, pulling herself out. Edmund was here. She froze.

'Good morning, Thing.' He stood by her clothes.

'Morning.' Water ran down her body as goosebumps appeared.

'Perhaps you should get dressed. As beautiful as you are naked, you know it won't incite me to passion, but I can't say the same for the gamekeeper who is on patrol because a young boy has been spotted wandering the grounds at night.' He crossed his arms.

She raced to her wet clothes and put them on as best she could. He was silent and she wanted him to speak. She twisted up her hair to put on the hat.

'You make a very pretty boy but leave the hat off,' he said.

She sent him a look.

'I don't need the gamekeeper spotting you.'

'Oh.' She curled the hat in her hands.

He ran his fingers through his hair, reminiscent of Zach's same action. 'Nanny suspects.'

'No.' Alice closed her eyes, blocking out the reality he was presenting.

He shook his head. 'Alice, you have been many things in the past, but never stupid.'

She swung towards him.

'Save the fight. You will need it to save yourself and him.'

She pressed her mouth into a line.

'Don't go defiant on me. I know you love him, and I'm not surprised.'

She began to speak but Edmund continued. 'Thing, if you love him, you will walk away. If your affair is discovered, he will be destroyed.'

Her hands clenched.

'You are a duke's daughter and he is a gillie who will never find work again. He has no other skills than a love of Shakespeare and that will not find him employment.'

She couldn't argue. Her shoulders sagged.

'That's better.' He cleared his throat. 'Nanny is peering out of her window as all nannies are wont to do. Make this look good, Thing, for all our sakes.'

Alice rolled the wet hat tighter in her hand and together they walked the last stretch to the house. The rain picked up its pace, lashing down on them. They took shelter in the loggia by the children's garden. Nanny walked out to meet them.

'Good morning.' He gave Nanny his most charming smile. 'I'm pleased I took my constitutional while the rain was kind.' He waved an elegant hand. 'I don't think we'll see any let up in this the rest of the day.'

Nanny looked across to the woods. Alice held her breath.

'No, I dare say we won't. Swimming again, Alice?' she asked, looking at the sodden clothing.

Alice nodded for she couldn't speak.

'I don't think it's advisable, do you?' Nanny arched a brow.

Again, Alice nodded.

'Change out of those wet things at once and come and see me when you are dry. The same applies to you, Edmund. You are soaked through.'

'Of course, Nanny.' He dipped his head slightly and slipped inside.

Nanny focused on Alice. 'I only hope that you haven't trodden too far, young lady.' She turned on her heel and walked back into the children's sitting room.

Alice raced to her room with her heart pounding, silently repeating the words she had said to Zach not long ago. This could still work. Today was the fifth of August and by Christmas they would be away from here and in America.

Susan stripped the wet clothes off her back without a word. Her stiff manner spoke loudly of her disapproval. She had warned her. God, how did she appear to the servants? A spoiled pampered princess of sorts. She wasn't now but she had been once. But she knew appearances could lie. So many had seen them this morning, most of the household.

Alice slipped into the hot water of the tub, letting the tears fall down her cheeks when Susan had left her in peace. This plan had to work. She would do everything in her power to make it succeed. She could be the model lady for a few months and convince them all that she would be biddable and marry a dull man with title, land and money. But she couldn't do this knowing that there was no way out. Her toes curled and her muscles clenched. She had known love. She couldn't go backward.

Constance's voice calling her name reached her before her cousin had. 'May I come in?'

'Yes.' Alice sank lower into the water.

Constance stood at the door, clutching a newspaper. 'War.'

'What?' Alice sat up.

'We are at war.' Her cousin's voice cracked on the last word.

'No.' Alice closed her eyes for a moment. In everything that had happened she had forgotten the prime minister's ultimatum. She looked at the paper in Constance's shaking hand. 'Hold it still so I can read it.' Her cousin came closer to the tub.

Great Britain Declares War on Germany

'Mummy called this morning,' Constance said, shaking her head. 'William has already signed up.'

'No.' Alice stood, and Susan appeared with a towel. 'I had hoped this wouldn't happen.'

'Lord Edmund is readying to leave,' said Susan.

'I must dress quickly.' Alice looked at Constance.

'He'll be doing the same as William.' Constance took a deep breath. 'They all will.' She left Alice to finish dressing.

As Susan fixed Alice's skirt, Alice tried not to think. She prayed they were right when they said it wouldn't last long. Sitting in front of the looking glass, she held her tears in check. Turning to Susan, she said, 'Do what you can quickly with my hair, please.' There was no time to lose. She had dallied too long in the bath.

'They will all be going, my lady.'

Alice took a deep breath in and gave Susan's hand a squeeze then raced downstairs. As she reached the hall Edmund, driving gloves in hand, stood waiting. Already he seemed different from the man she'd been with this morning.

'There you are, Thing.' He smiled. 'I'm off to the barracks at Bodmin to sign up.' He glanced out to the courtyard. Zach stood by the car, shifting his weight from one foot to the other.

'Now?' She turned from the window.

Edmund nodded. 'You left this behind.' He held the book of sonnets out to her. She focused on keeping her hand steady as she took it. It was part of the code. She turned to Zach. He held her gaze for a second then looked down.

'I think, Thing, this may be the best possible outcome. Now do buck up.' He lifted her chin as Nanny entered the hall.

'We'll all be back in no time.' He dropped his hand, giving her a penetrating glance then walked outside. She followed.

Constance raced ahead, asking, 'How many of you are going?'

'I have a car full of those with Cornish connections. I do believe there will be another group heading off to Tavistock and onto Exeter shortly.'

'Travel safe.' Nanny came out of the house and kissed his cheek. 'Do keep us posted.'

'Of course, I will.'

Alice clutched the book so tightly to her chest her fingers went white. Edmund turned and kissed Alice's cheek, whispering in her ear. 'This is best. Be good, Thing.' He gave her arm a squeeze, tapped Constance on the head and climbed into the driver's seat. The assembled men found spaces in the car. Zach was the last.

As the car pulled away, she caught his glance. There was sadness but she also sensed his excitement, their excitement. They were all going and she was standing here useless as if she didn't have arms and legs. They would have each other and she wouldn't have them.

God, she shouldn't feel like this. She should be proud of them for doing their duty, for serving king and country. For putting their lives at risk. But she wasn't. She looked around at the other women watching the car as their husbands, sons and brothers left. On their faces she saw tears and brave smiles. They weren't jealous. No, they were sad, worried and not angry. Maybe her mother was correct, Alice was awful and of no use to anyone.

Nanny led the way towards the children's garden where the three of them stood watching the car until it was gone from sight down Abbotswood Drive. She turned to Alice, studying her face. 'It is never easy to see those we love go to war.' She touched Alice's cheek and muttered under her breath, 'This couldn't have been timelier though.'

'Has anyone had breakfast?' Constance asked.

Both Nanny and Alice shook their heads.

'Not sure I have an appetite at the moment.' Nanny smiled at Constance. 'I doubt Alice does either.' She gave Constance a gentle push. 'Off you go.' She turned to Alice. 'You looked like you've seen a ghost... and—' her eyes narrowed '—perhaps you have. Go and rest. I will speak with you later.'

Alice nodded and half stumbled to her room, clutching the book to her heart. Once the door was shut and she was alone, she opened it, looking for one of the signs. The swallow feather fell onto the bed. She picked it up and slid it across her cheek. The swallow was the bird of true love. She looked at the sonnet it was placed in. It was Sonnet 116 where it had been before. She frowned. He wouldn't have given her the book back with no message but she read the sonnet.

> Let me not to the marriage of two minds
> Admit impediments. Love is not love
> Which alters when it alteration finds,
> Or bends with the remover to remove.
> O no! it is an ever-fixed mark
> That looks on tempests and is never shaken;
> It is the star to every wand'ring bark,
> Whose worth's unknown, although his height be
> taken.

He had recited this to her last night after they had made love.
Her hand shook as she pulled the folded paper from the page.

Lady of my heart,

*I have no time to write more than a few words. I must go.
This is one of the things that will bring us together. By
leaving you, I will make the way. I will not have to return
to Abbotswood when the war is over, but I will return
to you like the swallows return every spring. You are my
heart, my soul, my life.*

In haste and full of so much love, yours always,

Z xxx

His love was an ever-fixed mark. She wanted him beside her,
but she understood his decision. She stood and went to the
window. Outside the sky had cleared, the sun shone, the river
flowed and swallows flew, but her heart was in a motorcar on
its way to war and she didn't know when or how she would
hear from him again.

Chapter Thirty

Cat came into the kitchen and looked at Theo, still indignant at being left alone without food last night. Cat then complained bitterly about the lack of service here in Boatman's.

Theo laughed as she pulled the food bag out of the cabinet below the sink and poured a generous measure. After she had placed the bowl on the floor, she stroked Cat's head, thinking of what she needed to do today. Calling Karen and seeing how she was feeling post operation and apologising for any repercussions was number one on the list.

She walked outside and sat on the step, clutching a mug of coffee. The hydrangeas' blooms glowed in the dappled sunlight. Pulling out her phone it opened to the photos she had taken of the paintings. They took her breath away, even now. Her heart still ached at the thought of his short life and tragic end. She had seen his bike in the courtyard of the building. He had called the bike Galahad. It had been a detail of their time together that had been lost, until she had read a car had hit him while he was on it. He had died at the scene.

David. Through her restless night listening to the storm rage she had tossed and turned. The small doubt that she had placed in the back of her mind years ago that David was Patrick's and not Piers's wouldn't leave her. All the times when the thought had arisen, like when David had done so well in his A Level art, she had always dismissed it.

She and Patrick had taken precautions. They had made love four times but, as she reminded herself, she had slept with Piers before she went to Paris and when she returned after his confession. That time they hadn't taken precautions. They both had wanted a family so a week from the wedding it hadn't seemed important. In her mind David had to be Piers's. But there were times as he grew that she saw something that niggled. Now, having seen the portrait, she was positive. But what should she do? David was the son in Henshaw and Son. Piers would go ballistic and might even disinherit him. She should keep her own thoughts and not complicate David's life. But didn't he have the right to know?

She rose from the step and walked to the river. What had Martin said about secrets? They were better out. But what would he say about this? God, she couldn't tell him. Below the river was cloudy from the heavy rains. Across to Abbotswood a few people wandered the garden. Piers and his new wife would still be there.

When she left Swiss Cottage this morning there had been total silence in the early morning sunshine as she'd walked the riverbank, dodging fallen branches and puddles. Her boat had been full of water but still afloat. It had been a relief to return to Boatman's. Now she turned and walked back to the house. Rather than mull over David she would call Karen and apologise.

That done she began to look for a place to put the daphne

that Gayle had given her. She wanted it somewhere where the fragrance would be best appreciated so near the entrance to the cottage. She looked up to the clear sky. It was a perfect early August Sunday. Around her the garden, with the exception of the hydrangeas, was green. Now that the trees had been cut back, she might have enough light for crocosmia and maybe an agapanthus, but maybe not.

Her phone pinged. It was a text from David. There were no words. It was just a picture of Piers and his new wife who had clearly picked apart her bouquet or maybe it had been caught in the weather. She looked frightfully damp and windswept. It was perfect. No, that was mean. It was a shame. But she couldn't keep the smile off of her face as she walked into the house.

But what was David trying to tell her? Should she call him? If she did could she hold back what she knew? Her phone pinged again.

Thought I could come and see you today but it's all a bit of a disaster here. Will be in touch. Dxx

Theo walked slowly into the house and to the old oak bookcase. It was Grannie's and with a bit of elbow grease and a lot of beeswax it glowed in the morning light. She pulled her Baedeker's off the shelf. Sitting back down on the step, she stroked the faded red cover. Over the years, when in despair, she had looked at this old guide and imagined she had never left Paris. Now, knowing Patrick was gone, the light that that city always held in her mind dimmed.

Her phone rang. 'Hello.'

'Hi, it's Gayle.'

'How did it go?' Theo asked.

'I'll tell you over that drink that you definitely owe me.'

Theo laughed. 'I do owe you.'

'See you in the pub at seven.'

'Of course.' Seeing Hugo and Gayle would be something to look forward to and in the meantime she would clear some more of the bracken and not think, only work.

Gayle and Hugo sat outside the pub. The evening was warm and the air humid. The earlier wind had dropped. On the table was a wine bucket.

'I thought I was buying,' Theo said, sitting down.

'I felt I owed you both a drink for the disaster that was the Henshaw wedding.' Hugo turned to her. 'And I thought you should celebrate not being married to that man. He was the most unpleasant human I've dealt with in a long time and that's saying something.'

With her back to the river, Theo lifted the glass he had poured for her and said, 'I'll drink to that.'

'So, you are now going to tell us how on earth you married him.' Gayle eyed her.

Theo looked into her glass. This wasn't going to be easy. 'Youthful mistake.'

'Yes, but you were thirty-two years married,' Hugo said.

Theo twisted the glass in her hand. 'True, but there was a child involved.'

'Ah, yes, your son, David. Interesting.' He topped up Gayle's wine.

'How so?' Theo asked, studying him.

'Well, he reminded me of my uncle…' He paused, looking at her.

She glanced away, asking, 'Did he really?'

Hugo nodded.

'Don't leave me in the dark.' Gayle looked between them.

'Well, David is the spitting image of my uncle Patrick.'

Theo flinched. 'You didn't mention this to him, did you?'

'I did.' Hugo reached into his pocket and pulled out his wallet. 'I even showed him this.'

Theo swallowed. There was Patrick as she knew him and she assumed Hugo's father and mother. David looked like him.

Gayle peered at it. 'Doppelgänger, weird how that happens.'

'Yes,' said Theo, meeting Hugo's eyes briefly.

'He said something similar.' He put the photo back.

'Why do you carry that photo?' Theo asked.

Hugo smiled. 'It was the last time they were all together and they were all laughing and two of them are gone.'

She put her hand on his arm.

'It's you.' He said it so quietly she almost didn't hear him, but from the look on his face she didn't need to.

Theo nodded. There was no point in denying it.

'Have I missed something?' Gayle asked.

'I thought there was something about you that I knew.' He laughed.

Theo blushed and looked down at her hands.

Gayle looked at Hugo. 'I'm confused.'

'So, I think I met my cousin, my *first* cousin.'

'Yes.' Theo nodded. 'I think so.'

'Think?'

She pushed her hair behind her ears. 'I don't know.'

He nodded. 'So David has no idea.'

'No. I didn't know the connection until I stayed at your place.' She shook her head. 'I should have seen it. But to be honest it seemed unlikely.'

'Right, you two, should I go elsewhere or are you going to fill me in?' Gayle squirmed.

He looked at Gayle and smiled. 'You know the painting in my bedroom.'

She nodded and then she looked at Theo. 'Oh, you *are* a dark horse.' She laughed. 'Hugo's uncle is your son's father.'

'Gosh, you made that leap quickly.'

'But I can so see it,' Gayle said, squinting at Hugo.

Theo could see the resemblance and even the tone of voice was similar. She couldn't stick her head in the sand anymore. Theo wasn't sure how she felt having the information out in the open. But there were things she needed to say. 'It was a long time ago and I shouldn't have done what I did.'

'You weren't married then?' Gayle raised an eyebrow.

'No, but… ten days away.'

'Then you are not alone. Many people do this. My best friend did. Mind you, she didn't fall pregnant. She is still married and has never told her husband.' Gayle turned the glass in her hand. 'She just needed to be sure.'

'Hmm.' Theo pushed her hair back and said, 'I didn't know Patrick's last name.' Theo cleared her throat. 'Which sounds absolutely terrible when I say it out loud.'

Gayle's eyes opened wide. 'You never struck me as the type to be wild, free even.'

Theo laughed and looked at the darkening sky above them.

'I wasn't or at least I didn't know that side of myself. I was finishing work on my dissertation and Patrick was painting in Trocadero gardens. The rest, as they say, is history.'

'My father said Patrick never forgot you.'

Her stomach flipped. 'Oh.'

'So, you two are almost related.' Gayle looked between them. 'Can you tell me what happened?'

Theo poured herself some more wine. 'We met, we talked, we laughed, and then he wanted to sketch me.' She took a sip of wine. 'And eventually one thing led to another.' She sighed. 'Patrick was still sleeping when I left but I had to catch my flight. I planned to call off the wedding.'

'But you didn't,' Gayle said.

'No.' Theo shook her head. 'I was scared, confused even. Piers was the known and Patrick was the unknown. My father said I was suffering from nerves. My mother said I was lucky Piers would have me.'

'What?' Gayle gagged on her wine. 'He was bloody lucky to have you.' She shook her head. 'And you were stuck married to that bastard for all those years.'

'Sadly, yes, but there were some good things, like Higson Manor.' She smiled. 'All this time I've wondered about Patrick, but kept thinking that he was out there somewhere. I have been feeling bereft since I googled him.'

'I think we need more wine.' Gayle stood and went to the bar.

Theo turned to Hugo. 'I'm not sure what I should say.'

'Me either.' He smiled. 'But I am glad I finally met you, Theodora Grace.'

She blushed.

'He wrote your name on the back of the canvas and, in his journals, he wrote about you.'

'Oh God.' Theo put her hands to her face.

'Not in a bad way.' He touched her hand. 'He was never angry that you left. He'd written that you said you had to leave.'

She drew a deep breath and looked across the river to the flood plains. She was empty like they were at the moment. How did you feel the loss of someone you really didn't know?

'I do have his photos of you and all the sketches. You were a bit of a muse.'

She blushed. 'Oh God.'

He laughed and Gayle arrived.

Theo shifted a bit on the bench. 'Now, enough about my wild past. What happened post wedding?'

'Disaster at every turn, finishing with the bride wandering the grounds until one of the team found her down by Black Rock.'

'No!' Theo leaned back, trying to block the image from her mind.

'Oh yes. The groom was found asleep in the downstairs loo at three a.m.'

'Dear God,' she said. Piers always had a habit of doing that. Hugo shook his head.

'I'm so sorry.' Theo sipped her wine while her mind turned over it all.

Hugo waved his hand to dismiss her comment and asked, 'Will you tell David?'

'I don't know. More importantly I don't know what good

it would do and in fact it could make things worse for him. He is the son in Henshaw and Son.'

Hugo looked like he was about to disagree, but Gayle appeared with more wine. If Theo told David it would tell the world that her mother was right: Theo was a fool and no better than she should have been just like Grannie.

Chapter Thirty-One

1914

Alice's mind walked the riverbank while she diligently attempted sewing. Inside her was a restlessness unlike any she had ever known. Surely Edmund would be in touch soon and let them know what was happening. She stalked the cottages of the head gardener, the gamekeeper and the others who had gone off in that motorcar. The wives seemed to understand or tolerate her. They were all the same, losing their men to war. They too were powerless, and she was certain they thought it was for Edmund that she worried and she was, but Zach, dear God Zach, she worried for more. Each day she waited on the papers for news and each day she pulled a little more into herself.

'Nanny, I'm going for a walk. Would you like to join me?' she asked.

Nanny shook her head. 'Lady Constance?' She looked to Constance who was painting a watercolour of one of her butterflies.

She looked up. 'I would like to finish this.' She smiled.

'Very well. You may go on your own, Lady Alice.' Nanny's smile didn't reach her eyes. Alice took her chance but didn't race out of the room as she wished. Collecting her hat and gloves, she nodded at Burton as she left. He stood on the lawn, watching her, but she took a different route to the cottage. First climbing up through the garden, which was showing signs of the approaching autumn. The sedum had begun to colour in earnest and a few trees had started to drop leaves like they too were crying for the gardeners who would normally clear these away.

The journey across the river was easy. The water was so low she could walk across at the ford. She wove her way through the trees so she would not meet another soul and yet she still sought out Zach. Every shadow became him and she would turn and he wasn't there.

When she could, like now, she would come to the cottage and walk through the rooms and touch everything, trying to imprint it onto her like the fossils in the shell house. Upstairs she lay in the bed, remembering their last time together.

Let me not to the marriage of true minds

His voice resonated in the silence of the room. She wept until there were no more tears. Her logical brain told her that they were not far, only in Bodmin. They were not yet soldiers; they would not be sent out yet. Those who knew the world of war and fighting would go first. With all her prayers she challenged God to make the war short so that all those men signing up to do their duty in droves would never step on foreign soil.

A chill crept over her and she rose with one last sniff of his pillow. His scent lingered there. Lavender and woodsmoke touched with rosemary. She pulled the linen from the pillow and brought it with her. She stopped at the bedroom door, searching for the old looking glass but not finding it. Downstairs her glance was immediately drawn to the window and the pane where they had etched their initials. Its presence here had to be enough. It would stand as witness to their love, their promises.

She paused at the door, knowing her heart would lead her back here while he was away from her, but she must not cause suspicion. Nanny was eagle-eyed at the moment. But with more men gone from the estate this past month, Nanny worried less about Alice walking on her own.

Their lives here had taken on a quiet simplicity. In the evenings, Constance had taken to knitting socks. She had seen some article that said they would be needed, and Alice had never seen the girl happier. She was purpose driven in her speed, with socks appearing from her knitting needles at a tremendous rate.

Turning about the cottage sitting room, Alice's glance rested on the empty fire. Only a half-burnt log lay in the grate. It was a sad sight and she didn't need any more sadness. She was cocooned in it as it was.

Crossing the river, the house looked the same even though there was only Burton and an elderly footman left. Even the chef had gone and one of the maids had stepped into the role. Alice took solace helping in the kitchen gardens; working them she found some peace.

Her steps slowed when she saw Constance waving wildly.

'Edmund is on the telephone.'

Alice raced to it, nearly knocking Constance off her feet in her rush past.

'Hello,' she said, her chest tight.

'Thing, I thought I wasn't going to get to speak to you. I have been put through the inquisition from Nanny,' he said.

'How are you?' she asked, wanting to say so much more.

'Fine and so are *all* from Abbotswood,' he said.

She began breathing properly again. 'Thank you.'

'Any day we will be on our way north for training. Bodmin is a bit overrun.'

'*All* of you?' she asked.

'Yes, Thing, *all* of us.' He laughed. 'I will do my best to be in touch. You will write to me too.'

'Of course.' She couldn't write to Zach. If she dared, he couldn't reply. It was a terrible situation. She couldn't even sell the tiara because she didn't know where he had buried it. It was now lost until his return. She placed the phone down and walked into the hallway. Nanny was standing five feet away. Had she been listening? Nanny gave her a small smile and continued down the hallway.

Alice watched her go. Once she was out of sight, Alice raced to her room and dug out Zach's letter from its hiding place and read it again. Then went onto her knees and prayed aloud, 'Please let the war be swift and may all of them come home safe.'

15 September 1914

Dearest Sylvia,

I'm sorry I haven't written. With the outbreak of war and the need to keep everyone's spirits up, I have found that I have not been able to put pen to paper. Lord Edmund left here on the fifth of August with a motor car full of men, including Zachariah Carne, the gillie. This could not have come at a better time. He was a charming boy and a good gillie. But Lady Alice took to fishing again and she formed an attachment to him. I have been concerned and my concern has been proved correct.

Things have come to a crisis here as I had feared they might. However, I believe there will be a successful resolution for both your old charge and for mine.

You will agree that this will be the best in these circumstances.

I hope you are well, and I will endeavour to be a better correspondent.

Your loving sister,
Eve

PS My asthma has eased with these awful cigarettes. Have you tried them?

Chapter Thirty-Two

Theo sat on the quay. She had laid out a picnic rug and set up a meal for herself and Martin, who was due. Lady Alice filled her thoughts as she looked across at Abbotswood. It appeared that Lady Alice had had an affair with Zachariah Carne, which at the time would have been more than scandalous for many reasons. She was a young unmarried woman of the aristocracy and he was the under gillie on the estate. She must have risked everything to be with him. What courage that must have taken? But obviously something had gone wrong. Beside her were the letters she had found; Zach's sense of betrayal was so vivid in them that Theo felt the loss herself.

'Hello?' Martin's voice reached her.

'Down by the quay,' she called. Should she tell Martin her dilemma? He wouldn't tell her what to do. He would listen.

Martin dropped down on the blanket beside her and poured himself a glass of wine. His eyes were shining.

'What's up?' she asked.

'Sorry I'm late.'

'No worries.' She smiled. 'You look happy.'

'I met with the MOD this morning. It's a match,' he said.

'What?'

'We are St Loys! Get us.' He raised his glass.

'It's true?'

'No lying with genes.'

Theo took a sip of wine and looked at Abbotswood. That was part of their history. Penhale was part of their history. Then she saw a couple with a pushchair, heading down to the river. Even without being able to see details, Theo recognised Piers. Part of her wanted to leap up and shout that Martin was an earl or almost an earl and they were great-great-grandchildren of a duke. Then she closed her eyes. These things had never mattered to her and they never would. The couple opposite appeared happy and she was glad for that. She was happy too.

'You've gone silent, sis.'

She nodded. 'That's Piers, his wife and daughter.'

'Oh.' He tilted his head and studied her. 'Hurts?'

She laughed. 'Actually it's a relief.'

'That's good to hear. From where I sat it looked like the love had died years ago.'

Theo laughed drily. 'That obvious?'

'To me, yes, but to the outside world the two of you put on a good act.'

Theo took a deep breath. 'I guess we did.' She sipped her wine. 'I owed it to him.'

Martin shook his head.

'No, I did, really.'

'He was a lying cheating toad from the out,' he said.

'True, but he was good to me and… David.'

Martin sat upright. 'What are you not telling me?'

She sent him a look.

'I can tell by a mile when you are hiding something.' His glance didn't leave her.

'Like my journals.'

He nodded.

'Did I tell you the bloody cheek Mum had reading my old journals and then almost blackmailing me to send them to me.'

He laughed. 'No, you didn't, but don't tell me she read the one of you in Paris.'

'Oh God.' Theo closed her eyes for a moment. 'You read that?'

'I've read all your journals, each scandalous detail, I'm afraid. It scarred me for life, and I had to become a priest just to do penance.'

She hit him lightly. 'For spying.'

'No, for all the stuff I learned!' He chuckled. 'Let's see, there was Tommy and there was Fred and then there was the part that interested me most – the bit with Susie.'

Theo dropped her head in her hands.

'But what struck me most was that you were going to break it off with Piers because of a bloke name Patrick in Paris but you didn't. That was the last entry I read.' He shook his head. 'I waited for the nuclear fallout so that I could be the golden boy, the focus of all parental love, but you went ahead and married Piers.' He sipped his wine. 'That I never understood.'

'Well. Long story short Piers confessed he was sleeping with his father's secretary and asked would I forgive him.'

'And you did.' He slowly shook his head. 'And you felt guilty, therefore you went through with it.'

Theo laughed bitterly. 'Well, Mum always said I was a fool.'

'Never bloody believed it until now.' He shook his head. 'Is David Piers's?'

Theo's hand went to her throat. 'What makes you ask that?'

'Well, he doesn't look like him aside from the dark hair and he doesn't look like me or Dad.'

Theo looked down.

'I don't know is the answer.' Theo shook her head. 'He should be Piers's as I took precautions with Patrick.'

Martin cast her a sideways glance. 'But you have your doubts.'

She nodded.

'What are you going to do?' he asked.

'Short of handing David a DNA test there is little I can do, and it would cause more hurt.'

'Best not to keep secrets and David is an adult.'

Theo pursed her lips.

'I won't tell you what to do.' He sipped his wine, studying her.

'I know that.'

'Good, but I will say David deserves the truth,' he said.

'You beast.' She pursed her mouth, thinking about hitting him.

'Always, but don't hit me. I need to be filmed again tomorrow,' he said.

'Filmed?' she asked.

'Yes, a production company is making a programme for Armistice Day and that's what I was doing this morning.'

'You ham.'

'Absolutely. Me, I love a crowd all looking up at me.'

She laughed.

'They'd like to film you too.' He tilted his head and made puppy dog eyes.

She grinned but said, 'No.'

'Come on, sis. You're not bad for an old bag.'

'It's a wonder I love you.'

'But you do. Come. It will be fun. The filming is at Penhale. It turns out your gillie here—' he tapped the letter sitting on the blanket '—was originally from Penhale.'

'Really.' Theo looked through the trees to the cottage. 'OK, I'll come but may bolt at the last minute.'

Martin picked up the last letter. 'Have you read them all?'

'Not yet. They're deeply emotional.'

'May I?' he asked.

She nodded.

Martin opened the thin paper and read aloud.

20 April 1918

My lady of the river,

The morning light is just beginning. All is silent except for the men snoring. Water from the rain runs in little streams down the banks of the trench. At my feet the pool is brown and thick. The rats swim well, and we take bets on which one will first reach the piece of bread we placed out.

I don't know why I am telling you this. I don't know why I am writing to you at all. But I don't know how not to. Despite hating you, you are in my heart and my head and I talk to you all the time. Somehow that makes its way to my pencil and words appear on the page. You don't want to know about the rat races or the mud. You don't want me at all. It was a game, you said. No, you didn't use those words. Yours were much prettier.

But what of me. You ripped the heart from me. And, as I write this, I know exactly what that looks like. I have seen the heart blown out of a man along with other bits. I have seen the parts strewn on the ground. That is what I felt and still feel. How does one feel without a heart? With difficulty. Everything takes longer to penetrate my thoughts, especially beauty. The horror moves in quickly but passes through. I do not hold onto it. It does not matter if I live or die. I have lost you.

Z

Martin lowered the letter. 'I see what you mean.'

Theo shook her head. 'His words cut to the heart and I believe they were written to Lady Alice.'

Martin folded the letter carefully. 'Interesting.' He paused, taking a sip of wine as he looked across the river. Theo had often wondered what went on in his clever head but she could never tell.

'Do you think we should let Jeanette know about the DNA?' he asked.

Theo snorted with laughter. He had proved her correct again. 'If we don't, I think we will both be in the doghouse!' Theo handed Martin a plate. 'She'll want to come tomorrow too.'

'She'll steal all the limelight.' He grinned.

'Exactly what I was thinking.' Theo stroked Cat's head, who'd come to investigate why they weren't eating the chicken as she would like to.

Chapter Thirty-Three

1914

It was the first day of September. Leaves had begun to turn in earnest and here at Abbotswood the colours were jewel bright. Each evening at dusk Alice watched the swallows gather over the river feasting on the abundant insect life. Fish rose to enjoy the plenty as well. No one fished the river. Her uncle was in London. Her cousin, Charles, had signed up as well. Her mother was making twittering noises about lost chances and that Alice would never find a husband.

Pulling a long stem of grass, she twirled it in her fingers before she adjusted her skirt. It was tight despite her lack of interest in food and she was sick with worry all the time. The first reports back from France weren't good. Thankfully Zach and Edmund were still training in Aldershot. She tried hard to understand all the enthusiasm, but she couldn't.

However, Edmund's letter had made her laugh with the hardships and antics. She doubted the antics were true, but he knew his letters would lift her spirits and they always contained some news of Zach. Nothing that anyone else reading it would question. She stopped under the large oak and pulled the letter from her pocket to reread it.

Dear Thing,

Training is rolling on here. We have mastered marching. I can see you laughing but it's rather harder than you think, especially when you are attempting to achieve perfection with hundreds. Legs tangle, toes trip – many days it is like watching a comedy. However, I am pleased to report that all our Cornish men are a dab hand with a rifle. Of course, the gamekeeper is the best shot but the rest of us are not far behind in marksmanship. It is good to have my horse here now. Magpie is a constant comfort and I find myself gravitating to her company a great deal. I find Zach does as well. He's training to be my batman and he can keep an eye on me.

The mood of all the men is buoyant and the old hand officers that are working with us are a good lot. Many of them served in the Boer War and have tales to tell. Mostly they keep it light but some evenings the mood drifts down. Thankfully that is not often and usually only when the port comes out.

I am heading up to London shortly to sort the full kit of uniforms. I know you are still confined to quarters, which is a shame for I would love to see you and tell you all the news in person.

I'm hoping that there may be a chance of escape and I can come to Cornwall and then onto Abbotswood. Until then stay out of trouble or at least attempt to.

Yours,
Edmund

She folded it again and was putting it in her pocket when she saw Nanny heading her way. No chance of slipping across to the cottage. Although well-hidden during the day, she still clung to his old pillowcase each night despite his scent no longer being there.

'Lord Edmund's letter?' Nanny came to her side.

Alice nodded.

'He is well?' Nanny waited.

'Yes, he tells me the gamekeeper came tops in the marksmanship,' she said.

Nanny raised an eyebrow. 'And what of the gillie?'

She stepped backwards. 'He didn't say how well he shot, simply that all the Cornish men acquitted themselves well on the range.'

'I see.' Nanny's gaze narrowed.

'He says he'll be in London soon.' London was as far away to her as the moon these days. She felt less call to it than the bright orb in the sky.

'Uniform.' Nanny stared at the folded page.

Alice dropped her hand. She could offer the letter to Nanny; it might be easier. 'Yes. And he may be able to make a visit to Penhale and to stop here he hopes.'

'It will be good to see him. He is a good boy.' Nanny smiled.

'He's not a boy at twenty-one.' She shook her head.

'I think of you all as children.'

Drawing a deep breath, Alice began back to the house with the word children gnawing into her thoughts. A wave of nausea hit her. She made it to the cover of the shrubbery where she heaved up her morning tea and continued to dry heave for a while. Nanny rubbed her back as she used to when she was a small child. The action brought tears to her eyes.

When the heaving had stopped, Nanny led her to her room and tucked her into bed. She then brought her weak tea and a dry biscuit all the while saying nothing. Her face showed only love. Alice settled back into the bed, concerned at Nanny's silence, but despite her worries she slept even though it was before noon.

On waking she still felt unwell and she could no longer pretend it was only a stomach flu. Once on her feet a wave of nausea took over to confirm the situation. Susan appeared with a basin. The heaving subsided and Susan handed her a damp cloth. Alice wiped her face not wanting to accept that she was pregnant. She had missed her monthly and, even accounting for normal irregularity, she couldn't deny the truth any longer.

'What are you going to do, my lady?' The concern on Susan's face was almost comical.

'I don't know.' Alice sat on the bed and wrapped her arms around herself, glancing at Susan. Alice was carrying Zach's child. Her heart swelled with love. Their love had made a child. She closed her eyes. This was the worst possible thing. Now was not the time. Zach belonged to the army now. He couldn't desert. He couldn't rescue her. Dear God, what had she done? 'What would you do?'

'I'd marry him.'

Alice laughed bitterly. 'And that is the difference between us.' Alice smiled sadly. 'You have the freedom to marry whom you wish.'

'I do, my lady, but even so, once I married I could not be a lady's maid.'

'True.' Nothing came without a price.

'However, I could become a housekeeper.' Susan smiled kindly. 'Isn't there something you can do?'

Alice rose to her feet and Susan took her arm to steady her. If Susan knew then Nanny knew, and it wouldn't be long before everyone else knew. Time was not on her side. She was under no illusions what would happen if her mother and her uncle discovered her state.

At the small writing desk in the corner of the room she sat. There was only one person she could confide in, Edmund.

1 September 1914
Abbotswood

Dearest Edmund,

I hope you are well and enjoying army life. Things have taken an interesting turn here and a most urgent situation has arisen. I could use your assistance immediately. If there was any possibility of you visiting Abbotswood as swiftly as possible it might prove to avert dire results.

Always yours,
Thing xx

For the past few days she had avoided everyone except Susan. Alice didn't want to see Nanny or even Constance. Edmund had replied and would visit Abbotswood today. She knew what she had to do. This was her problem to solve.

Once safely inside the shell house she shut the door

behind her, hoping it would deter anyone from interrupting her. A warm light filtered in through the stained-glass rondels and the light caught the crystals of amethyst, quartz, and iron pyrites. Shells from faraway places and local were dotted about. It was a place of wonder.

She touched her mouth, remembering Zach's kisses. Did he still think of her or had the hard work and long hours of training pushed their love from his mind? No, they wouldn't. Just like fossils on the walls he was imprinted on her soul, she was on his. She sat on the bench where they made that fly together. Now they had made a child. She rose, left the shell house and her dreams behind. Her future and that of her child was what she needed to make now.

At luncheon Alice had not been able to hold down any food or liquid, her worry at Edmund's imminent arrival mixed with the baby sickness. She had no idea what to say to him. She struggled with her anger that she couldn't marry the man she was promised to, the man she had given her heart to and her dire predicament. If only they had run away then.

At the sound of the automobile arriving Alice went to the hall, her mouth dry and her thoughts racing. This was the right thing to do, for her child, herself and she hoped for Edmund. Her heart stilled as Edmund strode into the hall in his uniform. Handsome didn't begin to express his beauty. The uniform suited him, highlighting his shoulders and slim waist. He grinned at her. 'Come on, Thing, nothing is that bad.' He bent his head and kissed her cheek and slipped his arm through hers. 'Now let's take a walk on this fine September day.'

She nodded and followed blindly out into the warm

sunshine. Edmund's arm was steady and without speaking they strolled up into the garden away from the river and eventually stopped on one of the bridges crossing the stream. He lifted her chin. 'Look at me, Thing.'

She did as he instructed.

'Is it what I think?'

Alice nodded.

'I know whose child you carry, and you cannot marry him no matter how much your wild and loving heart tells you that you can.'

Alice pressed her lips together. This was harder than she expected. All last night she had tossed and turned and rehearsed what she would say. Now finding words was proving difficult. 'Edmund, I know this is most unusual—' she drew a breath '—but will you marry me?' She dared to look at his face before she continued. 'I know it's not what you wanted, it's not what I wanted, but it might be a solution for us both.'

'A solution.'

'Yes, a solution. You will have to marry someday and provide an heir.'

He nodded with a look of distaste on his face.

'I cannot marry my child's father though I want that more than anything but I now have a child to protect.'

'Thing.'

'We love each other but not as lovers. We both have secrets and there is no one else I would trust my secret to than you.' She looked up at him. 'Will you marry me?'

'Trust you to do this the other way around.' He laughed. 'As you knew I would, I read between the lines and had come prepared to ask you.' He pushed a curl from her face. 'But in typical Thing manner you have asked me.'

'Will you?'

'Oh, Thing, I know this is not what you want at all, but it is best.' He stroked her cheek. 'We don't need you committed.'

She shook her head. Part of her couldn't believe her mother would do that to her, but she would. Her uncle might insist for the sake of the family name.

'I had hoped to avoid marrying, and this of course would leave the earldom high and dry without a legitimate heir.' He rolled his eyes.

She cast him a sideways glance and he nodded.

'So, by marrying you, Thing, you give me an heir without the difficulty of begetting it myself.'

She looked down at the stream flowing under the bridge. Everything was rushing past her and she had nothing to hold onto. But Edmund was here as he had been in childhood. 'I will marry you, Thing, and as I anticipated the issue I have already asked your uncle's permission.'

She opened her mouth to speak to express her thanks but Edmund said, 'I suppose by marrying me you will be as free as it is possible for you to be.'

She swung around and looked up at him. 'Free?'

'Free as possible. You will have lovers and so will I. We will remain the best of friends.' He took her hand. She looked up into Edmund's eyes. They were smiling and full of kindness and love. 'And for my own vanity, may I ask you properly?'

She laughed and nodded.

He bent down on one knee. 'Will you marry me, Thing, and do me the honour of becoming my wife?'

She lifted the corner of her mouth in a half smile. 'I suppose I must as we tempted fate when you kissed me all those years ago.'

'Ah yes, we did.' He rose and pulled her into his arms, wrapping her in a bear hug. 'I will do my best for you and I will look after Zach for you.'

Alice laid her head against Edmund's heart and she listened to the steady beat. He was a good man and she was lucky. But that didn't stop her tears from soaking his uniform.

Chapter Thirty-Four

Susan packed the last of Alice's things except for Beatrice's wedding dress. Alice looked on it with distaste; she would have preferred to have simply worn one of her own dresses. But with one look from Nanny she hadn't argued and smiled politely to thank her aunt for her kindness.

It had rained since sunrise, suiting her mood, but now it had stopped. She longed, no needed, to take some fresh air. From her window she looked across to the southern bank. The cottage lay there awaiting her, but she had not been alone for one minute since Edmund's visit only days ago. Nanny had been hovering that day when they returned to the house as if she had known what had taken place. Her broad smile showed relief and Alice felt that too, but it was tempered with grief. Her dreams were dead. No Zach. No California with votes for women and men. No freedom. Today she would become Lady Alice St Loy, not Mrs Zachariah Carne.

The wedding had been arranged with haste. The war provided the perfect excuse. Edmund had been granted special leave. The ceremony was to be held in the private chapel at Penhale today. Before they could start fussing over her, she raced down the stairs and out into the garden. She walked deep into the woods wanting a moment to mourn what could now never be. There on the woodland floor she picked up a swallow feather. Last night as the twilight came the swallows fed before their long journey south. When they returned she wouldn't be at Abbotswood. She would be in Penhale or London. But her heart would return here always.

A showy male pheasant started in the undergrowth. He then made a poor attempt at flying, leaving behind a tail feather. She collected and clutched the two feathers tight in her fist. With deliberate steps she made her way to the kitchen garden where she found some rosemary. She would miss this too. Holding the feather and the rosemary buried in her skirts, she walked back to her room to find her mother and Nanny waiting.

It was time. She smiled briefly at her mother and turned to her bouquet on her dressing table. It held beautiful blue hydrangea blooms with spikes of blue and white veronica flowers. In amongst them she tucked the two feathers and the rosemary. They were mostly invisible and only she would know they were there.

'Stop dawdling, Alice, or we shall be late.' Her mother tapped her toe three times on the floor. Alice turned and let Susan begin her work. When the task was complete Susan gave her hand an encouraging squeeze and said, 'You look beautiful, my lady.'

'Thank you, Susan.' Alice turned to the looking glass. The only thing to mar her appearance were the dark smudges under her eyes.

'Alice, where is your grandmother's tiara?' her mother asked, running her hands along the lace of the veil. 'I looked for it in London but it wasn't there.'

Alice froze. Of course, today was the day she could wear it, but she wasn't the winner today. She shook her head.

'I asked your maid and she said it was here but she hadn't seen it in a while.' Her mother scowled. 'I do wonder if one of the staff hasn't taken it as they headed to war.'

Alice swallowed. 'I'm sure it's nothing of the sort and I have misplaced it.'

'Never mind. Use these.' She picked up clips with large pearls and handed them to Susan who secured the veil in place. With pearls roped around her neck, she was ready to end one life and begin another.

Penhale glowed in the September sunshine. Under foot, fallen leaves crunched and the whole of the estate that hadn't gone to war had turned up to celebrate Edmund's marriage. Alice hadn't expected that. Her palms sweated in their gloves and she tightened her grip on the bouquet as she walked to the chapel on her uncle's arm. Closing her eyes for a moment she thought of Zach. It should be him. Her heart longed for him and it would always be his. She raised her head and smiled at those standing outside in the hall courtyard. She had to do this, and she had to do it convincingly.

It took a moment for her eyes to adjust to the lower light in the chapel. Every pew was filled. Her glance flew over them to Edmund who stood proud in his uniform. He gave her a smile and a wink. The music changed and her uncle led her the short distance to the altar. There he handed her to Edmund who whispered, 'Hello, Thing, glad you made it.'

She suppressed a laugh. The look on the vicar's face was earnest. She couldn't tell if he approved of this match or not.

Maybe it was the haste in which it had been arranged. But weddings were happening everywhere she heard. The war went on and men were leaving in droves. Edmund had assured her that they weren't heading to France yet, but his leave was over tomorrow.

She didn't think she could go through with the farce if it wasn't for him. He paled when the vicar asked if any knew why they shouldn't be married. Alice didn't dare look towards the congregation, but she heard the shuffling. She kept her gaze on Edmund. Once the vicar spoke again his stance relaxed. No one else would have seen it but she had. As the vicar turned to Edmund, Alice looked behind him at the stained-glass window with the St Loy family crest, three hares circling, all linked. The child within her was the third hare.

The vicar said, 'Wilt thou have this woman to be thy wedded wife, to live together after God's ordinance in the holy estate of Matrimony? Wilt thou love her, comfort her, honour, and keep her, in sickness and in health; and, forsaking all other, keep thee only unto her, so long as ye both shall live?

'I will.' Edmund's voice was clear and strong. His glance didn't leave her as the vicar asked her to commit to Edmund. She took a breath and clearly said, 'I will.'

The vicar went on and Edmund held her hand in his as he promised to love and cherish her until death parted them. She closed her eyes for a moment. She had made these promises to one man already, although not in the eyes of a congregation but in the eyes of God who sees all. She stumbled on the words but made it through them. Edmund's fingers tightened on hers for a moment.

He placed the ring on her finger, saying, 'With this

ring I thee wed, with my body I thee worship, and with all my worldly goods I thee endow: in the name of the Father, Son and Holy Ghost. Amen.'

He held her hand steady as they kneeled. A wave of nausea hit her, and he kept her upright through the rest of the service. They walked down the aisle past her mother, his parents and her uncle and aunt. Constance and Nanny sat side by side. Nanny beamed but Constance was solemn.

Outside the chapel they were showered in petals as they processed to the great hall where the wedding breakfast was laid out. Garlands had been made with autumnal flowers and draped from the beams. It was spectacular.

She longed to sit down but she and Edmund and his parents were ushered out into the main house. They were arranged on a sofa and the photographer went to work. The first picture was of the four of them and then of Alice and Edmund only. It was all contrived and her face would look frozen in them. Nanny waltzed in with a glass of water. Alice drank it, grateful to her for the kindness.

Heading back into the hall, her new father-in-law, the Earl St Loy, took her arm for a moment and said, 'We cannot say how delighted we are about this marriage.' He smiled down on her and she shivered. There was something in his eyes she didn't care for. She wouldn't dwell on it as Edmund took her arm and everyone stood as they entered. He leaned down and said, 'Not the wedding breakfast you always imagined.'

She laughed. 'I suppose not; if I had imagined one at all it would have been in London.'

He led them to their seats. This was going to be difficult. She needed to eat enough not to cause any concern from anyone watching her. This was all a show. Edmund made it appear easy. He carried off the man head over heels in love well. There was a toast and then meeting and greeting of so many people from the estate. Thankfully the great and good hadn't been included due to the short time.

The sun had set by the time she and Edmund could flee. He led her up to a suite of rooms that she didn't know. The landscape out of the windows was no more than shadowy shapes. She sank on the bed.

'Your maid will be here in a moment to help you and I've asked for a light meal to be sent up.'

She looked up at him. He was studying her bouquet. 'Blue hydrangea for heartfelt emotion, veronica for fidelity, rosemary for remembrance, the swallow's feather for true love and the pheasant for...'

'You, or maybe good luck, I think.'

He smiled. 'This marriage is good luck.' He picked up one of her feet and unbuckled the shoe, giving her foot a rub. She sighed with contentment. He took the other one off and applied the same soothing motion to it. 'Well, Lady Alice St Loy, you are now free.'

'I'm a married woman and you say I am free.'

'I do and I shall not trouble you and in time you will take lovers, maybe even...' His voice trailed away.

She shook her head. He kissed the top of her head as the maid tapped on the door. He let her in and disappeared into the dressing room, returning once she was in her night gown and he in his dressing gown.

A tray of soup, bread and cheese arrived along with a bottle of wine and some tea. They sat opposite each other in armchairs. Alice was too weary to eat much but did manage some. Edmund sat cradling his wine glass, studying her in the fire light. 'You're exhausted.'

She nodded. There was no sense in pretending otherwise.

'Hop into bed. I'll sleep next door.'

She frowned. 'I think if we are going to make this appear real you will need to lie beside me tonight and be here when they light the fires.'

'Can you stand it, Thing?' he asked.

She laughed. 'Yes, I can. I might even find it comforting.' She stifled a yawn then went to stand behind him. Resting a hand on his shoulder, she saw his birth mark. Years ago she had made a matching mark on the other side of his neck in ink and told him that was where his wings would go. She touched it, saying, 'Thank you for being my guardian angel.'

She climbed into bed and when he'd finished his wine, he joined her. Holding out an arm, he said, 'Come closer, Thing.'

She curled into his side and fell asleep.

Chapter Thirty-Five

1915

As Alice had done every day since her marriage in September last year, she walked. She walked to forget, to silence her fears, to weary her body, but mostly to bury her hope. On a bright, warm, late-May day like today, hope could bubble to the surface and she had to be wary of that. Spring was rampant about her. Hawthorn bloomed in the hedges as she skirted the field. The white flowers were at first sweet to her nose, but as she came closer to them the sickly smell of death lingered in the air.

Edmund and the sixth service battalion of the Duke of Cornwall's Light Infantry were leaving for France soon. He couldn't say when, but his restlessness in these few days leave for her son John's christening told its story. Once so open with her, he now withheld more and more. Right now he was with his mother. His father had gone back to London last night but Clarisse had stayed on. She would leave at noon and Edmund shortly thereafter.

Then her life would fall into the rhythm it had found the past months. Of walking, learning about the estate, and evenings with Nanny and Constance. In a strange way it appeared as if nothing had changed except their location and the arrival of John six weeks ago. His birth had brought home the finality of her dreams and had opened her heart wider than she'd thought possible. That squirming scrap of humanity had changed her forever. John had taken her broken heart and smashed it to pieces with a love so huge, so painful, so all-consuming that it had reconstructed it differently.

Nothing looked the same, especially not herself. No preparation could have readied her for the reversal of her world. Once she'd been first, now she was last. Finally it was as it should be and yet... Constance was still passionate about bugs and she was diligent in her studies aided by an old Oxford don who had retired to the village. He was impressed with her swift uptake. Alice was as well but she didn't know how long this would last. With each letter from her brothers, or from Beatrice who was working with the Red Cross, Constance itched to be a part of things, but at fourteen she was best kept here away from the war. But truthfully the war was here. The absence of men brought it home daily with the empty spaces where they should be, whether at the table or in the fields.

Edmund had changed. Small differences that only those who knew him well would see. He laughed less, and when he did it wasn't with the joy that used to be there. The mischief in his eyes had dulled. Yet his body was stronger and she suspected his heart bigger. They hadn't spoken of Zach, but Jedidiah Carne had asked Edmund directly about his sons. Edmund recounted funny tales of their training and assured the old man his boys were well. But she doubted Zach was fine. Hour after hour, she tried to imagine what he must think of her. If he felt anything at all. He would be angry. She had betrayed him. Given a few moments with him she could explain. No longer could she put her own wants and needs first; she had a responsibility to this child, their child. John had to be everything now and he was.

God, how she'd struggled with it. She loved John more than she ever could have imagined and yet part of her was ashamed at how much she resented him when she had carried him in her womb. This tormented her. Every second she looked at her son she loved him, loved him for himself, loved him for his father and yet he was the reason she could never be with his father. As much as she had tried to keep that from her mind it wouldn't go.

If this was what she was feeling, how must Zach feel? She reached the top of the hill and paused to catch her breath. Below the land fell down to the Tamar and from this high point she could see Plymouth Sound. Above her swallows flew and her heart sank. She must love her son and be the perfect wife to Edmund. She owed it to them both. Sitting down on a fallen tree, she placed her head in her hands.

If she could tell Zach she still loved him with everything in her then maybe she could do her duty. It wouldn't be trapped inside her like an exotic bird at the London Zoo, wanting to fly but with no room. If she could explain he would understand. From her pocket she pulled out the letter she had written last night. It was not the first but the others she had destroyed.

Dear Zach,

There is so much I want to say. The most important is my love has not changed. Despite how things may appear to you I love you still. I have never stopped.

But our son John has changed everything. Yes, he is your son. Edmund saved me, saved you, saved John. He gave John a name. Edmund is my friend but not my lover. There are so many things I wish for, that I dream of nightly, but that is all they can be for John is now first. I will love you always and I will love your son and raise him to be a man you are proud of.

There is no sense now in wishing for things to be different. I am trying every day to make the now that I have the best it can be. I want the same for you. Every night I go on my knees and pray for your safe return.

Stay safe and know that you are loved and always will be.

Forever yours,
Ali xx

She folded it again and would burn it on her return to the house. Sending it wouldn't be fair since Zach could not reply. It would do no good. Nothing could be changed now. No, she couldn't write. She must hold this all inside. It must remain a secret. Not for her sake but for John and for Edmund. In Nanny's words she had been selfish, reckless and foolish. And she had been. She dropped her head into her hands again. Her life had no room for those things anymore.

Through her fingers she saw khaki-covered legs, a soldier on leave walking through the Cornish countryside at its best. The aroma of rosemary reached her. Zach. She leapt to her feet but didn't go any further towards him.

'Nanny Roberts said I would find you here.' His voice was

flat. She scanned his face, absorbing every detail. Her fingers twitched, wanting to feel him.

A cold breeze raced across her skin, pulling up the hair on her neck caressing the place that he loved to kiss her. She had longed for this moment and now he was here in front of her. All the things she thought she would say evaporated with the look in his eyes. She had expected anger and sadness but never pity. It undid her.

'Lady Alice.' He performed a mocking bow. 'Let me offer you felicitations on your marriage and the birth of your... son.' He held a small bunch of sweet violets out to her.

She took them and their fingers touched. Her breath stilled. His hand snapped away and he turned on his heel.

'Zach.' She grabbed his arm. He stopped and he turned. His eyes narrowed, assessing her, but with the sun behind him his expression was unreadable. She couldn't say she loved him; he would pity her more. She could take anger or even hate but not this. She drew a breath; her hand shoved the letter declaring her undying love deeper into her pocket. She knew what she had to do. 'It was never going to work,' she said, her stomach formed a tight ball.

'You could have said that at the start.' He stepped closer.

'I... I might...' she began, her voice fading away as his glance narrowed.

'I would have lain with you. How could I not?' He lifted a curl off her cheek and let it wrap around his fingers as she had around him. He studied it then pulled away. The curl tugged then sprung back and slapped her cheek. 'But I wouldn't have loved you. Love made it different... different for me, my lady.' The last words were not said as a caress as in the past. 'You wouldn't understand that.'

He was wrong, but the air in her lungs had left her as if he had punched her. She cast away the images of them together, his mouth on hers, his body on hers and their promises. But the more she tried not to see them, the more they came crashing in, knocking everything out of her head. Her glance rested on his mouth. Its flat line looked like his son's in a sulk. She lifted her head and straightened her spine. 'It was never meant to be real.'

'Real?' He grabbed her arms.

She held in the squeal of pain.

'This…' He kissed her hard and with such force her teeth cut her inner lip. When she felt a softening in him, he pulled away. 'That was real. Not your empty promises. Not a new life. That was nothing but fairy tales.'

Despite the pain in her arms, she hurt not there but in her heart. She closed her eyes for a second then opened them and said, 'It was all playing. I was always going to marry a peer.'

He bowed his head and pulled his forelock, saying, 'Maybe that is true, but you will find that this one doesn't do for you in bed what I did.' He turned and left.

Alice watched his shoulders rigid in the uniform, until he was out of sight. She raced after him, clutching the letter, then stopped. She couldn't go to him. She rubbed her arms where the flesh was bruising and swallowed down the metallic taste of blood. She wouldn't remember this. She would force it out of her head and keep only the memories of the loving gillie who had taken her heart.

Praying urgent words to keep him safe, she dragged her

feet through the fields to Penhale and her duty, knowing the door to Zach's love had closed forever and that her mother had indeed been correct. Alice was not good enough. If she had been, she never would have broken Zach's heart. She would have known like all fairy tales, it should stay in your mind, or on the pages of a book, or in your heart, not played out hurting someone else.

Alice stepped back from the window, hiding herself in the curtain. Below, Edmund stood with five men from his regiment including Zach. On her return from the walk, Nanny had informed her that the men including Zach had arrived last night and would be leaving with Edmund shortly. Orders had arrived. Nanny had studied Alice's face but Alice had given nothing away. But she hadn't expected to see Zach again after their encounter. She rubbed her arms, wincing at the bruises. The pain was good. It matched her feelings. She dropped her hands and walked from the window. John would be up from his nap shortly and she looked forward to the quiet time with him. Holding him, she held his father the only way she could.

'We are off in a moment.' Edmund stood by the door.

'You're heading to France, aren't you?'

Edmund studied her in silence for a moment then said, 'It's likely I won't survive this war and then, dear, dear Thing, you will be free.'

She shook her head.

He walked close. 'As a widow, Thing, you will finally be free as I will be in death, and a death that will make even my parents proud.'

'No.' She shook her head violently.

'Yes, you have given me a gift, an heir, and I can give you freedom.' He turned the ring on her finger. The one he'd placed there a few months before.

'But...'

'No buts. I am off to war and you are now my wife, but you have always been my friend.' He kissed her forehead and took her hand in his. 'I am only sorry that you can't have the love you deserve.' Then he smiled. 'But you have known love.' He squeezed her hands. 'And that is some comfort.' He looked down at her. 'Or is it?'

'Have you never known love?' she asked.

He laughed bitterly. 'I have known passion and maybe that is all I will ever have.' He looked at her. 'The law makes love too risky but you understand love's risks more than many.' He looked out of the window. 'Have you spoken to him?'

She looked down at their fingers threaded together.

'Thing?'

'I wouldn't call it that.' She turned her head away.

He lifted her chin. 'What happened?'

She pressed her lips together. 'Nothing.'

'I saw him head out to you.' He studied her face. 'You didn't tell him.'

'No, I didn't.' Her lips were swollen.

'Shall I tell him?' he asked.

'No.' She closed her eyes for a moment. 'You mustn't. He must not know.'

Edmund frowned. 'That's cruel. I don't mind if he knows. He must have guessed.'

'Do not tell him. It must be a secret.' She took a step back, but his hand still held hers.

'Secrets are hard, Thing,' he whispered.

She glanced out the window. Zach stood by his brother Brindley and their father Jed Carne. She raised her eyes to Edmund. 'It's our secret. He doesn't need to know. People mustn't know.'

'I've had to keep secret who I am.' He drew a breath and sadness settled on him. 'I cannot love openly. My type of love is illegal.' He looked her directly in the eye and Alice saw his pain. She clasped his hand tighter.

'I know what secrets do to you.' He paused and pulled her closer, resting his chin on her head. 'They eat you from the inside.' He paused. 'They discolour everything, including what joy you can find.' He shook his head. 'I know this, Thing. I will never be able to love openly.'

She touched his cheek, his pain so visible to her.

'You have known true love and still love now,' he said.

She began to speak but he continued, 'Don't lie. Tell him so that he can face whatever is ahead of us knowing that.'

Alice closed her eyes for a moment thinking back to an hour before. She wanted to. She could hand Edmund the letter in her pocket to give to Zach but that wasn't the way forward. He would only hold on and they both needed to let go. He would never be happy being her lover and that would never be enough for her either. She loved him and she must let him go. That was the fair and right thing to do. Holding on was wrong.

'My love and John's father must remain a secret. If Zach knows then it is possible that it will travel.' She clenched her hands. 'You have to see this to be true. Zach cannot know. For John's sake, for his future no one must know.'

He shook his head.

'Trust me. This is the best way for Zach. He will be able to forget me. If he knows about John then he will never forget. He will never find love with someone else.' She paused, looking into Edmund's eyes. 'You know him, you know this.'

His Adam's apple rose and fell.

'Promise me you won't tell him, Edmund.'

He looked out the window and then back to her. 'Are you certain?'

'The fewer people who know the better.' She closed her eyes, seeing Zach's pity all over again. He would forget her and their dreams. It was the only way to set him free. She owed him that.

Edmund shook his head. 'He loves you.'

'I love him and for his sake he must not know. He is free to hate me and therefore will forget me.'

'I'll do this for you, Thing. I will do it for John. I won't tell him, but I know you are wrong.' He pulled her into his arms and held her close. 'I simply hope we are not hurting him more.'

The clock chimed the hour. 'It's time.' Edmund stepped back and held out a hand.

She swallowed then stepped forward and clasped his hand. Together they walked out to join the men. Zach stood at the back, his face expressionless. Nanny arrived with John in her arms. Edmund kissed John's forehead and the baby held tight to Edmund's finger. Alice didn't dare to look at Zach. There would be pity but there would be something else and Alice couldn't bear it. Nanny handed John to her. She raised her eyes for a moment. Her glance met Zach's and she froze. She wasn't worthy of his love. All she could do was love his son with everything that was in her. It wasn't enough but it was all she could do.

PART FOUR

Alice laughed. 'There's no use trying,' she said: 'one can't believe impossible things.'

—ALICE'S ADVENTURES IN WONDERLAND,

LEWIS CARROLL

Case 752
Status: Open
15 August 2019

The remains of Captain Edmund St Loy, Earl St Loy, have been identified.

Plans for full burial with honours underway.

Chapter Thirty-Six

2019

Although it was only halfway through August, there were signs of autumn around and for Theo it was the sound of the wind in the trees. The leaves were drier and rustled more. A few floated to the ground as she and David walked to the riverbank. Their silence was filled by the sound of the water. It was not a comfortable silence for Theo had things to say but didn't know where to begin.

David walked with his hands in his pockets. She read his mood as tense. He used to be like this when he was about to sit an exam. Maybe seeing Abbotswood reminded him of the wedding. She wasn't sure but she knew enough not to push. Patience, as Martin encouraged.

'This place is so beautiful, Mum,' he said, turning to her.

Theo smiled. 'It is. I love it.'

'Boatman's is great.'

She nodded. 'How's things?'

He turned to her. 'To be honest, not brilliant.'

Her heart skipped a beat. 'Work or something else?'

He shrugged. 'Lots.' He stopped outside the cottage. 'Look,

it's been bothering me for years and I can't keep it inside any longer.' He looked at her with sad eyes.

'You can tell me anything, you know that,' she said, touching his arm lightly.

He half laughed. 'Yeah, I could tell you almost anything, I know that. We used to talk a lot about everything, but I wasn't able... no, I wasn't allowed to talk to you about this.' He looked down at his feet.

She saw the small boy who had broken a vase and she fervently hoped that whatever he hadn't been able to tell her was simply a broken vase. She took his hand. 'Tell me.'

He glanced at her. 'Dad.'

'Is he OK?' She searched his face, looking for clues.

'No, he's in full health and has come back into the office.'

'Is that the problem?' she asked.

'Yes, and no. Look, Mum, back when I first went to work during the holidays, Dad was having an affair with whatever secretary was there at the time. He swore me to secrecy.' He paused and looked at her. 'He said he loved you and this didn't matter.' He shook his head. 'I believed him for a while.'

Theo opened her arms, but David stayed where he was.

'He has had one affair after another and made me keep it from you and would have kept going if Tina hadn't fallen pregnant.' He rubbed his face. 'And I don't think the baby is Dad's as she was also having it off with the foreman on one of the projects.'

Theo laughed. She knew she shouldn't, but it burst forth. David stared. 'Mum?' Confusion was written all over his face.

She picked up his hand. 'I'm sorry you were put in that awful position. I should have seen it. For that I am truly sorry. But I knew about your father's repeated affairs right from the very start.'

'You knew?'

She nodded. 'I knew.'

'Why did you stay?' he asked.

'Let's have a glass of wine and I'll tell you.' She took a deep breath and walked into the cottage, needing more than wine. But she had to do this. He had to know the truth. In the kitchen she grabbed two glasses and took a bottle of Pinot into the sitting room.

David stood by the table, looking through Zach's letters. Had Lady Alice ever seen them? Lady Alice was brave and Theo could be too.

David looked up. 'These are so beautiful and so sad.'

'Yes.' She poured the wine then grabbed a folder. Only then did she sit.

David gave her a funny look. 'What's this?'

She took a deep breath. 'You asked me why I stayed with your father. The short answer is you, of course.' He was about to interrupt but Theo went on. 'Once, Piers and I were in love, or so I thought. He asked me to marry him and I said yes. I was in the last year of my degree.'

David nodded.

'I went to Paris to do the final research on my dissertation and while there I met an artist who was painting the gardens. For the two weeks we said no more than hello then on my last night there... well, enough said.'

'You had a fling.' He gave her a sideways look.

Theo steadied her nerves. This was awkward but she had to go forward now. 'Yes, I did. I was so ashamed and planned to call the wedding off even though it was only days away.'

'But you didn't,' he said, twisting the wine glass.

'No, because Piers confessed that he'd slept with your grandfather's secretary.'

'No.' David rolled his eyes.

Theo nodded. 'He asked me to forgive him and declared his love.' She took a deep breath. 'I forgave him and went ahead. Eight weeks into the marriage I discovered I was pregnant, and that the affair hadn't stopped.'

Silence hung between them.

'Is Piers,' David said slowly, 'my actual father?'

She took a deep breath. 'I have always thought so since I took precautions in Paris, but something recently made me wonder.'

He looked at her, eyes wide, but she saw no judgement in them. She slid the bulky folder over.

'What's this?' His hand rested on it, waiting.

She took a sip of wine. 'It's a DNA test and a picture of the man I believe is your father.'

'Why haven't you said something before?'

She blew out a long breath. 'Fair question. One, it would have made life complicated. Two.' She stopped and winced. 'Until the day of Piers's wedding I didn't know Patrick's last name.'

'Mounsey,' he said. 'Hugo's great and I couldn't but help notice we did resemble each other.' He laughed. 'So you want me to take this test?' he asked, opening the file.

'That's for you to decide.'

He moved the kit aside and revealed two photographs. One was a copy of the one Hugo carried and the other was

370

of the self-portrait with the painting of Theo resting in view. David looked from her to the pictures.

'He is my father, isn't he?'

She threaded her fingers together. 'I believe he is.'

He nodded. 'It makes sense.'

'What does?' she asked.

'I mean, I love Dad but we never see eye to eye on anything.'

'I'm so sorry.' Theo shook her head, wishing she could take the pain away but she knew she couldn't.

'Don't be, Mum.' He looked at the test. 'As I haven't had anything to eat or drink yet, there's no time like the present.'

'Are you sure?' She put a hand on his across the table.

'Yes.' He spat into the tube and sealed it. 'It doesn't mean that anyone else needs to know.'

'True, but in my experience these things will come out somehow.'

'Grannie,' he said.

Theo nodded.

He laughed. 'So, where did you find this painting?'

'In Hugo's sitting room.' She looked into her wine glass.

'And what about the one of you in the painting?'

She winced. 'This will make it sound worse.'

'Hit me,' he said.

'In Hugo's bedroom.' She took a large gulp of wine.

'His bedroom? Not covering yourself in glory.' He laughed. 'My mum the cougar.'

She raised her hands. 'Ha, ha. The night of the wedding I stayed at Hugo's and saw both paintings.'

'And I know that Hugo spent the whole night dealing with wedding guests.'

'Have you spoken to Patrick?' he asked.

Theo took a deep breath. 'He died in 1990.'

David's shoulders fell. Theo stood and walked around the table to him and hugged him while he remained sitting. He held her about her waist and she was reminded of the child he was.

'I love you,' she said.

'I love you too, Mum.' He stood and held her tight.

Chapter Thirty-Seven

1920

Had it not been for a call from Constance, Alice would not be making this journey to Abbotswood. In fact, she wished she wasn't, but Nanny Roberts was dying and she had asked for her.

Back in 1917, when she had last seen Nanny, there was still such a thing as hope in her breast, but that was before she'd truly understood loss. Days when she would race around the banks of the Tamar chasing rabbits and dogs were long gone. Her son now filled his time doing the same things. He didn't understand loss. Double death duties. Her father-in-law, taken by influenza weeks before she received the telegram announcing Edmund's death. Already in black for the Earl St Loy, she added an arm band. She couldn't add more. Then came word that Zach had died the same day as Edmund. Another arm band wouldn't begin to touch the sense of loss. Now she felt as if the colour was imprinted into her skin and even that didn't reveal the broken state of her heart. With his death she died. She was a few weeks from her twenty-fourth birthday and, if she wasn't careful, she would be old before her time. All emotion had leached out of her during her years in mourning.

A pheasant scuttled out of the way of the motorcar. Fishing flies, her wedding bouquet, more reminders of things past. Alice pushed the memories hovering in her peripheral vision away. This was why she hadn't wanted to return. It hurt to look at the landscape. She glanced up to the clear sky. For March the weather was fine. Alice would not think of the last time she had been here. It was pointless. She could not and would not change the past. Yet the love of her life was dead. Her best friend was dead. She wasn't ready to abandon the darkness of black and the hollowness that it represented so navy-blue was the acceptable choice.

The woodland floor was dotted with the bright-yellow cups of the lesser celandine and on the edges sweet violets and dog violets provided early food for the bees. The sight of them should bring joy but they didn't. She was numb. She knew it. Nothing felt as it should. Her heart didn't lift at the sight of the great magnolia at Penhale in bloom or even at John's laughter. That was what hurt the most. She was alive but she wasn't living. It was wasted on her.

The rhododendrons lining the drive were filled with tight buds waiting for the warmth of May to put on their vivid display. The banks along the drive should be filled with glimpses of primroses and daffodils but they were lost in uncut grass. The summer of 1914 there had been fifty gardeners at Abbotswood. All but the oldest and youngest had signed up immediately. Only one had returned.

The motorcar pulled up in the courtyard as the clock chimed two. The front door opened, and Burton stood much more stooped than when she had last seen him. The chauffeur opened her door and she swung out her feet as she looked at Burton's outstretched hand. He had lost a brother at the Somme. No one was left untouched by the war or the influenza. They were all the same.

Burton bowed his head. 'How lovely to see you, Lady Alice.'

'Thank you, Burton. Are you well?'

'Yes, my lady.'

She strolled past him into the hall. The space was full of shadows but the blazing fire welcomed her. A large tapestry covered one wall and a collection of watercolour paintings of salmon, trout and perch adorned the other. Nothing had changed. Not even the addition of electric light. Oil lamps were filled in readiness but not lit. Only the flowers adorning the table in the centre were different.

Pulling her gloves off, she knew what she had to do, but that didn't mean she wanted to. She readied herself and asked, 'Nanny?'

'Sleeping,' Burton said.

'My cousin?' She turned to him. All the suspicion she had felt years ago hung in the air between them. He could do nothing to interfere with her life now. She must let it go. She was no longer a wild and reckless young woman but a mother and a widow. He was only a man trying to do his job.

'She is out for a walk.' He held his hand in the direction of the library. 'I have taken the liberty of having tea laid out for you by the fire.'

'Thank you.' She entered the room and went straight to the bay window and she searched the bank for the impossible. Instead she spotted Constance, with her grey dress flapping, as she climbed out of the small rowing boat. At Abbotswood the distance between Cornwall and Devon was small yet like the past it was as far as an ocean. But standing here she felt him and her past.

Just for that second something inside stirred. If only she could hold on to it, but as she watched Constance make her way towards the house it died. What on earth had her cousin been doing on the other side of the river? There was nothing of interest to her now, not that there had been before. Was anyone using the old boatman's cottage? No smoke rose from the chimney. That was yet another thing the war had altered. Although not hindered by death duties like she was, her uncle struggled with the lack of staff to look after the house, the garden, the estate. The days of having a fire blazing so that the smoke rose from the trees were well past.

'Shall I pour?' Burton stood behind her.

Alice tensed. There were too many ghosts here. 'No, thank you Burton, I'll see to it myself.'

'Very well.'

She listened to his steps on the wide wooden planks of the floor until he reached the carpet in the hall. That sense of having been in the same place before covered her skin. She rubbed her arms while staring out of the window. Down by the banks of the river she caught sight of a hare being chased by a hound. It was as if nothing had changed but the feel of the cool gold on her ring finger weighed down by the emerald informed her everything had.

Alice heard Burton inform Constance of her arrival. She turned in anticipation. Alice smiled as her cousin walked into the library. 'Constance, how lovely to see you.' The soft grey dress she wore suited her dark hair and complexion.

Constance had become a handsome woman and right now she would say there was something about her that was different. Was it a glow on her cheeks or maybe a gleam in her dark eyes?

'You came.' Constance stood still by the door.

'Of course.' Alice felt her cousin's scrutiny. She knew that Constance would see the thinness about her and the pallid complexion. They knew each other too well. In their way they were both misfits.

'I wasn't certain after our conversation last night.' Constance poured the tea.

'I said I would,' Alice said.

'Did you? Why aren't you with her now?' Constance held out a cup and saucer.

Alice took it, saying, 'Burton said she was sleeping.'

Constance lifted her own cup. 'And you listened to him.'

Alice shook her head. 'Well, I do not wish to make things worse.'

'Really, a bit late.' Constance added a slice of lemon to her tea.

Alice put her cup down, not sure how to address that comment. 'She can't be dying. Surely it's her lungs playing up again, her asthma.'

'She is dying. She is suffocating from the weight of the secrets she has kept.' Constance picked up her cup. 'It's become a cancer within her, eating her from the inside out.'

'No.' Alice paled.

Constance put her tea down. 'Yours being the heaviest because she loves you the most.'

Alice stared at her cousin. What had she said? 'But...'

377

Constance interrupted, saying, 'No, we have done this, you have done this.'

Alice shook her head. 'I...'

Again Constance wouldn't let her finish, saying, 'The least you can do is to apologise. You owe her that if not more.'

Alice pulled her shoulders back. 'I don't owe her anything.'

'Yes, you do and not just her.' Constance stared at Alice.

'You, what do I owe you?' Alice pulled her head back. If anything, Constance owed her. She had kept her out of London and occupied during the war. Protected her.

'Think about it,' she said.

Alice shook her head.

'Try harder. How do you think Nanny knew about you and the gillie?'

'No.' Alice looked at her cousin again.

'I knew. You thought I didn't see.' Constance laughed drily, picking up her cup. 'I even knew you were pregnant.'

'No. You didn't, you couldn't have.' Alice took a step backwards.

'You would have been ruined or worse.'

'I contacted Edmund.' Alice sent Constance a hard look.

'Nanny was poised to act if you hadn't.' Constance picked her cigarette case flicking it open. 'And I watched and I learned. You taught me so much.' Constance sipped her tea then said, 'Now go to Nanny while you still can.'

'Is she in her old room?'

'No, I had them move a bed down to the children's sitting room so that she can look out over the fountain, the parterre and down to the river.'

'Sensible.' Alice rose to her feet.

Constance tapped a cigarette lightly against the case. 'I've always been sensible.'

Alice studied her. It was something in the tone of her voice. She walked to the door then turned, waiting.

'I'll finish my tea and have a cigarette. I'll join you shortly.' She put her cup down. 'I'm sure Nanny would like a bit of time alone with you.'

Alice walked the long hall to the children's wing. She could almost hear the echoes of laughter. In the memory of the raucous joy of the sounds of the past, she knew the words she needed to say, 'Nanny, I'm so sorry... for so much.'

She stopped outside the sitting room, closing her eyes for a moment. She could do this. Nanny had never passed judgement; if anything she had blamed herself. Alice opened her eyes and pulled the door open, holding her breath. She had no idea what to expect. She had seen death too many times with the influenza and the war, but this was different.

Nanny lay lost in the bed, appearing more like a frail child than an adult. Her eyes were closed and her skin sallow. Alice rushed to the bedside but didn't speak. The last thing she wanted to do was to startle her old friend, for Nanny had been a friend, an ally and a teacher. Nanny had given her everything and Alice had sucked it all up and never given back. She couldn't ask for forgiveness because she didn't deserve it. With great care Alice stroked the hand on the coverlet and lifted it next to her heart, willing some of her own health to flow into Nanny.

Nanny's eyes flickered open and a smile stretched her dry lips. 'Lady Alice, you've come.' The voice was barely audible, but still the sound Alice had loved. Her once bright-blue eyes were pale and yellowed.

'Of course I have.'

'I'm so—' Nanny coughed, and her small frame rattled. 'I've failed you.'

Alice drew back. This was wrong. 'No.' She shook her head.

'I have, I know I have.' Nanny drew a breath. 'I am sorry. Like your father I loved you too much.'

'No,' Alice said.

'My darling girl, I have failed you. I can see it now.' Nanny closed her eyes for a moment.

Alice shook her head.

'You aren't here.' Nanny coughed. 'You are dead inside.'

Alice slumped. Even now she couldn't hide from Nanny. Looking out the window at the bright spring sunshine, it was wrong. The sky should be leaden and pelting down with vicious, wild, wind-whipped rain. Instead the daffodils danced in the light breeze.

Nanny coughed and Alice took the glass of water from the bedside table and placed her free arm under Nanny's shoulders. Alice swallowed her gasp. There was nothing left of her. After a few small sips, Nanny looked at Alice as she lowered her back onto the pillows. 'Thank you for coming.' She coughed. 'I didn't know if you would...'

Alice picked up her hand. 'Of course I came.'

'How's John?' she asked.

Alice smiled. 'He's good and full of mischief.'

Nanny's eyes danced. 'You were full of mischief.'

'So you told me.' She looked about the room, seeing the toys she had played with, including her old rocking horse.

'Is he like his father?' Nanny's glance narrowed.

Alice turned away. 'Yes, very.'

'That's good.' She paused. 'His father was a good man.'

'Yes, he was,' Alice managed to get the words out.

'You are still young.'

'Is anyone young after a war?' Alice asked as she read the titles of the old children's books that lined one wall. *Alice's Adventures in Wonderland*. On rainy days when they couldn't see the river let alone the Cornish bank, she and her cousins had spent hours by the fire, listening to those stories. She had always felt it had been written for her.

'It does age you but don't let it take life and love from you.'

'There are so few men left.' Alice looked out to the fountain. Two fat wood pigeons were having a bath.

'Once you thought you didn't need one.' Nanny attempted to laugh, but it turned into a cough.

Alice nodded. 'I did indeed.'

'You don't you know.' Nanny closed her eyes for a moment.

Alice stroked Nanny's hand. 'You never had one.'

'No, that's not quite true—' Nanny coughed again and Alice's eyes opened wide. 'I loved once when I was young...' Her voice faded, and she drifted away. Alice tried to picture Nanny as a young woman. She would have had some beauty. Her eyes were a fine blue.

'He was the son of the house.'

Alice looked up. Nanny was studying her. She knew too much.

'We knew it could never be... but that doesn't stop love...' Nanny closed her eyes. 'Does it?'

Alice looked out at the clear sky.

'Look at me.' Nanny's voice croaked. 'Don't waste your

life not living. Don't miss a moment with John. Don't give up on love.'

Alice looked at Nanny, hearing the words but not wanting to.

'The past is behind us. Look forward. Chin up.' Nanny gasped.

Alice barely heard those last words and then Nanny was gone with eyes still open, watching Alice as she always had.

Alice rose from the bed strangely light as if she had been forgiven. But, of course, she hadn't. Nanny had witnessed it all and she had still loved her as her mother had never been able to. She had protected and directed her, and she was gone. Now Alice was free or freer. There was one less person who knew the truth.

Chapter Thirty-Eight

While Constance spoke to the doctor, Alice went into the garden. The nodding green flowers of the hellebores filled the long border. With each step she thought about Nanny leaving this world. Was it just another death? That was why tears weren't falling. Life was short. Nanny had had more years than many. But she hadn't lived the life she'd wanted.

For that matter neither had Alice. When she had last been here in 1914, she had wanted so much. Votes for women being one thing and that at least had partially come to pass. She still couldn't vote nor could any woman under thirty and without property but all men could. The old anger filled her, but she let it go. Her hands were filled keeping the estate afloat for John.

Alice reached the end of the rose walk and went down the steps of carved stone. The great stretching branches of an oak divided the view as she made her way to the shell house. It always seemed she never saw the same thing as her glance would pick out a different crystal or seashell. Stopping outside it, a shiver of memory covered her skin. A kiss had become the taste of desire and love. She opened the door and stood on the threshold. Her hand touched a fossil. A moment captured forever.

That day rain had pounded down but at this moment the sun was warm on her back as she walked through the gate beside the small building and down roughly cut steps, each one laden with memories joyous and sorrowful in equal measure. A pheasant started in the undergrowth and she watched the plain hen take to flight. Was that Nanny? No, Alice couldn't see her being attracted to the showy male of the species. Although it was now clear that Nanny had known more of life than Alice had ever considered. Questions circled in her mind.

The sound of the river rushing onwards filled her ears. She stood by Black Rock. Like the water racing past her feet, memories tumbled through her mind. They pooled and eddied around the ones made in 1914, that beautiful summer. Turning back towards the house, she strolled beside the river. The Tamar was swollen with all the rain of the past weeks. By the bank the water was clouded with the runoff of soil, bits of twigs and grasses a bit like her thoughts. It spoke of winter pursuits despite the coming spring. At the boat Constance had been using, Alice stopped. The old gillie was nowhere in sight.

She didn't hesitate. She climbed into it, put the oars in the rowlocks, released the line and let the boat into the current before she began rowing against the flow. She hadn't considered that her dress was not suited to the movement of pulling, or what anyone would think watching her. She could row and had done so many times but rarely so visibly. Her arms, legs and shoulders strained while her palms chafed on the worn wood. Eventually the boat began to move upriver and soon she saw the boatman's quay.

Once there she secured the boat and climbed onto the

quay. Smoothing her dress down, she breathed deeply. The scent of pine and leaf mould filled her lungs. She took a last look at the river and caught sight of an otter. It dove down and she knew the salmon were about. The timing was right, but the water's surface was too murky at the moment to spy the elusive prey.

Almost reluctantly she looked through the trees to pick out the cottage. It still stood. In her thoughts she had returned many times, imagining a life with Zach here in this little cottage. Her feet were rushing her towards it while her head said no. What good would it do to go back? There was nothing to be gained.

The door was closed and the wood dry and in need of varnish. The trees towered above it. Once they had been trimmed back to make space for the cottage, but not now. Nature had moved in close. The large window was blackened with grime, but she could make out the scratched letters on the upper right pane of glass. Done in haste six years ago but it could have been a hundred. The Alice who had stood here had been more girl than woman. She couldn't see it then, but she did now.

Lifting her skirt, she climbed up the granite step and checked the door handle. It swung open and sunlight fell onto the slate floor. Her glance immediately went to the fire. Even on the warmest day of the summer, that fire had blazed. Now the charcoaled carcass of a log was the only relic of the past.

The small round table with two chairs sat to the back of the room near the southern window. Otherwise the room was empty. Opening the door to her right she went through to the kitchen. All evidence of habitation was gone. No plate by the sink. No cup on the hook. She turned. A hollowness filled her chest as she climbed the stairs.

On the landing, she turned into the small bedroom. The bedstead was stripped of covers and some animal had nested frequently in what remained of the mattress. Alice stroked the corner, remembering. It seemed a lifetime ago she had been here. He had been here. But it wasn't a lifetime unless you looked at her son's five years. So many young men full of promise were dead. She didn't want that for her son. That was why his father had died. He and his comrades had died for the men and women of the future. She hoped they hadn't died in vain.

The cupboard was empty and the bottom shelf was untouched. She had searched Zach's secret place for anything of his after he left to war. He had shown it to her that final night they were together. It would still be empty now. She took a last lingering glance at the bed before leaving the room and closing the door tightly behind her. There was an undisturbed stillness about the cottage. When the war had taken all the men, this place was closed up. Since then it appeared no one had seen the need for it again.

Step by step she walked down to the kitchen, her heart squeezing with each one. All her dreams of the past floated away with the disturbed dust. The cottage would soon decay and that was best. She stopped and touched the table. It had all been so fleeting. She caught sight of herself in the looking glass. There was no flush of youth shown in her cheeks as she walked up to it. Why was this here and not in the bedroom as it had been? She ran her fingers over the frame and the small scar in the woodwork. Closing her eyes, she pictured him beside her, declaring his love. She prayed that he had died swiftly and was now in peace.

Outside, the sun was hidden behind a cloud and the March air had cooled. She shivered. She didn't turn to look at the cottage again. Nanny's death had unsettled her and had stirred the ghosts of the past. Love.

She had been reckless. Her actions had ruined Zach's life and, no matter what Edmund had said, she had limited his as well. But she hadn't seen it in the moment. She had only thought about herself and not others. She was selfish then and still was now. Yet she loved John with everything in her and that would be enough.

Constance stood on the bank, watching her as Alice rowed. Her face was expressionless as Alice struggled with her own thoughts. She didn't want to deal with Constance's. During those war years, Alice had watched her grow up and she had become like a sister. But now more than the Tamar stretched between them. Constance loved Nanny and she would be devastated with her passing. But Alice didn't see that, only the anger that was apparent earlier. Constance had many reasons to rage. She'd lost her brothers bar one. And she had lost the future that had been certain in that summer of 1914. Or did she truly believe that the weight of secrets caused Nanny's death especially Alice's?

She tied up the boat and walked to her cousin. Indecision slowed her steps. Having blocked all emotion for so long, too many vied inside her. Visiting the cottage had opened her up. Tears that hadn't come earlier pricked her eyes. She took a deep breath, attempting to force everything back inside, into its locked place. But, as Constance opened her arms to her, everything tumbled out. They clung to each other.

When the tears subsided and Alice looked at Constance's tear-blotched face, she took her cousin's hand and they walked to the house in silence. There was too much to say to even begin.

Inside, Constance waved Burton away and went straight to the brandy decanter. She poured them both a large measure. After she handed a glass to Alice, she raised hers and said, 'To Nanny.'

Alice bowed her head for a moment then joined her cousin and said, 'To Nanny.' After taking a sip she turned to her, saying, 'Constance, I...'

Constance interrupted, 'It's done. Let it lie.' She knocked back the contents of her glass and Alice opened her eyes wide.

'I do need to say...'

'Sorry,' Constance said with a dry laugh. 'Life is made up of apologies. Your list may be longer than mine but shorter than others.' She shrugged and poured herself more brandy. She glanced at Alice's barely touched glass before placing the circular cut-glass faceted stopper back into the rectangular decanter.

Constance took a sip and glanced at Alice, asking, 'Where do we go from here?'

Alice studied Constance. The woman in front of her was different to the docile, inquiring child she had known. Her time working in the hospital with the wounded soldiers had changed her.

'I suggest we put the past behind us.' She raised her glass

again. 'To the future and whatever it may bring.' A tear slipped down Constance's cheek. Alice reached out to her, but Constance pulled herself up to her full height and drank the rest of the brandy in one go. She smiled at Alice then left the room.

Alice shivered. Putting down her glass, she walked into the hallway and to the small room her grandmother used to use. It overlooked the fountain and caught the last of the afternoon light. She pulled a chair up to the fire and wrapped her arms around herself. Everything was different now, including her.

Chapter Thirty-Nine

The light was drawing in and behind her a fire was being lit. She had spoken to Constance on the telephone regarding arrangements for Nanny's funeral. Her trip to Abbotswood had a dreamlike quality to it. The river, the cottage, and Constance, all in the aftermath of Nanny's death. Alice walked to the window. John was running with his nanny watching. In a way she had achieved freedom yet she was tied to Penhale. Constance, thanks to the war, had no husband or likelihood of finding one. Her dreams, like so many others, had disappeared. So few men.

Guilt furrowed Alice's brow. Arthur Carew. She had no right to him and yet he had been so courteous throughout the war, visiting when he came to Cornwall and now over a year had passed and his visits had become more frequent. She looked forward to them and to his smile. She huffed. Once she hadn't considered him in any way other than someone who had listened to her. But as she saw two hares break from the tree line on her lawn and spar, something entirely different stirred in her.

She leaned her head against the glass then straightened and went to the desk. Opening the middle drawer, she pulled out Edmund's last letter.

31 October 1918

Dear Thing,

It is All Hallows' Eve and I can feel the many souls around me in the earth. So many men mourned but unmarked in this mud. I pray for them and I am not a praying man. But sometimes when everything is stripped away prayer is the only power left, that and love. Somehow they are connected.

Your last letter filled me with hope and good things. I am so pleased that John is outdoors for as much time as he is allowed. I want him to know every hedge, every tree, every fish, every bird, every animal, every flower that surrounds him. It's funny but I never valued them as I do now. I see joy in a tiny field mouse managing to survive in this hell. I pray that John will never know the horrors I have seen.

Yes, before you ask, I have written to Mother. Thank you for looking after her. I think because of all the death of the young and strong and brave I have seen about me, my father's death is nothing. Not meaningless but carries no emotion, or possibly emotion in me has been deadened.

Death is every day, hourly, sometimes every minute. Therefore news of my father's passing is just one more. I sound cold, unloving even, but I think the war has dulled the edges of my nerves to protect me. Looking back, I remember fighting tears when my first subaltern fell. Now, I think only Zach's death would trouble me. He has been a stalwart, a friend, a brother in arms.

Do speak to the solicitors regarding the death duties and all the mess that death leaves in its wake. Be kind to my mother, which I know you will be. Love John with everything in you. I didn't need to write that but as I listened to the barrage of guns it seems the only thing that is important. Love. I love you, dear Thing. Be brave. I know you are. Be strong. It is in you. Be kind, possibly the hardest thing I ask of you. You are too clever, too beautiful, too head strong. All the gifts have been yours; be kind to those who don't have them like me.

I will write again when time permits. I leave everything in your capable hands, dear Thing. Love you.

Yours,
Edmund

Be brave, be strong, be kind. She held the letter to her heart. He knew her so well. She could do it.

Alice placed the letter from Edmund's commanding officer into the drawer with the telegram and the last letter she had received from Edmund. The major was now fully recovered and had written, as he said, to help. But had it helped reading about Edmund's bravery? His goodness? Or had it simply opened the wounds that had barely scabbed over? Everything inside her was disturbed. Nothing made sense as she stared out the window. The major had enclosed a photograph he'd come across. It was of the major and Edmund and in the background stood Zach, Edmund's shadow.

She had been faithful, truly faithful to them both. But

what of Arthur her heart called out. Could one be unfaithful to the dead? Drawing a breath to ease the tightness in her chest, she glanced at the desk where a note from Arthur sat waiting for a reply.

In the distance she heard John's childish laughter then she bristled at the sound of the thump of footsteps behind her. Wilfred always announced himself by his noisy tread. He held out the silver salver holding the post. She picked the envelopes off the shining surface.

'Thank you, Wilfred.'

He bowed and left the room. With a distracted glance, she flipped through the heavy cream envelopes. Her ears tuned into the sound of her son. She shouldn't be worried about him. He was strong and robust like his father. But she couldn't help but be worried. Everything rested on his young shoulders.

She watched him from the window. In the distance the Tamar sparkled. Although the first of April the sun held the warmth of summer today. Late daffodils danced in the breeze. What was it that Shakespeare had said of the flower? That it… 'comes before the swallow dares'. That had certainly been true at Penhale this year when the first sweetly scented narcissi had bloomed on New Year's Day. Her son who always dared, raced after a ball to the garden wall.

She put the letters on the desk. Whatever was in them could wait. She wanted to run with John and feel the heat of the sun, the caress of the breeze and to laugh. She took a last look at the post. There would be bills, demands, responsibility.

The daffodils waving in the breeze reminded her of 1917. They had lost so much to the blight. Yet another casualty of the war. No one to lift the bulbs. The loss of income came at the worst time. Only this year, having lifted all the bulbs last year, were they able to begin to earn from them again. And they needed to. All of this was hers to protect for John. She browsed through the envelopes until she came across one with a Paris post mark. Slipping it into her pocket, she left the others behind as she walked into the garden to join her son and his nanny.

Halfway across the lawn she stopped. Arthur walked towards her. He had mentioned he might come to Cornwall from Saturday to Monday, but today was Friday. His jacket flapped open in the wind coming up from the river. He waved to her. Her heart lifted. It shouldn't, she knew it shouldn't, but it did. His pace quickened and his smile widened the closer he came to her.

'Alice,' he said.

'This a surprise.' She held out a hand. He took it in both of his, not letting it go.

'A good one I hope,' he said.

'It is.'

He raised an eyebrow. 'Is that all?'

She smiled, hoping it said what she wasn't willing to put into words yet. She looked up at him from under her lashes. A corner of his mouth lifted in that half smile of his she found so attractive. But she couldn't explain why. Arthur Carew was a neat man of thirty-six years. His fair hair was thinning. But his eyes, yes, it was all in the eyes. They were moody grey and spoke so eloquently of what went on in that clever head of his, but only hinted at the depths of his heart. It was those depths that called out to her.

He lifted her hand to his mouth and left the lightest of

kisses on the back of it. She held her breath, letting the feeling travel through her. Their eyes met.

'Alice,' he whispered.

'I know...' This was so unexpected and should be unwelcome, but she wanted him.

John ran towards them and Arthur let her hand go. He had been about to propose. It was in his eyes. Their expression had declared his feelings more eloquently than his words ever could. Steadily he had been leading them to this point over the past months. Only recently had things intensified.

John threw his arms around her legs. 'Mumma.'

'My darling.' She kissed the top of his head before she peeled him from her skirt. Taking his hand, they walked down through the garden. He sang a silly song he made up as they went.

Arthur matched his pace to hers and John's. He would fit so well into their lives in one way. But much of his time was in London. He served his constituency well. His estate was not far from here. Although knowing him for years, she had never seen him, truly seen him, until lately. Now it felt like he was always in her sights whether he was beside her like now or on the end of the telephone line. What was she going to do?

Chapter Forty

2019

It was a glorious September day as Theo and David walked from the Trocadéro metro station to the entrance of Passy Cemetery. So many memories floated about her but this wasn't a trip down memory lane for her. This trip was for David. His DNA results had arrived and there was no surprise. Piers was not his father and Hugo was his first cousin. Piers did not know this yet. With new courage and the assistance of his girlfriend, David was going to leave Henshaw and Son and follow his heart and go to art school. Theo was thrilled beyond words, despite her worry over how Piers would react.

David was holding the map with Patrick's grave marked on it. When she had suggested this trip to him, she hadn't thought they would make the journey so soon but he was eager and she was ready. Hugo and his father Ron, Patrick's older brother, had been supportive and welcoming as had the rest of the Mounsey family. Theo had let David do this without her. Her feelings didn't need to be a part of his exploration. They had plenty of time ahead.

He stopped at the entrance gates. 'Ready?' he asked.

She nodded, her mouth suddenly dry. Together they walked in silence first to the left to the Avenue Chauvet then onto Chemin Heugal and down to the back. The variety and beauty of some of the monuments was overwhelming, or it could be her own state of mind. David may be ready for this moment, but she wasn't sure she was.

Looking away from the graves, she studied the tall plane trees lining the outside. The Eiffel Tower was not far away. The distinctive sound of a siren mixed with traffic noises. She allowed these things to stay in the forefront of her thoughts until David took her hand.

That contact broke the wall of sensory detail she was building around herself. She lifted the flowers in her hand and breathed in. Jasmine for love and sensuality, freesia for innocence, hydrangea for heartfelt emotion and white dittany for love and passion.

As they approached the far reaches of the cemetery, David stopped. Theo kept her eyes on the flower petals and slowed her breathing. This was hard and she hadn't anticipated it. David's fingers tightened around hers before he let them go. Without the warmth of his hand, she shivered.

David bent low over the long piece of black granite that marked Patrick's last resting place.

PATRICK DANIEL SEBASTIAN MOUNSEY
ARTIST

17 MARCH 1962
25 AUGUST 1990

Theo closed her eyes, holding the flowers close to her face. Jasmine.

'Mum?' David touched her arm. 'You OK?'

She opened her eyes. 'Yes,' she lied. She bent and placed the flowers down. Had she stuck to her plan things might have been different. She laid her hand flat on the cold stone. He had been so warm, so real, so loving. Pulling herself back up she looked at the contrast between the smooth stone and the colour and shape of the flowers. She thought he would have appreciated that.

David put his arm on her shoulders as they stood silently in the warm September sun.

'I want to bring Natasha here,' he said.

'That would be good.' She turned to him. 'Before or after the wedding?' He'd proposed and the big day was on the twenty-first of December at Abbotswood.

'In the new year.' He smiled. 'I'll take a few pictures now.'

She stepped back as he did and they both tripped, landing on the grave behind.

'Are you all right?' she asked.

'Yes, but I feel we need to apologise to the occupant.' He smiled, turning and tapping the grave.

'Me too,' she said, rising to her feet. She looked at the poor soul they had fallen on. Theo did a double take, looking at the name.

'Zachariah Carne,' David said.

'Can't be the same one,' Theo said, walking around the side of it to read it from the front.

ZACHARIAH CARNE

8 JANUARY 1896
15 MAY 1920

LOVED

Below the inscription there were three hares in a circle with the ears touching. Theo thought about the St Loy crest, hers now.

She looked at David who was scrolling through his phone. 'Uncle Martin has done some more research.' He continued through his phone then looked up, 'Zachariah's birth was registered in February.'

She bent down and touched the cold granite tracing the hares.

'This can't be a coincidence.' She looked up at David. He nodded and she took a picture and immediately sent it to Martin.

Theo turned back to Patrick's grave and removed a single hydrangea flower and then placed it on Zachariah's. She didn't think it could be possible but something inside her called out to the soul buried there.

The following day Theo was emotional before they began. Being at Masnières Cemetery with Martin, David and Jeanette felt surreal. Martin would be reading and Theo knew then that the tears that she just had control of now would flow. TV cameras were around but they were giving them time before they began to record. All the families of the men who went missing on 2 November 1918 were here, including Zachariah Carne's family. After discussion with Martin they had decided not to share that she and David had discovered his grave. Martin had said that this secret had lasted this long, and they didn't need to know that Zachariah Carne must have deserted. That knowledge would help no one. Both she and David agreed. She glanced over at them and smiled.

In the distance, lines of headstones all alike were a powerful reminder. All the men buried here were equal. All had died serving their country and the saddest thing, standing there now, was that they had thought it had been the war to end all wars. Theo took a deep breath and studied the men and women in uniform now. She was grateful to them and all who served.

The woman from the TV production company came up and spoke to Martin. It was time. Sgt Bowman would be buried first then Captain Edmund St Loy. David grabbed her hand and they walked down into place. Martin had Jeanette beside him. They had asked Toby but he would only be back from his Stateside travels next week.

Theo was grateful for her hat. The sun beat down relentlessly as she watched the proceedings, thankful for her family, new and old. Martin read without a wobble in his voice even when saying, 'At the going down of the sun and in the morning, we will remember them.' However his voice faltered at the end reading,

'As the stars that are starry in the time of our darkness,
To the end, to the end, they remain.'
The silence after his voice faded away hurt. All the images

of the day ran through her mind. Then the bugle played the last post.

Theo could no longer be strong; she wept.

Chapter Forty-One

1920

Outside in the courtyard Arthur stood with John, hand in hand. They were in deep conversation. John squinted with focus and Arthur was relaxed with a smile on his lips. He would be a wonderful father. Back in 1914 he would never have been considered a suitable suitor. Now her heart filled watching him with her son.

The Carews were an old Cornish family but Arthur was the son of the younger son. However, his father had been successful in both mining and politics. Arthur had built on both and hadn't lost himself in the process. He crouched down to John's level, listening with full focus. John was showing Arthur the stones he had collected on his walk. Arthur's study of geology at Oxford was being put to use answering all John's questions.

John's nanny went out to meet them and he raced with her towards the kitchen. Arthur looked to where Alice stood in the doorway. He waved and she went out to him.

'Walk with me?' He held out a hand and she took it. The great magnolia tree was in full blossom. They both paused to look up. 'Beautiful,' he said, turning to her.

'Yes.' She smiled at him. He wasn't looking at the tree. She was no longer vain, but she knew she was beautiful. It didn't hold the value it once had. Beauty had made her briefly the more attractive prize. Now she was a mother, a widow and the controller of her own destiny. She caught her breath. If she said yes to Arthur then that would no longer be the case.

'Where have you gone?' He touched her cheek before he dropped his hand.

'Many places?' She smiled ruefully at him.

'How do I hold your attention?' he asked.

'Very easily, as it happens.' She picked up his hand, loving the feel of it.

'Pleased to hear that.' He paused. 'I didn't think I'd be lucky enough to be able to enter into your affections.' His intense grey eyes met hers.

She held his glance. 'I…' she began, but he stilled her words with the touch of his finger on her mouth and she turned it into a kiss.

He moved his finger across her lips and along her cheek. 'I want you.'

'Yes,' she whispered.

'I've waited to speak my mind…'

Her maid came running out of the house down to them. 'My lady, the telephone for Sir Arthur.'

'Timing,' he said, letting his hand slide down her arm before he went to the house. She hoped this wasn't something earth-shattering, but simple. It was a Monday afternoon, the sun was out and the world wasn't at war. She watched a dove nesting. It was that time of year and she felt its call.

Below, the Tamar worked its way to the sea. It was a hive

of activity with barges moving goods. Around her the ancient buildings of Penhale stood. Jed Carne nodded in greeting as he made his way up the hill. There had been times that she had almost told him about John but held back. It must remain her secret, but she tried hard to make certain the old man was fine and that Zach's older brother, Brindley, had employment on the estate, despite the loss of his leg to the war. She rubbed her temple. Life was complex.

Arthur's footsteps sounded but she continued to study the river. She knew he was leaving for she had heard his car being brought to the front of the house.

'I must go,' he whispered from behind her. His breath brushed the sensitive skin behind her ear. She wanted him but she would wait. They had reached this point and they would go forward. She turned.

'I'm sorry,' he said, taking her hand in his. She shook her head then stood on tiptoes and kissed him. She tried to give him the answer to the question he hadn't yet asked.

'Alice,' he managed to say as she stepped away from him, missing the feel of their bodies touching.

'Yes.'

He lifted her hand and kissed the inside of her wrist. She closed her eyes, holding onto the feeling. Desire. It raced through her. Opening her eyes, she looked at him. He had been watching her.

'I must go,' he said.

'I know.'

His fingers wove through hers as he said, 'I'll be back soon.'

She nodded and their hands fell apart. He walked with quiet determination to the car and she suppressed the desire to follow. Desire. Passion. She hadn't thought she would ever feel it again nor had she wanted to. But it was there, sparkling on the edges of her vision, making everything a bit brighter, from the cloudless sky above to the green of the grass. It was spring and the world was full of promise.

Why had she agreed to leave Penhale and John to come to Castle Harkness? It was the first of May. She would rather be walking through the bluebells in Cornwall than be here. None of the Saturday-to-Monday activity interested her. It had mild intrigue when she was young as she eavesdropped on the servants about the comings and goings from bedroom to bedroom. But now it bored her.

Alice had always been a light sleeper and woke to the bell at six thirty, the reminder to return to your own room. The consequences of being in the wrong place were weighty. When Lady Helen had overslept, and the butler found her in bed with the foreign minister, she was ruined. Divorce was costly and, as her mother had told her, unnecessary. Once you had produced the required heir you were free to pursue your own interests. As a widow her mother's interests were many and still didn't include her daughter or her grandchild more than was necessary. For this Alice was grateful.

Her hostess, Nancy, Countess of Dunloch, was a distant cousin and her daughter was the same age as Alice. They had begun the season together in 1914. Now, she too was a widow. There were too many husbandless women and she wasn't sure how the countess would balance the numbers at dinner unless she borrowed bodies from the family crypt.

Alice closed the door on her bedroom. In neat black ink

it read: The Dowager Countess St Loy. Walking down the hall she noted that her mother was two bedrooms down the corridor. These days away would be bearable if Arthur were coming. But he was due to be in Cornwall and her mother had insisted that, now Alice was out of mourning, she needed to be seen. Alice couldn't think why her mother was meddling now? Being a widow gave her freedom and for this she was grateful, but she would rather have had Edmund alive. It didn't take much to hear his wicked commentary and scandalous gossip as she walked along. She pictured him whispering at her side.

'Thing, did you hear that Anthony what's his name… you know him. Well, last night at Topping's old place, he leapt into Lady Grace's room, whipped off his dressing gown, shouting, I'm all yours, darling.' He would pause, waiting for her reaction, and then continue with the story, 'The Bishop of Portsmouth was a bit taken aback to have a peer of the realm dancing naked in front of him when he'd turned on the electric light.' Edmund would laugh. 'Not flattering at all on his middle-aged two stones and a yard. Electric light is cruel, Thing, cruel.'

She paused at the top of the staircase and took a deep breath. God, she missed him. These few days would be full of fun and laughter if Edmund were at her side. But instead he was in some field in France and she must face this alone for John's sake.

'Buck up, Thing,' he would say to her if he was here and she must do just that. She went in search of her mother and a strong drink.

Dinner dragged on. Rather than find men from the family crypt, Nancy had pulled on the local professional class, which was wonderful, except for their age. A solicitor in his seventies spoke to her endlessly and she nearly nodded off at one point. Never had she been so relieved to leave the men at the table. Standing by the French window, the cool evening air took away the edges of the wine she had consumed, praying that the evening would come to an end.

The butler walked in the room. 'My lady, Sir Arthur Carew.'

Nancy clapped her hands and rose. 'Thank goodness.' She kissed Arthur's cheek and Alice's body tightened in anticipation of his glance meeting hers. 'Carew, darling, how wonderful, you made it.'

'How could I refuse?' He looked over Nancy's head, scanning the room. A smile lifted the corner of his mouth and a lantern of light exploded inside Alice as their glances met each other for the briefest moment.

Alice's mother said, 'Carew, how good to see you. Are you going to join the men or take your chances with us?'

'Your Grace, I thought I might freshen up.' He smiled and sought Alice's glance again. She could be wrong, but it would appear her mother was flirting with him.

'The men will have joined us by then. Do tell Simms if you require anything.' The countess sat back down and leaned towards Alice's mother and continued their conversation.

Alice drifted out into the garden. The air was cold on her bare skin, but it only heightened her sense of being alive. He was here. She couldn't figure out how or even why but her heart sang.

The dew was heavy on the lawn and the light from the salon was caught in the water drops on the tree branches. Above, the sky was filled with thousands and thousands of stars. She focused on the Plough and felt a hand on her elbow.

'Shouldn't you be inside?' she said, turning into Arthur's arms.

'How could I be when I saw this angel wandering in the garden alone?'

'Angel?' She pulled back to look at his face, half in light and half in shadow.

'Yes, mine I hope,' he said.

'Possibly.' She laughed softly.

'Only possibly.' He tilted his head and considered her.

'Well, one must look at all the options.' She forced herself to keep a straight face.

'Let's see.' He ran a finger down her cheek. 'There's Lord Effingham.'

'Yes, the ear trumpet is a bonus.' She grinned.

'Or maybe the Earl of Bloxham takes your fancy.'

'I think he rather prefers his dogs,' she said.

'True.' He leant down and put his forehead against hers. She enjoyed the feel of him as she slid her hands along his arms until they reached the back of his neck. His hair tickled her fingers.

'Alice,' he whispered, pulling her closer and kissing her.

There was a discreet cough and a glowing end of a cigar. 'Good evening, Carew; pleased we found the right attraction to pull you away from Cornwall.'

Alice and Arthur stepped away from each other. 'Indeed, you have.'

The Earl of Dunloch strolled with them back into the house.

*

Alice opened the note the maid handed her.

Come at once.
Mother

It was obviously penned in haste. Alice peeked in the looking glass then went to her mother's room and tapped on the door.

'Come in.'

Alice opened the door and entered.

'Alice, how could you?' Her mother paced her bedroom floor.

'What have I done?' Alice sat on the end of the bed. It was obvious that her mother had not spent the night on her own, unlike Alice.

'You were seen.' She turned to Alice with disapproval in her glance that Alice knew too well.

Alice frowned. 'Seen?'

'Last night Effingham saw you and Carew in an embrace,' she said.

'Oh.' Alice released the tension holding her rigid and met her mother's glance. 'And?'

'It's not done.' She shook her head.

Alice held up a hand and said, 'I'm a widow, he's unmarried...'

'That's the whole point.' She turned and fixed her glance on Alice. 'You are free. Carew is a lovely man, but a serious-minded one. He will want a very dull marriage.' She peered into the looking glass on the dressing table.

'Mother,' Alice said.

'Don't tell me you love him.' She tossed a glance over her shoulder.

Alice pressed her mouth into a thin line.

'That never works. By all means have an affair with him. But do not marry him.' She sat down and rubbed some cream onto her cheeks.

Alice began to speak but stopped. Her mother stood up and rang the bell for her maid. Alice had already been up and dressed for an hour. She had gone for an early morning ride alone and the whole time she had been thinking about Arthur and saying yes. This would not please her mother at all but it would please Alice.

Chapter Forty-Two

Standing at the window while Susan fixed the belt, Alice considered her attire. Fashions had changed, as she had been made aware of while at Castle Harkness. But for visiting sites about the estate this was a practical solution and economies must be made. Her clothing was an easy one. Although her figure suited the new dropped-waist style, her life right now didn't require the latest fashions from London, let alone Paris. She laughed to herself as she looked in the mirror. Not that long ago fashion was the one thing she and her mother could agree on but now things had changed.

Those days away had shown how far apart Alice's life and her mother's life had drifted. Alice scanned the horizon, looking for John. She could hear him heading off to the river. John loved watching the boats.

Down in the hall Wilfred greeted her. 'The telephone. Sir Arthur.'

Alice forced herself to proceed slowly to the telephone. The servants wouldn't be pleased if she married.

'Hello,' she said formally, just in case it wasn't him. It could be his secretary.

'Alice.'

'Yes,' she said suddenly breathless. Despite what her mother had said Alice knew what she wanted, and she didn't have to listen to her any longer.

'Aside from wanting to hear your voice I needed to tell you that I won't be in Cornwall on Saturday.'

'Oh.' She couldn't help it, her disappointment crept into her voice.

'I thought possibly you and John would enjoy a visit to London, the museums, the parks.'

She could see Arthur leading John through the displays, taking time to answer the millions of questions. She smiled. 'It might be possible.'

'Please make it happen.'

'Are you sure you want us around?' she asked.

'I couldn't think of anything I want more.' His voice dropped.

'Oh.' She flushed. He was talking about a few days in London she reminded herself. But she was sure that wasn't all. 'I'll check and see if I may stay with my mother… or my aunt.'

'Thank you.' He rang off and Alice closed her eyes for a moment then she walked out the front door and paused, taking a few steadying breaths. Clouds scudded across the sky, promising rain, but for now it was dry. On the occasions when the sun appeared then the landscape transformed. The greens were brighter, the sky bluer and her heart lighter. Arthur was becoming like the sun in her life. Dare she love again? It had all gone so wrong, so very wrong before.

Listening to John's happy cry in the distance, she stopped her thoughts. John was not wrong. Alice raced through the garden to be with him down by the river. The estate manager would wait. The call to her mother would wait but the spring sunshine would not.

Down on the quayside, the old gillie, Jed, doffed his cap. His glance followed her son who went straight to the river's edge. Jed bent low to chat to John. Looking at her son's intent face she saw his father and that was her burden to bear. John was safe and some day she would take him to France to see where his father had lost his life. She reached for a handkerchief in her pocket of her skirt and she felt paper. She paused. When had she last worn this? It was unlike Susan not to have found it and given it to her. Sitting on a large stone, she looked at the envelope. She broke the seal as she read the address, 7 rue de la Chaise, Apt 7, Paris, France.

Inside it she felt for a letter but found a photograph. Squinting, she swallowed a sob. The picture showing the back of two men close together. Shoulders touching, hands touching. They were looking to the Seine and the Eiffel Tower and not at the photographer. Edmund. His stance, his lean body, his shoulders and the birth mark on his neck, below his hair line, clear. How he'd joked about it. He was marked for life he'd said. He knew she would know him from this. Angel wings.

With shaking hands, she turned the photograph over. In pencil was the year, 1919. The photograph slipped from her fingers onto the grass as her son ran towards her. She swooped down and grabbed it and placed it and the envelope into her pocket before John or the nanny could see it. How was her husband alive and who was he with in Paris?

The evening sky above was pale and still light. Her fingers worried the envelope in her pocket. Edmund was alive. She wasn't a widow. For the past few days that had been her only thought. That and Arthur. But Edmund still walked this earth. His words to her on a May morning five years ago as he was off to war ran through her head.

Alice pulled the photo out of her pocket and studied the picture. There was love. It was there where the bodies touched. Intimacy. She could remember love. Edmund had found it. He had been right. She was free and her father-in-law died a happy man. Edmund's death in war was honourable, Alice had produced a male heir and the St Loy family would go on.

But dear God, she was jealous. She was angry and she should be none of those things. Sadness and longing for all that was lost, for what could have been was what she should be feeling. Those feelings she would allow to exist within her, but hurt bubbled to the top. She looked at the stones that made Penhale and the walls of the garden about her. She was not free.

Glancing at the nursery above, she placed the photograph back into the envelope. A lump the size of a peach stone formed in her throat. She had known love but had never understood it until John was born. But passion, she'd had it once and that would have to sustain her through the years ahead.

Along the far wall she saw a shadow; this shadow limped. It was Brindley. He had returned from the war minus a half a leg and most of his mind. She could not have borne it to see Zach broken.

Brindley looked up and bowed his fair head. Two brothers could hardly look more different but then Brindley took after his father. She turned back to look at the nursery window. The last rays of the setting sun reflecting off of it. She would head up and kiss John goodnight, even though she had done that hours before. It must be nearly nine thirty now. He would still be awake, looking through one of his picture books.

Entering the house, she plucked the fallen rose petals off the table. The fragrance was still strong as she raised them to her nose and the texture soft and smooth like John's skin. She raced up the stairs to the nursery, needing to hold her boy in her arms and against her heart. He was more precious than life itself.

He was asleep with the chapbook on his chest. She lifted it and tucked the blanket about his small body. Taking the book, she placed it on the window seat so that he would find it first thing when he woke. She tiptoed out of the room and down to hers. The sky was still light in the distance. Despite the joy that John brought her, her heart was heavy. She was living a lie. She wasn't a widow; she was a wife and that was something entirely different.

On the table beside her bed was a letter from Arthur. He was in love with her and she had been about to... to what? Let him in to her life but he was already in her heart. Most of the men of her generation were dead and this whole man wanted her.

Now she couldn't marry Arthur. The freedom that Edmund so badly wanted for her was gone. She dug out the envelope from her pocket. 7 rue de la Chaise, Apt 7, Paris, France. She ran her finger over it. Paris. She hadn't been there since before her season. Her French was now rusty but then she had been fluent. At seventeen she had been so full of so many things but able to do so little. Had she known then what she did now would she have changed her actions? No.

She walked slowly down the corridor to the morning room. She had letters to write but her thoughts were restless. Life hadn't come out as she had wished. She touched the photograph again.

At the desk she placed it standing against the ink pot and took a clean sheet of paper.

12 May 1920
Penhale

Dearest Edmund,

I find I am at a loss as to what to say other than thank God you are alive. I am filled with happiness. But as this is you I am writing to, I cannot lie. I am filled with anger too. My inside is twisted with relief and fear. I need to see you to know what you are doing, what you are thinking and how we will go on.

Know that in amongst all the fear and anger there is huge love and happiness. I eagerly await your reply.

Thing xx

Alice looked at it knowing it wasn't enough, but it would have to do. She addressed an envelope and placed it with the photograph in her pocket. She would post it herself tomorrow.

Chapter Forty-Three

Alice's feelings were mixed as they arrived at Abbotswood but John's were not when he saw Constance. He raced out of the car, straight to her coming out of the front door. Constance swung John up into her arms and twirled him about as she used to a few years ago. 'You have grown.' She put him down and looked to Alice. 'Our other guests haven't arrived so I thought I would walk John up to see the waterfall.' Constance looked closely at Alice. 'If you wouldn't mind.'

Alice smiled. 'He'll love it.'

'I thought he might.' Constance reached out and touched Alice's hand, giving her a searching look.

'We came via Brent church.' Alice looked at the roof line of Abbotswood. The sky behind it was a bright blue, making it look a bit like a cut-out of a gingerbread house.

'I'm sure Nanny likes the view up there,' Constance said, as John tugged on her hand, and they were off. Constance gave Alice a look of pure joy. If any woman deserved to be a mother, it was Constance but the likelihood of that happening now was slim with so few men. Although the daughter of a duke, Constance had no real fortune of her own and no great beauty. She was clever and kind and once that would have been enough. Alice clenched her fist. It wasn't right but there was nothing that could be done.

Burton stood by the door. 'There is tea in the library.'

'No thank you, I will take a walk.' She smiled at him and headed to the riverbank. A cloud covered the sun and the vivid spring green of the new leaves dulled. A shiver ran across her skin. She looked across the river then turned away.

She headed towards the swimming pond on her way back to the house. It gleamed in the sunlight and two men walked down towards her. One was her cousin, the Earl of Bath, but the other she did not recognise. Bath raised his hand and she strolled towards them. The gentleman on the left was foreign. It was obvious from the way he carried himself as much as his clothing.

'Darling Alice.' Bath kissed her cheek.

'Bath.' She smiled, pleased to see him. He wore a patch over his left eye. Rather than take away from his looks it added to his mystique. Had the war left any man whole?

'Allow me to introduce Baron Conrad Villiars.'

'Lady St Loy, your beauty is far greater than I had heard.' He bowed over her hand, raising it to his lips.

Her glance narrowed at this over the top compliment. She had forgotten how generous the continentals could be. Before she could reply, John was racing towards her at full pelt calling, 'Mumma.'

Trailing behind were Constance, Arthur and the nanny twenty yards behind them. She bent low and scooped John up. Once perched on her hip, he looked shyly about at the two strangers.

'Is this your son?' Baron Villiars asked.

She nodded.

'He looks like his father,' he said, his glance narrowing before he smiled.

Bath raised an eyebrow. 'Isn't it a good thing he does.' He chuckled. 'It is always a relief when that happens.' Alice nuzzled her son's head until she regained her composure. It was easy to forget that many people had known Edmund well. Bath intended no harm.

'Here's our hostess and the esteemed member for parliament. This is quite the gathering.' Bath adjusted his eyepatch. With a wicked grin on his face he looked a bit piratical.

Alice looked at her feet then said, 'Indeed.' She glanced to Arthur, her heart breaking, and then back to Baron Villiars. She didn't like the way he was studying John and her.

Bath had ensured that lunch had been a jovial affair, but Alice found herself exhausted. It was difficult being so near Arthur and not being able to say everything had changed because she couldn't tell him why. It was a relief when the meal was finished and they went into the garden. Alice watched her son race down the lawn by the long border full of spring colour.

The woman now beside Alice – Hester, Constance's companion – had been the biggest surprise. When Alice had heard that Constance had left the family home in London and moved into a small house with a companion, Hester Clifford, she had pictured a stout woman of undefinable age. She had not expected a beautiful woman of thirty, a childless widow. In between the witty comments from Bath, Alice had seen Hester watch Constance. And also noticed Constance's glance stray to Hester frequently. She read the signs.

'You don't appear shocked.' Hester pulled a bloom to her nose.

Alice studied her, trying to see where this was heading. In the distance Constance was in an animated discussion with the baron. Her cousin was happy, blossoming even.

She turned to Hester who was now focused on her. 'No, should I be?'

'Constance didn't think you would be, but I wasn't sure.'

Alice pressed her lips together. Had Constance spoken about the past to this woman? Isn't that what lovers did, share secrets? 'Constance knows me well.'

'She does and she speaks of you and John with great affection.'

Alice cast her a sideways glance. 'We adore her but sadly don't see enough of her.'

'You rarely leave Cornwall.'

Alice looked across the river. 'I love it and London has no real appeal.'

'Once it did.' Hester smiled.

'Ah, my infamous past.' Alice searched her face for maliciousness but found none.

'You were right. It was inhuman,' she said.

'Yes, but it was not the best time to do it.' Things might have been different, but the odds were that she would still be a widow.

'Do you regret it?' Hester asked.

'No.' Alice's thoughts travelled to the time after.

'You were brave making a stand.'

Alice laughed. 'It wasn't much of a stand. I was banished to the country and married a peer. So much for women's independence.' She laughed bitterly.

'Yes, this is true but as a widow now… you have choices.' Hester looked over her shoulder at Arthur.

Alice took a deep breath and closed her eyes for a moment. Arthur. 'Yes.'

'But, of course, John is your first thought,' she said.

He was waiting at the door of the shell house and calling her name.

'Always,' she said.

'I so wanted children.' Hester's voice dropped away.

Alice turned to her.

'But it is not to be. I was married for ten years and never blessed.'

'Your husband?' Alice asked.

'He had a child with his mistress.' The words were spoken without rancour, which Alice didn't think she would have been able to achieve. 'I am the broken one.' Hester gave a self-deprecating smile.

Alice watched Arthur take John's hand and open the door to the shell house. When Alice reached it, she hesitated but John took her hand, pulling her to the wonder inside. Wide-eyed, he seemed to have lost the power of speech as he took her hand and placed it on crystal after crystal. He wasn't interested in the shells, only the stones and fossils. Arthur put a name to each of them for him. Her heart swelled. John needed him and dear God she needed, no, wanted him. But she had wanted before and that had placed her here, in this situation now. She left the confines of the shell house.

With each step down the hillside she attempted to stop her circling thoughts until she reached the bank. The water was clear and, as the afternoon sun broke through cloud, the woodland floor across the river became a sea of violet blue. A flash of movement caught Alice's eye. Was the woodsman about his work. Did Abbotswood still have a woodsman? Or was she imagining things.

Behind her she heard a splash. Her fingers twitched, remembering the feel of the rod in her hands. She hadn't cast a line since that summer.

'Lady Alice,' Baron Villiars said, walking towards her. 'May I join you?'

'Certainly.' She turned to him. 'Forgive my directness but what brings you to Abbotswood?'

He smiled. 'I could say the fishing but that would be a lie.'

'You are missing something special then.' She glanced at the river.

'So I have been led to understand,' he said.

'Abbotswood is famed for the quality of its fishing,' she said as he fell into step beside her on the Abbotswood drive along the river to Horsebridge.

'But it was you I wanted to see.'

Her eyes opened wide. 'That is a surprise.'

'I thought it might be.' He nodded.

She stopped walking.

'It's about Lord St Loy,' he said. Although there was nothing odd in his appearance, she became uneasy as he scrutinised her.

She narrowed her glance. 'My son or my husband?'

'Husband.' He spoke so softly she barely heard him over the sound of the water.

A shiver covered her skin and she took a step away from him. 'Did you serve with him? He fought with the Belgian army at one point.'

'Yes.' Again, his voice was not much above a whisper and Alice's throat dried. Was he about to reveal Edmund as a deserter? This thought had been moving around in her mind, but she had pushed it aside. Never mind that he was alive, but if it came out that he had deserted. She must stop this man from saying more. Did he intend to blackmail her?

'Your husband was—' he waved his hands searching for a word '—not the… man you thought he was.'

Her mouth dried. 'I knew Edmund since I was able to walk. There was little I didn't know about him.' She forced a pleasant smile.

'I wonder if we can truly know another human being,' he said. The sun vanished behind a cloud. The water went from glistening to a sludgy colour, not reflecting the joyous apple crisp greens of the unfurled leaves.

'That is a rather philosophical statement and no, I do not believe we can.' She looked him directly in the eye. 'We have all done and thought things we would never want another human being to know.'

He appeared to be about to speak.

'I have found the bible stands one in good stead in this area, Baron Villiars.' She said his name almost as a caress. 'He without sin…'

'Mumma.' John raced towards her and she met the baron's eye before focusing on her son. She didn't flinch nor show any sign of fear.

'Villiars.' Bath walked up to them. 'We need to set off.'

Bath kissed her cheek. 'My dear, you become more beautiful with each year.'

'And you become more outrageous.' She smiled. 'I look forward to meeting your fiancée.'

'You'll like her. She has spirit like you.'

Her mouth twitched. One kind person had called her spirited rather than wilful years ago. It might have been Bath's mother.

'Lady Alice, a pleasure to spend time with you.' The baron bowed over her hand. 'I am certain we will meet again.'

Alice resisted the urge to pull it away from him but prayed this would be the last time she would ever see or hear of him.

Chapter Forty-Four

London had been fraught. She had missed John as if her heart had been ripped out. There was a ball. Her aunt, the duchess, was hosting and it had been the right thing to do but as she walked London's streets and parks, she was a stranger. This landscape, once so familiar, was wrong. She only found ease when beside the Thames, yet it was nothing like the Tamar. Its murky depths brown and smelly unlike the clear water of her river. The river had become her soul, or more her lifeline.

Her time there had been a tease. She had spent evenings dancing in Arthur's and other men's arms. Most of them were either far older or far younger than she was. She witnessed the madness that was taking hold of the young. Could she blame them, no. What Alice's generation and older ones had done was destroy their world. The past was gone, obliterated by the war to end all wars. But life tried to act as it had before. The season was in full swing. Yet the walking wounded stood on the edges of the dance floors, unable, unwilling, or not wanted. The sparkling faces of this season's debutantes parading by but for what? A broken man, one barely out of the schoolroom, or one so old her flesh crawled at the thought of a sexual act with them. It was so different to her season.

And yet, in the midst of it all, Arthur was there with her. His hand firm against her waist holding, tempting, reassuring her. But he hadn't asked to marry her. Had he sensed her reluctance? It had been odd to find herself standing on the same balcony as she had as a naïve girl. Now both of them were different. His hand sought hers in the cool evening air. She thought maybe that he would propose then and there. She hadn't wanted him to because she must refuse. Yet it was the only thing she desired. How she had changed. Once the thought of marrying a respectable man and being a wife was her last wish, and now she yearned for it.

London and Arthur were far away now. Relentless rain battered the thin glass panes. She sat, mesmerised, watching the drops burst and pool down to the thin metal sash bars. The wind increased and threw everything at the fragile barrier between wet and dry. Motionless, she waited for the first crack as the wind pushed it harder still. But it held.

Alice touched her mouth. Thinking about Arthur helped nothing. She would be better to resolve the things she could. She must set him free. It was unfair to him and to all the other women he could love. She put her hand on her heart. It was selfish to hold onto him. Edmund was alive. She would not think of herself. She would put the man she loved first.

Moving to the desk she pulled out paper and filled her pen with ink.

15 June 1920
Dearest Arthur,

She balled the paper up and began again. She must not give him any reason to hold onto hope.

Dear Arthur

Again, she threw the paper away.

Carew,

She tapped the pen against her teeth thinking of all the words she wanted to say. Hold me. Love me. You have my heart entirely.

> *For some time, we have been close and becoming closer.*
> *It must and will cease. I am sorry if you were under the*
> *impression that I returned your feelings.*

She lifted the pen from the paper. She loved him more than life itself.

> *But that is not the case. If I have caused you pain, I am*
> *sorry. But by parting now you can find the right woman*
> *to share your life.*

Alice closed her eyes as she leaned back. A fat tear hit the bottom of the paper. She dried it and her eyes with her handkerchief. She could do this. She was made of iron.

Thank you for your kindnesses, especially with John.

Yours sincerely,
Lady Alice St Loy

She pushed away from the desk. The rain had not let up. A walk would help but instead she was trapped in this house and in her own thoughts. She folded the letter and addressed the envelope. It was done.

The dawn chorus was at full volume. Alice walked to the window, her heart heavy. She had heard nothing from Arthur but what had she expected? He was a proud man and she had sent him away. He wouldn't come chasing. That story was finished and she needed to move on.

She might be living a lie, but she would be living it honestly. Holding her breath she looked down below. On the edge of the flower bed a small rabbit was merrily eating the flowers. Brindley would be furious.

She needed to do something though. She couldn't marry Arthur. Digging out the envelope from where she'd put it below her bible, she studied the address 7 rue de la Chaise, Apt 7, Paris, France. She touched it. Paris. That was the answer. She must go.

Below, she saw Wilfred striding towards the courtyard. What had ruffled him this time? Wilfred didn't approve of some of the decisions she had made about the estate. And like Burton he had a way of making his views known without directly stating them. She walked to the nursery and found John playing with the aeroplane model that Arthur had given him. She put her hand to her heart. It would all be fine, and it was time for the communion service in the chapel. She held out her hand and reluctantly John put the plane down and picked up a rock that he slipped into his pocket. He was silent, which was most unlike him, but maybe he felt her melancholy.

Honeysuckle scented the air as they walked through to the chapel. She much preferred worshipping at this hour and the vicar was pleased to humour her. The congregation consisted of her staff and a few villagers. John squirmed beside her, rolling the stone between his fingers. She pulled a small book out of her pocket. The vicar would keep this service blissfully short. He had other places to be. John could be quiet if not still for the duration.

Out of the corner of her eye she saw Jed Carne, Brindley and Brindley's family take a seat in the back. They came for the hymns. They were more chapel people, she knew, but both Edmund and Zach and all the other men lost to the war were remembered on the walls here at Penhale. As with every estate across the country, the legacy of loss was far too long.

John shifted closer to her and hummed. It would be down to him to look after all of this and she would make sure he was prepared for the task. She hadn't been but she was learning and learning fast.

They stood and sang 'All Things Bright and Beautiful' but Alice's mind wasn't on it. She glanced to the ceiling and noted the three hares of the St Loy coat of arms on one of the wooden roof bosses. She hadn't noticed when having luncheon at Abbotswood whether the St Loy coat of arms had been added to the dining room. It might have been, but even before Baron Villiars had mentioned Edmund, he had unsettled her.

John snuggled in next to her when they sat for the sermon. She looked down at the book she'd brought to amuse him. *Alice's Adventures in Wonderland*. He was studying the page with the March Hare. She smiled and took his small hand in hers. Sunlight broke through and illuminated the stained glass depicting a fish, the symbol of Christ and, in a way, her downfall. She suppressed a smile at the irony.

They rose for the bidding prayers. Alice mouthed the words. She prayed but no longer for her husband's soul, but for him still breathing. Anger tightened her chest. He was off in Paris finding love and she had had to push love away.

She put a smile on her face and thanked the vicar who stood by the door. John tugged at her hand, which gave her the excuse to slip away without any more than the perfunctory words. The vicar had looked at her encouragingly, but she wasn't going to be drawn. No matter how nice a man he was, no one could be trusted with her secret. She now carried two. One was her son's true father and now that her husband was living with his lover.

Out in the main courtyard, John raced away from her, towards the kitchen, and she walked through the garden to the woods. There was solace to be found in the woods or was it memory? She and her lover had taken refuge among the trees, which shaded them from the summer sun and the prying gaze of others. But as she reached the gate she turned back.

Inside the private chapel the scent of extinguished candles hung in the air. She stood in front of the memorial listing

Edmund's details. It was all wrong but that might appeal to him. A tear ran down her cheek. She lifted her hand from the stone and brushed the tear away. So much had been lost but not her husband, it would seem.

Everything was almost in place for her journey to Paris. She had found a plausible excuse to be in London. Once secrecy had been easy, necessary, but now it frustrated her at every turn. She was irritable and this didn't help anything. The weather was beautiful as it had been that summer six years ago.

Alice studied the accounts in front of her. The daffodils had come back and the rents from the tenanted farms helped but there must be some other way to build the income. She couldn't and wouldn't increase rents. Every one of them were still suffering from the effects of the war. She tapped the numbers in front of her. This should have been Edmund's problem but then she doubted he had a better head for these things. He had not been a practical soul in any way. God, she mustn't think of him as gone because he wasn't. Her head ached with it all. She rubbed her temples and closed her eyes. When she opened them, Constance was standing in front of her.

'Doesn't the estate manager sort that for you?' Constance asked.

Alice rose to her feet and embraced her cousin. 'Yes and no.'

'Does that mean he does but he doesn't do it to your liking?'

Alice laughed. 'You know me too well.'

Constance took her gloves off. 'Clearly, I don't.'

Alice frowned as she pulled the bell, hoping that Wilfred already had refreshments in hand.

'I am just from London and Carew.' She cast Alice a sideways glance.

Alice looked down.

'I may not know much but I do know a broken heart when I see one.'

Alice rested a hand on the desk. The room swayed.

'You are not cruel without reason.' Constance stared with an unblinking gaze.

Alice looked at her cousin. There was no reply she could give.

Wilfred entered. 'I have arranged coffee in the drawing room.'

'Thank you, Wilfred.' Alice walked down the hall, trying to compose her thoughts.

'Is John about?' Constance asked, entering the room and heading straight to the piano. On it sat the one of three photographs that Alice had of her and Edmund together. She was in evening gown and he uniform. It was a friend of Edmund's who had taken it and he had captured a moment of lightness, togetherness. Anyone looking at it would have thought that they had been the perfect couple. For two people who had never shared anything more than a childhood kiss they were intimate.

'My lady, the post.' Wilfred placed the silver salver down by the coffee and Alice saw the second letter she had sent to Edmund returned. Return to sender, not known at this address, written clearly in French. She scooped it up before Constance could read it and discover Alice was writing to her dead husband in Paris. God knows what Wilfred thought. But then she was certain he had seen so much over the years that he was part of the fabric that held the building together.

When Alice straightened, she saw Constance picking up the Baedeker's Guide to Paris. Her throat constricted.

'Planning a trip?' Constance asked, flipping through the pages. The envelope with the photograph dropped to the floor. She picked it up.

Alice's hands shook as she poured the coffee. No one but her must bear this secret. Edmund had deserted and was living in Paris with his lover. The latter Constance would understand, but the former she would never forgive. Alice herself struggled with this every day. She handed the cup to her cousin and Constance placed the book and envelope down. Alice must be careful.

'You don't appear yourself.'

Alice cleared her throat. 'Worries about the estate may have caused a few sleepless nights.'

'Hmm. But you do look better than Arthur.' She sipped her coffee. 'He loves you.'

Alice studied her hands in her lap. She loved him.

'He's a good man. Maybe not as exciting as some, but I thought you cared for him.' She sent Alice a hard stare. 'In fact, I'd wager the fortune I don't have on it.'

There was nothing Alice could say that wouldn't make things worse.

Constance put her cup down. 'You have a chance to love again.'

Alice looked out the window. The sky was brilliant blue, simply perfect weather to be happy. 'Did Arthur send you?'

'No, he has no idea I'm here.'

The tension in Alice eased. It would be fine. Everything would resolve itself. Arthur would find a fine wife and he would forget her. Men were few and he was one of the best.

John raced through the door and straight to his cousin.

'My, you are growing so fast.' Constance hugged him tight. Alice smiled but that vanished when she saw Constance studying her. She must avoid scrutiny at all costs. Too much was at stake.

After coffee Constance drove them to the quay and John raced off to find the gillie.

'Thank you for visiting.' Alice watched her son rather than see the expression of disapproval she knew Constance would be wearing.

'Call him,' she said.

Alice shook her head, knowing every time she passed the telephone she wanted to pick it up and hear his voice.

'Don't throw this away.' She picked up Alice's hand. 'You will regret it.' Constance stood. 'He wouldn't want you to mourn him forever.'

Alice remained silent as she rose.

'I'll be at Abbotswood for the week. Why don't you visit?' Constance kissed her cheek.

She smiled and waved as her cousin returned to her car. 'Maybe.'

Constance was off in a cloud of dust. Alice coughed, thinking of her cousin's words: he wouldn't want her to mourn forever. Edmund or Zach?

'Mumma, look.' John strolled towards her, bearing a small trout. 'I wanted you to see it before we put it back.'

'Wonderful.' She smiled and walked with John to the gillie. Carefully the old man set the fish back into the water and after a few moments it wriggled and moved into the current. She ran her fingers through John's glossy hair. Someday she would have to let him go, but for now she could hold him close.

Chapter Forty-Five

Alice stood at the bottom of the staircase in the grand hall of Exeter House, trying to find a way to leave, to do anything but be there. Arthur had just walked through the vestibule. He hadn't seen her, thank God. Of course, she had known that seeing him was a possibility. Constance took her elbow trying to lead her towards him but Alice pulled away, heading to the furthest corner of the room and stood behind a pillar. She was behaving like a child, a naughty child who had been caught out. She had done nothing more than let a kind man down.

'Here, this might bring some colour back to your cheeks.' Arthur held out a glass of champagne. Her hand trembled. 'I'm not a ghost nor do I tend to frighten women.'

Alice took a deep breath. 'No, I wouldn't say that was your mode of operation.' She looked up at him. Her chest tightened. She hurt from the inside out.

'It was bound to happen that we would meet,' he said.

She nodded. He touched her hand and even through the glove her skin tingled. This was madness. She sipped the champagne without tasting it.

'I wanted to say my feelings haven't changed.' He looked at her.

'No.' She closed her eyes for a moment. These were not the words she wanted to hear, but it was what her heart wanted more than anything. She opened her eyes. She had to be strong. Forcing a bright smile onto her lips, she said, 'If you'll excuse me, I haven't seen my uncle yet and it would be rude of me to ignore him.'

His knuckles brushed hers and she paused a moment before she fled. Another second in his company and she would give in and she couldn't. Tomorrow she was leaving for Paris. She had to find Edmund and have him promise that he would be careful, that he would be discreet. If people discovered he was alive, that he had deserted, it would kill his mother and cast a black cloud over the name of St Loy that would never leave.

The Gard du Nord was as she had remembered it, crowded and foul-smelling. The July heat didn't help. A porter retrieved her baggage and, once in a taxi, she suppressed the small bit of excitement at being in this glorious city again. Everything had been full of promise the last time, and now she wasn't sure what to think. She had been so innocent. Then her only concerns had been suffrage for women, the dresses and how to make it through the season without being sold to the highest bidder.

She had heard talk of war, but it hadn't seemed real. Now so many men were in the ground and her innocence and joy had gone with them. Yet Paris was still exhilarating. Excitement oozed out of every stone.

Alice had lied to everyone about this trip and Constance suspected something. Susan was the only one who knew where she was, and she was sworn to secrecy. She had told the story of the Paris trip for clothing. Her appearances at various social events this past week had made it all seem feasible. She was truly emerging from her period of mourning.

The taxi pulled up to the Hotel Meurice and Alice stepped out of the automobile. There was a strange freedom in travelling alone. She had never done it before and it was as if she should be off to meet a lover and not to find her husband.

'Lady St Loy, it is a pleasure to welcome you to Hotel Meurice.' The concierge bowed and her bags were taken to her room. She wanted to immediately head out and discover this address, but she was travel weary. A bath, a cup of tea and a nap would be best before she went on her search.

'Shall I send a maid up to assist you?'

She nodded and followed the manager to her room. The suite overlooked the Jardin des Tuileries and, as soon as he had disappeared, she flung the doors to the balcony wide. Looking down, she drank in the wide boulevards, the beautiful gardens and the Seine. Somewhere out there was Edmund. She thought for sure she would feel his presence in the city but she didn't.

The maid bustled about the room behind her, unpacking her things and running the bath. A knock on the door caught her heart. She didn't turn. It would be tea and not Edmund somehow knowing she was here. She longed to see him.

The last time she had was when he was recovering from gas exposure. He had spent so much of that time with John. As her son had grown, she had watched Edmund's love for him grow. He had not been interested in the peaceful bundle at the christening. Her mother had whispered in her ear that few men enjoyed babies. But on Edmund's next leave, when John could smile at him, things had changed. And on that final visit they had played with Edmund's old tin soldiers. She'd loved watching their joy at being together.

When the letter had come from Edmund's commanding officer, it had said that his men had loved him, and he was one of the best to have served in the regiment. But Edmund wasn't dead. He had deserted her, John and his men, all in the last days of the war. And what of Zach? He was never found. The wind outside stirred and leaves lifted on the plane trees lining the boulevard.

The door caught the wind and slammed. Alice poured the tea, inhaling the fragrance of bergamot, and watched the leaves collecting in the silver strainer. She didn't add any milk or sugar. She wanted to taste something clean and clear. The tea didn't disappoint. She poured another cup, thinking about what she would discover when she found Edmund. The one thing she knew was that he had found love and this was good. She needed to see him. To talk with him and then she could resign herself to the lonely years ahead.

The staff were watching as Alice left the hotel unaccompanied, having refused a taxi. This was not the way a lady behaved but at this moment she was not a lady, rather a wife in search of her husband. The afternoon sun was hot as she strolled past the rose garden in the park and once she was sure that she could no longer be seen she exited through the nearest gate by the Seine and walked across the Pont Royal before upping her pace.

Sweat beaded under her hat and slowly trickled down the

back of her neck. She would be both hot and damp when she saw Edmund again and she didn't want that. She was vain enough to want to appear her best. She slowed down. The address was not far. Just before she was due to turn onto the street in question, she stopped and entered a church.

Cool air filled the dim atmosphere. The scent of incense lingered on the air. Candles flickered below statues and she sat in the last pew, cooling down and collecting her thoughts. Beneath her gloves her palms were sweaty. It wasn't because of the heat of the summer day. She could pretend it was, but the pain in her chest told her a different story. How do you face a man you've grieved for? She had loved Edmund for so long. Now as she sat in the silence of the church, she did not know what to feel, to think, or to do.

A beam of sunlight pierced the gloom, highlighting the feet of the crucified Christ suspended above the altar. Somewhere in the back of her mind the words of an old vicar resounded. He died for us. The men of the Great War had done that too. Edmund hadn't died but absconded. He had served bravely up until that last moment. Wasn't that enough?

In her pocket was one of his letters. She knew it by heart, which was just as well as her tears had caused much of the writing to bleed across the paper.

My dearest Thing,

I woke this morning feeling I had truly fallen down a rabbit hole and lived in a nightmare. Instead of mad queens and madder hatters, I was surrounded by desperate men and mud. But what woke me this morning was the sound of a wood pigeon, and in that moment I was home and waking in my own bed as I had the last time I was there. Young John was there tugging on the blanket whispering, 'Wake up, wake up.' His sweet face full of joy and mischief. It was a blissful moment as I remembered your beautiful smile and then came the sound of an explosion so close that it shook the ground and brought me to my senses.

I don't know what will happen in the next few days. I wanted to let you know that I love you and John more than I could have ever imagined. It has made my life so very different and entirely richer. Would that the dream was all true and not just an illusion. But love is always real in whatever shape it takes and I am grateful for yours and John's. I hold it tight. Know that I love you as I can, and that darling John has taken hold of my heart.

I don't know when I will be able to write again. Keep well.

Yours always,
E

A tear slipped down her cheek and she brushed it aside. What message was he trying to send her with that photograph? She stood and looked at the altar. Love. Christ had sacrificed himself because he so loved us. She must show nothing but love when she faced Edmund. Of that she was certain, but of nothing else.

Outside the address Alice stopped. The building was not what she had expected. There was nothing grand about it.

She had anticipated Edmund's love of beautiful things to be evident, but she would have walked right past it had she not been following the numbers. A woman eyed her from behind a curtain. Alice adjusted her hat and walked up to the gate. She glanced at the apartment numbers and rang the bell. There was no response. She tried again. Still nothing.

Pulling the letter and the photograph out of her bag, she double checked the address. It was correct. The curtain twitched. Alice needed to speak to her. This was not the time for holding back. She was here in Paris and the longer she was here, the sooner someone at home would discover her real reasons for the trip.

She walked towards the window and the woman pulled back, but Alice wasn't going to give up. She tapped gently on the glass. The woman watched her from the centre of the room. The window was open an inch and the smell of boiling cabbage surrounded Alice. Her nose wrinkled.

She signalled to the woman who continued to stare. There was no choice. She bent down and said, '*Excusez moi, s'il vous plaît.*' The woman continued to watch, and Alice forced down her revulsion of the aroma and went on to ask about an Edmund St Loy who lived in the building.

The woman shook her head. '*Non*, Edmund St Loy.'

'Please come to the gate and speak with me,' Alice asked.

The woman narrowed her glance but nodded at Alice. She disappeared from view and Alice straightened, ready to step away from the window. Heaven knows what anyone would think, seeing her behave in such a manner.

The sound of shuffling footsteps and the turn of the lock preceded the gate opening. Alice smiled then said, '*Merci.*'

The woman summoned her into the small dark passageway. The smell in here was worse than the cabbage wafting out the street side window. Alice's stomach turned, but she kept a pleasant expression on her face while she went on to ask again about Edmund.

The woman repeated that no Edmund lived there. Alice was about to give up when she pulled the photograph out of the envelope and in desperation showed it to the woman. The woman took it and squinted at it. It was the back of two men. Alice had little hope, but she tried.

'Ah, Philippe and Zachariah.' She handed it back, shaking her head muttering '*non naturel*' and blessing herself. Alice's chest tightened. Zachariah? Edmund?

Alice asked if they were in and the woman tutted before telling her that they were not. Philippe left after Zachariah had died. She turned to walk away. Alice grabbed her arm. She needed more.

'*S'il vous plaît…*' Alice spoke twisting her hands together. The woman turned and Alice asked if she had an address. The woman walked away and Alice closed her eyes. What should she do now? She opened them again when she heard the woman's feet shuffling on the tile floor. She held out a piece of paper. In French she told Alice that Philippe was there as she pointed at the paper, and that the other one was in Passy Cemetery. Buried six weeks ago.

Alice thanked her then hurried out of the gate. She walked up the street, clutching the paper. The address was in Bruges. She couldn't do anything about that right at this moment, but it was possible she could visit the graveyard. Pulling out her Baedeker's she looked at the map. It wasn't too far, but it was further from the hotel. It didn't matter. She needed to know.

Clutching her guidebook, she strolled past cafés now filling with people. Couples with heads leaning close together and hands touching across the table. Music carried on the evening air. An elegant couple strolled into the park together. The Eiffel Tower appeared in view down streets and boulevards as if it was playing hide and seek with her. Arthur came to mind. Paris, the city of love. She longed to be here, enjoying a summer night with him. Dreams were lovely things, but that was all that they were.

Shop windows were beautifully dressed but they couldn't hold her attention. Her mind worked through the things she was certain of which were few. A clock chimed the quarter hour and she picked up her pace, remembering the graveyard might be closing for the evening. Slightly out of breath she waited to cross the street and saw a man locking the beautiful gates to the cemetery. Tomorrow she would come and look for Zachariah. Nothing made sense. He couldn't be here.

Unlike yesterday's sunshine the morning was wet and not ideal for a lady to wander the streets of Paris alone. Not that that was easy at any time, but with insistent rain pounding down she couldn't say she was taking the air; it would be more like taking a swim. She paced the suite. What was John up to? His nanny would keep a close watch. Maybe she should have brought them with her. John would have enjoyed the parks and the Eiffel Tower. But then there would have to be explanations.

That may well come. All night long she had tossed and

turned. Philippe and Zachariah. Who was the man with Edmund? She knew they were lovers. She hadn't needed the woman's muttering. If Edmund's lover had died why would he have moved to Belgium? God, she didn't know who was whom.

She spun on her heel and picked up the telephone to inquire about travel to Bruges. If the weather cleared this afternoon she could go to the graveyard and proceed to Bruges as soon as possible. There she would find Philippe or Zachariah and hopefully find answers.

By the time she had gathered the necessary information for travel, the rain had all but stopped. She, again to the dismay of the staff, left the hotel on foot, heading into the park. The raindrops pooled on every surface and the flowers all had drooping heads from the onslaught of the morning precipitation. She felt a bit like them. With each step she knew that this would be a fruitless exercise, but as she was here she would follow through.

At a flower stall she stopped and bought white and yellow roses for remembrance and friendship. It was awful thinking that she might have lost Edmund again. She needed to know because her heart couldn't take much more. She had overcome the anger in her but now she was filled with sadness. And what of this Zachariah? That couldn't be a coincidence.

She confused the woman by buying three tight red rose buds and three stems of tuberose. The fragrance tickled her nose. She had not been allowed to mourn Zach differently to any of the other men they had lost from the estate. So rose buds and tuberose expressed it all... passionate love only beginning with dangerous pleasure.

Her strides shortened as she left the Jardin du Trocadero and she turned towards the cemetery. Once through the gates she went to the office but it was closed. She turned and strolled past grand tombs mixed with statues expressing the love and the loss of those left behind. How was she going to find this Zachariah? In the distance she saw the gravedigger leaning on his shovel. Avoiding puddles, she made her way to the gravedigger.

'*Bonjour*,' he said, bowing his head.

'*Bonjour.*' She asked about the office and he explained there had been an emergency. She asked about a Zachariah that was buried six weeks ago. He remembered and in silence they walked down the path to the far end by the tall brick wall. He left her there to give her privacy, but she wanted to stamp her feet. There was nothing more than a mound of earth. No head stone, but of course it would be too soon. Her hand, clutching the bouquet, fell to her side. She stood there, not moving, not thinking. The mud was wet and dark. A cold chill passed around her. She looked over her shoulder, but she was alone among the many souls buried here. Would she never know?

She placed both bouquets on the earth. A bit of mud tarnished the brightness of the blooms. She didn't know what to feel. She didn't know who she was here mourning or indeed what she was doing here.

The rain began to spit, and she raced towards the gates, stopping when she saw someone in the office. She tapped on the door. Hopefully they could give her the information she needed.

After managing to explain in convoluted French, the man

confirmed that six weeks ago they had buried Zachariah Carne, an Englishman, a soldier living in Paris. Alice drew on all her poise in completing the conversation with the kind man. She turned slowly out into the rain and returned to the mound of earth and fell to her knees. At first tears wouldn't come and her hands dug in the wet earth wanting to hold what couldn't be held any longer. Then deep sobs wracked her body and she understood nothing except the pain of loss tearing her apart.

Chapter Forty-Six

Alice obtained a tourist map from the concierge and discovered the address was not far from the hotel. Again, she set out alone and with trepidation. But the beauty of the city spared from the destruction in the war soothed her. She was well aware that, although the buildings showed no damage, the people within them had suffered greatly.

During the journey from Paris, she had pondered the information that Zachariah Carne was buried under that mound of earth. Rather than go immediately to Bruges, she had spent a few days in Paris, mostly in churches lighting candles. She didn't know what else to do. There were so many things going around in her head that it hurt. The hotel maid thought she was insane, and she could be correct.

Now the day was bright and almost too warm. She paused outside a beautiful mansion. The contrast was so great to the apartment building in Paris. It couldn't be correct. Who had sent her the photograph? The writing had looked like Edmund's but now she wasn't sure of anything.

Did Philippe work in this house? She walked up the stairs to the front door. She had come too far to turn back now.

The door opened before she could change her mind.

'*Bonjour*,' she said, not turning and running away like she wanted to. '*Je cherche Philippe*,' she blurted out. The manservant looked her up and down and obviously deemed her suitable to speak to as he stepped aside and opened the door further for her to enter.

'*Un moment, s'il vous plaît*.' He bowed and she stood clasping her hands together. The interior was opulent with a grand staircase in the centre of the hall which rose to a landing before splitting and rising again. The manservant had disappeared into one of the rooms to her left. Beneath her feet the coffee-coloured marble glistened and reflected the light from the golden chandelier above. This was so far removed from the cabbage-smelling building in Paris that she was certain it was going to be a horrible mistake and difficult to extricate herself from. Silently she thought of things she could say to exit with her dignity intact. It might be simpler to walk out the door now before another second passed.

At the sound of footsteps, she turned. Her heart fell. It was Baron Conrad Villiars.

He walked towards her with his hand extended. 'Lady Alice.'

She held her hand out and he bent over it. When he straightened, the look on his face was full of sadness. Hers, she was positive, was full of confusion.

'Tea?' he asked.

'Yes, thank you,' she said.

'Please come this way into my study.' He held out a hand directing her.

This small room was restrained compared to the opulence of the entrance hall. Here the walls were lined with books.

Most in French or German but scattered with English titles. However, it was the desk that captured her attention. In an ornate silver frame was a photo of Edmund as she remembered him with a slight smile on his lips and his eyes gleaming with laughter. It looked as if he was about to say something outrageous as he frequently had.

'Please take a seat.' Villiars gestured to the red armchair. She sank into it, relieved. She was shaken. The picture of Edmund unnerved her as did Villiars.

He sat in the chair opposite her. 'Have you been to Bruges before?'

'No.' The last thing she wanted was small talk. Edmund. Zach. And so many things raced in her brain.

'Once the tea has arrived, I will try and answer your questions.' He smiled kindly.

'Thank you.' She heard a child call out and looked at him.

'All I will say first is that we live complicated lives.' He raised his eyebrows.

This was something she couldn't argue with. She looked down at her hands and pulled off her gloves. The tea arrived and he dismissed the servant before offering it to her.

'I wondered if you would come and find me.' He handed her the cup and saucer.

She frowned. 'Why?'

'The letter I left for you that day,' he said.

She shook her head. 'I did not receive it.'

He tilted his head to the side. 'Curious, but it does not matter now that you are here.'

'Forgive me, are you Conrad... or Philippe?' she asked.

'Both are my names,' he said.

She nodded and added a bit of sugar to her cup in the hopes it would steady her for what was to follow. 'I see.'

'Do you? I think these things are complex.' He placed his fingertips together in a thoughtful pose.

'What was in the letter you left for me?' She sipped the tea.

He shrugged. 'I don't know. It was from Edmund and I did not read it.' He looked at her. 'I believe you have received a photograph from him.'

She nodded.

'They were supposed to be together, but he was not well, and he was trying to hide the letter from me.'

She took a deep breath. 'Why?'

'Our life together needed to be totally secret.' He looked around the room. 'But he wanted you to know that he had found love.' His face softened.

Alice closed her eyes and let air return to her lungs. Opening them, she scanned the baron's face and said, 'Edmund loved you.'

'I loved him.' He looked directly at her.

She smiled. 'I am pleased.'

'He knew you would be, and he didn't want to hurt you in any way.'

She put her cup down. 'I'm afraid I'm confused.'

He smiled ruefully. 'I'm not surprised. I'm not sure where to start or what you do and do not know.'

Alice went to pull out the picture. She had carefully slipped it under the paper lining the back inside cover. But it wasn't in her bag. She had last looked at it on the train. She must have left it on there. Her chest tightening. The picture. What would people think if they saw it? But then she relaxed. Only she would know it was Edmund. 'The photograph?'

'Yes, I had argued with him, but he wanted you to have it,' he said.

She closed her eyes and she felt his fingers touching hers. 'I thought he was dead.'

'A double loss, no?' he said.

She nodded. 'You didn't say anything.'

'I tried but it proved difficult.' He held his hands out in an almost pleading gesture.

She understood, but here she was now dealing with his loss all over again. 'What happened?'

'As you know Edmund suffered from a mustard gas attack.'

She nodded.

'Well, although he was fit enough to serve again, he caught pneumonia this past winter and could not fight it.'

She entwined her fingers squeezing them tight.

'He died in my arms.' He looked down as his emotions took hold.

She glanced away, trying to compose herself. 'I'm so sorry.'

'I was honoured to be with him.' The echo of children's voices in the hallway interrupted him.

'Your wife?' Alice looked to the door.

'Understanding.' He smiled.

'I see.' But she wasn't sure she did.

'I love her, but not as I loved Edmund.' He took a sip of his tea. 'We found something I could never have with my wife, a passion, a love... and we fought together.'

'Zach?' she asked.

'Ah, yes.' He stood and walked to the window.

'He was in Paris with you?'

He turned to her. 'No, the good Zachariah was never in Paris.'

'But I saw his grave.' She rose to her feet.

He shook his head. 'That is Edmund's.'

She closed her eyes for a moment before speaking. 'I don't understand.'

'I am not surprised but your Zachariah was the best of men. He saved Edmund's life and lost his own in the process.'

She went to speak but he held up a hand. 'Let me explain.'

She nodded.

'During fighting that day Edmund had been hit in the leg. Zach had gone to find him that night.' He paced. 'And he did find him. He bandaged the leg and began to carry him back. That was when Zachariah was hit.'

Alice flinched.

'It was a fatal wound. Edmund held him until the end.' He closed his eyes for a moment.

Edmund and Zach. She took a deep breath, not sure she wanted to hear more.

'From what little Edmund told me after Zach died, he could take no more. He was broken.' He shivered.

'Edmund's letter...' She paused, trying to remember what he had written. 'Only Zach's death would trouble him.'

He nodded his head. 'Shortly after the armistice was signed, he contacted me.' He sighed. 'Like you, I believed him dead.'

She squinted, trying to understand but none of this made sense. 'How did he survive?'

He shrugged. 'I don't know, and he never spoke of it. He

was less himself, but I had hope.' He paused and studied her. 'Edmund was a good man.'

She nodded.

'The war had made him and then it broke him.' His hands tried to express what his words could not.

'Yes,' she whispered, sitting back down. 'And Zach?'

He walked to his desk, unlocking a drawer. 'He still loved you. I found these after Edmund died. They are Zach's letters he'd written to you but never sent.' He handed her the stained bundle. 'Edmund had kept them, and I could not destroy them.'

Her hand shook and she dropped them on her lap. 'I still don't understand.'

'I believe, piecing together the little Edmund told me, that Zach's death broke him. When he came to his senses, he decided he didn't have to be Edmund St Loy and as someone else he could love whom he wanted; he didn't have to conform any longer.'

'I see.' But she didn't. Her hand touched the rusty-coloured spots on the letters. Zach died in France. He wasn't in a grave-yard in Paris.

'My dear Lady Alice, your confusion is evident.' He poured more tea. 'How can I help?'

'I don't know.'

'Edmund and Zach were very close.' He looked at her intently. 'Closer than brothers usually are.'

She gasped.

'You didn't know they were half-brothers?'

She shook her head, but it explained so much. Why Zach had spent so much time with Edmund growing up.

'Edmund marrying you was the right thing, but it drove a wedge between them for a while.'

'Oh.' She stroked the envelopes.

'I can see I have surprised you,' he said.

She shook her head, not sure what her thoughts were. 'But they forgave each other?'

'Yes, even before the end. War can do that. It can take the greatest rift and mend it.'

Alice pictured John and her heart tightened. 'I'm so pleased I found you.'

'I am too. It was important.' He smiled.

She nodded.

'Edmund was my true love but that is now behind me.' He placed a hand over his heart. 'There are many types of love, but one grand passion is enough.'

A grand passion. Zach. 'Thank you.' She rose, clutching the letters to her chest.

'I am pleased I was sentimental enough to keep them and now they have found their true home.'

'Yes.' She stepped towards the door.

'Will you read them?' he asked.

She paused. 'I don't know. Maybe there was a reason he didn't send them.'

'You may be right.' He pulled a bell chord. 'Pierre will see you out.' He bowed deeply over her hand.

'One last question?' she asked.

'Of course.'

'Do you know where Zach died?'

He nodded. 'Near Cambrai, Saint-Waast.'

She bowed her head for a moment trying to pull her thoughts together.

'If you wish to know more, call again, but I think you have had enough of a shock.'

She nodded and said, 'You may be right. Farewell.' She followed the manservant out the door.

She blinked in the bright sunlight then adjusted her hat. Across the street she saw a church. With shaky legs she headed to it.

Chapter Forty-Seven

Alice stepped off the train and prepared herself for explanations she might have to make. That done she would return to Cornwall and stay there. She would not be dragged back into society but live a quiet life with John, honouring both Edmund and Zach. When he was old enough to understand she would let John know the truth of his parentage. She would tell him how she had loved both Edmund and Zach and that they had loved each other as half-brothers could. Half-brothers. That explained so much, including her father-in-law. What a vile entitled man. She shivered, thinking of Zach's poor mother and Jed having to live with that knowledge the whole time. So much was wrong with the world and the way it worked. She couldn't make a difference anywhere else but she could at Penhale. Not that she could say a word to Jed Carne or Brindley but somehow she would make their lives easier, better.

In order to avoid a collision in the crowd, she kept her head high and caught sight of the station clock. Below it she saw Arthur standing on the platform, searching the crowd. He wouldn't be looking for her. No one knew she had been in Bruges. Behind her the porter carried her bags and she lowered her head so that her face wouldn't be visible under her hat. She didn't want to see anyone, especially not Arthur when her emotional state was confused at best and at worst in pieces. The whole journey back she had held Zach's letters. But she hadn't opened them. Doing that would lay her open to too much emotion and she hadn't the strength for it. But Arthur had filled her thoughts on the journey as well.

The crowds on the platform jostled her and she looked up. Arthur was standing in front of her with arms out to steady her. 'Alice.'

She blinked. 'Why are you here?'

'You,' he said.

'How?' she asked.

'Let's move out of the crowd.' He spoke to the porter then took her arm. Swiftly they were through the station and into his motorcar. Once underway Alice turned to speak but Arthur shook his head, pointing to the chauffeur and she held her questions. The short journey was a form of torture. He was so close but she mustn't touch him. Instead from under her hat she studied every detail of him. She wanted to imprint the details onto her heart and take them with her to Cornwall. This was the one way she could hold him close.

They arrived at his house in Chelsea and once inside the drawing room, she turned to him, ready to speak. He handed her a sherry while he poured himself a whisky.

'Arthur, explain please.' As she said these words, she knew she would need to as well. This wonderful man deserved to know why she had turned him away. He would keep her secrets.

'I received a telegram from Villiars,' he said.

'Villiars?' She tilted her head.

He nodded.

'I don't understand.' She thought of their departure.

'You met with him.' He took a sip of his whisky.

She nodded.

'He was concerned.' He studied her. 'He told me you had received some distressing news and he thought you may need some support.' He put his glass down. 'He was aware of my feeling for you from his visit to Abbotswood.'

Alice sank onto a chair. She looked up at him, expecting anger, but there was none.

'Would you care to tell me about it?' He sat opposite her and took her hand in his.

'It's complicated.' She looked at his fingers holding hers and tried not to feel.

He gave her an encouraging smile. 'Life is.'

'True, but right now mine seems more so.' She tried to put everything she had learned into the proper places.

'I'm here to listen.'

She looked away, but she needed to tell him. Turning back to him, she began, 'Arthur, you are a good man and I...'

'I want you to be my wife,' he whispered.

She drew a breath. He was so fair that his eyelashes could barely be seen. He wore no moustache and she imagined for that reason this gave his handsome face a youthful appearance despite his thirty-six years. 'Once you hear what I have to say you will understand why I must say no.'

His fingers tightened a bit on hers, but he did not let go. 'May I have any say in the matter?'

She shook her head. 'No, for you deserve only the best and as you will see with me that is far from the case.'

He began to speak but she interrupted. 'The story begins back in my suffragette days.'

'When you spoke to the king?' He raised an eyebrow and a smile hovered on his lips.

She resisted the urge to lean forward and place her mouth on his, for that is what she wanted to do. 'Yes, but also before too.'

'Some women have gained the vote, so you were right.'

'I was right about that, but so reckless and careless of people and of their hearts, including my own.' She looked into his eyes. 'I have since learned how precious people's hearts are and I have no wish to hurt more.'

'Alice.' He placed his other hand on hers.

'When I was banished to Abbotswood I was angry and bored. While there I met and fell in love with the most wonderful but most unsuitable man.' She took a deep breath. 'He is John's father, not Edmund.'

Arthur smiled. 'I never thought Edmund was.'

She opened her eyes wide and studied his face trying to read his thoughts.

'Edmund was wonderful, warm and witty, but it was known that he was queer.'

Alice's eyes opened wide. 'So, everyone knew?'

'I'm sure they thought that, until they saw John who looks much like him.'

Finally, Alice understood why that was, thanks to Villiars explaining Edmund's and Zach's relationship. Did Arthur realise this too? Did he know who she was speaking of?

'And the world provided many other things to think about and talk about,' he said.

'True, but...'

'Dearest one, you would not be the first nor the last woman to find herself in that situation and I should imagine Edmund was relieved to help.'

She nodded. 'So now are you beginning to see why I can't be your wife.'

'No.' He shook his head. 'I fell in love with you a long time ago. You were ardent, rash, wilful even, but mostly you were you.' He leaned closer. 'It's why I fell in love with you.'

She tilted her head. 'What?'

'You are fierce, passionate and loving,' he said.

She was so filled with love and longing for this man.

'Say you will marry me,' he said.

'You still want me to marry you, knowing I set off to France on my own to find my husband?'

'Edmund is dead.' He pulled back a small distance, studying her face.

'Yes, I know that now, but when I went I believed him alive and living with...' She paused, almost about to say his name, but that was not fair. 'A man in Paris.'

'That explains things,' he said.

She frowned.

'When I last saw you, you were different. It was because you were uncertain.'

She nodded. But she hadn't been uncertain. She loved Arthur then as she did now. That was never in question. She was certain that he deserved more than her and what she could offer him.

'Glad it wasn't because of your mother's desire for you not to marry me.' He smiled. 'She made her views quite clear.'

'I've had years of being used to my mother and her disappointment that I was not the son she longed for.'

He grinned. 'For that I am grateful.'

He sank to one knee and took both her hands in his. 'Please accept my heart and my love and agree to be my wife.'

Her breath caught and everything in her called out to him. Dare she say yes? She glanced out the window, and early evening sunlight glinted on the water of the Thames. She knew her answer because there was only one that was possible. She wanted him with her whole heart and soul. She looked back at him. 'Yes, I will.'

Chapter Forty-Eight

2019

As soon as she opened the sitting room door, Cat strolled in, weaving through her legs. It was a glorious misty October morning with the rising sun sending slanting rays across to Abbotswood. Jeanette was due shortly and they were collecting Martin from Bodmin Parkway train station en route to visit Tregare and Toby Carew.

Her phone pinged with a message from David, checking on her. She replied that all was well and why didn't he ring tonight or on the weekend for a chat. Life was funny. She never expected to discover that the John Grannie had been engaged to was an earl, nor had she expected to make new friends when she'd bought her hidden cottage. The latter was a huge bonus, and this gave a lightness to her step as she readied herself for the day. She grabbed a slice of toast and went to the table in the sitting room.

The last remaining letter sat on top of the pile. She would bring it with them today and show it to Toby. Taking a bite of toast, she picked up the letter. She fought the feeling that she was invading someone's privacy, because of course she was, but it also felt like she was meant to find them.

20 October 1918

My lady,

The war is now four years going and, somehow, I am still alive. I have moved through the desire to die to the need to live and see you again, even though we can never be together. But I am happy knowing that you are in Penhale and young John will know the joys of the river and the fields. That it will all be his. I know he is mine even though I have no proof other than knowing Lord Edmund would never lay with you or any woman.

I have chased this thought around in my head until I couldn't see clearly anymore. But then I watched him with a Belgian officer and it became clear as these things do.

I want to survive the war. I want to see my son. I want to see you to apologise for everything. You did the one thing you could to protect yourself and our son. You have given him what I never could have.

Pray for me, my lady. I want to live. I want you to live, knowing that loving you has been the best thing I have ever done even if it was wrong. I want you to live a full life. You need love. You blossomed so when you had it. If something happens to Lord Edmund, promise me you will marry again. That you will love again. I will always love you, but if I survive, I must keep my distance and still hold the past close to my heart.

We are about to go check for bodies.

I am forever yours,
Zach xxx

PS I left a map showing where the tiara is buried. You'll find it where you see your beauty reflected.

Tears threatened. These men, that generation, had lost so much. Cat nuzzled her hand. Theo wasn't sure if she was doing it because Theo was suddenly tearful or Cat was reminding her that she would like some breakfast.

After feeding Cat, Theo studied the picture she had taken of Lady Alice's portrait. Maybe Toby could shed some light on the affair but would she have told her son about the gillie? Probably not. If her own circumstance had been different she wouldn't have told David about Patrick. Parents' love life was taboo full stop, let alone a forbidden love affair.

Theo was still angry with Piers for putting David in the situation he had, making David cover up and lie for him. He hadn't protected David; he'd used him. However, being kind, David had invited Piers to his and Natasha's wedding. Theo was not looking forward to seeing him. But he had raised David and she owed him something for that. David hadn't yet told Piers the truth. She had said she would do it with him if he wanted. But David wasn't ready and may never be. This was entirely David's choice and she would respect it no matter what.

'Hello,' Jeanette called, walking into the sitting room. She instantly picked up the letter. 'Have you read them all?'

Theo shook her head and picked up her handbag, making sure that she had the copy of Grannie's photo.

'Are you bringing them?'

'Yes.'

'Shall we go and collect your delicious Martin?' Jeanette asked.

Theo laughed. Martin being delicious was something she didn't want to contemplate. She gave Cat's head a good scratch then they went into Jeanette's car. As they set off down the drive, Jeanette said, 'I've been doing some digging of my own through my mother's papers.' She turned down the radio. 'Much of it is tedious academic work but she was a keen journal keeper.'

'How does it feel, reading your mother's thoughts?'

'Good question. I'm not sure.' Jeanette followed the twisting country roads with an ease that Theo hadn't yet acquired. Outside her window, autumn was truly taking hold. Trees were turning, fields were golden.

'I haven't yet found her journals for 1914, or the years she spent at Penhale during the war before she came to London to work as a nurse's aid.'

They joined the A38 and Jeanette turned into Bodmin Parkway. Martin stood waiting, dressed in full dog collar. It always shook Theo to see him that way. In her head he was simply her pesky little brother.

He climbed in the back while Jeanette said, 'How very dashing and yet disappointing. I think I prefer the leathers and the Nirvana.'

'I had an important meeting this morning so didn't have time to change. Plus this shows a bit more gravitas.'

'For Toby?' Jeanette laughed.

'Yes,' Martin said, grabbing onto the ceiling handle as Jeanette took a sharp turn at speed.

'This is a short cut to Tregare,' Jeanette said as she sped over the dry track until they came to substantial gate piers. The drive smoothed and eventually a stately white house appeared in all its Palladian grandeur.

'Wow,' Theo said. The house in front of her did not match the image the biographies depicted of the rebel that was Lady Alice Carew. But Theo understood it was because she had been Lady Alice Carew that she had made headlines and had made a difference by bringing publicity and her voice to those who had little or none.

'It's a lovely home and my aunt adored it and she adored Arthur. They were so in love. You saw it in the way they looked at each other and in everything they did.' Jeanette brought the car to a stop. 'He was a dear and so instrumental as an MP, urging the government towards change.'

A tall gentleman walked out the front door and stood between the pillars with a big smile on his face. 'Jeanette, it's always such a delight to see you,' he said when Jeanette abandoned the car, leaving the door open and racing to him.

'Oh, Toby, it's been far too long and you promise me that you are prepared for this.' She pulled back and Theo watched as he nodded.

Only then did Theo climb out of the car with Martin right behind her. Her palms were sweating but she put a smile on her face. Toby looked youthful for his seventy-nine years with hair that was more fair than grey and lively blue eyes, which watched them both.

He took Jeanette's hand in his and said, 'I can see why you warned me.' He stepped onto the gravel and held out his hand to Theo. 'You look so like my mother, it is unnerving, but what a delight to meet my brother John's grandchildren.'

'Thank you.' Theo's voice faltered.

He turned to Martin and said, 'I can see John in you.' He shook Martin's hand, saying, 'Do come in.'

He led the way into the hall, which was flooded with afternoon light. Theo's eyes were immediately drawn to two things. She walked straight to the larger of them. A life-size portrait of Lady Alice. Theo would guess at her own age, mid-fifties. The resemblance had not diminished but had grown. Theo touched her own cheek.

'If you doubted what we know,' said Jeanette, coming to stand beside Theo, 'this says it all.'

Theo laughed. Alice was standing in a rose garden with a flower trug over her arm and secateurs in the other.

'Uncanny,' said Martin, coming to stand beside her.

'My mother loved gardening.' Toby came up to them. 'She said it began during the war when she helped in the kitchen garden then grew when she ran Penhale.' He looked at Theo. 'You are so like her.'

'Thank you,' Theo said, turning to the other portrait. It was of a handsome fair-haired man in uniform.

'My father Arthur Carew.' He paused. 'He was one of the lucky ones.' They all stood in silence thinking of those that hadn't been.

'Come into the dining room where I've set out photos of John and the rest of us.'

Reluctantly Theo left the portraits. An image scratched the back of her mind, but she couldn't place it. There was something familiar about this place but she couldn't say why. Maybe it had featured in a magazine she had read. She followed behind, listening to Toby saying, 'And Martin, you are so like my brother, except he was fairer than you. I am so delighted that Jeanette has found you and brought you to us.'

'We are too.' Martin stopped by a dining table, which would easily seat twenty, covered end to end in photos.

'I've organised them chronologically, but I think the ones you might want to see first are in the middle.' Toby smiled. 'They are the ones John sent home to Mother.'

Martin reached the centre of the table seconds before Theo. She held her breath, almost afraid to look down, but, sure enough, there was Grannie. There was a less faded version of the same photo in her bag, and others too.

'I'm going through Mother's letters now. Should have done it years ago.' He shrugged and continued, 'But you know life, children, grandchildren intervene.'

'How is the family?' Jeanette asked.

'All well and—' he grinned '—they are all moving back to the UK in December. Tregare will be full again.'

'How wonderful. We shall all have to get together.' She walked back to the table asking, 'Your sisters' families?'

'Good. I spoke with Janie last night and caught up on the news.'

Theo shut their voices out and studied the pictures of her grandfather at Penhale, at Oxford and in his uniform. So much loss for Alice. Theo turned to look at Toby. He looked like his father.

'Tea?' Toby asked.

'Yes, thank you,' said Theo. 'I'm afraid I have a thousand questions for you.'

Toby laughed. 'I'd be surprised if you didn't. Fire away and I shall try my best to answer them.' They walked together into the drawing room then Toby poured the tea.

Theo sat down, pulling out all of Zach's letters. 'I don't know if Jeanette mentioned the letters I found at Boatman's Cottage.'

'Ah, yes, she did.' He looked to the door where Martin and Jeanette were standing, chatting.

'It appears that…' Theo's voice faded away.

Toby laughed. 'My mother had an affair with the gillie.'

'Yes, this last letter.' They opened it and placed it on the table. 'I don't mean to…' She didn't know what to say.

Toby picked up the letter. She watched him scan it. 'Ah the tiara. The missing laurel tiara. My great-grandmother left it to Mum.'

'Yes, I didn't understand that.'

'I shall explain and no need to worry that you are telling me something I was unaware of at all.'

He poured tea for Jeanette and Martin before saying, 'My mother later in her life didn't want any secrets lingering. She told me of this gillie, this Zachariah Carne who was, as she put it, her grand passion, whereas my father was her enduring love.' He paused. 'She, however, was his grand passion, his heaven and his earth.' He took a breath. 'Zach was John's father.'

Martin looked at Theo. 'So, it's not Edmund St Loy that we buried at Masnières Cemetery.'

Theo immediately thought of the grave in Paris.

'No, it was Zach.' Toby sipped his tea. 'Mum only told me this before she died.'

'We are not St Loys,' said Martin.

'Oh, I love a bit of intrigue.' Jeanette picked up a biscuit and snapped it in half.

'But you are St Loys.' Toby put his cup down.

'How?' Martin asked.

'This becomes even better,' Jeanette said.

'Zach was Edmund's half-brother.'

Theo sank back into the chair, saying, 'What complicated webs we weave.'

'Exactly.' Jeanette stood and poured more tea.

Martin leaned forward. 'Did John know?'

'I asked my mother that.' He smiled. 'She told me when he reached twenty-one she had told him the full story.'

'I wonder if he told Grannie?' Theo said, putting her cup down.

'Knowing John, he would have. He was the best older brother. Always full of mischief, poetry and fun.'

'I am relieved in a way as this morning I was filming,' said Martin, rising to his feet. 'Not that it mattered one way or another to me but one of the researchers for the production was intrigued by the story and is digging into it.'

'Are they trying to make you the Earl St Loy?' Jeanette shivered. 'How absolutely delightful.'

'As a priest it doesn't work but if they can make the case and, if there is a special remainder on the St Loy title, you could be looking at the Countess St Loy, or failing that it would pass to David.'

Jeanette clapped her hands. 'This would be perfect and my aunt would be thrilled.'

'She would indeed as she was all about equal rights for

women.' Toby paused and pointed to a picture on the piano. 'She was about equal rights for all.'

Theo rose and went to the picture. Her great-grandmother was in the front of a crowd carrying a banner that declared 'End Racism' with the George Washington memorial obelisk in the background. Martin joined Theo.

'Was that the Martin Luther King march?' Martin asked.

'Yes.' Toby walked over to them.

'I wish I had known her,' Theo finally managed to say.

Toby joined them. 'I do too, but I am thankful you are here today. My mother, I'm sure, would be smiling in heaven especially.' He turned to Martin. 'To have a priest in the family. She converted to Catholicism two years before she died.'

Martin laughed. 'So it's not just me that's a radical.'

Theo laughed. 'Well, now we know where it comes from.'

Chapter Forty-Nine

Walking back to the cottage with her post Theo was grateful for what December sun there was. She loved the lower light at this time of year coming through the bare branches. The architecture of the trees was revealed silhouetted against the sky. David was arriving shortly, and Natasha and the small wedding party would all be descending on Abbotswood. Piers had declined the wedding invitation, possibly out of spite due to David's resignation. David had not told him about the DNA test or the results. Theo was pleased Piers was happy with Tina and their daughter, but he could have shown some affection for David.

Outside the cottage she stopped. The garden had been neglected but the cottage was fully finished. She had yet to plant the daphne that Gayle had given her. December had been wet and they hadn't had a frost. Maybe she should plant it today and begin work on her plans for spring planting.

Martin walked out of the cottage, holding a letter. 'I've been looking at these and this last one about the tiara.'

'Toby said they had looked but his mother had no idea where Zach buried it.'

'Zach says, I left a map where you'll see your beauty reflected.'

'By the river?' Theo shrugged.

'That was my first thought but then it struck me it would be a mirror.'

Theo walked past him and straight into the sitting room. She lifted the heavy mirror off the wall.

'Let me help.' He took it from her and she threw a blanket across the table and he laid the mirror down glass first.

She shook her head. 'There's nothing there and it's a long shot that this mirror would have been here the whole time.'

Martin ran his fingers along the wood that lined the back then he pulled at one side. 'These nails are not flush like the others.'

'Let me get my tools.' Theo dashed to the utility room and came back clutching a small hammer and a flathead screwdriver.

Martin stepped back, saying, 'You are far better at this sort of thing than me.'

Theo gently tapped, lifting the wood off the mirror, expecting to see nothing at the back of the mercury-coated glass.

'What's this?' he asked, lifting a sheet of paper, which he took to the table. It was a hand-drawn map of Abbotswood.

Theo looked for an X to mark the spot but there was none. 'It doesn't say.' She sighed. The map was simply drawn with Abbotswood, the Tamar, the cottage and a few key landmarks like Black Rock shown. Stick-like trees marked the location of some of the specimen trees and it showed a daphne. Daphne. Daphne laureola, wood laurel. 'It's here.'

Martin leaned in closer. 'What?'

She took the map and collected her gloves and shovel. She studied the map and then surveyed the garden to see where the daphne was marked. Nothing was there now. Walking to the spot, hoping it was right, she handed the map to Martin and began to dig a hole. Putting her foot on the shovel, she heard a metallic sound. She stopped and used her hands to dig away until she saw a flour tin. It took time but she managed to pull it out while Martin looked on.

The lid had rusted and she couldn't budge it. Once inside she used the same flathead screwdriver and hammer and tapped it gently open.

A faded blue leather box with the engraved initials DN on the top rested in the tin untouched by the earth that caked on its container. Theo released the clasp and gasped. The missing tiara. She lifted it out and the diamonds glistened in the light from the lamp. In the bottom of the box was the large central pendant diamond. 'Wow.'

Theo turned to see Hugo, David and Martin standing together, staring at the tiara.

'Where did you find that?' David asked.

'Would you believe me if I said where X marks the spot?'

'You're joking...' said Hugo.

'No, I'm not,' she said.

Hugo asked, 'May I?'

Theo nodded and he lifted it. 'Stunning.' He turned it over and looked for the maker's mark. 'Garrards.'

'It should be easy enough to find out its history.' He smiled.

'We know it belonged to Lady Alice,' she said.

'Shall I ring Toby?' Martin asked.

'Yes, it's his.' She laughed as she attached the large diamond in place and said, 'David, can you put the mirror back on the wall?'

'Sure,' he said and she followed him. Once it was in place, she placed the tiara on her head. The diamonds caught the light, sending prisms onto the wall with every move of her head.

'It suits you, I have to say,' Martin said, coming back into the room. 'By the way, Toby sends his love and is looking forward to tomorrow. He also said the tiara is yours. And he points out every countess should have one.'

Theo laughed. 'I'm not a countess and I will never have a reason to wear it.' She paused and turned to David. 'Do you think Natasha would like to wear it tomorrow?'

He grinned. 'I think she might. In fact, I think she'd be honoured to be asked.'

There was a tap on the bedroom door. Theo looked up from putting her shoes on for tonight's pre wedding party at Abbotswood. 'Come in.'

'Hey Mum.' David walked in and perched on the end of her bed.

'Don't you look handsome.' She stepped up to him and adjusted his tie. He looked up at her. 'What's wrong?' she asked.

'Dad, Piers, him.'

'Ah.' She sat next to him. 'I'm truly sorry he's not here to celebrate with you.'

'It's just that—' He threaded his fingers together.

'What?'

'Well, when he turned down the invite, I went to see him and, well, it all came out.' He rubbed his chin.

'I see.'

He shook his head. 'I'm not sure you do. I wasn't nice.'

Theo tilted her head. 'What did you say?'

'Well, I was angry and I told him I wasn't his son and he laughed.' David shook his head. 'I then went on to say I had proof I wasn't.'

'Oh, dear.'

David nodded. 'Yes, and he called you every name in the book but kept repeating the C word.'

Theo flinched.

'He ranted about raising a cuckoo and made demands for compensation and everything.'

'Oh no.' Theo had feared Piers's reaction but hopefully this was all wounded bluster.

'Sadly, yes, and I'm afraid I was so angry that I told him not to rush to change the name of the company to Henshaw and Daughter because I wasn't the only cuckoo he was raising.'

'Ouch.'

'That stopped him. He then wanted to know what I knew.' David laughed bitterly. 'I didn't have to say that but he was so vile about you.'

Theo put her hand out and took his in hers. 'I'm so sorry you had to go through that.' She drew a big breath. 'He was angry and hurt and lashing out.'

'But—'

Theo stopped him. 'No buts, he has a right to be angry and he has a right to happiness. I hope his daughter is his and not the foreman's.'

David huffed.

'Let it go and let's focus on happiness and true love, your true love. Tonight, we dance and tomorrow you marry the woman who is everything to you and that lifts my heart no end.'

'Thank you, Mum.'

She stood and pulled him to his feet. 'All will be fine.'

Chapter Fifty

1921

Arthur rowed Alice across the river. She was carrying their child and he was worried about everything and she loved him for it. He secured the boat then helped her ashore.

'Wait here,' she said.

His glance narrowed.

'I'll be safe. I need to do this on my own.'

He nodded and she kissed him before she walked the path to the cottage. These woods were filled with memories and they walked with her as the scent of warm pine rose with each step. Reaching the cottage, she opened the door. A damp smell greeted her, and she had to pull the curtains back to let light in. A and Z were still visible. She smiled, heading up to the small bedroom and into the cupboard to where Zach had kept his precious things. She paused, thinking about her grandmother's tiara. Somewhere it was buried and it would remain so.

Pulling the piece of wood up, she placed Zach's letters in the hole but found a metal box that hadn't been there on her last visit. She pulled it out and inside were two letters. She recognised Zach's writing on one of them. A sad smile crossed her face. Her poor cousin carried all of this; Constance had taken on the burden rather than add to Alice's grief.

There was an unopened letter addressed to her. She ran her finger over the ink. She didn't know the writing and it had no stamp. Using her fingernail, she broke the seal. The paper was already yellowed but the writing was clear. Her heart caught. Edmund.

My dearest Thing,

This letter will come as a shock. It is the seventeenth of March 1920 and I am alive and not in the ground in France. There is much I should say but as my days on this earth near their end I am not sure where to start. I, who am never short of a quip or a story, am indeed at a loss. I hope you will find that amusing. As death approaches, I want to amuse, I want to laugh, for strangely only dark humour lifts me. It was the same in the war. Death was everywhere but laughing at it helped.

It didn't help me cope with Zach's death. I was wounded in the leg and couldn't move. Zach was at my side. I made him fight on and he swore he would come back and find me. He was true to his word. In the darkness, lying next to the dead, he found me and bandaged me up. He half carried and half dragged me towards our line.

We were some distance away when the sniper found him. He fell on the spot. I held him as he died. I held my brother as he died. Yes, he was my brother. My father had a roving eye and Zach's mother was exceptionally beautiful, everyone had said. She died in childbirth, but I think it was of shame. She was a good Methodist woman. My father forced Jedidiah to stay and for Zach to be there. There was a month's difference in our ages. I think we both knew, but nothing was ever said until he lay dying in my arms. Despite the resemblance between us, no one said a word, not even you, dear Thing.

I made sure he knew that John was his as if he had any doubt. I also made sure that he knew you loved him. He died with that knowledge. I broke my promise to you but I knew it was the right thing to do. It was in my power to give the truth to him.

What I did next was not honourable but the act of a desperate man. Immediately after Zach died, I swapped clothes. I placed my ring on his finger. At least in death he was a St Loy. I wasn't in a good state, but I knew I couldn't fight anymore. I found shelter and when I began to remember what I had done the war was over and I made my way to Paris.

I am weary now. But I wanted you to know that I found love. I enclose a picture of my love and me. Finally I know what you had with Zach: an all-encompassing love. I pray, despite all that has happened, that you are well. I picture John in my mind's eye and see a strong healthy boy running across Penhale's lawns.

Dearest Thing, forgive me. I should have come back to you. I should have brought Zach back to you and I failed on all accounts.

I am not long for this world. Live well, dear Thing. And love, always love.

Yours,
E

She clutched the letter to her chest then carefully folded it and put it in her pocket. The rest of the letters she placed back into the box and the hole in the bottom of the cupboard. Someday she may retrieve them and give them to John. But for now they belonged here, safe from the world in a forgotten cottage.

She rose and took a last look around. Zach died knowing the truth thanks to Edmund. She placed a hand over her heart. They both resided there. On the landing she stopped when her child moved. She was living life. She had found love again as Edmund had wanted her to do. And, most importantly, as he had asked so long ago, she had learned kindness. It was not always easy, but his words were always there. *Be kind, Thing.*

Down by the fireplace she took the letter out of her pocket. The matches she found were damp and wouldn't light.

Arthur coughed. She turned to him. 'Can you help?' She held out the matches.

'Of course.' He rummaged in his pocket and produced a lighter. He raised an eyebrow as she handed him the letter.

'Edmund,' she said.

'Are you sure?' he asked.

She nodded and he lit the corner of the paper, making certain it had caught before dropping it on the grate. She took his hand and they waited together until the flames died out and only ash remained. In silence they walked back to the riverbank.

Alice took one last look at the cottage as they pulled away from the bank then placed a hand on Arthur's knee, grateful for love.

Chapter Fifty-One

2019

Standing in front of the fireplace, Theo adjusted the red rose in David's buttonhole. He grinned. 'Ready, Mum?'

'I should be asking you that,' she said.

'I am. I love her more than life.' He smiled, and, as she kissed his cheek, the string quartet began to play. He went to stand beside Hugo and Martin, who was presiding. Hugo's father, Ron, sat beside her, and Virginia sat on the other side of Ron. She hadn't said a word to Theo and for once Theo didn't mind. Theo hadn't told her that David wasn't Piers's because she didn't want to hear what her mother had to say. No doubt she suspected anyway, due to Piers's absence today. It didn't matter and it was more peaceful this way.

Across from them Natasha's mother and her grandparents sat. While behind Theo were Gayle, Jeanette and Toby and his daughter and her family.

Jeanette leaned forward and whispered in Theo's ear. 'I'm feeling emotional.' Gayle handed her a tissue as they all stood when Natasha walked into the room with her father. Her gown had been her great-grandmother's and the beautiful dropped-waist lace dress in a soft ivory suited her. Her veil was held in place by the tiara. Many things old celebrating a love that was new. The bride's bouquet nodded to the season with rich red roses, white dittany and rosemary sprigs.

As they spoke their vows, Theo fought to control her tears. Ron smiled at her and handed her his hankie. When David kissed Natasha, applause broke out then they walked down the short aisle.

Hugo took her hand to lead her to the drinks in the library. She looked up at him and whispered, 'It's your turn next.' He grinned and turned back to smile at Gayle, who flushed.

The quartet played as the pictures were taken in the west-facing sitting room with the glorious hand-painted wallpaper as a backdrop. Theo managed to always have someone in between her mother and herself. She did not want this day celebrating love to be ruined.

Pictures finished, they moved to the dining room where the wedding feast awaited them. After the first course Natasha's father spoke, and after the main course Theo stood to make a toast to their small company of thirty people. Raising her glass, she looked up for a second and noted the many family crests around the room. Her glance fell on the three linked hares of the St Loy coat of arms. Alice, Zach and Edmund.

'Thank you all for coming today. Natasha's father has already said so much about this wonderful couple, I need only add that I am so thrilled that Natasha is now officially part of my family.' She lifted her glass in her daughter-in-law's direction. 'I also want to thank all who have helped to make this day a wonderful celebration, from the chef, whose glorious food we have been enjoying, and to all the staff for making sure nothing is missed.' She took a breath. 'And in view of all the information that has come to light, there is something rather special to be celebrating here at Abbotswood.' She smiled. 'To the people in our pasts who have brought us to our present here and now, celebrating love, the love of David and Natasha.'

They all rose and lifted their glasses. 'To David and Natasha.'

She sat down and Ron leaned closer and said, 'Patrick would be pleased.'

She nodded, for words were not possible as she watched her son kiss the woman he loved.

After dinner they headed into the large sitting room where the carpet had been rolled up and dancing was about to begin. Virginia walked up to Theo. Theo tensed, waiting. 'Well, you did one good decent thing in your life,' her mother said so quietly only Theo could hear. 'David.'

'He is a wonderful person, and I'm proud to be his mother and the role I played in that, but I have done more than be a mother.' She fixed Virginia with a look.

'You have wasted every gift given to you,' Virginia said through lips still forming a smile.

'In your eyes possibly, but I know I haven't.' Theo pulled her shoulders back and looked down on her mother.

'You play with flowers.'

Theo smiled and saw the beauty of her work around them. 'I do indeed and it is a fine thing.'

'You betrayed him with this Patrick.'

'If that's what you choose to think then do.' Theo turned and took two steps away.

'You are just like Claire.' Virginia kept her voice low and even.

'That is the nicest thing you have ever said to me. I'm also like Lady Alice too, and I thank God for that.' Theo smiled and took Martin's outstretched hand and began to dance.

Theo breathed in the fresh air clearing her head of the wine. The night was bright and the moon was rising. The dew on the grass dampened the edges of her dress as she made her way down to the shell house. She stood at the fence, looking down on the moonlit Tamar and Boatman's only turning when she heard footsteps.

'What a beautiful wedding,' Toby said.

Theo nodded, looking back to the house. 'Very.'

'The tiara looked beautiful on Natasha.'

'It did but it's yours.'

'No,' he said. 'My mother had others and in the end my sisters had them made into brooches and the like.' He looked down on the river. 'My own daughter has no interest and Tregare will be hers when I go. But I have something else for you.'

Theo frowned.

'As I'd mentioned I've been going through my mother's papers and found this.' He held out an envelope.

Theo took it. 'It's not opened.'

'Look at it,' he said.

She turned it over and squinted.

Miss C Pascoe
24 Gunterstone Rd
London
W14

Scrawled on it was 'No longer at this address, no forwarding address'. The postmark was 5 August 1940.

Theo looked up and said, 'You haven't opened it.'

'No, I would imagine that my mother had written to your grandmother and I felt you should be the first to read it.' He gave Theo a half smile and walked back to the house.

Theo turned to the river. There wasn't enough light to read, but she carefully opened it and pulled her phone out of the pocket in her dress. Using the torch, she read.

Tregare
1 August 1940

Dear Miss Pascoe,

I am so sorry in my delay in writing to you. John had told me all about you, but it wasn't until his effects were sent to me that I found your letters.

My heart is with you as you digest what I have just written. I do not know if you had heard that John was shot down over France. I hope I am not the one to bring you this news and so long after it happened. I pray that one of his wonderful friends has told you in person.

From what John told me, and from your letters to him (forgive me for I have read them), you two shared such love. This has given me comfort as I grieve for my son. His love for you showed in his eyes when he spoke of you. He talked of bringing you home to meet us. I know his intention was to marry you as he asked for the St Loy emerald. I gave it to him and told him not to waste a minute. I trust he didn't.

There are no words that can take away the pain of loss. Only love can cause such pain and only love can ease it. Hold tight to the love that you had together. Let it comfort you and ease your grief. I hope that love may find you again in the future. I have known such loss and I have known such love.

Please know that we are here. If you wish, we would love to meet the girl who made our boy so very happy. You are part of us.

May God bless you.

Yours sincerely,
Alice Carew

Theo couldn't breathe. Her heart ached. Claire had soldiered on alone, never hearing these words of comfort so freely given. She traced the writing. Tregare. She thought of her most recent visit and that sense of being there before. Grannie had held her hand when they had viewed the open gardens there that first visit to Cornwall when she was six. There had been a beautiful older woman that Grannie had spoken to. The woman had bent down and given Theo a boiled sweet from her pocket.

Her hand went to her heart. Grannie had taken Theo to all the places of John's past and even to meet his mother.

Grannie had known great love, maybe just for a short time. But, as Theo had learned, sometimes that was enough. She folded the letter and put it carefully back into the envelope and then into her pocket. She had found her home and in the process had found herself and she was enough; in fact she was far better than enough.

In the house behind, her family and friends celebrated love. Taking a deep breath, she looked down on Boatman's across the river in Cornwall. All those months ago when she sought a new start, she had no idea a ramshackle cottage on the Tamar would bring her so much. That it brought her her past and led her to her present. She raced back inside to join the dancing. She didn't want to miss a minute of her now.

Case 752
Status: Closed

_____

Captain Edmund St Loy and Sergeant William Bowman were buried with full honours at Masnières Cemetery on 6 September 2019. Family for both men were in attendance.

Acknowledgements

There isn't a way to express sufficient thanks to all those who served in both World Wars. The more I read their stories, the more I am in awe of what they sacrificed.

This book would not have come together without the unfailing support of Brigid Coady and Deborah Harkness. They have held my hand, consumed sherry, read and re-read draft after draft of this book and simply wouldn't let me sink into despair or rest until I had carved out the best story I could. Their belief truly pulled me through.

My husband, Chris Fenwick, is the most patient and understanding soul, who accepts my bad moods when characters go rogue. He will walk endless miles with me while I wrestle with the story. He has become adept at coping with random questions, apparently out of the blue, which he understands is just how this writer's brain works. Huge thanks go to my children: Dom, Andrew, and Sasha for putting up with their mother and supporting her work even when it's deeply embarrassing. And a special shoutout to Andrew for taking my version of Zach's map of Abbotswood and making a far better one, especially with the fantastic lettering done by Annabel Harper.

Thanks to John Jackson, friend and early reader. A huge thanks goes to Gwen Hammond for reading the proof pages to spot the mistakes I didn't see. The continued support of the whole Book Camp team. After the first draft of this book, I had the privilege of attending the Breakout Novel Intensive Retreat. The insights gained propelled me deeper with more confidence to find the story I wanted to tell. A special thanks to all the Boni Retreat crew, especially Don, Brenda, and Lorin.

DNA and its wonder led me down a rabbit hole and once there I couldn't see a darn thing. Deborah Harkness put me in the expert hands of Shelli Carter, a molecular biologist, who pulled me out of the ground and set me straight on exactly what DNA could and couldn't do. If there are DNA mistakes, they are all my own.

A massive thanks to the many people, who wish to remain anonymous, who assisted me in my research into identifying soldiers' remains. Again, any mistakes in this area are entirely my own.

The garden at Endsleigh is glorious. The head gardener, Ben Rushcombe-King, took me through it and opened up its history, revealing the joys of a Humphry Repton garden and the magic of the setting itself. Any mistakes on depicting a Repton garden are mine.

When I asked at Hotel Endsleigh who was the best person to speak to about the history of the hotel, they said Amanda Randall Cox of Flowers et al. Amanda provided a wealth of insight into the property and its history for which I am grateful.

There are two characters named after Gayle and Ron

Mounsey, who won the bid at an auction raising funds for the charity Hope & Homes for Children, which takes children out of institutions and into families – with a mission to end institutional care in our lifetime. When I met Gayle and Ron, I felt fate had stepped in. I knew there would be a head gardener in the story and Gayle had been a gardener at stately homes.

There are many people who are part of a writer's life and agents are a huge part. Both Alison and Luigi Bonomi have steadied my nerves, calmed my fears and simply been there. Thank you.

Team HQ, wow! A huge thanks to all, but special thanks to Kate Mills, who believes in my stories and will work to pull the best out of me every time. She is ably supported by Becky Heeley who has endless patience with all my queries. Then the art team, the production team, the marketing team and the sales team… they are all brilliant. A special shout-out to Janet Aspey, Joe Thomas, and Isabel Smith. And thanks to Donna Hillyer for copy-editing the manuscript so thoughtfully. As a dyslexic writer, I am extremely grateful to my proofreader, Mary Chamberlain, for the attention and care she put into checking my words.

Author's Note

Lady Alice's story was a joy to research and to write. The fun of taking actual events and creating fiction around them can be frustrating if timing doesn't fit, but when it does it is magic. 1914 was a year of so much history and I loved wading through it. Mary Bomfield did speak to the king at her presentation and someone did protest at the Peace Ball.

Endsleigh Cottage, the model for Abbotswood, was built in 1815 as the hunting lodge for the 5th Duke of Bedford. I wove as much of the actual history of Endsleigh into the story as I could. The grand cottage orné is now the magic Hotel Endsleigh and it still feels like a private home with its quirky rooms and eclectic decor. I loved my time researching there.

The gardens at Endsleigh are enchanting. None of Repton's magic has been lost even if some of the giant specimen trees are sons and daughters or even grandchildren of the original trees.

The Shell House has the most fortunate outlook over the Tamar. When I could tear myself away from the view and ventured inside, my sense of wonder grew. Fortunately, my husband Chris is a geologist by degree and he was able to name many of the stones inside. However, although mentioned in the story there are no fossils in the Shell House.

And Boatman's Cottage itself... I was looking at an old ordnance survey map of Endsleigh when I spotted a boatman's cottage on the Cornish bank. It captured my imagination. The old chimney and some of the walls still stand today but it is mostly hidden by the wild growth of nature.

ONE PLACE. MANY STORIES

Bold, innovative and
empowering publishing.

FOLLOW US ON:

@HQStories